INTO _{THE} LIGHT

CLAUDIA GRAY

LOS ANGELES·NEW YORK

STAR WARS TIMELINE

THE HIGH REPUBLIC	FALL OF THE JEDI	REIGN OF THE EMPIRE

THE HIGH REPUBLIC

YOUNG JEDI ADVENTURES

THE ACOLYTE

FALL OF THE JEDI

THE PHANTOM MENACE

ATTACK OF THE CLONES

THE CLONE WARS

REVENGE OF THE SITH

REIGN OF THE EMPIRE

THE BAD BATCH

SOLO: A STAR WARS STORY

OBI-WAN KENOBI

STAR WARS REBELS

ANDOR

ROGUE ONE: A STAR WARS STORY

AGE OF REBELLION

A NEW HOPE

THE EMPIRE
STRIKES BACK

RETURN OF
THE JEDI

THE NEW REPUBLIC

THE
MANDALORIAN

THE BOOK OF
BOBA FETT

AHSOKA

SKELETON
CREW

RISE OF THE FIRST ORDER

STAR WARS
RESISTANCE

THE FORCE
AWAKENS

THE LAST JEDI

THE RISE OF
SKYWALKER

To Mike, Jen, Charles, Justina, Cavan, Daniel, Lydia, Crash,
George, Tessa, and Zoraida—thanks for taking me along for the ride.

Printed in the United States of America

First Edition, April 2025

10 9 8 7 6 5 4 3 2 1

FAC-004510-25072

ISBN 978-1-368-09518-1

Library of Congress Control Number on file

Design by Kurt Hartman, Soyoung Kim, Scott Piehl, and Leigh Zieske

Visit the official *Star Wars* website at: www.starwars.com.

SUSTAINABLE
FORESTRY
INITIATIVE

Certified Sourcing

www.forests.org
SFI-01681

Logo Applies to Text Stock Only

STAR WARS
THE HIGH REPUBLIC

TRIALS OF THE JEDI

The final confrontation between the Jedi and the Nihil looms. The valiant Jedi are spread thin as they are put to the ultimate test on four separate fronts.

Some rally against NIHIL MARAUDERS who plan to punish the planet ERIADU for its resistance to their rule. Others patrol the dangerous border of the OCCLUSION ZONE, protecting planets from vicious Nihil raids. A brave few struggle to stop the mysterious BLIGHT, an infection moving from planet to planet, draining worlds of life. Still others battle the sinister MARCHION RO and his monstrous NAMELESS CREATURES.

To save the Republic, the Jedi will face their fears in their most daunting challenges yet. If they fail on just one of these battlefronts, the wave of darkness will extinguish the light of the Jedi forever....

ONE

The planet Inad hung in the darkness of space as a perfect shining bauble, its shades of blue and green hinting at abundant foliage and wildlife. Many generations prior, the Inadi had decided to keep their world healthily pristine, unpolluted by large-scale industry, their skies free of all but the most needful satellites, the better to maintain the peace and harmony of their way of life and the inheritance of their children.

A few generations after that, the Inadi had decided they would also like to make more money.

Money involved industry—but, it was determined, it need not require sacrifice. Inad's larger moon, Inad Komesh, had a breathable atmosphere, ample ore deposits, and gravity within Republic-habitable norms but otherwise was almost entirely barren, housing little but microbes. With shuttles, it was possible for the trip between planet and moon to take no more than twenty minutes. Why not place new industry on this moon, while preserving Inad in all its natural glory?

And so Inad Komesh became the site of all Inad's factories, its refineries, its mines, and its interplanetary trade. Citizens of Inad awoke in lovely homes amid primeval forests or along a coastline with sand white as the stars; they then traveled to spaceports (carefully camouflaged within natural rock) and commuted to Inad Komesh—which, unsurprisingly, became everything Inad was not: hyperdeveloped, grimy, noisy, and so crowded with structures that in some areas the actual ground was hard to see. Some called it a little Coruscant, a nickname that would have fit well had Coruscant been built with no thought of beauty, elegance, grandeur, or even comfort. In truth, most of the Inadi liked the contrast, as it made each homecoming sweeter at the end of the day.

Yet one danger of Inad Komesh had gone overlooked: On a world so overbuilt, so dense, certain threats could take root and spread for a very long time before anyone noticed.

Threats such as the blight.

As the Inadi worked happily on, the blight spread so slowly that at first it was not recognized. Then, within a few terrible days, the moon changed dramatically. One building collapsed, then another, and another again; lives were lost, and power shortages flickered for dozens of klicks around each disaster site. The artificial waterway system suddenly drained, precious water seemingly sucked down into the moon's core. People began to argue that all activity on Inad Komesh should be suspended until a thorough survey was done, began to blame contractors and developers, called for inquiries. All this would have occurred in short order had the next building to collapse not been the Orbital Operations Tower—the one in control of air and space traffic, communications, and all satellite functions.

In other words, as soon as the tower fell, the Inadi on the moon were trapped. The blight was finally identified. Panic spread, and no one could flee to safety—not without help.

"Everyone remain calm!" Jedi Knight Reath Silas called to a crowd that had thronged one of the larger Republic haulcraft that had recently landed at one of the central spaceports. Hundreds of beings, perhaps more than a thousand, had gathered together in mutual desperation to escape. The air seemed to crackle with fear. "We have ships enough to get everybody to safety, but it will take time. The more disorganized we are, the longer it will take—so stay calm, avoid contact with anything showing signs of the blight, and *listen*."

His words were projected by amplifier device; those who could hear them settled down somewhat. Unfortunately, most people *couldn't* hear—knew only that some Important Instructions had been issued and that they didn't have them, which only increased their panic.

Reath cast a despairing look toward his friends and fellow Jedi Bell Zettifar and Burryaga, who were each working at the edges of the crowd and having no more luck restoring order. Even Jedi Master Adampo, their team leader, had become so caught up in trying to assist the injured that he could not use his calming influence to help. So far this was only a mess, but within minutes the next transport would land, and at this rate, Reath feared it would be met by a stampede as dangerous as any building collapse.

He looked up toward Inad Komesh's pale sky and saw the dot above that marked the transport's descent. As others saw it, too, the murmuring of the crowd became louder and more frenzied.

Suddenly, a loud crack rang out amid a brilliant flash of purple light. Silence fell as everyone, including Reath, turned to see his fellow Knight Vernestra Rwoh striding into the middle of the throng, her lightsaber whip aglow in her hand. "Listen uuuu-*uup*!" Vernestra shouted. The crowd went completely still, which allowed her next words to ring out far and wide: "The next transport is coming! The only chance you have of being on that transport is by paying attention to what Reath says and following his instructions! Got it?" A few nods and low murmurs indicated that it had, indeed, been got. Vern nodded with satisfaction. "Okay, then. Let's get this done!"

By the time the shape of the transport had fully formed in the sky above, the Inadi had been guided into long lines, with children and others of special need at the front. Reath made sure his path crossed Vernestra's long enough that he could say, "I hope I learn how to do that someday."

Vernestra laughed. "Sometimes a little sternness isn't a bad thing." Reath's doubt must have shown on his face, because she put one hand on his shoulder as she added, "It's not the same as giving in to anger. It's about shocking people out of their fear, into a state of mind that allows them to do what they need to do."

"Of course." Reath should have considered this himself, and no doubt he would have, had the prior two days not been such utter mayhem. He had not slept five whole hours since the arrival of the Jedi team on Inad Komesh, and somehow it seemed as though every transport they managed to launch added to the number of people they had to help, rather than subtracting. The gritty dust in the moon's dry air had grayed his robe and, to judge by his fellow Jedi, probably his hair, too. (Burryaga looked as though he had been powdered like a buttersweet puff.) Reath had to believe that it was merely dust—not infected with particulates of the blight—mostly because there would be no other way to go on. They'd find out the truth after the evacuation was complete and until then had to try to ignore the horrific threat of the blight. Meanwhile, the Inadi became tenser and more desperate by the hour.

Who could blame them? Reath thought as he continued setting the crowd to order. In the distance, Bell's charhound, Ember, barked happily while actually herding a few more Inadi into position, exactly as she would have urged muunyaks toward their shearing; he welcomed the sound, the only current evidence that life still contained joy. On the periphery of the crowd, Jedi Master Adampo struggled to establish order, hampered not only by the general terror but also by his evident deep weariness after three years of conflict and loss. *The blight somehow went unnoticed for so long here that they didn't even know any risk existed until the very moment their lives were in danger.* Horrifying as the blight was, it was a creeping menace, one that devoured worlds slowly but relentlessly. On Inad Komesh, its late discovery meant that the entire moon seemed to be falling apart within a matter of days. Perhaps overgrown construction and overburdened bedrock were a particularly bad combination when it came to vulnerability to the corrosive power of the blight.

Reath felt a moment's gratitude that the blight on Coruscant was, thus far, still contained to the Jedi Temple. But for how long?

Swiftly he set his doubt aside. That was for a later time; the Inadi needed help now. He checked on a few of the more seriously injured, who were being attended to by Padawan Amadeo Azzazzo and medic Dorian Innes. "The ship's coming in," he said to an older woman, who shivered with pain on her stretcher. "Don't worry. It won't be long now."

"I'm hallucinating," she said, her voice wavering. With a shaky hand, she pointed toward a nearby tower. "It looks like that one's dancing."

Reath opened his mouth to tell her she shouldn't be worried— but then he caught his own glimpse of the tower, which swayed in the wind. Anyone raised on Coruscant had seen tall buildings sway before, but to Reath's practiced eyes, the movement seemed exaggerated. Dangerously so.

He grabbed his comlink just as Indeera Stokes's voice came through: "Transport here—don't worry, we're landing in less than two minutes."

"I need you to take as many people on board as you can without crashing," Reath said. "People don't need to sit. Everyone still able to stand should stand. And we have to call for more transports, as many more as we can get here, as fast as we can. We're looking at an imminent building collapse that could set off a chain reaction throughout this area."

Indeera responded, "Understood, and I have a few extra Jedi with me, but—you know we already have almost as many on hand as possible."

"I know," he said. The Jedi Order had been stretched thin for months—years, now—due to the Nihil insurgency and the machinations of Marchion Ro; Reath could hardly recall how it had felt to go on missions with a full complement of his fellow Jedi, to know that they were adequately staffed and prepared for anything that might come. "But Inad Komesh may already be on the brink of collapse."

Indeera Stokes swore under her breath. "Calling Coruscant now."

The transport by this point had lowered to within a few stories off the ground, displacing air in great gusts that scattered more ashen dust everywhere; Reath sneezed, then wished he'd kept his mouth closed as the grit crunched between his teeth. His gut clenched as he imagined particles of the blight—invisible and fatal—in all that dust. Still, there was nothing for it but to keep going. He spat once on the ground before calling out via amplifier device, "We'll begin loading as soon as the ramp lowers, so everyone—"

He ceased speaking as the squeal and crunch of twisting metal drowned him out. Even as the transport landed behind him, Reath turned and saw—too late to act—a distant building, not even a quarter klick away, collapse. Screams of horror rang out through the crowd as the ground shook, and a thick wave of dust rolled through the streets until it overtook them—a wave so thick that Reath could not see. He managed to kneel before he fell, but the cries of pain and alarm all around him meant not everyone had escaped injury.

"Come on!" a familiar male voice shouted through the swirling dust. "Follow the light!" With that, the brilliant blue glow of a lightsaber cut through some of the murk, providing just enough illumination to reveal the indistinct lines of the transport entrance.

Reath began guiding people toward that blue light, his consciousness once again focused on the task at hand. As he came closer to the lightsaber, a smile spread across his face—grit in his teeth be damned. He said, "I *thought* I recognized that voice."

"Nice to know you haven't forgotten all the times I kicked your ass in the sparring ring," said Dez Rydan. Through the dust he could make out Dez's answering grin. His old friend and mentor looked like himself again, at least so far as Reath's limited view showed. He knew only that Dez's time away after taking the Barash Vow must have done him good, restoring a formidable Jedi to the Order when they needed him most.

But the jubilation of the moment was immediately drowned out by the screech of tearing metal. Reath looked upward to see the hazy outline of the largest nearby tower—the dancing one—toppling toward the transport, the crowd, and Reath himself, threatening to crush them all.

TWO

One building collapse had been jarring to the Jedi, shocking to the throngs surrounding them; a second might well incite massive panic, not to mention blanketing them all in another, larger wave of dust and debris potentially contaminated with the blight.

So there could be no second collapse.

Reath flung his hands up toward the sky—unnecessary, to call on the Force, but often moving the body in a way that mimicked the desired effect helped center and clarify the mind. From all around him, he drew on the Inadi people and his fellow Jedi, focusing not on their terror but on their desire to live, their attempts to help each other, the sense of unity that disaster brought—all of it powerful in the light. At his side, Dez shoved upward, as well, and Reath sensed all the other Jedi joining forces, desperate to prevent this from becoming utter devastation.

As he stared up at his hands, the weight of the tower settled so strongly against the resistance he had created in the Force that for a moment Reath seemed to feel the sun-scorched brick warm and rough on his skin. Yet settle it did, hovering halfway through its collapse, a looming finger pointing over the crowd, as if in judgment. Its shadow darkened the faces of the panicked people who cowered beneath it.

"To the side," said Dez, who sounded winded. Both of them shook slightly, just as they would have done if they were attempting to lift an immense weight with their muscles rather than the power of the Force. "Let's just edge it to the side, bring it down slowly."

Reath nodded. In truth, no words were needed; he could feel the unified intention within every Jedi currently standing amid this disaster-struck zone of Inad Komesh, all of them thinking and acting in harmony. Yet words, like hand motions, helped with the focus that was so important in their efforts—and rarely more so than now, when they held hundreds of thousands of kilos worth of bricks above the heads of so many helpless people. He moved slowly, turning just as Dez turned, angling the half-collapsed tower away from them, toward other buildings that he hoped were empty. Just in case they weren't, though, he began settling the tower very slowly downward so that no structures beneath it would be instantly crushed. Enough of the dust had cleared for him to see Vernestra in the middle distance, as well as

Bell and Burryaga farther away, all of them joined in the effort. Every Jedi moved in unison, as though these were the steps in a dance they had all performed many times before.

The slow settling of the tower still made noise—the crash of breaking windows, the thuds of tumbling duracrete—but after another moment, Reath felt the weight lift from him and the others. Immediately, he got back on task. "Come on! We have to fill this transport now!"

Dez turned to the entryway, the better to count and organize the rescued, but he paused just long enough to say, "Where's Master Adampo?"

Reath scanned the crowd, realizing only then that the Council member had been standing at the edge of the crowd—near the place where the first tower fell. "I'll find him."

Attempting to simply push through the frenzied crowd shoving its way into the transport would have been futile. Reath bounded up over them in a leap that sent him at least four meters into the air and was long enough to take him over Vernestra's head. His feet skidded into the dusty walk not far from where Burryaga stood. The Wookiee roared his approval and encouragement as he carried two injured persons—one cradled in each arm—toward the transport.

"Master!" Reath called as he began lifting fallen beams and blocks, searching through the rubble. Was Adampo half-buried by it, injured, unable to speak?

Then he hauled up another plysheet and found Adampo . . . or, rather, what remained of him. One piece of crashing debris had fallen unchecked, even by his skill in the Force. As a result, very little of Master Adampo's head was left; in its place was only blood and gore.

Another member of the Council lost? Another dead? The sheer horror of it swept over Reath, but he could not allow himself to feel the weight of this, not at this moment when there were so many lives to save. Would not any Jedi Master place the good of others beyond all personal concerns? *Brace up. Move on.*

No time to retrieve the body in full, Reath decided with fresh resolve. The space on their transports must go to the living. From the looks of things, the collapse of Inad Komesh was likely to serve as Master Adampo's funeral pyre.

He went back to helping the crowd into the transport and signaling the next transport's landing place. From the comlink at his belt, messages kept coming through from other rescue teams in other quadrants of the moon, all of them reporting the same: more collapses, more sinkholes, more catastrophic damage, the rate of each accelerating by the minute.

"Come on, Silas!" Bell Zettifar yelled. He and Ember stood at the entry to the second transport—which, clearly, would be the last transport capable of ever leaving this place.

The last of the straggler civilians were running on board, so Reath followed, making one more great leap to land nearly at Bell's side.

This won him half a smile from Bell. "Show-off."

It was a small joke, not one likely to amuse either of them for long in a situation so dire. Both Reath and Bell grabbed on to the entry-jamb struts as the transport rose upward, blowing around yet more grayish dust. Once again Reath thought of the chance that the blight could lurk within those particles; he forced himself to trust their initial surveys and to accept that there was nothing to be done about it at this point but to keep going.

The dust clouds could not conceal the way the ground had begun to cave in beneath them—all around them—the circle widening more and more into a shatteringly enormous maw, into which yet more buildings began to topple. Burryaga whined in dismay as Inad Komesh continued to collapse and contract, the damage spreading ever wider as the transport rose. By the time the Jedi had to step inside and seal the door shut for upper atmosphere, the scene beneath had become one of pure horror: structure after structure calcifying into deathly white, then dissolving into ghostly dust. Here a shuttle port collapsed, layer upon layer, losing more substance and shape with each consecutive crunch; there a land-vehicle bridge swayed and sank as if to its knees. Soon it looked as though nothing remained intact on the surface—and as though the surface itself had crumbled many meters deeper than before.

The Jedi stood in silence for a few long moments, breathing hard. All around them, Inadi wept, shook, or stood numb in utter shock. It was Bell who finally said, "Come on. Let's queue up for the sterilization booths. I've never wanted a wash so badly."

Bell's jaunty tone fooled no one. Nearly everybody in the galaxy knew the danger of potential contamination by the blight at this point. Reath wanted to believe in the results of their earlier scans, and in the few moments he had been able to spare for meditation in the past few days, he had sensed, as deeply as his current circumstances allowed, that probably he *could* believe in them. Still, that was instinct, not certainty—and such delicate predictions could be no reassurance to the Inadi.

So everyone, rescuer and rescued alike, did as Bell said, quietly shuffling into lines. What else could they do? Reath joined them, wishing he could give those around him a moment of greater comfort and hope instead of this slow, bureaucratic set of cleanings and checks that would determine whether the blight, like a malignant shadow, had followed them onward.

Around the dying moon of Inad Komesh orbited a small satellite, one that would easily fit in a humanoid hand. At that size, it escaped the notice of all organic life-forms and most droids; it might as easily have been a random bit of space junk, the flotsam that circled every inhabited planet until the day it sank into the atmosphere, heated, and burned away in a spark of light too brief for anyone to notice. Nor would it have been picked up by an energy sweep, as the satellite used very little power. Its solar batteries only needed capacity enough to fuel a few sensors and a transmitter.

That transmitter fed its signal to a router, deep in the Occlusion Zone, one that had its own broadcast coordinates changed every few days. Only at the second destination—a specially modified Nihil Spider Squall cruiser called the *Firebringer*—was the death of Inad Komesh viewed.

"How very interesting," whispered Dr. Mkampa. Her tiny skittering servitor droids rolled and tapped closer to her; proximity was safe when she was happy. At the moment, she was very nearly ecstatic, a broad, bright smile contrasting against her darker skin. Even her many cybernetic enhancements seemed to gleam in the laboratory lights. "Not at all what I was told—but precisely as I anticipated."

With one hand she optimized the information fed to their location, creating a detailed record she could analyze in depth later, on the very slim chance that she was wrong. With the other she pressed the *Firebringer*'s main comm signal, the one that called to—and delivered messages from—the leader of the Nihil, Marchion Ro.

He did not reply immediately. Mkampa did not expect him to. At this point, Ro very nearly ruled not only the Nihil but also a growing swath of the galactic space once governed by the Republic. The demands on his time had grown exponentially. Yet she had a feeling that her message would attract his attention, and soon.

In this, too, Mkampa was correct, because it had not been ten minutes before the holo appeared in her ship, life-size, seemingly only paces from her: Marchion Ro in his helmet and full battle gear. The eye of his helmet appeared to swirl as he said, "Dr. Mkampa. Surely we have no pressing business?"

They did, and he knew it, or he would not have bothered replying. Still, Mkampa played along. "Your trial of the cure for the blight—it appears to have failed," she replied, lifting her chin.

"There was no test."

"Really? We had agreed that Inad's industrial moon would make an excellent test subject. . . ."

"I decided against it," Ro said. "The evacuation began too late.

Too many witnesses would have reported the moon's survival, and quickly—thus giving the Republic false hope and uselessly extending this conflict."

"Indeed," said Mkampa. Only a few weeks prior, he had argued that a populated world or moon would be a better place for the trials to be run, because then the effects of the blight, and its supposed cure, could be tested on multiple levels of plant, animal, and sentient life, as well as on constructions and technology. Ro had argued this after Mkampa had suggested that they run the test on an asteroid—a suggestion she had made only after Ro had said that only something similarly deserted would allow them to keep the result entirely secret. "Should we then begin our search for a previously inhabited world now abandoned? So you might study the effects on such structures as remain?"

The one swirling eye of Ro's mask seemed to contract. An illusion, perhaps—Mkampa's cybernetic eye occasionally focused too sharply for her liking—but one perhaps inspired by the irritation and suspicion she knew must have been hidden by that mask. "An excellent suggestion, Dr. Mkampa. Please begin immediately."

"And you will continue with the current seeding protocol?" She took care to make it sound as though this were an afterthought, no great concern to her.

"Of course. But leave that matter to me, Dr. Mkampa. Your priority should be your search."

"Certainly, my lord," Mkampa said before cutting communication with Marchion Ro for what she expected to be the last time.

When Marchion Ro had stunned the galaxy by going to Chancellor Lina Soh and offering to save the Republic—to save everyone—from the blight, Mkampa had been intrigued. What cure had he devised? Who, among the Nihil, could have found such a cure, other than herself? She had requested samples, had asked for a role in the study of this cure and its potential further development, had all but begged for the chance to deploy it herself. The dance of Ro's ever-shifting priorities had then begun. By now, Mkampa knew the truth, the one the Eye of the Storm hid from Republic and Nihil alike:

He had no cure for the blight. His promise was pure falsehood. Neither he nor anyone else could stop it.

Rational responses to this would have included deep shock, shrieking outrage, or overwhelming horror. Mkampa, infused as ever with the roiling enthusiasm of the zealot, felt her smile spread wide.

"The lie of the Eye will be known to all eventually," she said to the silent droids surrounding her. The mute shining audience was the only one she needed. "Teeth will gnash and voices will wail, but their fates are inevitable. The Galactic Republic and the Nihil Storm will both collapse, and afterward . . . only a very different sort of power can hope to prevail."

It would take a long time for even the insidious blight to destroy the entire galaxy. Distant stretches of Wild Space might prove both safe haven and raw material to those enterprising individuals ready to seize the opportunities present.

Mkampa went to her personal vault within the *Firebringer*, one even her own droids could not possibly open; she had synced the lock with her cybernetic eye so only her own gaze had the power to reveal what lay within.

She had found it approximately a year prior, during her initial searches for a "cure" test site. At that time, her loyalty to Marchion Ro had been all but absolute—yet she had kept the device secret, knowing the power within was too great to give away to anyone. Mkampa would either use it herself or see that it ceased to exist. Had Ro made good on any of his promises, she might well have hurled the object into a sun to melt.

But he hadn't. That made this her power to wield.

"Deep within the ruins, it lay," Mkampa whispered as she leaned into the scanner light of the lock. Her face flickered with green light; the whir and click of releasing tumblers made her smile. "Covered in dust. The scanners had no idea what to make of it. How fortunate that I figured it out. You might even say it called to me. . . ."

The door of the vault slid open, revealing within the faint glowing pyramid of a Sith holocron.

Mkampa smiled. "Let's have some fun."

THREE

Mkampa's insight regarding Marchion Ro's long-term strategy for ending the blight—or his lack of one—was information she kept to herself. Perhaps the enormity of her ego prevented her from understanding that she was not the only person capable of reaching this conclusion.

Throughout the rest of the Nihil, others were realizing that Ro's vision of the future was somewhat lacking . . . and they did not respond like Dr. Mkampa. Ghirra Starros could see the signs.

When Ro had made his grand offer to cure the blight—had proposed to play galactic savior—Ghirra had been as surprised as anyone else. They should have discussed this together, debated the pros and cons of offering help, determined a way to negotiate the price of such assistance, even worked out the exact wording he would use in speaking to Chancellor Soh. Instead, not a word. Ghirra had been stung that Ro had not shared this amazing cure with her, nor his thought process regarding how to use such powerful knowledge, and she had seen it as a sign of distrust. Since then, she had come to fear precisely what Mkampa had divined: that there was no cure, that Ro's promises of salvation were empty.

Were all the rest of his promises equally false?

She knew she was not the only one asking. With the Nihil at unprecedented power and influence, the mood aboard their ships and within any of their gatherings ought to have been ebullient, near ecstatic. Instead, where any group of Nihil came together, one heard the mutterings of discontent. There had always been rivalries within the Storm, backstabbing and skulduggery galore—but the rivalries had at least always had stakes, consequences, something at the center worth fighting for. More recently, the fractiousness had become not only more plentiful but also pettier, sometimes bordering on the childish. It was only a matter of time, Ghirra thought, before schism.

Most frustrating to her was that all this was avoidable. If Marchion Ro would step up, if he would become the leader she had once believed she saw in him, all this could be remedied. The Nihil were in such a position of strength, and Ro on the verge of such domination, that nothing should be beyond Marchion's grasp.

But still, he refused to truly *govern*; Ro exercised his power while ignoring most of the responsibilities that came with it.

Ghirra tried explaining this to him. It didn't go well.

"You talk like a bureaucrat," he said between quaffs of teal Alderaanian wine. They sat at a ridiculously resplendent dinner table, laden with dishes and decorations as though they were having the entire Senate to supper when in fact only the two of them were eating. "You would be so much more comfortable if I set up forms for government officials to fill out. If I issued codes for Stormwall access. If I *licensed* ships." He spoke the word *licensed* with contempt so harsh it bordered on venom. "I didn't rally the Storm so I could become a mere office drudge."

"You don't have to do any of those things," Ghirra said, though privately she thought it might not be a bad idea to order someone else to do them. "But there's no way to rule without authority, and authority isn't only about power. Authority is about having the ability to get things done. As much as everyone loves to ridicule red tape, a certain degree of bureaucracy is necessary to ensure that systems and governments run smoothly."

"You think we can't operate without it?" Marchion gave her his curved-blade smile. "Watch."

Thanks to a career in politics, Ghirra had become very good at holding her tongue. On this night, she decided not to. "Oh, you can operate without it . . . for a few months. A year. Maybe even two. But the longer you go without providing a functional government, the more quickly you bring about your own ruin."

"The Jedi are no threat any longer—"

"Will you *shut up* about the Jedi?" Ghirra slammed her hand down on the table; plates, goblets, and utensils all jangled. Marchion gave her the kind of look that reminded her of the exact location of the nearest airlock. She moderated her tone but not her words. "Your domination of the Jedi is one of your greatest triumphs, but the Nameless are not infinite in number . . . and the Republic is not solely defended by the Jedi. If the people rise up against you, Marchion—the people who don't use the Force, who don't care about the Nameless—how long do you think you can stand?"

He shrugged lazily. "We'll find out. And when we do, my Storm will be ready."

Your Storm is made up of people who were once not so different from the Republic citizens you scorn, Ghirra thought that evening after dinner as she walked back to her quarters alone. *Let the downtrodden of the Republic realize that the Nihil are nothing but witless thugs, and they will offer up thugs of their own.*

There had been a time she believed that the Republic needed amendment so badly that even the rough edges of the Nihil could be acceptable, because only such destruction could effect real change on an institution that was literally tens of thousands of years old. Ghirra now had trouble remembering what she had thought needed amending in the first place.

None of this would have mattered much had Ro already, finally, decidedly *won the conflict,* as Ghirra had once thought inevitable. His position remained powerful, but the longer he failed to capitalize on that position—to expand and solidify it into enduring authority—and the more damage the blight did to all that she had once believed he would rule, the more she heard the whispers in the back of her mind hinting that she might have backed the wrong fathier in the race.

As she turned a very rounded corner within the corridor, she nearly ran into Thaya Ferr—mousy and omnipresent as ever—and the girl called Nan. As always, the sight of this would-be intelligence operative, so inexplicably in Ro's good graces, irritated Ghirra past patience. "How does Thaya announce you, anyway? Don't you need a second name?" Ghirra snapped at the girl.

Nan hesitated. "I could use Hague, I suppose. He was good to me. It's as proper a second name as anything else."

"Well, Nan Hague, if you're hurrying off to ingratiate yourself with Marchion again, don't bother," Ghirra said. "He's done with dinner but not done with his wine. By the time he's free, I doubt he'll be conscious."

In her usual clipped voice, Thaya replied, "The Eye just sent for her. She is responding to his summons."

He had thrown Ghirra out before doing business? Business with this scrap of a girl? Galled beyond the ability to speak, Ghirra hurried past them, the cold air within the *Gaze Electric* sharp against her shame-warmed cheeks.

She had no idea what he wanted with Nan, nor did she much care. Whatever it was, it no doubt involved more secret intelligence–type maneuvers, all of which would be cleverly concealed and potentially devastating and would not bring them one bit closer to an actual functioning government.

I shouldn't have spoken to him so sharply, Ghirra thought. *He's tired of hearing it from me, and I'm the only person he hears it from at all. If I lose all influence over him, disaster will no longer be possible—it will be inevitable.*

But the question was not when or how she might lose that influence. The question was whether she already had.

So Ghirra Starros is out, Nan thought as Thaya Ferr showed her into Ro's chamber. Yet another of the inner circle had been cast aside. *All the people I once looked up to, the ones I thought would lead us forever—they fall, and I remain.*

Marchion Ro lazed in one of his high, broad chairs, the type that wouldn't have appeared out of place for the Chancellor's seat in the Galactic Senate. The translucent goblet in his hand was nearly full, certainly not for the first time that evening; Starros might have lost her grip on many aspects of her place within the Nihil, but she hadn't been wrong about the Eye's indulgence.

"Nan Hague, sir," said Thaya. "I'll be waiting outside to escort her back at your convenience."

If Ro registered that Nan now had a surname, or even that he hadn't known it before, he showed no sign. "Thank you, Thaya."

He thanks few people, Nan thought, casting a glance toward Thaya, who was already walking out. *Probably because his little minion would die for him and would even make sure not to leave a mess behind. He's always aware of loyalty and disloyalty. He is not an easy man to deceive.*

"You have had quite a journey with us, have you not?" Ro began. "You are one of the children of the Nihil—the first generation to be born within our ranks, the first who will live in a galaxy that never knows the taint of the Republic."

"Yes, my lord." She tried, as she sometimes did, to remember the faces of her parents. They had become all but lost over time. But she remembered Hague holding her up, showing her the swirled-cyclone symbol of the Nihil and saying, *That's us, Nan. That means we've been here.* After her parents' deaths, it had felt so good to be part of something bigger than herself. Hague had taught her about the Nihil dream and all it promised.

"The very first time you had a chance to help us, at that Amaxine station where you were marooned by the Great Hyperspace Disaster—you exceeded our wildest expectations. Or, I should say, you would have done, because as yet we did not even know you well enough to expect anything. But you infiltrated the Jedi. You won their trust, learned their stories, gained a purer source of intel than some operatives who had been working for years."

"With Hague's help, my lord."

Ro showed no sign of having heard her. "Then you manage to bring me stories of the fall of Starlight Beacon. To pay witness to its demise, to thwart the Jedi's hopes of saving the station, and then to escape intact. And then you serve on the Lightning Crash under Dr. Mkampa and feed me information on her loyalty, or lack thereof?" He took another deep quaff, then studied her, head cocked, like a salt hawk spotting a juicy toad. "It is rare to find people capable of both taking initiative and following orders. You appear to be one of them."

"I have always sought to serve the Nihil as best I can," Nan said. She knew he had not mentioned Dr. Mkampa at random, but it would be better to show no curiosity about that or any other topic. Ro always wanted his underlings' attention focused primarily on him. "It's good to know that you think I've done well."

"You have long wished to be a spy, have you not? A true intelligence operative?"

Nan knew her answers must be both complete and very careful. "I feel that I've already acted in that capacity on several occasions. But those moments have always been—improvised. Making the best of a difficult situation. I've often wondered what it would be like to undertake intelligence-gathering missions on a larger scale, with an established objective."

Ro nodded. "You know the difference, then, between what you have already done and what you wish to become."

"Acutely, my lord."

"I may have such a mission for you," he said. "You will go alone. You will have no backup, no security, and only minimal weaponry. There will be no communications between you and our Storm until the end—unless, of course, you learn something of such import that you consider it worth breaking mission protocols. If you do so, however, be aware: If I do not agree that your information merited that sacrifice, you will pay the price."

Nan wondered whether that meant a quick death or a slow one. Ro dispensed both at his whim. "I would expect no less."

"Young as you are, your experience—particularly your gift for improvisation in times of both risk and opportunity—tells me your judgment can be relied upon. So let us test that, hmm?"

He asked her questions as though she still had the ability to turn the mission down. Nan knew better than that. The task before her was not optional; refusal meant disobedience, which would be answered with death.

But it didn't matter. Nan did not want to refuse. She had a

rough idea of what he might be about to ask her, and if she was correct, this mission was the last task she would ever wish to turn down. It might well be one she had dreamed of for months now. If so, this would be the single greatest opportunity of her life.

Ro rose from his chair and walked toward her. His considerable height towered over Nan, who was rather small for a human and had only just given up hoping for a late growth spurt. Being small, she had learned how to avoid being intimidated. She had also learned that it was very easy to convince larger people that she *was* intimidated, the better to keep them off their guard. With the Eye of the Storm, she decided, a middle path was best; she lowered her head enough to suggest respect, even awe, but she stood as straight as she could. When he looked at her, she wanted him to see a weapon shaped perfectly for his hand.

"Tell me, Nan," he said. "Have you never been curious to see Coruscant?"

I was right, she thought, and she managed not to smile.

FOUR

There had been a time when the cargo vessel *Cathar Crown* flew as proudly as a banner, a magnificent tribute to its home planet's prosperity and engineering skill. Its captain, Gabs Marise, estimated that this time had ended no less than three centuries prior. Ever since, a series of owners had been keeping it in the air through a mixture of intelligent repairs, slap-dash repairs, and no small amount of prayer to various planetary deities. The current owners, in Gabs's opinion, only continued sending the *Cathar Crown* out in hopes of a disaster that might allow them to collect on insurance. Not a comforting thought for its crew.

And never was that less comforting than at a moment like this, when ominous signals showed up on the very fringes of the system. The Ithorian navigator clucked, low and concerned, as he ran another sweep—which confirmed the worst.

"We have the Nihil approaching!" chirped their Chadra-Fan pilot. "No more than a Cloud, maybe even just a Strike, but . . ."

The pilot didn't need to finish that sentence. What few defenses the *Cathar Crown* possessed had grown rickety and unreliable. Gabs doubted they could stand up to a single Nihil ship for long.

"Send a distress signal," Gabs ordered. "All channels, all frequencies, flood it."

The pilot's pointy ears drooped—she knew as well as anyone how thin the Republic resources were stretched—but she said only, "Aye, Captain."

Gabs thought fast. "Okay, we all know we can't outgun them. We can't leap to hyperspace this close to Viasyl." They were currently collecting heavy gases from the outermost layers of the gas giant Viasyl, tedious work that tasked the engines to their limits merely resisting the tremendous gravitational forces at work. "Do you think we can make it clear before the Nihil reach us?"

"We'd have to fly toward the Nihil to do it," the pilot replied. "Which gives us a couple of minutes to navigate our way out—"

The navigator purred in hope, but too soon.

"—but if they realize what we're doing and accelerate, we'll have flown straight to our deaths," the pilot finished.

They won't blow us up right away, Gabs thought. *They know we're mining volatile gases and won't risk an explosion that could take some of their ships out, as well. Besides, they're raiders. They* raid. *Probably they'll board the ship and ransack it for the little it's worth. But afterward—*

Sometimes the Nihil took hostages and charged exorbitant

ransoms, when they thought they could get the money. One look at the *Cathar Crown* and they'd know the owners were unlikely to pay any ransom large enough to even buy lunch. No, if they got caught, Gabs and the crew were dead.

"Maybe they haven't seen us?" Gabs said.

The Ithorian navigator shook his enormous head and gestured toward the readings, which showed the Nihil already assembling into attack formation.

"Right. Time to hide." Gabs pulled up the specs on Viasyl, which like all gaseous planets was surrounded by vast klicks of haze before approaching anything as solid as a surface. "Any chance we can dive into the upper layers of the planet, confuse their systems?"

"They'll probably realize what we've done," the pilot said, "but they might not pursue. Their ships are smaller, and escaping from that gravity will be harder for them than for us. That said, it won't be easy for us, either."

Gabs didn't want to die being sucked into the full density of a gas giant and ultimately crushed by gravity. But if the choice was between that and being tortured by the Nihil until they were thrown out of an airlock, the gas giant it was. "Take us in, then. Go carefully."

The Chadra-Fan pilot shot her a dark look—she knew how careful they needed to be; only a fool wouldn't—but she did as Gabs said. Slowly they began to approach the gas giant, which loomed larger and redder before them. Soon it would blot out all the darkness and all the stars of the sky—

"Damn!" The pilot's cry was followed by the horrifying

appearance of another Nihil Strike. Gabs's hearts sank as the truth set in: The other Nihil had been hiding behind the gas giant all the time.

A suicide run? Dive into the core, hope the Nihil would follow closely enough that a few of them would be taken out by the ultimate explosion? No good choices remained, but that might have been the best one. Gabs spared a moment to think of her home—its beautiful night sky, the three moons in their various phases overhead—then lifted a hand to give the order.

The pilot shouted. "Look! Incoming!"

Gabs's eyes widened as another entire small fleet appeared, silver streaks zipping into view. But they weren't Nihil—or Republic.

"*Cathar Crown*, this is Affie Hollow of the Byne Guild ship *Vessel*!" a young woman's voice called. "Hold position as close to the planet as you can—we've got you!"

Some of those on the bridge cheered as the Byne Guild fleet swarmed closer, positioning itself between the *Cathar Crown* and the Nihil. The Guild fleet was a motley bunch: cargo ships like their own, smaller haulcraft, a few starfighters, and even one repurposed pleasure yacht. But they all appeared to be armed and ready for battle.

The Nihil didn't react immediately; if Gabs had to guess, her theory would have been that the Nihil saw just another bunch of civilian ships and expected them to scatter or surrender. As the Guild ships took attack formation, however, the Nihil began to swerve, but too late. The same flight patterns that were ideal for surrounding a lone ship were also spreading their defenses too thin to oppose a fleet of any size.

An oddly bulbous bluish ship zoomed forward, not firing—Gabs nearly froze in disbelief—but the little ship had a skifter in its deck. The Chadra-Fan navigator chirped, "It's activating a tractor beam!"

"A tractor beam? A ship that size?" Gabs had rarely seen such a thing. But never had she seen what happened next: the little ship focusing its beam on the lead Nihil craft. The two ships spun in an ellipse around each other, the bluish ship seemingly winding up the Nihil as though their enemy were a stone in a sling. Then the tiny ship cut its (apparently *extremely* powerful) tractor beam completely at just the right moment to send the Nihil craft hurtling uncontrollably into the gas giant, past the point of escaping gravity, until it disappeared from sensors in a flash. Gabs imagined hearing the crunch of its hull.

The other fleet ships were attacking the Nihil with regular weapons, but this Strike had been after the easy kill. Now that the *Cathar Crown* required effort to capture, they lost interest. Within an instant, the ships began to peel off—and not in any organized manner. Those Nihil craft would soon be scattered across half a quadrant.

They know how to win, Gabs thought, *but they don't know how to lose.*

The little blue ship brought itself nearly nose to nose with the *Cathar Crown* as the holo transmitter switched on, revealing a shockingly young-looking captain. Her long straight dark hair hung over one shoulder in a single plait; her coverall had been decorated with patches from various planets and systems. "Affie Hollow of the *Vessel*," she said. "Are all of you okay?"

"We are now, thanks to you," Gabs said. The navigator murmured, calling attention to a few blinking orange panels that hinted at damage. "Actually, it looks like we have a few hull braces that could use shoring up—but we'd be in much worse shape if you lot hadn't arrived."

"That's what we do here with the Byne Guild," said Hollow. "I'd like to talk with you more about us, after we get you some repair help. We've got a priority path charted to a friendly port on Alderaan. Would you care for an escort?"

Gabs had been to Alderaan once, long ago. Its beauty lingered in her memory like a fairy story. Given how close they had just come to death, going to Alderaan sounded a bit like going to heaven. "An escort would be great."

☽☾

Affie hadn't had as much opportunity to explore the Core Worlds as she would have liked, but she already knew: If you had the chance to go to Alderaan, you *went*.

Her small fleet wasn't sad about the stop, either. Those who were still hauling some cargo had the chance to sell; those with empty holds had opportunities to haul. Ships that needed repair could get it done here with confidence in top craftsmanship and a fair price. All this on a world where the air seemed always to smell of conifers and freshly fallen rain.

For her part, Affie found a table at an outdoor cafe with a stunning view of distant snowcapped mountains. This was less difficult than it would've been on many worlds, as stunning mountainscapes seemed to lie in every direction in Aldera. Her table had three chairs: one for her; one for her ship's pilot, Leox Gyasi; and one for the *Cathar Crown* captain yet to join them. The *Vessel*'s navigator, Geode, preferred to stand.

"He's kinda got a thing about mountains," said Leox as they drank their caf and watched Geode staring wistfully at the distant snowcaps. "For Vintians, they're—I guess you'd say aspirational."

"I get it," Affie replied. "Mountains are kind of the ultimate rocks, right?"

Despite common belief to the contrary, Vintians were not rocks. It was just difficult to tell the difference between Vintians and rocks unless you were a Vintian yourself (or, Affie supposed, a rock). Yet, as a mineral life-form, Geode did sometimes betray a certain soft spot for various cliffs, outcroppings, stalactites, stalagmites, and the like. Mountain ranges often touched him deeply, as this one apparently had. Affie, less sensitive to geological wonder, was content just to enjoy the view.

At that moment, Captain Gabs Marise appeared; almost instantly, a servitor droid poured a third cup of steaming caf. Gabs looked wrung out—beige fur frizzing in all directions— which Affie felt was fair.

"We came way too close to being Nihil prey today," Gabs told them. "Thank you, all of you."

"That's what we do," said Leox. "That is, when we're not working like any other set of pilots throughout the galaxy."

Affie had been polishing her sales pitch ever since the Stormwall went up; she thought she was getting good at it, and Leox had set her up perfectly. She began, "See, the Byne Guild— we used to be under pretty strict control. A lot of pilots and their ships were indentured, and many of them were forced to take risks they should never have been faced with. All that has changed now. Our founder"—she knew better than to specify *my mother* at the recruiting stage—"was sent to jail for her crimes, but we've stuck together. We're an alliance of independent pilots who come to each other's aid—and sometimes, like today, we come to the aid of other ships, too."

"Make no mistake," Leox said. "We're no match for Nihil firepower—"

"It looks like you hardly have any weaponry on the *Vessel* at all," Gabs interjected. "One cannon, and not a large one at that."

Leox nodded. "I'm opposed to armaments on philosophical grounds."

Gabs sputtered over the rim of her cup. "During a *war?*"

"Well, naturally. It doesn't require much of a philosophical stance to remain unarmed when there's nothing dangerous going on." Leox took another deep sip. "It's staying unarmed in a conflict that takes guts. Ultimately, our responsibilities to our clients led us to take on the cannon, but we don't fire it unless we have to. Risky, you might say—and you might not be wrong—but I'll remind you that the *Vessel* faced off with a Nihil Strike leader today, *without* using the cannon, and we're not the ones who wound up being crushed in a gas giant."

This tangent was turning into a distraction, Affie thought. "Individual ships within the Guild make their own decisions about whether they want to be armed, and if so, with what and how much of it. That's the whole point: Ships remain independent, yet within a framework that allows us to help and protect each other."

"You have no warships?" Gabs looked dubious. "Only a few starfighters?"

"Put the right pilot in the cockpit of a starfighter, and that's all you need." Leox grinned. "Besides, as you saw, we've learned a few tricks that help us get the better of the Nihil most of the time."

"Not all the time," Gabs said, in a tone that suggested they'd been caught out.

Affie nodded. "No. Not all the time. The risk is real. I'd be lying if I even suggested otherwise. But we're making a living out there, despite all of this, because we do it *together*."

After a few moments, Gabs shrugged. "I guess I can hear you out."

Leox leaned back and grinned. "Then let's sit and chat for a spell."

He'd take the lead from this point on. Leox was better at this, and Affie generally didn't mind turning the conversation over to him. But at that moment she would have welcomed the distraction talking provided, because the enormity of the crisis facing them all had just hit her anew, yawning dark in front of her like the vastness of space but without a single speck of starlight. They all made their living in a galaxy where the Nihil called the shots, where all the powers and wisdom of the Jedi could fail, where nobody knew what to do about the blight. Alderaan seemed like one of the last oases of peace and harmony in the galaxy—and Affie knew they couldn't stay.

FIVE

Through some miracle of the Force, no one who had escaped the moon Inad Komesh turned out to have been exposed to the blight. Reath Silas dwelled deeply on his gratitude for this unlikely but welcome circumstance; gratitude became even more important as it became harder to come by, as it certainly was these days.

After taking the Inadi survivors to their homeworld, the Jedi transport began the journey back to Coruscant. Reath watched through one of the oblong viewports as the ship went past Inad Komesh, which now resembled nothing so much as a bit of crumpled refuse, with its once-bustling megacity reduced to ashen rubble. It was as though Marchion Ro's malevolent fist had reached across the galaxy to crush the moon in its remorseless grip.

For a moment Reath's encounters with the Nameless welled up again in his mind, hinting at the cold shivering nausea of dread. . . .

Then Reath shook his head. He didn't have to deal with a Nameless right now. Marchion Ro wasn't some deity of legend or some immensely powerful creature of myth. He was a man; therefore he was fallible and his abilities limited. Therefore, eventually, Ro would make a mistake—a fatal one—and the so-called Eye of the Storm would be revealed for the sham he truly was.

All the Jedi had to do was keep looking for that mistake and their chance to strike back.

He was startled from his reverie when the sanitation droid chirped, "Will you wish to postpone your final sterilization shower?"

"No," Reath said, turning his mind back to the present. "I'll take my turn."

Because scientists remained uncertain of how the blight was spread, those who had come into near contact with it were obliged to undergo a vigorous cleaning process before entering the ship at large or setting foot on another planet. Even though scans had confirmed no blight particulates had entered their ship, protocols had to be obeyed to the letter; this was not only a matter of regulations but also a chance to reinforce habits that might save their lives on some future day. Reath placed his robes in the appropriate hamper for their own sonic clean before submitting his naked self to a spray that was part water, part chemical, and all nasty. Wincing from the smell, he scrubbed his hair as per protocol.

At least I don't have as much hair to scrub as some, he thought as he heard a lot of whirring and loud growl-howling coming through the wall from the booth next to his. Burryaga's thick pelt meant that he essentially had to undergo a thorough vacuuming; from the sound of things, this was not an enjoyable process.

Reath couldn't help grinning, but the smile didn't last.

Elsewhere on the transport, his fellow Jedi also struggled with what they had just seen.

Indeera Stokes had only witnessed the mayhem for a few moments and from the safety of the transport cockpit, but that had been enough to horrify her. Even if they had not already discerned the connection between the Nameless and the blight, she believed she would have sensed it. The terrible injuries she had suffered from her near encounter with one of the Nameless—it had *felt* the way the blight looked: gray, desiccated, crumbling. Sometimes, in her dreams, the sensations returned to her so vividly, so horrifyingly, that she would awake panting, convinced that she had not been saved, that the horror still waited inside her, ready to hatch.

Vernestra Rwoh remained among the steadiest of them all. She meditated within the ship, as placidly as though she were within the heart of a temple on some peaceful little outworld untroubled by greater galactic cares; that day, her mind was filled with memories of her former master. Stellan Gios had never stopped fighting, not even when the Nameless had damaged him, not even when he'd ridden the burning remnant of Starlight Beacon into the sea, to his doom. Vernestra intended to do no less.

Bell Zettifar had had an easy time in his own sterilization booth but afterward needed to console both Ember and Burryaga after the vacuuming processes they'd had to endure. They were so put out by it—Ember bristling, Burryaga's sour expression in sharp contrast to his fluffed-out fur—that Bell couldn't help laughing. Burryaga didn't resent it. They had to seize what few chances for laughter they got these days.

In the sick bay, Amadeo Azzazzo was being seen to by Dorian Innes. To be specific, his shoulder was being seen to, having been dislocated in the effort to help a heavily pregnant woman to safety. Amadeo was untroubled by an injury acquired in the line of duty, but he was struck by Dorian's calm.

"You have to have been shocked by what we've seen today," Amadeo said to him.

"I haven't looked beyond my patients," Dorian replied.

"It's got worse," Amadeo said. "We thought it couldn't get any worse, and now it has."

"The people I'm seeing are no more or less injured than before," Dorian insisted. His hands braced Amadeo's shoulder as the anesthetic medpatches kicked in. "Let me know when you're numb."

Within seconds, the sensation of Dorian's palms against Amadeo's bare shoulder faded away. "Now."

It took only an instant for Dorian to pop Amadeo's arm back into its socket with a sickening wet crunch. Brave though Amadeo was, he took a moment to be grateful for painkilling technology.

"I've administered meds to keep post-injury swelling down," Dorian said, looking upon Amadeo's restored form with satisfaction. "It's going to be hard to use that arm while the medpatches are still in place, and you'll be tempted to remove them. Don't. The aftermath of this injury can hurt almost as badly as the injury itself."

"The medpatches are going nowhere," Amadeo promised.

The Jedi, wise as they were, could occasionally fall prey to pride—in particular the idea that they had much to teach the galaxy beyond their temples but had little to learn from that galaxy in return. Amadeo felt he would never make that mistake again, not after watching Dorian in action. While he and so many of the others became discouraged by looking at the larger picture, Dorian stayed solely focused on the tasks before him. He lived in the moment. And by doing so, he was able to truly help. It was a lesson Amadeo had needed, one he intended not to forget.

꧁꧂

Dez Rydan had never undergone the blight protocol before, had never before even witnessed the blight doing its corrosive work. He stood in the sterilization shower, numb to thought, as the chemical fumes stung his nose and eyes. Again and again, he remembered the toppling buildings, the frightened crowds, the blinding grit of endless dust.

The Jedi need to work on their process for welcoming back those who have taken the Vow, Dez decided as he dried off afterward. Meditations encouraged for this process talked about reentering duty as though it would be a very ordinary thing. *During wartime,* he thought, *those returning should be more carefully braced and briefed for what is to come.*

Maybe other Jedi would benefit from this insight. Dez had done without, and he hoped he had nonetheless done well. From past experience, he knew that the queasy, unsettled feeling within him could be quieted through meditation, certain koans, or the far more prosaic method that had always been his personal favorite.

So a few minutes later, Dez was sitting in the transport mess, helping himself to a large bowl of Mirialan porridge, when Reath Silas came in.

"The Barash Vow hasn't changed one thing about you, at least," Reath said. "You're still hungry practically every minute of the day."

Dez shrugged good-naturedly. "A good solid meal is always settling. You ought to know—you used to keep up with me, bite for bite. Master Jora always used to say she wanted us to compete."

"She did, didn't she? I'd nearly forgotten that." Reath shook his head. "These past three years—the intensity of the events we've all lived through—it doesn't leave much time for thinking back about Master Jora. We've lost so many people since the Great Hyperspace Disaster that we never have enough time to mourn, or to remember. And I want to remember everything about our master."

Dez had been Jora Malli's Padawan before Reath; oftentimes a young Knight would befriend their master's next apprentice, becoming a mentor who was more of a peer than a teacher. When Dez had done this for Reath, he had only thought of it in those terms, little realizing that—in times as dark and desperate as these—their shared memories of Master Jora would become so precious and so fragile. Their bond served a purpose beyond Reath's training. It connected them to the life they had both known, the one they still hoped to find again after the Nihil fell . . . if they fell.

Reath looked even more dismayed than Dez felt, his expression clearly showing the grief he still felt for Master Jora. Dez put down his spoon. "It's all right, you know. She'd understand. Master Jora's returned to the Force; we still bear the burdens of the living."

"Which is the greater burden?" Reath asked. "Memories of what's been lost or the tragedy of forgetting?"

It was a rhetorical question. Dez understood that. But he also knew this question actually had an answer. "Memories. Always, memories."

"Your memories of encountering the dark side on the Amaxine station—they still burden you?" Reath took a seat opposite Dez.

"They always will. I've just learned to carry the weight." Dez sighed as he gazed toward some of the other Jedi who had begun filtering in for their own meals. "When I left to take the Barash Vow, I thought I was . . . broken. Unable to serve the Jedi. Now I've returned to find the entire Order almost as broken as I was."

"Not broken," Reath said, "but scarred. Humbled, maybe. And fewer in number. We just lost Master Adampo, which makes almost a third of the Council who have died since the beginning of this conflict. The task of identifying the Nameless, the search for the rods—"

"Rods?" Dez said.

Reath sighed. "Long story short, Ro has a way to control the Nameless with these rods. We've found a counterpoint to it that might negate his control."

The explanation that followed was so detailed Dez could scarcely keep track of it, but he got the gist. So often, non-Force users thought of what the Jedi did as magic, when it was anything but. This, however? *This* felt like magic. When Reath had finished, Dez shook his head in wonder. "It's like something out of legend."

"It *is* from legend," Reath said. "The tales of the adventures of Barnabas Vim—yes, I know, some of those have been mythologized in the centuries since, but the truth about Master Vim is astounding as any legend. I can show you in the Archives sometime, when all this is over." This small promise evidently lifted Reath's spirits for a moment. Dez imagined he was buoyed by the mere thought of someday being able to hang out with a friend and return to his beloved research.

"So we're chasing myths now, hoping for deliverance." The words sounded more pessimistic than Dez had intended, but it was hard to look at the situation with any real hope. "Do you think Chancellor Soh will capitulate to Ro in the end? Take his deal to stop the blight and save the afflicted planets?"

"I hope not," said Reath. "But if we cannot stop it, and if the blight continues to accelerate as we saw today, accepting Ro's solution—as much as I hate the idea, it might be the only way to save trillions of lives. Looked at in that light, the only option left to prevent death and devastation on an unprecedented scale may be . . . surrender."

Speaking that word had clearly cost Reath. Yet there was courage in facing the worst squarely, head-on, without gentling the words.

Dez decided to match Reath's bravery. "There's another option, and we're going to find it."

"We are closer than ever before," Reath said. "We just have to act fast enough to save these afflicted worlds . . . starting with Coruscant."

⚜

Dr. Mkampa had work to do in her arboretum.

Her scientific interests were as far ranging as they were cold-blooded, but she'd always had a particular fascination with botany. In most cultures, the majority of plants were regarded as purifiers of air, bringers of scent and beauty, wellsprings of medicine, even symbols of the sacred and divine. Many species kept them indoors in little pots, so tame and harmless did plants seem.

Mkampa knew better. Plants were no more uniformly benign than any animal form of life. They claimed territory by sinking their roots deep—choked and suffocated would-be parasites— even poisoned those beings fool enough to nibble on the wrong stem or leaf. On some planets, trees grew enormous bellflowers that tempted insects close, then trapped them for food. On others, little ground shrubs had spiky-edged leaves that would snap shut on an unsuspecting lizard before beginning to ooze digestive fluids, dissolving and absorbing the creature while it was still alive. Mkampa knew well how much thought various sentients had put into devising sadistic deaths, but had any among them come up with a means of murder more horrific than that?

Well, yes. But not many.

"There, there," Dr. Mkampa crooned as she tended to the cuttings salvaged from a recent run-in between a Nihil Cloud and a Drengir hunting party. The saplings were young, not yet liberated from the soil, but already they slowly twisted and turned, gaining strength, preparing to break free and join the great hunt for meat. "Be patient, little ones. Your time will come soon. Come, come. Bathe in the light."

With that she snapped at a droid, which began shining a beam of specially calibrated light on the saplings. What had been gentle movement instantly turned frantic, every leaf and stem whipping about in a wild frenzy. An observer might have thought they were being tortured—that they were suffering—when in fact, they were overcome by the desire to *cause* suffering.

She ran one of the long acid-green fingernails that grew from her synth-skin glove along the length of a Drengir sapling leaf. It thrashed at her, and one of the tiny spines that grew along the leaf veins scratched Mkampa's finger, slicing through the synth-skin entirely. She looked down at the wound, saw the glitter of metal within, and smiled.

A chime alerted her to the fact that the *Firebringer* was receiving a communication from the *Gaze Electric*. What could Ro want with her? She'd pretended to be fooled by his increasingly shabby lies about the supposed "test site," and that should have freed her from his oversight for a long while. Attracting his attention at this point was the last thing Mkampa wanted.

So she was both relieved and irritated when the holo came on to reveal the face of Ghirra Starros.

"Dr. Mkampa," Starros said with barely masked distaste. "What progress have you made on finding a test site?"

Mkampa's half-cybernetic face allowed her to utterly freeze her features, revealing little to nothing of what she felt. Usually she didn't bother, but this called for caution. "Did the Eye of the Storm delegate this task to you? He has not informed me of this change in your responsibilities."

Starros drew back as though struck. "It's not your place to question me, Doctor. Remember that I stand at Ro's side."

There was much Mkampa could have said to that, much she wanted to say. Taking Ghirra Starros down a peg would have been a pleasure—but business came first. "Then it is very strange that he did not tell you. It seems our lord has changed his thinking on the ideal site. He gave me new instructions only hours ago. Have they changed again already?"

Obviously Starros knew nothing of this. The small crease between her eyebrows suggested that she only now was doubting that Marchion Ro might have a cure. How thoroughly he had addled this woman's mind! "Of course not. Continue on—but remember that time is of the essence."

Mkampa's cybernetic eye picked up images just as clearly

from the periphery of her vision as from straight ahead, so she was able to look upon her enraged Drengir samplings and Ghirra Starros's face simultaneously. It was easy to know which one of these mattered more.

"Time is of the essence," Mkampa repeated. She decided not to resist a small smile. "On that, we entirely agree."

SIX

"**Y**ou don't seem to understand the assignment," snapped Professor Hastmon Chross of the Galactic Academy of Sciences. "We are analyzing the various reasons the attempted cures for the blight have failed."

Avon Starros had fully understood the assignment, which meant she understood that it was ludicrous. How was she supposed to make her professor comprehend this without stepping on his pride? "Isn't it more important to look for what will work, instead of concentrating on what *hasn't* worked?"

"Yet again, Miss Starros believes she is teaching this course." Chross breathed out in a huff, his broad Lannik ears twitching in irritation. "Student work is supportive of expert efforts, not the other way around! Leave the high-level theorizing to those who have already achieved a high level of accomplishment—and think a little more on how you might someday accomplish something yourself."

Avon had, in fact, accomplished quite a lot for a scientist of any age, much less a girl of fifteen. Unfortunately for the purposes of this argument, most of these accomplishments were classified. She could only nod and turn back to her work, cheeks hot with embarrassment.

For all Avon's knowledge, she lacked credentials. So she had enrolled in advanced courses at the Galactic Academy of Sciences with the goals of broadening her knowledge and acquiring the degrees that would qualify her for future work. It was an act of bravery—focusing so resolutely on a future that seemed murky to so many—though Avon did not see it as such. To her, knowledge was its own reward; the degree was nothing more than the tool that would make her knowledge more useful.

However, the Academy had so far proved to be a disappointment. She'd had to argue her way into advanced classes, only to find most of them overly simplistic. The majority of her teachers at least recognized her acumen and allowed her latitude with independent study . . . but a couple of them seemed determined to patronize her, and Chross was the worst of them.

She went back to work, obediently crunching equations, wondering if everyone else in the class had the background to understand that all these failed attempts were abysmally, fundamentally wrong. Whatever the answer to the blight might be, whatever cure it was Marchion Ro had hidden behind the Stormwall, the Republic wasn't only unaware of it; they were completely on the wrong track.

Avon just wished she had some idea what the right track could be.

She headed home from class in depressed spirits, hardly taking in the rush and glow of Coruscant's twilight traffic surrounding her in all three dimensions. Once she had returned to her tiny apartment, she knew she should either make herself some dinner or get back to her studies. Instead, she activated a small holocube. There, projected into the half darkness of her apartment, was a glowing three-dimensional map of the Coruscant Federal District. It illuminated her face in gold and green as she examined the small area—shaded dark in her holo—beneath the Jedi Temple. She was one of only a handful of people who had access to such a map, who knew that the darkness shown represented the blight. If the galaxy at large had found out that Marchion Ro and his Nihil had successfully infected the capital of the Republic itself . . .

Well, Avon hoped they never found out. That they never had to find out.

(And it wasn't like they could know for certain Ro was even responsible! The blight might have found its way to the Jedi Temple on its own. But if word ever got out, Ro would claim he had planted the infection there, nobody would be able to prove otherwise, and he'd get all the credit. Most people weren't as stringent about proof as Avon was.)

More senior scientific minds were studying this, as well, and she imagined that few of them expected any major breakthroughs to come from a girl fifteen years of age. Certainly Professor Chross didn't. But what she lacked in experience, she intended to make up for with determination.

The buzz on her comm unit jolted her back into the mundanity of her apartment. Avon ran one hand through her hair, took a deep breath, deactivated the holo, and answered the signal. From darkness appeared the face of her mother.

And somehow—after betraying every single person in the Republic and arguably in the entire galaxy—she had the *absolute gall* to look like she was the one with reason to be angry.

"Avon," said Ghirra. "I'd begun to think I would never see you again. It seems that's what you would prefer."

"Of course I want to see you again, after all of this is over—"

"When the blight has overrun the Republic and you've blackened your name with Marchion and the Nihil and there's no place left in the galaxy for you?"

By this point, Avon could hear some of the concern beneath the anger. It helped her remain calm and civil. "That's not the only ending to this story."

"This isn't a story. This is reality." Ghirra had gathered herself together by this point. "I wanted to check on how you were."

Avon scoffed. "I have work to do, Mom. Science to create. Equations to solve. Crises to fix. Of course, you're busy, too— *causing* crises to fix."

"We're not going to litigate this again, *Miss Sunvale*." Ghirra spat the name out as though it burned her mouth. Avon managed not to cringe. Despite all the many ways mother and daughter were opposed, somehow Ghirra Starros was angriest about Avon's short-lived attempt to live under a pseudonym. That was the only part she seemed to see as a rejection—which meant she had never taken seriously anything else Avon had ever said to her.

"I'm not going by that name much anymore," Avon said, hoping to cut off that subject at least.

She had hoped in vain. "So you're still going by it sometimes," Ghirra said. "You pick and choose when to be a Sunvale and when to be my daughter. Do your beloved Jedi know your true identity? Or are you still lying to them?"

"They know." That revelation had been painful—not just the fact of Avon's identity but also that she had been a liar. Worst of all had been lying to Reath Silas . . . but thinking about Reath was even more of a no-win scenario than arguing with her mother. "Everyone who matters already knows. So you can stop trying to hold that over my head."

"I'm sorry to hear that," said Ghirra, and she no longer sounded petulant; her tone had turned grave. "I wish fewer people knew. Because that knowledge—Avon, that information can never be widely known on this side of the Stormwall."

"That I once used an alias? I doubt that's going to fire up the Nihil."

"That you're helping the Jedi. That you've sided with the Republic. As my daughter, you had status here. Influence, if you'd chosen to cultivate it."

"Some of the Nihil tried to *kill me*."

Ghirra hardly even slowed down; either she wasn't really listening, or her time with the Nihil had significantly lowered her standards for appropriate conduct. "You shouldn't let a rabid fringe drive you away from opportunity. Have you ever considered that you might have had more impact by staying here than running away to be one lowly science student among thousands seeking answers?"

Avon had, in fact, considered this, and in enough detail not to buy it. "Like the amazing influence you have over Marchion Ro? Where you snap your fingers and he just . . . does whatever he was planning to do in the first place while totally ignoring you?"

That dart landed; Avon could see the glint of fresh pain and anger in Ghirra's eyes. It never felt good to hurt her mother, even when it meant she'd scored a point.

The moment of vulnerability didn't last. Ever the politician, Ghirra Starros had soon wiped every trace of it from her expression, and when she spoke, she used the low "sincere" tone that she used to say anything she meant to be *for your own good*. "Someday, Avon, this will all be over. As long as the blight spreads across the galaxy, Marchion Ro is winning. The Nihil are winning. The galaxy is taking on an entirely new shape, one in which the Republic is not the only power—one where authority will be shared. I believe that's a worthy goal."

"The Republic does share authority among its member worlds," Avon said, realizing even as she spoke that she might have saved her breath; her mother showed no sign of having heard a word of it.

Ghirra continued, "After the Nihil victory, there'll be no more hiding on the other side of the Stormwall. People will be held accountable for their actions in this war. So far I've been able to conceal your disloyalty from Marchion, but that doesn't mean I'll be able to do so forever. I don't want to see you hurt, Avon. Can you understand that?"

That part Avon fully believed. A darker possibility occurred to her, though: "Mom—if Ro found out about me, about my work with the Jedi—the Nihil wouldn't hurt you, would they?"

Her mother tossed her hair. "Nonsense. My position would always forestall that, as you should be well aware."

Did anyone really have any "position" among the Nihil that wasn't merely the whim of Marchion Ro? Avon wasn't sure, and she suspected her mom was less confident on that score than she was letting on. Still, she had no way to know. "Well, if you have so much status and sway, you should be able to save me. Right?"

Ghirra's casual act finally faltered. "My influence may not go that far."

Fearmongering. Had to be. "Come on. Marchion Ro's got a long list of people to hate in the Republic before he works his way down to a student scientist. Thousands, if not hundreds of thousands. Every officer in the Republic Defense Coalition, every member of the Senate, every Jedi Knight from every temple—"

"You forget that one of the things Marchion hates most is disloyalty," Ghirra said. "Betrayal. As my daughter, you had an honored place among the Nihil. You were privy to our most secure areas, even many of our secrets. Marchion made you welcome, and you repaid him by defecting to the enemy."

Avon shrugged. "Kinda sounds like how the rest of the Senate probably feels about you."

"The Senate doesn't use capital punishment."

"Oh, hey, you're right, it doesn't. Wow. When you look at it that way, doesn't it seem at all, just a little bit, like you might be on the *wrong side*?"

Once again Avon glimpsed vulnerability in Ghirra's eyes, but this time the fear wasn't for herself but for her daughter. For the first time, Avon's anger toward her mother faltered—not because she was any less angry but because she couldn't feel it through a sudden wave of unease. It *was* just like Ro to indulge his petty grievances through outright murder. During her brief time with the Nihil, Avon had heard of people being thrown out of airlocks for less. She had heard of other killings, too, but it was the thought of the airlock that haunted her, the terrible seconds of waiting, the spiraling open of the ship, the loss of any air to breathe, the possible explosion of her lungs, the agonizing utter cold that would seize her to the bone but leave her just enough time before she died to feel her eyeballs boil—

Avon tried not to think about airlocks.

Instead, she changed the subject, or attempted to. "I heard what happened to the Nihil's 'Minister of Advancement,' you know. Baron Boolan's capture by the Jedi was pretty big news. Does that make Dr. Mkampa the new Minister of Advancement? Or did Ro finally rein her in?"

This didn't make much impact on Avon's mother, who shrugged. "Marchion sees the sciences in a strictly utilitarian light. As long as Dr. Mkampa keeps providing useful discoveries, she'll have her place within the Nihil—but that position will never rise to the ultimate heights. Her ambitions have a ceiling that will never shatter."

"But Mkampa remains important as long as she keeps figuring out more ways to hurt people—and you still think you're on the right side."

Ghirra sighed. "I still believe that the Nihil, over time, will settle into a true governmental body. However, in the first flush of victory, there will be . . . overcorrections. Extremes of behavior. Examples will be made of those who worked against Nihil victory. I don't want one of those examples to be you."

"I don't either, Mom," Avon replied. "But *I* believe in the Republic and in the Jedi."

Ghirra shook her head sadly. "Just promise me you'll think about what I've said. That you're taking this seriously."

"I'll think about it."

Avon kept that promise for several long moments after they ended their conversation. She sat in her small, murky chamber— mid-level apartments on Coruscant only got direct sunlight for a few minutes a day, if that—hugging herself, forcing herself to imagine a Nihil victory. A galaxy without all the security and freedom provided by the Republic. One susceptible to the vengeance of Marchion Ro.

Her mother's belief in Ro's specific vengeance toward Avon herself might be no more than maternal paranoia. But it might not. If she lost the protection of the Republic and the Jedi Order collapsed or was even made extinct by the Nameless, there could be no guarantees that Avon would ever be safe again.

That was no reason to give up.

I don't avoid execution by bowing down before Ro before he's even won the fight, Avon thought as she straightened and got back to her feet. *I avoid it by doing everything in my power to make sure Ro loses that fight.*

If that's even in my power.

If it's within anyone's power at all.

⚜

Half a galaxy away, Dr. Mkampa stood within the heart of her Spider Squall cruiser, the *Firebringer*, holding the Sith holocron in her hands. Ever since she had found this precious relic, she had understood it to be of paramount importance—but she had restrained herself from attempting to use it until she fully understood what it had to teach. This was the sort of restraint Marchion Ro did not comprehend and, therefore, the reason she had not shared it with him, even when she had still been loyal to his cause. Opening it had proved a challenge, but a dying Jedi prisoner on the wrong side of the Occlusion Zone had eventually provided the means. Conveniently, he had died before even fully registering what he had done, much less telling anyone else among the Nihil about it.

Since then, Mkampa had researched the holocron and its contents as best she could. Impatient as she was to act on the potential power it promised, she had restrained herself. Science demanded discipline. Just as she had waited to obtain her own Spider Squall until she could do so in secrecy—until she had been all but sure her time with the Nihil was ending—she had waited for the right moment to act.

Now, however, she was on her own, and the time was as ripe as fruit dangling low from the branch, peel splitting to reveal the softness inside.

Mkampa gazed at the material once more, then went to an emitter she'd worked up specially. The purple crystal within wasn't *quite* right—but she suspected it was close enough for her purposes. One quick trip through hyperspace, one pulse of this light, and her plan would be properly set in motion. Then, at last, she could chase her goal, confident that her army would soon follow.

She nodded to herself as she whispered, "Let them awaken."

SEVEN

Someday, all the humans and near-humans of the galaxy would speak Basic, thought Romila Kaveh, acquisition negotiator for Czerka Corporation—soon to be *senior* acquisition negotiator, if she could lock this deal down. Also someday, protocol droids would be programmed to handle even more languages than they already did, including the most obscure. Until that blessed day came, certain backward planets would require people to work as translators.

Sometimes maddeningly irritating people such as Tolor Patewick.

"Of course we appreciate the exquisite biome you have here on Kenari," Romila said as she made her way through the lush undergrowth, trying not to grimace as her designer shoes encountered vines and snails. From far overhead, through the clouds, a shaft of light bathed the nearby meadows; the scene would have appeared idyllic to anyone attuned to nature and its beauty. It was of no interest to a Czerka negotiator. "Rest assured that any gas mines established by Czerka will be built to the highest environmental safety standards."

Tolor spoke to their guides, a small party of local leaders, all of them with wary dark eyes. He then turned to Romila and translated—or, rather, did his version of translation: "They very politely indicate that they know you're full of mudhorn poodoo, just like the corporation that sent you, and they're almost positive that you're going to make a mess of it like you have on countless other planets."

Romila held on to her temper. "How much of that was the Kenari, and how much of it was you?"

The reply came with a shrug. "Language doesn't break down into mathematical percentages."

That meant almost all of it had come from Tolor, who seemed to think he could make a principled environmental stand while still getting work as a translator for major corporations. This was a misapprehension Romila couldn't wait to cure.

"Tell them, via a *faithful* translation, that our technology is constantly evolving, and the gas mines built here would represent the very highest state of the art. Past incidents have sometimes been . . ."

"Fatal?" Tolor said. "Devastating? The Kenari have a word that can encompass both—"

"Have sometimes been *unfortunate*," Romila cut in, "but they have also provided opportunities to learn, and Kenari will benefit from that education."

Tolor spoke to her next, rather than the Kenari: "Do you ever get tired of lying for Czerka?"

She shot back, "Do you ever get tired of working as a translator? Because you're steering yourself towards another career."

"The answer is that sometimes I do tire of it," Tolor said, "when I'm obligated to have conversations like this one." He looked so weary then, so sad, that Romila felt a small, rare quiver of remorse. Accidents did happen, too often—but Czerka didn't profit from accidents, either! Their profit and local safety ideally went hand in hand. If Czerka focused more on profit, well, didn't the locals focus more on safety? That meant they had people looking out for *both* interests!

Before she could say any of this, though, Tolor had launched into his latest translation for the Kenari. He raised an eyebrow. Then he smiled. Romila didn't like the look of that smile.

"What?" she asked as a breeze softly rustled the leaves surrounding them. "What are they telling you?"

Tolor turned to her with his arms crossed over his chest and a huge grin. "They've just informed me that they'd feel better signing over the gas rights to the Republic, who actually happen to have sent a team here last week."

Damn them! Czerka did its best to beat the government to the punch, but they didn't always succeed. Romila knew the Republic offered better terms and higher safety standards; still, there were other negotiating tricks to try. "Tell them that governments change. Regulations change. What if the Republic loses this system to the Nihil? Do you think Marchion Ro will give you as much consideration? Or what if the Republic chose a much more profit-minded chancellor than Lina Soh someday? Those regulations they're tempting you with—they can be repealed and replaced at any time." Romila raised her voice slightly as the rustling of the leaves became louder. "Whereas with Czerka, you'll have the benefit of contract terms, *in writing*, that—"

"Hang on," Tolor broke in. "Do you hear that?"

The Kenari, too, were glancing at each other in confusion. This, in turn, confused Romila. "It's just the wind through the branches," she said brightly. "A bit loud, but nothing we can't manage."

Tolor gave her a look. "If the rustling is just the wind—then where's the wind?"

It hit Romila then that the breeze gently touching her hair wasn't nearly strong enough to cause so much noise. She turned to see the greenery behind her waving violently, moving constantly—

"They're plants—but they're moving, they're coming. They can't be the *Drengir*?" Tolor cried.

"What?" Romila had heard of the Drengir—who in the galaxy hadn't, at this point?—but she'd never seen one, never expected to. Wasn't there some kind of truce? Weren't the Drengir in stasis? Still, as the murderous copse rushed toward her, she suddenly recalled a corporate "safety briefing" she'd half watched while lunching in her work pod one day: the thick sharp leaves, the writhing tentacle vines, the harsh maw-mouths, which even now were opening wide. Images had far undersold the terrifying reality, a point she intended to make to the corporate training group if she lived long enough to get the chance.

She scuttled backward as the Kenari rushed forward; Romila had thought the primitive weapons they carried to be purely ceremonial, but apparently not. The blades at the ends of their sticks pierced Drengir trunks and sliced at vines, winning shrieks of pain from the Drengir . . . but no retreat.

"Tell me there's a security drone above us!" Tolor shouted as he and Romila kept backing away. One of the Kenari fell with a cry that sent shivers through Romila's flesh. "Or a craft you can summon for emergency pickup?"

"Those are only for *senior* acquisition negotiators!" Romila remembered her last performance review with sharp regret. Oh, why couldn't that promotion have come through one mission earlier?

"They left you out here with no cover?" Tolor asked before wincing as another of the Kenari went down.

Romila couldn't answer. She could see far enough behind them to realize they were nearing a tall, steep ridge—one that couldn't be safely descended in a hurry. They'd just have to fling themselves down it, assuming they made it that far.

Tolor had begun to laugh, a terrible, desperate sound. "The one time Czerka could've done something helpful," he said. The Drengir surged forward, violent foliage only centimeters away. "The one time! And they're useless!"

For the first and only time, Romila heard a Drengir speak, the very last word she heard in her life: "Meat."

Everything that followed was only screams, and thrashing, and the crushing grasp of tentacle vines, and the brief taste of blood in her mouth before all went dark forever.

After the feast, the Drengir curled in a sunny patch amid the Kenari glades, leaves unfurled, soaking up light and heat. Their need for meat consumption did not totally replace the necessity of, or pleasure in, photosynthesis. Had any Drengir ever discussed this with any animal life-forms, they might have realized that sunshine often fulfilled much the same function as "dessert."

Of course, they had never had such a conversation, nor did they intend to. Meat could talk all it liked, but it would never make any sense. Their words would never matter. A handful of Drengir had suggested they might at least attempt to learn something from the meat before consuming it, but when the moment came, the prey just tasted so good. Who could stop at only one bite?

Luckily, in this case, the meat had not communicated with any others of their kind before dying. This meant that no counter-attacks could be expected for some time, if at all. The Drengir preferred long periods to digest, to allow the acids to fully break down their meal, before moving on. It was also neater to spit out inedible clothing and any inorganic matter at the dining site, rather than on their spacecraft. (Though it was fun, once in a while, to keep a belt or vest in reserve and spit it out just before falling upon fresh prey. This generally froze the new meat with terror, which made that first bite much easier to get.)

Dimly they recalled that there had been conversations in the past—something about a truce, during which they had taken to the ground like their rooted brethren. Something about the Jedi.

It all seemed very fuzzy at the moment and not nearly as important as either sunshine or meat. A recent bath in the light had reawakened their hunger, and their anger, and they were inclined to follow their appetites once more.

It was the Great Progenitor herself, seed and stalk of the people, who curled her leaves, signaling the end of their rest. "Soon we shall depart this place. One of the prey carried many inorganic items with electrical charge. These items do not fall silent for long before others come, and when those others arrive, they often bear weapons. We must make haste."

This would normally have earned some disappointed rustling; green worlds like Kenari were rare, and they felt so homey that Drengir preferred to stay in such places as long as possible. Furthermore, despite the rich repast they had just enjoyed, they knew their hunger would not be kept at bay for long. The Great Progenitor assured them, "We will return here soon, after they are no longer looking for us. Then, perhaps, we will be able to feast for days."

This compromise pleased everyone. Good hunting had become more complicated of late; the unfathomable infighting among the meat beings had led to ships being destroyed, barriers being erected in space that parted Drengir copses, and vast amounts of innocent flora being destroyed—this last yet more evidence of the meat creatures' barbarity. Worst of all was the monstrosity called the blight, which devastated all that it touched. The Drengir were repelled by its utter emptiness—a chilling void missing the dark side of the Force, from which their entire species drew its energies. The accompanying absence of the light was no consolation.

Wherever the Drengir sensed the blight, they were both disoriented and disturbed by this utter lack of the Force. They had repeatedly been compelled to alter their paths and trajectories to avoid it.

Yet the blight continued to spread. Havens like Kenari, which were green enough for pleasure and rich in relatively unarmed meat life, had become more difficult to find. The Drengir would keep this world as a sort of treasure in which they could indulge whenever the time seemed safe, unless the blight found this planet, too.

They were lucky still to be led by the Great Progenitor, who had briefly been thought dead but had escaped the planet Eiram after a battle with the Jedi. (Delicious, the Jedi, but difficult to eat.) The Great Progenitor had a destination in mind for them, they knew, and it never occurred to them to ask where it might be. If all was as the Great Progenitor wished, then all was well.

The Drengir party began the slithering journey back toward their craft, the *Innovator*. Only then did the Great Progenitor wish for them to know their ultimate destination. (The most important statements never came in the form of words but in the purer communication of pollen or scent.) Their spirits were lifted by the rest of the Progenitor's message, which told them that the world they traveled to was very green indeed, yet possessed meat life. The feasting would be plentiful, more so than ever before. So the light had told them, and light did not lie. For the light had reached all the way to Eiram, to speak of their new goal.

Kashyyyk, they all thought, tellers and listeners at once. *We go to Kashyyyk.*

EIGHT

At that moment, another leader spoke to her people throughout the Republic, hoping she was being heard even beyond its bounds—even through the Stormwall.

"The new evacuation technologies we have announced today," said Chancellor Lina Soh into the array of cam droids and recorders that would broadcast her message far and wide, "will allow us to swiftly transport even substantial planetary populations to safety within a matter of a few days. More and more worlds are joining the resettlement treaties, making room for the displaced to stay, whether that be for weeks, for years, or even forever."

Of course, Chancellor Soh knew that most of the planets who had joined thus far were not wealthy, thriving Core Worlds where nearly anyone would be happy to live (Alderaan being a notable exception). No, these were planets that had had trouble attracting industry and settlement in the past, whether due to harsh climate, difficult geography, a reputation for lawlessness, or a combination thereof. This crisis provided an opportunity for such worlds to increase their populations at last, with people who had lost their former homes and were in little position to choose their next one. She did not include this information in her public address—not out of any desire for concealment but because everyone already knew it.

"Our greatest scientific minds continue to study the blight," Soh continued. "We learn more every day, and thus we are coming closer and closer to a solution. Some are frustrated, I know, that this quest has already taken so long—but when we consider that the blight is a totally new phenomenon, one never before recorded, the amount of knowledge we have gained about it already is extraordinary. I have faith that these efforts will bear fruit, and I urge the people of the Republic to continue to hold to their own faith. Only by standing together, by believing in each other, can we face this crisis and ensure that someday soon we will emerge triumphant."

On the Jedi transport, Bell Zettifar shook his head. "I wish believing in each other was enough."

"Belief is necessary," said Reath Silas. The ship's passengers had all started to gather in the bay, preparing to disembark, as the transport began its approach to Coruscant. Weary but extremely clean Jedi were helping the Inadi survivors form lines, the better to be swiftly processed upon landfall. "But not sufficient."

Vernestra Rwoh, who had been petting Ember, looked up. "I

don't know how much belief people have left, or how much longer they'll hang on to what they've got."

"Not much," agreed Reath. He had already done this bleak extrapolation inside his own head. "People are tired of fear and threat. They're fed up with not having answers. Soon they won't want to listen to Soh anymore."

After a pause, Bell spoke the words they were all thinking, yet dreading: "They may be ready to listen to Marchion Ro."

Burryaga roared in defiance. Even if the peoples of the Republic doubted Lina Soh, surely they could not be fool enough to put their trust in a disreputable megalomaniac like Marchion Ro.

"Let's hope you're right," said Vernestra.

The transport descended through unusually thick cloud cover to find its landing pad, one very near the Jedi Temple. Fine misting rain silvered the skies and rendered many of the surrounding towers and spires no more than shadows against the gray. Hovering canopies had been installed so the Inadi refugees were not immediately soaked, but once the disembarkation process was underway, Reath left for the Temple. He needed to walk, to clear his thinking.

Rather than zigzag through the various bridges and connector tunnels, Reath took the lift down as far as it would go, all the way to the ground. Dark as it was down there, he could make the trip faster on foot. He tugged up the hood of his cloak as protection against the drizzle as he wove his way through an open market, peddlers and vendors on every side hawking everything from droid repair kits to bucket hats; the only thing all products available had in common was a highly dubious provenance. A few of the sellers cast wary glances at Reath; despite the heavy cloak he wore, it was possible to catch glimpses of his mission attire. This meant he was known to be a Jedi, and the denizens of these lower levels had their reasons for distrusting anyone who might be considered an enforcer of the law—but he scarcely noticed them. His thoughts were all for the blight they had left behind on the now-dead moon of Inad Komesh . . . and the blight that lay ahead.

The blight that had taken root beneath the Jedi Temple itself.

Deep in the Archives, Reath had read the tales that told of how the Jedi Temple had begun as a Sith shrine, in the far-distant days of the ancient Sith. He himself had once unwittingly played a role in bringing ancient Sith idols back to this same shrine, little realizing their true nature. They'd been taken away years ago, of course—sent back to the same Amaxine station where they'd been found, albeit too late to contain the Drengir—yet Reath still felt the weight of knowing how they had unwittingly released the Drengir on an unsuspecting galaxy. Sometimes he dreamed of the sharply carved faces of those idols, sneering at his naivety.

But those were the least of the influence of the Sith even in a place that should have been so sacred and pure. Centuries ago, some of that fallen empire's dark power had rooted itself in place beyond even the Jedi's ability to exorcise, and it was in the very location of the ancient shrine to the dark side that the blight had appeared. Had darkness itself called the blight, summoned it into being? Reath didn't know if that was true. It felt true, but if it were, wouldn't the sheer power of the light emanating from the Temple now have been sufficient to hold the blight back?

A man's voice interrupted his train of thought: "Reath."

Looking up, Reath saw Cohmac Vitus standing before him, similarly shielded from the mist by his coat. Cohmac smiled in welcome.

In the aftermath of the death of Reath's first master, Jora Malli, Reath had requested that Cohmac Vitus be the one to take over his training. From their time together on the Amaxine station, Reath had already known Cohmac to be an unorthodox Jedi, one who gave voice to doubts others either never felt or would not express. That had been one of the main reasons Reath wanted such a teacher. Master Jora's last act, accepting the mission on Starlight Beacon, had shown Reath how much he still needed to stretch—to reach beyond his familiar, comfortable limits—and he'd trusted Cohmac to take him along that less-traveled path. It had been a great act of faith, undertaken at one of the most vulnerable points in Reath's life, and at first their partnership had promised to be all that he could have wished.

Then, only months later, Cohmac had become overwhelmed by his own doubts regarding the Jedi Order and had paused only long enough to knight Reath before leaving. Leaving the Order, leaving Reath, leaving everything.

This utter abandonment had ultimately helped Reath stand on his own. After the first hurt had subsided, he'd even understood some of the reasons Cohmac had done what he'd done. If you weren't sure of your own path, of course you wouldn't want to lead an apprentice down that same path after you. No doubt Cohmac had felt that he was protecting Reath, not wounding him.

They had come to a greater understanding, even forgiveness, since Cohmac's return to the Order. Cohmac had joined Reath on several missions since then. They went on a quest to learn about the Tolemites, an ancient civilization with connections to the blight, and Cohmac also joined Reath and Padawan Amadeo Azzazzo in the search for the mysterious Rod of Ages. Cohmac had even given Reath an ancient Jedi shield, an object of legend, one that could not fail to thrill either a warrior or a historian, and especially not someone who was both. Though the bond of master and Padawan had been severed, they had become friends again.

All this Reath knew to be true. And yet—still, somehow—a faint sense of unease crept into many of their conversations.

"Hi," Reath said evenly. "I'm on my way to report to the Council."

Cohmac nodded. "We received Burryaga's message from the transport. I came to meet you—I recalled that you sometimes liked to take this path."

They had spent little time on Coruscant together; Reath's preference for walking on the ground there was something he had mentioned only once. Cohmac had not only remembered it but had met Reath there, no doubt in an effort to deepen the rapport between them. This both touched Reath . . . and reminded him that he was not the only one who still sometimes felt awkward. He said only, "What did Burryaga tell you?"

"That you came with dark news that must be delivered in person," Cohmac replied as they fell into step side by side. Distant thunder roiled through the dim sky. "Which can only mean someone has been lost."

"Yes. Master Adampo fell on Inad Komesh. We were unable to retrieve his body."

"Not another from the Council!" Cohmac stopped in his tracks. "Another. Again. Sometimes, Reath, I fear this crisis could be the blow from which the Republic cannot rise again."

"The rest of the galaxy doesn't put the same stock in the individuals within the Council as we do. They just have faith in the Jedi Order, and we're going to vindicate their faith. Our discoveries on Tolis and our success in obtaining the Rod of Ages will turn the tide against the Nameless." He ignored the faint queasiness in his belly as he spoke the word, did not allow himself to remember his encounters with them. "There's no other choice."

Just as their clothes had become all but sodden with rain, they reached the Temple. Reath handed his cloak to one of the droids, trusting Cohmac to follow as he made his way into the Temple depths. Protocol should have taken him first to one of the lifts so he might report Master Adampo's death to the Council the very first moment possible. Instead, however, he went to the deepest sanctum. To what had been the Sith shrine.

To the infection of the blight.

Cohmac paid Reath the courtesy of not questioning his choice, merely following. They walked into the dimly lit chamber where more than a dozen Jedi sat in various meditation poses around the perimeter, all of them calling on their full strength within the Force to hold the blight at bay. Indeed, so far, the blight had not progressed more than a millimeter or two.

And yet it still lay there, an uneven indentation gray-fuzzed at the edges like the rot of fruit that had spoiled, ominous and inexorable.

We need answers, Reath thought. Those answers apparently lay somewhere beyond those sought by Republic and Jedi scientists up until now. They needed to know how this blight was tied to the dark side.

Which meant speaking to someone who did not turn away from the dark side: Azlin Rell.

Reath left the shrine without a word, Cohmac still by his side.

"You are wise to delay the report to the Council no longer," Cohmac said. "But I sense a different sort of urgency in you."

"After I speak to the Council, I'm going to talk with Azlin Rell. I want his take on this."

Cohmac seemed uncertain. Reath wanted to ignore this but could not keep himself from pausing. "Reath . . . I know you've spent a great deal of time with Azlin of late, and you've had good reasons to do so, but this is not a connection you should continue to cultivate. He's a dangerous man. His thoughts lead in dangerous directions."

"They also lead to new directions," Reath said. "Which might lead us to new answers, and the galaxy needs those now more than ever."

"His malign influence—"

Reath cut in, "I wasn't asking permission from you or anyone else. I'm merely keeping everyone informed, as a courtesy. My decision is made."

Although Cohmac remained visibly uneasy, there was also a grudging respect in his gaze. "Very well, Reath," said Cohmac. "Where the Force leads you, you must follow."

NINE

Azlin Rell had become no more than a shadow of a man—emaciated, haggard, every aspect of his appearance bearing testimony to decades of neglect or, in the case of his eyes, horrific violence against the self. He looked as though he might topple over at any moment, faint dead away.

But shadows fell long, and any Jedi who forgot that in the presence of Azlin Rell did so at their peril.

Reath never forgot.

"So Marchion Ro has successfully murdered one third of the Jedi Council," said Azlin, his voice acidic with cruel glee. "A formidable foe, indeed. To think that, not so very long ago, there were those in the Senate who still ridiculed him as a bully from the middle of nowhere, one who'd managed to land a few lucky punches. I imagine they aren't joking as much any longer."

"Nobody's laughing," Reath replied. "But, with all due respect to the Jedi Council, I'm much more concerned about the millions of other people who have died or been displaced by the Nihil. This is not only a military crisis; it's also a humanitarian one. I'm sure Master Adampo would never have considered his own fate as important as that of those suffering from these disasters."

"No doubt," said Azlin, his tone so deferential that it became mockery. "And yet . . . the Jedi Council will find time, amid this 'humanitarian crisis,' to schedule a grand funeral ceremony for Adampo, won't they?"

Reath was used to Azlin's barbs by this point, but that struck low. "Remembrance is important. Ritual has purpose. Services like this bring us together when we need it most."

Azlin shrugged, not mocking the idea any longer but not conceding defeat, either. His posture suggested that he was, at the moment, more taken with his own private thoughts than anything his visitor had to say. This was not unusual. He paced about his chamber slowly, not like a caged beast but like a scholar in the Jedi Archive carrels, deep in reflection. Reath understood that the best strategy during pauses like these—not infrequent— was to remain silent and see which direction Azlin's curiosity would turn next.

An encounter with one of the Nameless had done this to Azlin: shattered him into the shell he had become, thrust him into the grasp of darkness, apparently never to escape. After his own experiences with the Nameless, Reath felt greater compassion for this fallen former Jedi; he knew exactly how devastating, how hollowing it was to be cut off from the Force, to know the galaxy could exist without it, to confront the vast yawning emptiness that forever waited to smother the light.

Yet sometimes he felt more impatience, too. Reath might not have had as severe an encounter as Azlin had endured, but it had been the greatest anguish imaginable . . . and yet, he still stood. He still served. It was possible to endure an attack by the Nameless and emerge intact. *Was that mere luck?* he wondered. *Or did Azlin suffer something so much worse that there was no coming back?*

But what could ever *be worse?*

Reath was sitting in a chair in front of Azlin's chamber, if *chamber* was the right word for it. It remained stark and unwelcoming—but nonetheless it represented an upgrade from the cell Azlin had been inhabiting since Master Yoda first brought him to Coruscant. This upgrade had been earned when Azlin had helped his fellow Jedi during a battle with the Nameless, even saving the life of Master Arkoff. Azlin now behaved as though he had chosen this new room, even become proud of it. He had etched hash marks along the edge of his table, his bunk, his seat; not a design, exactly, which would have been pointless to one without sight, but perhaps the tactile equivalent. The shield he wore over his eyes was incongruous in such a small, dark space; however, it disguised the empty sockets left behind after Azlin had gouged out his own eyes in an attempt to free himself from the ghastly hallucinations that had haunted him ever since his encounter with the Nameless. Azlin's strength in the Force was such that he could move around the room as easily as though he still possessed full sight—which as a Jedi Reath completely understood, and yet he found it unnerving to see Azlin doing it.

The unnerving part was knowing that Azlin's greater power in the Force flowed from the dark side.

Too many fellow Jedi had endured their own close encounters with the Nameless. Those creatures' effect—the absolute severing of a Jedi from the Force—provoked an agony that lingered long after the Nameless was gone, one that in some ways was worse than death. A Jedi who died without the Force . . . could that person even find their way back into the eternal ocean of life and energy, the ebb and flow of the Force throughout the galaxy? Or were they lost, a permanent break in the chain?

It was better not to dwell on such thoughts too often.

"Why have you come here, Reath Silas?" Azlin said at last. "Why report all this to me?"

Reath had been asking himself that same question, but he believed he was starting to understand the answer. "To confront the Nameless, we must confront the feelings that lead to the dark side. You know that path better than anyone else."

"Better than anyone else you should trust," said Azlin with his short bark of a laugh. "Assuming you do trust me?"

"What you know about the Nameless," said Reath, wisely ignoring Azlin's question, "may make the difference between the Order's salvation and its downfall. Yoda believes that. I think I've come to believe it. But you won't be able to do it alone. Someone has to balance the darkness within you, and . . . I guess that's me."

Azlin laughed again, but he didn't insult Reath outright. Was that progress? Reath didn't know, but at the moment, positive signs were few and far between; he had to take them where he could find them.

⚜

That night, atop the roof of the Jedi Temple, hundreds of members of the Order gathered to honor the late Master Adampo. As his body had not been recovered, no true funeral pyre could be built, but a large ceremonial bonfire was constructed and, not long after nightfall, set brilliantly ablaze. The leaping bright tongues of flame were reflected off the shiny surfaces of countless towers all around them, organic and alive amid so much artificiality, and therefore all the more compelling.

In many respects, this service was not only for Adampo but also for the other Council members who had fallen in the Nihil conflict: Jora Malli, Pra-Tre Veter, Ada-Li Carro, and Stellan Gios. Yet those who stood there thought of the dead not as former leaders but as comrades and friends they had lost.

Vernestra Rwoh mentally relived her earliest days as a Padawan, how serious she had been, how earnest, how dedicated—and how Stellan Gios had been a wise enough teacher not only to take advantage of her dedication but also to show her that rest, relaxation, and even play could also provide their own pathways through the Force. Noble and valiant as he had been, she thought the man's true greatness also lay in the fact that he had remembered how much children needed to laugh.

Burryaga recalled a mission he had gone on with his late master Nib Assek not quite a year before Starlight Beacon's loss, rescuing settlers from overwhelming floods on Yisbon Minor.

She'd injured her knee as they helped citizens into rescue ships—not horribly, but enough that she couldn't walk. Together, Nib and Burryaga had tied their cloaks into a sort of makeshift sling, which allowed him to carry her across his chest in much the same way that many species of parents carried their young children; they had laughed about it together. She had been such a little thing that the weight had been nothing to him. Sometimes he dreamed that he carried her still.

Master Yoda's ears were lowered. Though he bore more hope than almost anyone else in the Order, even he could not remain untouched by the severity of the losses they had suffered. Yoda's lessons with the younglings, and the centuries through which he had carried those out, meant he individually knew nearly every Jedi in the galaxy—a feat few others could claim. But this meant that he had more to grieve than almost anyone. When he looked at the blazing bonfire, he saw those who had been lost not as the capable, experienced Jedi most had become, but as the little children he had first guided.

Dez Rydan had only just learned of many of these deaths; he had sworn himself to isolation as part of the Barash Vow, and while he'd remained aware of the Nihil threat as it increased, some of the particulars had eluded him. For some reason, the loss that struck him most forcibly was not that of his old master, Jora Malli—her fate he had known as he went into exile; her death he'd had the chance to grieve—but that of the Wayseeker Orla Jareni. He'd only known Orla for a matter of days, mostly the ones they spent marooned on the Amaxine station, and yet that had been time enough for Dez to be struck by her courage, her wit, her flinty determination, and the boldness with which she carved out her own path to follow the Force. Unique as she had been, she had become a model in Dez's mind for her bravery and her independence. For the kind of Jedi he hoped ultimately to become.

If the Nameless could rip Orla from the Force, he thought bleakly as he stared at the ceremonial flame, *they can do it to anybody.*

After the ceremony, Dez sought out Reath Silas in the crowd and found him on the outskirts. While some were gathering to tell old tales of those fallen, it appeared Reath preferred to be alone—but when he caught sight of Dez, he gestured toward him. Dez had the distinct impression he was being paid an honor.

(In truth, Reath's transformation had surprised Dez as much as anything else he'd witnessed since his return to the Order. The scholarly kid who'd hated the frontier and dreaded even a hint of adventure had become confident and courageous. How proud Master Jora would have been, if she could have seen it!)

As they fell into step beside each other, Dez confessed, "I had no idea how many people I would know among the lost."

"It's awful," Reath replied simply. "It comes at us fast, yet it sinks in slowly. It's everywhere, all the time—the knowledge that your friends and mentors and fellow users of the Force have died. That they're continuing to die every day."

"You're the historian, Reath. When's the last time the Order sustained losses like this? Since we wrestled with this much dread, both existential and very, very literal?"

Reath took a moment to consider that. "You'd have to go back centuries. The only question is how many centuries. We've never faced a foe like this, at least not in recorded history. Yes,

Jedi fell during the Night of Sorrow on Dalna. In the Battle of Jedha. During the Shaw Uprising, and on Ord Mantell, and in the Zeitooine Schism—"

"You might want to stop there," Dez said, "before you depress us both."

The small smile Reath gave him lasted hardly a moment. "Now, though? What we've been up against throughout this conflict? The blight, the Nameless . . . it's as if they're stronger than the Force. And they *aren't*. They *can't be*. That's not how the galaxy works."

He spoke as though it were a matter of science rather than belief. Dez wondered if he agreed. His reply was short: "The living Force always falls to death eventually. Death is part of that cycle."

Reath's footsteps faltered, and his expression suggested that his thoughts had turned sharply inward. He said to Dez, "You must have learned a lot about the Force through taking the Barash Vow."

"The Vow requires us to forgo any activities that tie us to the Jedi Order, to separate ourselves from those who remain within it," Dez said. "The ideal is to commit to gaining ultimate communion with the Force, on our own, as individuals. In reality, most who take the Vow . . . we come as close to that as we can."

"How close do you think you came?"

Had the gloom of the evening been any less pervasive, Dez might have laughed. "Ask me in the distant future, after I do find that communion, and maybe then I'll know. Sometimes I think I left too soon. Other times, I think I could have meditated in silence forever and never reached any greater understanding. For now, the only thing I'm sure of is that I found peace. The darkness aboard the Amaxine station loosened its grip on me. I'm myself again."

By now they were on their own—or as close as anyone on Coruscant ever came to being alone—walking along a connector between two towers; the running lights of various speeders and cruisers glittered off the multipaned surfaces of the towers that surrounded them. A sharp breeze ruffled Dez's black hair, and he glanced upward to see that the clouds were low and dense tonight, enough to subtly catch the colors of the city illumination beneath. A storm was coming.

"That's the cruelest thing about the Nameless," Reath said. "Dying that way—it steals us from ourselves. Cuts us off from the living Force."

Dez decided he and Reath knew each other well enough for him to be honest. "I still feel that falling to darkness would have to be worse. To die consumed by fear and loneliness is terrible, but to die consumed by hatred?"

Reath did not seem convinced. "I've been questioning Azlin Rell. His darkness torments him, even as he still believes it to be his strength—it's sad. But he isn't cut off from the Force."

"You think even the dark side of the Force would be a comfort?" Dez said. "Think again. Azlin's gone down a path no person can turn back from. He's miserable every moment of every day, because that's what darkness means. Those who serve the darkness have to constantly stoke their pain, their resentment, their fear, their hate; those bitter feelings are the only things that make them feel alive."

"You aren't the first person to tell me to steer clear of Azlin," Reath said, "and I doubt you'll be the last. But I still believe there's a lot we can learn from him, as does Master Yoda. Azlin truly helped us on our mission to Banchii. He *saved* Master Arkoff."

Dez raised an eyebrow. "I didn't tell you to steer clear of him. Be careful, sure—but get every answer out of him that you can. It sounds like this Azlin Rell owes the Order whatever service he can give, and we can't afford to ignore even one person, one fact, that might help us save the galaxy."

❧

One of the smaller ships piercing the Coruscant cloud cover at that moment was a spaceport transfer shuttle; lower-cost commercial interplanetary vessels often docked at these small orbital platforms, rather than paying exorbitant landing fees. From there the shuttles carried their motley crews of people, creatures, and droids from across the galaxy straight to the heart of the capital of the Republic. A Rybet and her husband cooed at the tadpoles they carried in little baby-safe water-tank backpacks; a traveling salesman reviewed his presentation, whisper-reciting his lines about how their propulsion systems were superior to all others; a red-billed Kassowarian watched a current-events debate show on her datapad without a headset—grievously rude, but nobody could be bothered to confront her about it.

One passenger, at least, was grateful for this rudeness, as it gave her a chance to learn more about what the Republic was telling itself without betraying her own interest in the matter.

"I heard not all the Jedi Council members they've reported dead actually died," whispered one person in a nearby seat to another. "Some of them have given up hope and quit. Just walked out of the Temple to hide somewhere safe."

Her companion didn't want to hear it. "This is rumor! This is misinformation! You know as well as anyone that stories of every kind are running rampant throughout the galaxy—"

"How could it be otherwise? The Stormwall has severed the galaxy in two. People are cut off from their families, their friends, their employ. Where fact is unavailable, fiction will fill the gap."

A servitor droid rolled up at that moment, holding a small tray of complimentary beverages and snacks. "Would you enjoy some refreshment?"

The gossiping passengers waved the droid away. Nearby, Nan Hague was briefly tempted to help herself to a glass of Toni-ray; it was said to be some of the finest wine in the galaxy, and Marchion Ro himself had stockpiled many cases of it. But she hadn't come to Coruscant for fun.

"No, thank you," Nan said, looking down at the pattern of lights below her. She had studied enough to recognize the Jedi Temple from above. "I'm doing just fine."

TEN

In the interest of leaving no stone unturned in the quest to understand and stop both the blight specifically and the plans of Marchion Ro generally, Reath was willing to research anything and speak to anyone—and had in fact been doing so for more than a year. (As it happened, one of his few criticisms of the Jedi Council and the Republic leadership in this crisis was their mutual tendency to assume that the best answers would come from people and institutions they already knew. Not that such input wasn't valuable, but if ever there was a time to cast a wide net, surely this was it.)

So when Avon Starros had reached out about discussing her work on the blight, Reath gladly made the time.

They met in the Jedi Archives, both because Reath always

welcomed a chance to go there and because he knew the effect the place had on anyone else who loved knowledge—and Avon certainly did. The cavernous vaults, the holos depicting scholars and adventurers of bygone days, the soft glow of lamps calibrated to shed only light that would not damage fragile antiques—all of it created an atmosphere that suggested magic as much as scholarship, which seemed fitting to Reath, who believed those were often the same thing. He got Avon set up with a visiting researcher card and ushered her inside. As she took in the vast stacks of holocrons, informational pads, and even books, some of them centuries or millennia old, the sheer rapture in her widening eyes made Reath chuckle.

"This place blows my mind every single time I see it," she said as she hugged her datapad to her chest, gazing all around. "You could come here every day? Why do you ever go anyplace else?"

"I used to ask myself that same question. Honestly, I still think I'll return as a full-time archivist someday. But my late master, Jora, taught me that sometimes it's good to push ourselves away from what's comfortable, more toward what's challenging."

Avon made a face. "Isn't dealing with the Nihil and the blight challenging enough? We're full up on challenge. Supplies are plentiful. I'd love some *not*-challenge for a change. Something simple. Even humdrum. I could *kill* for some humdrum right around now."

Reath had to laugh. "Humdrum sounds amazing. I admit, I miss it—hanging out, researching whatever caught my imagination that day. Intergalactic astrology, obscure planets, crystallography and gemology, even Toydarian ceremonial flight patterns—whatever it was, I would always argue to Master Jora that it might come in handy sometime. She would just say that knowledge didn't have to justify itself, but my messy room did, and then she'd pack me off to clean it up."

"I wouldn't have thought you were the messy type."

Reath shrugged. "She had high standards. I was fourteen. Bad combination."

Once they had claimed one of the secluded research booths, Avon laid out her most recent findings on the blight. Young as she was, she possessed a streak of true brilliance; Reath had reviewed everything issued on the topic by the top research foundations in the Republic, but Avon's information was clearer and even potentially visionary. "As you can see, the rate of decay has remained constant—almost too constant. Natural variation should include a wider range of results than we're getting here, or from any of the blight samples we've received."

"Suggesting that this is a manufactured contagion?" Reath asked.

To his surprise, Avon shook her head. "More like—like it ties into something extremely fundamental, extremely basic. Something that physics itself regulates. In other words, the blight appears to be . . . attacking the very fabric of the galaxy."

Reath hadn't asked permission to reveal this next piece of information, but he trusted Avon. "You should know that we believe there to be a link between the blight and the Nameless."

Avon frowned. "Wait. What? *How?* Like, they carry the disease?"

"Nothing so prosaic. The Nameless cut the Jedi off from the Force, and the blight—the blight is basically the loss of the Force itself. The energy that should emanate from all life and matter disappears, leaving behind only desolation."

He saw the realization sink into her, weigh her down. "Then my professors at the Academy have us looking for solutions in all the wrong places. They're not even close to understanding this. Which means a potential cure is even farther away, if—if there's any cure at all."

She had spoken aloud the doubt Reath had been carrying for far too long now. It was so heavy a burden for such a young girl to bear—but she lifted her chin, determined to bear it. Deeply touched, he put one hand on her arm, for just a moment. "There's an answer. There has to be."

It was a simple thing to say, and a friendly gesture, no more. But Avon looked up at him, all astonishment and affection, her face betraying the crush she so patently had on Reath. This crush was unrequited—Reath was newly an adult and Avon only just into her adolescence—but he did admire her for her intelligence, insight, and dedication, and he had hoped to thread the needle of encouraging her for those traits without ever encouraging the crush itself. Had he crossed the line?

Before he could backtrack, though, Avon proved it was unnecessary. She turned back to the materials she'd brought. "So, instead of wildly brainstorming new ideas for a potential cure, I need to determine whether or not a cure is even possible."

Reath wasn't sure he wanted the answer to that. But they'd

find the answer eventually, regardless. Better to know sooner rather than later. "The resources of the Archives are yours, Avon. Good luck."

⚜

Under normal circumstances, interplanetary travel involved relatively few customs checks. Some planets were more secure than others, and droids occasionally scanned bags for contraband, but many worlds kept no comprehensive record of who came or went. Who could keep track of such things when any individual could own a starship?

The answer to that question: highly developed planets that had to tightly control atmospheric traffic to prevent collisions, of which Coruscant was the busiest of all. During various crises, Coruscant had been obliged to increase controls somewhat, but this still mostly began and ended with answering a few questions at a customs station.

A bored, half-asleep agent at the station asked the passenger before him, "Reason for visiting Coruscant?"

Nan smiled. "I'm catching up with an old friend."

⚜

Not every planet currently labored under the weight of the fear and gloom that shrouded Coruscant and so many other worlds. A few of them—those farthest from the violence—were even able to embrace joy. One of those planets was Kashyyyk.

The Wookiees of Kashyyyk were neither unfeeling nor oblivious to the gravity of the conflict between the Republic and the

Nihil. Far from it. But theirs could be a deeply spiritual culture; it was also a culture that loved a good party. And this day—Planting Day—combined both.

For the most part, Wookiees allowed the trees and the plant life of their planet to govern itself. The biome had formed in perfect balance, one they did not wish to disturb. Nor was anyone in any great rush to disturb the lowest levels of Kashyyyk, which were home to both animals and plants that were intensely dangerous, even to beings as strong as Wookiees. What modest agriculture they did practice concentrated mostly on prized fruits and important medicinal plants. The great wroshyr trees would forever remain the masters of their own destiny . . . except for this one day each year.

On Planting Day, the Wookiees in certain honored villages scouted the forest floor and gently dug up wroshyr saplings that had taken root in places where the trees ultimately could not grow to full adulthood. They then carried the baby trees to more promising sites and replanted them with fertilizer, chanting, and a dance. After that, the mead kegs were cracked open and the ensuing festival often lasted until dawn . . . that is, dawn two or three days later.

By tradition, only the most senior Wookiee matriarchs gathered the wroshyr saplings. For everyone else, the morning was time to prepare for the celebration. Children collected slender vines to braid into their hair or wove crowns of twigs, grasses, and flowers for their friends. Adults cleaned their tree houses thoroughly and put away any breakables, just in case the evening's party proved exceptionally lively. In the early afternoon, the mead kegs were due to be brought up from the deep root cellars—but that was when the first howls of alarm sounded. Then warning horns were blown. Within moments, virtually every Wookiee in this particular village was hurrying toward the sound, gathering in one large frightened group.

The howls had come from the matriarchs. One of them gestured to a wroshyr sapling, one that had been found and marked for transplant only a week before, when it had been slender but strong and flush with new leaves. Now the sapling was shriveled and dead, wilted to one side, half its leaves gone and the other half faded almost completely to brown. Its slender trunk had a telltale pallor. It appeared as though the ground around the dead sapling had turned ashen—as if it had been poisoned—and therefore the young tree growing within it had been utterly cut off from nutrients, water, all the stuff of life.

Normally such a death would have required months of neglect and privation. For it to have happened within days . . .

This, they knew, could only be the blight.

ELEVEN

The next day, a new rumor caught fire within the Chancellor's inner sanctum, and within the Jedi Temple. These whispers had it that Marchion Ro's ship, the *Gaze Electric*, had been sighted by a probe droid in the Thraisai system, in Wild Space . . . and most significantly, beyond the boundaries of the Stormwall. As for Thraisai itself, it had a reputation as a vector for the slave trade, as well as being a known hideout for bounty hunters. If Ro was extending his evil influence in either of those vile directions, this hinted at his confidence that he would claim yet more Republic territory, and his intention to rule it with no thought for any value except profit. The Council—what remained of it—immediately went into conference with Chancellor Soh, but other groups of Jedi gathered together in enclaves in and near the Temple, eager to discuss this news.

If, indeed, it was news. Not everyone agreed.

"It can't be real," said Dez Rydan, who stood among those who'd gathered on one of the open-air terraces. "Why should Ro expose himself like this? He's never left himself this vulnerable before, has he? I can't believe he's done so without an agenda of his own."

"What's the one weakness Marchion Ro has shown us so far? Overconfidence." Bell Zettifar, fierier than usual, argued the point. "He knows there's a lot of fear on this side of the Stormwall, and a lot of dissent. If you ask me, it's just like him to think that right now he can do whatever he wants. To get messy. To make a mistake." This was met with a few nods and murmurs of assent.

Dez, however, was neither convinced nor alone in his doubt. He said, "He hasn't made that many mistakes so far, and if we assume he's made one now, then we'll be the overconfident ones."

Overconfidence was not the general feeling around the Temple after three years of conflict, to put it lightly. Dez was not fool enough to believe otherwise. But he had returned from the Barash Vow clear-sighted, fully aware of the flaws inherent in the Order, and thus in every Jedi, including himself—one of which was hubris. He'd come to understand that it was impossible for anyone to wield the Force without running the risk of confusing the Force's power and wisdom for their own.

At the very corner of the terrace sat Reath Silas, who had been listening silently, his expression unreadable. Only now did he speak. "If Ro has traveled beyond Nihil-controlled space, he did so for a reason. Searching for the man himself isn't nearly as important as learning what he went to Thraisai for."

"Precisely," said Cohmac Vitus. "This is one of the other dangers Marchion Ro presents: He is so vainglorious, so egocentric, that he convinces everyone else—even us!—that he's the enemy, not the Nihil at large. We cannot be so caught up in the desire to catch him that we lose sight of actually winning this war."

To Dez's relief, this sentiment seemed to carry the day. *May the Council chamber prove as wise as this gathering!*

Yet not everyone was convinced. Bell, in particular, crossed his arms before his chest. "Bringing Marchion Ro to justice matters. No matter how many battles we win or how many Nihil ships are destroyed, or even if we bring down the Stormwall tomorrow—no one in this galaxy is going to feel safe until he's in custody, or dead."

Burryaga whined, acknowledging this, but then pointed out that focusing too much on Ro was dangerous for the Jedi, because it brought them too close to hatred.

He might have gone on had not young Padawan Condola Oquine appeared in the doorway, pale and panting. "Is it true?"

"If only we knew," said Cohmac. "The Council is evaluating the intel about Ro as we—"

"Not about him," said Condola. "About the blight. Wait. None of you know yet, do you?"

Dez's gut clenched. "Oh, no. What now?"

All became clearer when Condola then turned and spoke to Burryaga alone. "I'm so sorry, but . . . they've found the blight on Kashyyyk."

Though none of the Jedi conversing on the terrace knew it, a figure on the street far below had been observing them with interest.

Nan's goggles looked like any other pair of distance viewers a person might wear, even if such devices were more common attire for adventurers on unsettled worlds than for those who dwelled in the capital of the Republic. Wearing them on Coruscant came across as more of a fashion affectation. So Nan allowed those around her to believe she was a shallow chaser of style, all the while adjusting the magnification levels until she could make out the faces of some individual Jedi above. Most of them were strangers to her, but not Reath Silas.

So close, she thought, watching him speak. He'd grown up a great deal in the past three years; so had Nan. How much would they recognize of each other? How meaningful was the contrast between the people they'd been when they met on the Amaxine station and the people they had become?

She slipped her goggles up over her forehead to hold back her thick dark hair, then looked down at the base of the Temple ziggurat. Other than a few tourist booths selling commemorative Temple holos, she could make out little sign that anybody on Coruscant paid attention to the authority of the Jedi in their midst. Instead, blasé city dwellers hurried past without a glance, on their way to wherever it was they considered more important.

Nan had studied the publicly available information about the Temple interior—as well as the privately available information, much of which had been wrung from the suffering of the late

Jedi Master Loden Greatstorm. Some uncertainties remained, but she knew enough secrets to hazard an extremely good guess as to where the ancient Sith shrine lay.

And she had seen enough of the blight to imagine it hatching there, growing, threatening to rot the Temple from the inside out.

I'll be back, she thought before turning and walking away.

The underworld on Coruscant—the alleys and avenues where trade laws were less stringently observed, where the illicit could thrive—wasn't actually that difficult to find. Nan had sense enough to understand that, in a city like this one, shadow followed light; beginning at a bastion of virtue and respectability, all she had to do was turn one hundred and eighty degrees and take a good long walk. The buildings became slightly less grand, the vehicles overhead a bit less shiny . . . and then, the first sign of a poorly lit alley cavern. Twenty stories higher, probably, the residents and businesses would still be entirely legitimate. Down here, not so much.

Her path took her past a wall of shiny green vines that had managed to cling to life this far below, probably due to a high tolerance for darkness and a lucky hour or so when a sunbeam made its way down through the skyscrapers and the endless ribbons of sky traffic. Nan let her hand trail against the waxy leaves, a sensation that reminded her of the mission to the Amaxine station. The arboretum there had housed a mysterious garden that managed to live in the depths of space. She and Hague—and the Jedi—had walked through that green space unaware that the Drengir were slumbering all around them. Until the Drengir woke up, of course. Things had become much livelier then.

Nan wandered into another alley, glancing from shop to shop, individual to individual. She was glanced at in return. Given her young age and her short stature, many of these were no doubt looking at her as potential prey. She looked forward to enlightening anyone fool enough to act on that assumption.

A low arched doorway beckoned those who sought a cantina; the bouncer droid flickered intermittently, obviously providing little security. Nan ducked inside and blinked quickly as her vision adjusted to the low lighting. Most of the room's illumination actually came from the luapite counter, which faintly glowed a sickly shade of yellow and cast the drinkers in silhouette. Only a handful were inside at this hour, and most of them would be seeking the oblivion of drunkenness, not business deals. But at least one individual present would know somebody in a better position to get Nan what she needed.

She went to the bar. "A mineral water, please," she said, taking out a coin that ought to earn some attention.

It did. The bartender said, "What kind? We stock eleven planets—got Chandrila, Alderaan, and Paucris Major in bottles, and on draft we have—"

"Paucris Major sounds fine," Nan said. "I'm also looking for someone who could help me source some equipment." She didn't elaborate on what kind of equipment, and she knew she wouldn't be asked to.

A burly Houk nearby chortled. "What's a little girl like you need with a blaster? Scared there might be monsters under your bed?"

Nan reached into her pocket and then, in one fluid move,

activated her short vibroblade in the instant before she slammed it down onto the countertop. Its point stabbed through the Houk's sleeve but not his flesh. Only then did she say, "I'm not a little girl."

The Houk laughed again, more meanly this time. "You didn't even hit my arm. You'll have to work a little harder if you want to—to intimidate . . ."

His voice trailed off and was lost under a faint hum, one that became louder every moment. It emanated from the luapite bar itself, the glow of which had begun to brighten and dim at irregular intervals.

"Vibroblades plus luapite means a kinetic feedback loop," Nan said. Her hand remained a tight fist around her blade's hilt. "Should be getting warmer, too. Is it?"

"It's hot," whined the Houk. "It's going to burn me!"

She replied, "Just wait until it overloads. My guess is this stuff will hit a high enough temperature to burn through to the bone before then, of course—but if you're still here, the explosion might just cut you in half."

The Houk swore violently, wriggling in an attempt to get his jacket and shirt off, but it wasn't easy to accomplish with only one free arm, and nobody else was in a hurry to help him out, particularly if it involved getting closer to the bar that was busily turning into an explosive. "All right, all right, you've had your fun," he finally said. "But it's time to end this!"

Nan smiled. "Then it's also time to stop patronizing the lady and tell her where she can find a weapons dealer who doesn't ask a lot of questions."

She strode out of the cantina not five minutes later with all the information she needed and her Paucris Major water in a to-go flask. Time to do some shopping.

◈

By the next morning, the Jedi Council had determined two things:

First, the intel regarding Marchion Ro's presence on Thraisai was too solid to be easily discounted and therefore required investigation. A party would be assembled to follow up on the intel, to prove or disprove his presence in that star system, determine why Ro had been there and examine whatever that might be, and—of course, if possible—act to capture the Nihil leader.

Second, the Kashyyyk blight outbreak was real, and therefore it must be the latest planet to benefit from the Jedi efforts to hold back the blight. A team would be dispatched there to do what it could, for as long as it could. By this point, everyone knew that the best-case scenario for dealing with the blight was buying enough time to get answers.

As soon as Reath heard this, he went straight to the Council and asked to be on the Kashyyyk team.

"To aid in evacuations?" Yoda tilted his head.

"No, Master Yoda. If all Wookiees are anything like Burryaga, then I know they won't leave Kashyyyk."

Yoda nodded. "Wise in the ways of Wookiees are you. No evacuation will there be, unless in the very final hours of the planet. What, then, do you hope to do on Kashyyyk?"

Reath took a deep breath and hoped he would sound reasonable, not irrational. "To save that world, if it can be done. If not, to learn something from it that may save another planet, if not all future planets, from the blight. And to prepare the Wookiees for the evacuation that must inevitably come, unless an entire people are to die. Either way, I want to help them as much as I can, and to learn more about the blight if possible."

"An interesting request, you have made," said Yoda. "Other Jedi I have heard from, yet other than Wookiees, all ask to pursue Marchion Ro. All, that is, until you."

"I still have hope," Reath said. "The blight seems undefeatable—but I still want to defeat it. And if there's any chance to defeat it, first we have to fully understand it. The Force alone can't kill the blight; if it could, we'd have eradicated it months ago. We need more study. We need *research*—and research is still what I do best."

Yoda's ears rose along with the corners of his mouth. "Self-knowledge you have gained, Reath Silas, and greater wisdom, too. Never sought we to deny your gifts, only to show you in how many other ways those gifts could be used."

Reath smiled back. "Is that a yes?"

"Take part in the Kashyyyk mission you will, Reath. And may the Force be with you."

❈

The verdant globe of Kashyyyk swelled large on the viewscreen of the *Firebringer* as it exited hyperspace not far beyond the planet's atmosphere. Instantly, the ship's comms lit up with an automated warning: BLIGHT QUARANTINE. NO UNAUTHORIZED ACCESS. LANDING PROHIBITED.

"Already, it has begun," Mkampa murmured. "Excellent."

Her good mood was threatened when her scans confirmed the location of the blight on Kashyyyk, which was far, far too close to what she had come to Kashyyyk to find. A moment's paranoia pierced her: Could Ro have guessed her intent? Had he specifically planted the blight in this place to spite her, and perhaps destroy her prize?

If the Eye of the Storm's need to parade the blight around had cost her this prize—if the blight had destroyed what she sought (though she was not convinced it had the power to do so)—then she intended to dunk Ro headfirst in a Kennerla swamp. That was only the first of many humiliations she intended to visit on the man if he had gotten in her way. . . .

But a few minutes soon confirmed what the lush green vista beneath suggested: The blight had only just been detected on Kashyyyk, and apparently at its very earliest stage. She had time to search the area before the affliction grew too much larger.

Time to seek, and time to find.

TWELVE

Almost all Jedi came to the Order as babies or toddlers—either found by the Knights who wandered through various star systems or sometimes even brought to a temple by parents who had observed some of the phenomena that can surround infants already strong in the Force. Given the lifespans of most sentients, this meant most Jedi retained little, if any, memory of their birth families and home planets.

For longer-lived species—such as Wookiees—the experience could be profoundly different.

Yes, Wookiees came to the Order as very young children, but within that species, "very young" meant "not yet thirty years old." Although Wookiee youth did not form as many memories as most sentients had by that age, they generally retained strong recollections of their family and powerful bonds to the trees and forests of their homeworld. Complete separation was not only more difficult under such circumstances but also cruel.

Therefore, Wookiee Jedi were not entirely cut off from their families and all the beings and places they had known before. They made occasional visits, knew their relations, and went to Kashyyyk for various festivals. Although the Order did not permit stays so long that deep personal attachments would be inevitable, Wookiee Jedi remained connected to their origins in ways few other Jedi could even imagine.

So when Burryaga learned that the blight had reached Kashyyyk itself, the horror he felt was both intense and personal. It mattered little that the area affected was nearly on the other side of the planet from where he had been born, far distant from Bree and Toko; he knew well that all the forests of Kashyyyk were in fact the one Great Forest, that the untimely fall of even one tree burned a scar in the rings of all. The planet had to be saved, and the Wookiees among the Jedi would be invaluable in those efforts. By the time Reath Silas came to ask him to join the Kashyyyk team, Burryaga was already packed.

(Of course, packing didn't take very long for beings who wore little clothing. Still, he was proud that Reath had found him ready.)

"We won't leave for another day or two yet," Reath said. "They want to complete scans by probe, to make sure we're tackling the whole problem at once."

This made sense. On a densely forested, little-developed planet such as Kashyyyk, even a sizable patch of blight might go unnoticed for days or weeks. Directing all their efforts at one section of the blight would be meaningless if it was spreading elsewhere unchecked. Still, Burryaga whined in impatience.

"I know," Reath said. "I promise—we'll move as fast as we can."

As soon as Reath had left, Burryaga went to find his friend Bell Zettifar. They had become good friends even before the fall of Starlight Beacon, but since Bell had rescued Burryaga in the aftermath, they had been all but inseparable. He entered Bell's quarters, petted Ember, and asked whether Bell was ready to see Kashyyyk. Those Shyriiwook lessons were about to come in handy.

Bell, who sat at his small desk, didn't reply for several seconds. "Actually, I—I think I'm going to put in for the Thraisai mission."

Burryaga whined curiously. Marchion Ro's presence at Thraisai remained nothing but a rumor; the blight was fact. Did that make no difference to Bell? He'd been studying the Wookiee language, hadn't he? Wasn't this an ideal opportunity to use it?

"No," Bell said, then grimaced. "I mean, yes, of course it is—on some level—but we have enough people who understand Shyriiwook that I don't know that any of my skills would really be needed on Kashyyyk. Obviously it's very different for you. For me . . ."

He thought several moments longer. Burryaga said nothing, knowing how important it was to listen.

At last Bell said, "What you said on the terrace, about making sure our focus on capturing Marchion Ro doesn't turn into hatred—there's truth to that. Wisdom, too. But it doesn't change my need to go after Ro. Maybe he's a bloviating figurehead, maybe he's a thug who just got lucky, but he's also the one who captured Master Loden. The one who tortured him and made the last months of his life pure, unending pain. I swear to you that I don't want revenge. I just need to see it through. Does that make sense?"

Burryaga agreed that it did. When Bell looked surprised, Burryaga chuckle-growled. Had his friend believed that if they parted ways here, Burryaga would take offense?

"Not offense, exactly," said Bell. "But I thought you might not understand. Obviously I underestimated you."

A common mistake, Burryaga pointed out, preening his fur in a way that made Bell laugh. Inseparable friends, it seemed, remained connected even when their paths traveled in different directions.

※※

"Lovely, isn't it?" purred the Zygerrian shopkeeper. "That's Meliccan wool, some of the best you can buy. The Melicca shear themselves as a sign of submission to their deities only once every seven years, you know. That's why the fibers are so rare."

Nan had heard of Meliccan wool but never felt any herself. She lifted the shawl from the display; its softness against her palms nearly made her shudder with delight. How could a mere fabric feel almost like a caress?

"That color is perfect on you," said the shopkeeper, stroking her ear fur. "It might have been woven with you in mind."

Nan knew sales patter when she heard it, but she couldn't help feeling flattered. Perhaps the rich green shade of the woolen shawl she held contrasted well with her dark brown hair and eyes. "How much?"

The shopkeeper blithely named a price that would've paid for a quality landspeeder, at least the previous year's model. Nan had been given ample funds to carry out her work for the Nihil and great discretion in how to spend them, but she doubted Marchion Ro had imagined this might be a necessary expense.

"I'll take it," she said. "In fact, I'll wear it out."

A few moments later she exited the luxury shop, newly swathed in deep green. The shawl's large size had allowed her to wrap it around herself almost as a cloak, complete with a make-shift hood. Nan ran her hands down it, reveling in the luxurious texture. She decided to walk along the next passageway over—the most expensive area of what was already the planet's most expensive shopping center—before she left.

Nan made her way up, then down that passageway, looking at finely made boots and belts and jewelry so attentively that no one watching her would have detected how carefully she was also eyeing the security droids and personnel. When she had first entered this center, they had all taken note of her because her clothes weren't quite right. They were neat and decently made—better than she'd once had as a ruffian Nihil orphan—but to the careful observer, even on a subconscious level for the sentient guards, something about her would always seem *off*.

Wrapped in a luxurious shawl, however, Nan had become invisible. The same garment that would have marked her as extraordinary in most places made her ordinary here. And now that she looked like any other wealthy young inhabitant of Coruscant, nobody would take much note of her, no matter where she might go.

(It didn't hurt that the bulk of the shawl also concealed certain devices on her person, ones that the security droids wouldn't have been on the lookout for in the shopping center but that might have been of more interest to other security yet to come.)

Nan strolled out of the shopping center onto one of the elevated walkways, so high up that layers and layers of traffic zipped by below, bright ribbons of color and light woven beneath her feet. The sun was shining, and the Jedi Temple basked in it, waiting for her.

* * *

Most of the traffic moving along below Nan at that time was made up of the usual skimmers and speeders licensed for Coruscant. However, one vein of traffic was reserved for larger cargo haulers and small interplanetary craft with clearance, which at that moment included the *Vessel*.

"Man, I remember the first time I saw this planet," drawled Leox Gyasi as he deftly maneuvered through the thick traffic. "I didn't want to be impressed, but I couldn't help it. After Alderaan, though? Coruscant looks downright shabby."

Affie laughed out loud. "Watch it, Leox. You're becoming jaded."

"Far be it from me to lose appreciation for the many spectacles of the cosmos, and I'm glad to see our navigator hasn't, either," Leox said with a nod. Certainly, Geode hadn't lost his childlike gaze of wonder upon seeing Coruscant. "However, I maintain that Alderaan is a jewel among jewels, and that deserves appreciation, too."

"I guess people can get used to anything after a while." Affie, too, had once found Coruscant both awe-inspiring and intimidating. She remembered her mother taking her to a luxury hotel here, buying her fancy desserts, and how excited she'd felt. Had she still been that much of a kid only three years ago?

Not all years are equal, she reminded herself. The whole galaxy had aged a lot since the Nihil conflict began.

Besides, she'd traveled to Coruscant a lot in that time, and now that she was running the newer, better iteration of the Byne Guild, Affie found this was becoming one of her principal hubs. Her coalition of independent, allied pilots couldn't be summoned with a snap, the way Scover Byne had gathered the Guild ships together back in the day. If Affie wanted to meet with her crews in person, Coruscant was one of the few planets that everyone flew to eventually.

They piloted the *Vessel* to its berth, one in the general vicinity of the Jedi Temple. Upon realizing this was the area she'd chosen, Geode gave Affie a knowing look. "Oh, stop it," she said, laughing. "It's not like I'm *hoping* the Jedi are in the market for transport. Those are always the missions where we nearly get killed."

"From where I'm sitting, lately it seems like all the missions are the missions where we nearly get killed," Leox pointed out.

"The Nihil make sure of it. But you'll get no guff from me even if you *are* hoping for a Jedi run. Say what you will about those trips, but they're never dull."

Once the *Vessel* was safely berthed, they set out on their various errands: Leox went to replenish their food stores, and Geode had the responsibility of fueling them up, as few coaxium dealers could long withstand his cold stare on the other side of a bargaining table. Affie had only a small gathering of Byne Guild pilots to meet with later on, but every meeting she could get was worthwhile.

As she walked through the catacomb of archways that connected the buildings in this area of Coruscant, Affie's thoughts at first dwelled on the meeting to come—the need to hear their intel about various Nihil movements, their thoughts about different signaling protocols in future—but slowly, her surroundings demanded more and more of her attention. When she had first come to Coruscant, the viewscreen banners and hologram displays everywhere had proclaimed the glories of Chancellor Soh's Great Works, or advertised festivals to come in the near future. Now they broadcast various safety warnings and information about rerouted space traffic. Although the flight patterns in the upper atmosphere were still busy by any normal planet's standards, Affie's experienced eye could tell that they had slowed since her first trips to this world. People were staying home if they could. They were shipping fewer goods to fewer places. As for the pedestrians who surrounded her—there was no such thing as a single public mood in a place like Coruscant, but she could see more signs of stress, fewer smiles. The capital of the Republic, the bright center of the galaxy, had been shaken. Dimmed. The confidence it had carried so easily before had all but vanished.

There's more than one kind of blight infecting the galaxy, Affie thought.

If the Nihil could shake even Coruscant—could anyone stand against them forever?

It was the first time she had ever allowed herself to wonder whether the Nihil might actually win.

Free walking tours in Basic! The holographic words levitated in midair near Monument Park, along with starting times. As the next tour was drawing near, several beings had begun collecting beneath the sign. Tourism on Coruscant was at less than one third of its pre–Hyperspace Disaster levels—but this being Coruscant, that meant there were still thousands of visitors eager to look around. A large family of humans from some dim world with a lot of cloud cover had gathered, all of them dressed alike in their tunics and protective goggles. An affectionate pair of Twi'leks only had eyes for each other but seemed ready to wander through the tour hand in hand. A Godoan was taking holo-images every two or three seconds, to the annoyance of the Bith standing nearby. Other humans seemed to be from other Core Worlds, to judge by their elegant jackets, dresses, and shawls.

The Trodatome guide slithered up right on cue. "Hello there, everyone! I'm Occo, and I'll be sharing the 'Wonders of Monument Park' with you today. Hopefully our sign droid here has transmitted our guidelines to your devices, but just in case, let me run through the basics with you." Nobody was listening much. Nan wasn't listening at all, until Occo reached the one relevant part of his spiel: "—and those same security regulations mean we won't be able to enter the Jedi Temple today, but we will be able to stroll along the grounds, appreciate the beauty of this galactic landmark, and learn more about its incredible history!"

Once the tour began, Nan walked along, nodding when everyone else nodded, drawing no attention to herself. Only very slowly did she begin to trail behind, falling farther back until she was at the rear of the group. They were used to her being there well before the tour's path took them onto the Temple grounds.

So this is where they're from, she thought, looking up at the epic structure, which hinted at greater wonders inside. *While Hague and I were sleeping in the cockpit, running on battery only, so cold we could see our breath—the Jedi were resting in luxury here.*

The Twi'lek couple had deviated from the group to the very edge of the security perimeter of the Temple. A few sentries lazily noticed the two of them taking holo-images of themselves in various affectionate poses. Just as a guard began to wave them on their way, Nan hurried out after them, making *Oh, just let me do it, too!* gestures as she went. Nobody stopped her, even when she stepped just over the edge. She reached into her shawl, as though for her holoemitter. . . .

And she pulled out a dull-sheened spherical device, which she activated with a twist. As it glowed bright orange, people gasped and shrieked; the sentries suddenly woke up, too late. Nan shouted, "Take one step toward me and this thing goes off!"

"Is it a thermal detonator?" one of the goggled humans whimpered.

Occo answered, "Worse! It's a rupture flare—capable of aerosolizing poisonous fluid, or poisonous gas, basically anything poisonous you can micro—"

"It's a rupture flare loaded with the blight," Nan said as loudly as she could while remaining cool. "You want to see Coruscant rot to nothing? Do what I say, or that's exactly what you'll see. We can all watch it together, *today*."

People started to scream and run. Others stood as though frozen. The security guards took her seriously enough not to approach, though she could see them muttering frantically into their comms. Nearby buildings' indicator lights began to blink red; no doubt evacuations had begun all around them. Only a handful of people remained completely calm; these, she realized from their white-and-gold robes, were Jedi. The one closest to her, a Mirialan just within earshot, said, "You don't want to detonate that rupture flare."

Nan had been warned about this sort of Jedi trick—had steeled herself against it—but she hadn't been ready for the sheer power of that mental suggestion. Weariness settled over her like a weighted blanket, rendering her limbs loose and heavy, urging her toward relaxation and rest. How long had it been since she had felt really, truly at rest? So long. Too long. She didn't *want* to extend this standoff, did she? There was no point to it. And the device had become so cumbersome. It would be so easy to set the rupture flare down, just to put it down and walk away from it forever. . . .

Snap out of it!

"Nice try," she said to the Mirialan Jedi. "But no luck."

The Jedi remained calm. "Then perhaps you should tell us what you want."

"I want to tell the Republic everything I know about Marchion Ro and the blight," Nan replied, "and I know quite a lot."

"You don't have to threaten anyone to make that happen," the Jedi said.

Nan shook her head. "I don't trust the Republic. I don't trust any random Jedi just because they're wearing fancy robes. There's only one person I'm willing to speak to—Reath Silas. Take me to him, *now.*"

THIRTEEN

Reath walked toward the chamber housing Azlin Rell, his steps slowing only slightly as he heard Azlin softly crooning, *"Shrii Ka Rai, Ka Rai...."* That lullaby remained profoundly creepy, and yet . . . somehow, Reath was becoming accustomed to it. If Master Yoda was correct and both Azlin and the lullaby contained knowledge about the Nameless that lay beneath the conscious realm, then Reath's search could only be strengthened by familiarity. Fear occluded vision. Calm provided clarity. He had been growing toward this goal from the beginning, slipping closer so slowly that progress had been almost invisible but very real.

That or, by this point, Reath just didn't scare that easily anymore.

When he shared these thoughts with Azlin Rell, the response was a laugh—short and hard, like a sliver chipped from bone. "They tell you not to be afraid," Azlin said, rocking back and forth on his cot. "Then they send you into the depths of danger, where fear is the only sane response."

Fear was a sane response to many risks, Reath felt, but never the only response possible. He would have told Azlin that, too, had the organizer droid JJ-5145 not rolled up in an electronic yet unmistakable state of alarm. (Elzar Mann had instructed the droid to take its issues to Reath whenever he himself was absent; Reath wasn't certain yet whether that had been a kind gesture or an excellent practical joke.) "Jedi Silas!" it trilled, lights blinking frantically. "A terrorist is threatening the Jedi Temple with a rupture flare, which she claims contains particles of the blight!"

So far, the blight on Coruscant was contained within the Jedi Temple, which meant the terrorist was threatening to infect the one place on the planet already infected. Yet blight beyond the Temple walls would be disastrous. Reath imagined the vast towers of Coruscant toppling like the buildings had on Inad Komesh, then wished he hadn't. "All right, Forfive," Reath said to the droid. "Are we evacuating? Sheltering within the Temple? And will this be a Jedi or Republic response?"

"The terrorist wishes to speak only to you, Jedi Silas."

"To me?"

"She named you specifically," JJ-5145 confirmed, then projected a small holo of the scene outside.

Automatically, Reath began describing what he saw for Azlin.

"The Temple perimeter, usual crowds more or less, one young woman standing with what appears to be a rupture flare—" The woman in the image turned, revealing her face to Reath's view; he very nearly swore. "By the Force . . . that's *Nan*."

"Nan?" Azlin and the droid said in unison. It was Azlin who continued, "You know this terrorist? You're becoming more interesting, my boy."

"She's not a terrorist exactly," Reath said, wondering if this could still be considered true while she was essentially holding the Temple hostage. "But she is a member of the Nihil."

Azlin asked, "How did you come to know her, then?"

"Amid the Great Hyperspace Disaster, the ship I was traveling on was marooned at an abandoned ancient Amaxine station," Reath explained. "So were several other ships, including a small two-person craft that looked like it was held together by weaving twine and prayer. That ship was Nan's. During the time we were trapped there, we talked a lot. Got to know each other—"

"Ah, I understand now." Azlin was smiling smugly. "Don't feel too bad about it. For all the Jedi Order's efforts to pretend otherwise, virtually every Padawan experiences a clandestine attachment during youth."

Reath shook his head before remembering that Azlin couldn't see. "It wasn't like that between us. Not for me, anyway. But I believed we'd become friends, and as a result, I wound up telling her too much."

"She fooled you."

"Yes," Reath said evenly. "She did. But she won't again." He pulled up the hood of his robe and nodded to the droid, which promptly began rolling away, leading Reath toward Nan and the confrontation she so desperately sought.

❀

The droid parted the crowds of Jedi and visitors who milled about on the lowest level of the Temple, clearing a swath for Reath to walk through. Outside the windows, he could see Nan standing there, still holding her rupture flare aloft. He wondered if her arm hurt by now.

After Azlin, am I developing a specialty in dangerous characters? Reath wondered. *If so, how do I stop developing it?*

He strode out onto the plaza, ignoring the murmurings of the panicky crowd nearby. Nan tensed—probably expecting physical resistance—but then relaxed when she evidently recognized Reath. She looked well, with fashionable clothing and a luxurious shawl, hardly recognizable as the ragamuffin girl he'd met only three years ago. What did it mean, when someone looked better in the heart of a war than they had before it? Reath wasn't sure, but he doubted it was a sign of anything good.

Once he was within several meters of her, he called, "You know, you could've just sent a holo."

Maddeningly, Nan played it just as cool. "Would you have watched it?"

"Eventually." Reath came to a stop only a few strides from her. "Please put that thing away."

"We have to talk," she said. "I don't intend to set this aside and then get thrown into a cell where nobody ever hears what I have to say."

"I can't promise you're not going to be thrown into a cell. In fact, I'd say that's about the only place you can go from here while both of us remain alive. What I can promise is that I'll hear you out. You didn't come all this way just to pull some kind of stunt. Whatever it is you want to tell me has to be important. I get that."

Nan blinked. "I didn't think you'd tell the truth about my arrest."

Since when am I the liar here? Reath thought but did not say. "You knew you'd be arrested before you even decided to come to Coruscant. You're too smart not to have known that was the inevitable result. That's one of the things that tells me this truly is important."

"Then let's get this over with." Nan clicked the rupture flare, deactivating it. Security guards and a few sentry droids began rushing them, but Reath held up one hand, halting them all in their tracks. She cocked her head. "You're escorting me to jail? What a gentleman."

Something about the way she said it made Reath think of what Azlin Rell had said about "clandestine attachments." He didn't feel that for Nan, but did she think he did? Were such emotions part of her calculations about whatever she was attempting here?

Or were those emotions something she felt for him?

Nan had spent time in a Republic cell once before, a makeshift brig on the late Starlight Beacon, which had very nearly wound up becoming her tomb; she'd have gone down with the station if she and Chancey Yarrow hadn't managed to break out. The cells on Coruscant were a lot nicer, but Nan suspected they'd be harder to escape from. Luckily, escape wasn't one of her current objectives.

"Okay, Nan," said Reath as he took a seat on the bench opposite the energy field holding her within her cell. "Whatever it is you came to say, say it."

She stood, keeping her face as blank as possible as she said, "I think Marchion Ro's losing this war."

"I wish I were as confident about that as you seem to be. Please, convince me."

"Ro's an outlaw by his nature. He lives to break the rules. But he has no capacity for *making* the rules, now that he can. I think he's dealing with more complexity and breadth of responsibility than he can even fathom, much less manage, and I think he's enough of an egotist that he has no idea of the limits of his capabilities. It doesn't matter whether or not the Republic or the Jedi figure out how to defeat Marchion Ro. He's going to self-destruct, given time."

"I don't know that the galaxy has that much time to spare, thanks to the blight." Reath studied her, giving away as little emotion as she. Where was that idealistic boy she'd met on the Amaxine station? "So this is you, what? Switching sides?"

"I never expected to receive a warm welcome on this side of the Stormwall," Nan replied. "This is me being a realist. Once

Marchion Ro finally realizes that he can't actually govern an entire galaxy, it would be just like him to smash up the place as much as possible before he vanishes. That means more blight. And *that* means a galaxy nobody gets to live in safely, regardless of what side a person fought on. Which means, except for Ro, everyone loses."

"That probably sums it up," Reath said. His gaze had turned inward as he considered her words. "But I doubt you came all this way just to wash your hands of Marchion Ro. You must have actionable intelligence, Nan. So what is it?"

"I know the blight is already on Coruscant, within the Temple." Nan saw Reath go pale and took satisfaction in the knowledge that she had finally scored a point. He hadn't expected her to have that information. "I also know where it's going to strike next—on Kashyyyk."

"It's already on Kashyyyk," Reath answered. "We found out earlier today."

This took some of the wind from Nan's sails, but she had little choice but to carry on. "I have reason to believe that Dr. Mkampa is also heading to Kashyyyk, for reasons of her own— and that she may be not only leaving the Nihil but also hoping to create schism. If she can persuade even a few ships to come with her, she'll have her own Storm, which means the Republic will have a whole new enemy in a war they're already losing."

"You have my attention." Reath stood up slowly. "How do you know this?"

"Marchion Ro, of course," Nan said. "He's forever paranoid about other leaders among the Nihil gaining enough power to stand up to him. As a result, he's murdered everyone else even remotely competent, which is how you wind up with our current mess."

"You think Dr. Mkampa is on Kashyyyk?" Reath said.

Nan nodded. "Or she's headed there, and will be soon. I think I can help you find her—but only if you take me with you."

FOURTEEN

"**B**elieve this Nihil spy, you do?" Yoda's ears swiveled in a way Reath had learned signaled considerable skepticism. "A trap, you do not suspect?"

"With Nan, I don't think we can entirely discount that possibility," Reath answered, "but I don't think we can dismiss her statements out of hand, either. She knew about the presence of the blight within the Temple, which is a closely guarded secret. It appears Nan has been on the rise within the Nihil as an intelligence operative, and if she knows that much, well, that suggests she's risen high in those ranks. And if she's willing to *tell* us that she knows—that indicates one of two things. One, she's actually on the level. Two, Nan has another agenda. In my opinion, option two is a lot more likely . . . but I don't have the slightest idea what that agenda could actually be."

"This could be a Nihil ruse, intended to distract us from Marchion Ro's movements around Thraisai," said Teri Rosason.

Reath shook his head, though a part of him wondered when he'd become a person who could contradict a member of the *Jedi Council* without sweating and stammering. "I can't see the point. We're capable of responding to both the situation on Kashyyyk *and* the rumors of Ro's whereabouts. The Nihil know that."

Yoda had been contemplating deeply, it seemed. "Some rivalry between the Nihil spy and this Dr. Mkampa, there may be."

"I hadn't considered that," Reath said. Nor did this strike him at first as especially likely. Why should a scientist and a spy need to compete with each other? Surely each played a very different role within the Nihil.

Yet as he examined the concept, he began to sense what Yoda might be thinking. For one, Baron Boolan's recent capture meant that a power vacuum had been created within the Nihil ranks— one many would rush to fill. Furthermore, the Nihil was not a meritocracy; it was a group of piratical raiders who believed that might made right. Proximity to Ro meant power. Therefore there would always be bitter rivalries at work between those desperate for Marchion Ro's time and attention. If Nan and Mkampa had wound up on opposite sides of some issue and Ro was now favoring Mkampa, then Nan might want to turn the tide.

But how would a stunt such as this one help her accomplish that?

"What worries me is the possibility that Ro himself sent her," said Keaton Murag. "Surely he's setting a trap for as many Jedi as he can kill. This woman is only the bait."

"Yet why on Kashyyyk, hmm?" Master Yoda asked. "Why in this particular place, rather than any other planet in the galaxy?"

"And why now?" Master Rosason added. "Why should Ro set this particular trap just as he has promised a cure to the Republic?"

Reath shrugged. "It's all about as clear as a Kennerla swamp, I know. Regardless, I don't think we can afford to ignore what Nan's saying. If there's any chance she's on the level, we should follow up on her intel, and besides—we were headed to Kashyyyk anyway."

Yoda nodded. "Wookiee Jedi you will have with you there. Strength enough to contain one Nihil spy, hmm?"

"I hope so," Reath said. Weirdly, when he imagined Nan going up against, say, Burryaga, he wasn't 100 percent confident of Burryaga coming out on top. Nan was little, but she was tough, and she'd had to fight her way through life. Sure, Burryaga would always be stronger, would always have the Force as his ally, yet Nan's wiles, intelligence, and sheer obstinacy gave her a shot. This was the greatest compliment Reath could have given Nan, not that he planned to ever share a word of it with her. "If I may ask, have you decided yet who will lead the Kashyyyk team? Obviously I should discuss this with the leader in depth."

The Council members exchanged glances that Reath couldn't understand at all. His confusion turned to astonishment as Yoda said, "Lead the Kashyyyk team, *you* will, Reath Silas."

"Me?" Not exactly the dignified response he would have

wanted to give for his first leadership assignment from the Council, but it was an honest one. "I wasn't knighted that long ago. And this mission is vitally important, doubly so now that Nan is involved and we may be seeking this Dr. Mkampa—"

"You," Yoda said. "You and no other."

"As the Force wills it," Reath said, pulling himself together. "Thank you. I hope to deserve your trust."

"Assemble your team," said Rosason. "Report back to us tonight, and arrange for the earliest possible departure."

Reath hurried from the Council chambers, still dumbfounded but understanding Yoda's reasoning more and more as he walked away. There had been four empty chairs among the twelve in the chamber, silent testimony to the many Council members who had fallen. It was simply impossible to send a senior Council member to every outbreak of the blight any longer.

Besides, this was surely not about Reath's individual status— he was, after all, not so strong in the Force as many other Jedi were. No, this had to be about the sheer toll the Nihil conflict had taken on the Jedi Order. The deaths had not been limited to Council members. He could easily think of so many other Jedi who would have been more obvious choices to lead the Kashyyyk team, like Master Jora Malli. Mirro Lox. Pra-Tre Veter. Orla Jareni. Estala Maru. Ada-Li Carro. Loden Greatstorm. Stellan Gios.

Every single one of them was dead, killed by Marchion Ro, the Nihil, and the Nameless.

The scale of this conflict had become too great. The Jedi

Order was stretched thin, and that stretching was worsened by the many who had fallen in the struggle. Reath had gone to Yoda and volunteered for this assignment; he might have been the only non-Wookiee Jedi to do so. In an age when so many had been lost and so much remained to be done, a simple request such as that one might be enough to justify authority.

Now, to deserve it.

First came the Wookiees. Burryaga, who had already volunteered, introduced Reath to a Knight in his prime called Kelnacca, perhaps a century Burryaga's senior. Kelnacca, who wore his lighter brown head fur in a topknot, was both more reserved and more gruff than Burryaga, but this did not disguise either his intelligence or his considerable strength in the Force. Reath felt profoundly grateful for this addition to the team.

His lone hesitation was something he voiced only to Burryaga. "I feel like maybe—maybe a Wookiee should be the one to lead this mission," Reath said. "This is your planet. You have a connection to Kashyyyk I can't duplicate."

But Burryaga growled in the negative, reminding Reath that it was exactly this connection that made it difficult or even impossible for a Wookiee to head this team. When on their homeworld, Wookiees strong in the Force were greatly affected by the forests; some trees on Kashyyyk were sentients, at least in the Wookiee view, and they had to be listened to and respected. In other words, he and the other Wookiees would be so caught up in listening, translating, and communicating that their attention would be divided. Not ideal for the leader of a mission as dangerous as theirs could prove to be.

Reath kept his expression utterly serious as he said, "So, you're telling me Wookiees can't see the forest for the trees?"

He ducked quickly enough to avoid the swing of Burryaga's claw-sheathed hand—just. That was it for joking around about such an important assignment, but it felt good to grin.

Reath was somewhat surprised to learn that Bell Zettifar had not volunteered for the team; it had become second nature to think of Bell and Burryaga as an inseparable unit, but even good friends might be drawn in different directions by the Force. Reath could potentially have overridden Bell's preference to search for Marchion Ro, but he saw no need, particularly not after Dez Rydan volunteered to go to Kashyyyk. Dez's skill with a blade would make him a valuable asset.

Cohmac Vitus came to Reath personally to volunteer, which felt awkward; it hadn't occurred to Reath until that moment that, regardless of his sometimes-stormy relationship with the Order, Cohmac might have been a more natural person for the Council to call on for this mission. However, the awkwardness appeared to exist solely in his own head, because Cohmac earnestly explained: "My own presence may or may not be helpful to you on Kashyyyk, but I would urge you to consider inviting Padawan Amadeo Azzazzo on the mission. After the death of Mirro Lox, he greatly seeks a stronger sense of purpose. This mission would give him that. More importantly, perhaps, Azzazzo has a . . . gentleness to him that is too easily overlooked during a time of conflict. We need that gentleness for a mission that is as much about healing as about war."

"I already intended to ask Amadeo—we make a good team." Did that sound like Reath was saying he and Cohmac *didn't*? Quickly he added, "And yes, please, join our mission. You'll be a strong asset."

Cohmac accepted with grace, and yet Reath could not help questioning his own words for a while afterward. Why did so many encounters with his former master still feel unnatural? He'd forgiven Cohmac and come to comprehend the pressures that had led to their untimely schism. In many ways, they now had a far deeper understanding of each other than they'd ever shared as master and Padawan.

So why did these odd moments still arise?

Reath reminded himself that this was far from the most pressing matter at the moment and went on his way to find Amadeo Azzazzo. Indeed, Amadeo was clearly awestruck to have been chosen, and accepted almost before Reath had finished inviting him.

Nan's inclusion was a given, albeit a very dangerous given. She would be treated like the prisoner she was, tagged to their camp location, unable to travel far. If she was leading the Jedi into a trap, then she was going to fall into that trap alongside them.

Many more senior scientists would've gone with the team if asked, but this was another area where Reath was willing to trust his instincts. The scientist he chose wasn't as certain.

"You need somebody *good* on this," Avon Starros said.

"That's why I've asked you," Reath replied.

"Yeah, of course I'm *good*, but I mean—megagood. Expert. Mind-bendingly fantastic. The best in the galaxy."

"Exactly," Reath said. "Your work on the blight compares to that performed by scientists with decades more experience. More than that, you aren't wedded to any one theory—unlike some of your professors, it sounds like. That's the kind of thinking we have to avoid. But you keep an open mind, and we're going to need that."

"I don't know if I'm comfortable being your sole scientist on this."

"We'll have analysis equipment along, and some of the scientists from the top research institutes will be on call. You'll have as much collaboration as you need."

Avon nodded, considering this, studying him carefully. "Are you trying to show people I'm useful so I'm not only defined by my mother and what she's done?"

"I wouldn't choose any member for this mission based on that criterion alone. It's too important for that. But you deserve to be recognized for who you are, not who you're related to. So let's say it's a side benefit."

"That's not your motivation," she said, realizing her own thoughts out loud. "It's mine." Their eyes met, and she shook it off. "I mean, I *am* also strongly motivated to save the galaxy—"

Reath had to laugh. "I understand."

One of their primary concerns would be keeping the blight at bay, to preserve as much of Kashyyyk as possible, as long as possible. The Order had begun developing meditation teams specially trained for the kind of extended, in-depth concentration that worked best against the blight; one such team would accompany Reath's mission. Formidable mystics one and all, these Jedi were capable of entering meditative trances that could last for days, even weeks, without ever once relaxing the pressure they exerted on the blight. This not only would allow Reath and the others more time to study and investigate but also represented the best chance of preserving Kashyyyk from ruin . . . at least, for a time.

He decided that both the meditation team and his own unit should travel on non-Republic ships, with no military presence. The Force had seen to it that the *Vessel* was on Coruscant, and he was able to hire other civilian transport, as well.

All these choices met with the Council's approval, until Reath informed them that the final member of the team would be Azlin Rell.

"Out of the question," thundered Keaton Murag, with an appalled expression that was reflected on the faces of most of the masters in the chamber. "He's been taken on too many missions already. The man is dangerous!"

"Saved lives, did Rell, on his last mission," Master Yoda pointed out.

But Murag would not be so easily calmed. "How do we know that wasn't only because it gave Rell an excuse to kill?"

"I've spent a lot of time speaking to Azlin Rell these past months," Reath said. "And I've come to believe—as Master Yoda believes—that Rell is not permanently lost to darkness. He's gripped by fear and hate, yes, but neither of those are directed toward the Jedi Order. And he has a sensitivity to both the dark side and to the Nameless that we may very much need."

Master Yoda nodded. "A risk it is, but risk must ever be the companion of hope."

"Exactly. Besides, Rell needs something to do—something positive, something that lets him feel less powerless against his fear. If we give him that, as we can on this mission, I think the transformation might be extraordinary."

Master Murag was not convinced. "What happens if there is no transformation? If Rell lashes out to harm others the way he has harmed himself?"

"In that case," Reath said, "it's going to be a great time to be surrounded by hundreds of Wookiees."

A couple of masters smiled despite themselves, and Reath knew that particular battle was won. The battles to come wouldn't be so easy.

FIFTEEN

From the moment Master Yoda had reappeared in his life, Azlin Rell had known that the Jedi Order would want to make use of him. Oh, Yoda had had many fine words to say about learning from the past and repairing the future, none of which Azlin had put much faith in. He had suspected that the Jedi would expose him to the Nameless again—they were fools enough to seek the Nameless out—but Azlin intended to strike back. Already he had made at least one of them pay for what they had done to him. But he knew there could be no ultimate victory against such Force-negating devastation. No matter what else he did, it would all end with Azlin as a hollow husk. Despite the endless misery his life had become, he was still in no hurry to die.

All this he was ready to tell Reath Silas when the young Knight came to him with a mission . . . until he heard what the mission was. "Kashyyyk?" He had been there once, when he was very young—or was that no more than a dream? One, perhaps, brought about by the tales of his former Wookiee master when he was a Padawan: Master Arkoff had loved to speak of his time there.

"We're bringing along a team to meditate and hold back the blight through the Force itself," Reath said. "Of course we're going to study the blight, try to make progress against it—and failing that, attempt to talk the Wookiees into evacuating. Beyond that, we've received intel that suggests a top Nihil operative may be in the vicinity. It's important to find out if that's true."

"So you've invited me to a planet that might collapse in on itself before the week is out, complete with Nihil vandals to attack us," Azlin said. This sounded more like his usual luck.

"No evacuation has been ordered yet." The footsteps on the floor of Azlin's chamber brought Reath closer to his side. How could this young Jedi not fear him, when even the Council did? "Besides, consider the possibilities. The blight on Kashyyyk was caught earlier than anywhere else, we think—within a day of its arrival. We've never been able to study it at such an early stage, so this presents an incredible opportunity. Every new opportunity might be the one that gets us closer to an answer."

Azlin usually scorned such hopefulness, but this was so extreme a denial of the galaxy's rot that he almost had to admire it. "You truly think you can twist the galaxy into whatever shape you like. One stroke of luck, and lo! The blight is defeated, the Nameless sent home, the Nihil no more."

(Within his mind, the soft lullaby whispered, *Shrii Ka Rai, Ka Rai.*)

"We don't need luck," Reath said, "and I don't think we'll be reshaping the galaxy. We're working to save one world, and I think you could help us."

Angry words crowded Azlin's mind and throat so he couldn't speak at all for a moment. He was glad of the pause. If he'd spat out what he truly felt about the Jedi's naivety, how badly he still needed revenge against these creatures—even the foolishly courageous Reath Silas would have stepped back from Azlin forever. But he couldn't get revenge while he was locked up here, could he?

"What the hell," he muttered. "Anything to get out of this room."

"Welcome to the team," Reath said.

⚶

On Coruscant, repair droids and sentient mechanics were available to help with any issue a ship might have—for a price, which tended to be higher than it would've been on most other planets. However, Affie Hollow believed that pilots ought to be responsible for their own ships, ought to know them down to the smallest nut and bolt. That was why, less than an hour before they were due to depart for Kashyyyk, she lay flat on her back beneath the *Vessel*, staring at a power coupling that wasn't operating at top efficiency. Still within safety parameters, but she didn't understand *why* it wasn't operating well. Affie knew the most dangerous problems were the ones that were hard to understand. So, new power coupling time.

"Leox?" Affie yelled. "Pass me the T7 anx, will you?"

An arm circled by a few braided leather bracelets emerged from the interior side of the open panel and gave the hull a solid thump over one of the exterior tool pockets, which obediently flipped open. Leox withdrew the crescent-shaped T7 anx, still not poking his head out, but he guided it expertly into Affie's hand. They'd worked together so long that sometimes they operated like two parts of the same being. "You got it on your end? I think some of our Jedi friends are starting to arrive."

"I got it. You and Geode can be the welcoming committee."

Yet she got the work done swiftly and was happy to join the rest of the *Vessel* crew in greeting their passengers. In a time with so much conflict and pain, reunions with old friends were even more precious. She hugged Reath Silas, which made him laugh—but he also hugged her back. Unexpectedly, Cohmac Vitus embraced her, as well. The young Jedi apprentice Amadeo Azzazzo had traveled on the *Vessel* previously but in a state of extreme shell shock that kept him with the medic most of the time; she and her crew took the opportunity to reintroduce themselves to him under better circumstances. Amadeo turned out to be one of the very few *Vessel* passengers ever to be unsurprised by Geode.

"On my very first mission with Master Mirro, on Gatalenta, we met a Vintian sculptor called Shale," Amadeo said. Then, realizing he'd made Geode uneasy by even hinting at chisel and hammer, he hastily added, "No stone carving! She only worked in metals. Made amazing stuff."

Next came two Wookiees—Burryaga, whom Affie knew slightly, and a solemn, even taller Jedi Knight called Kelnacca, who had to duck almost comically low to get through some of the passageways. *Mental note,* Affie thought, *maybe put in some seats that can expand for passengers of larger species.* The Wookiees would fit, barely, but it would've been nice to accommodate them in more comfort.

Avon Starros showed up carrying a full array of scientific gizmos, none of which Affie was familiar with, all of which Avon seemed convinced they would need. "This one is calibrated for superfast analysis of most cellular samples," Avon said, "and this one checks for rates of mineral decay. The tubes—careful with those!—they contain various chemicals that I think we can use to create a spray that might detect pre-blight particles."

"Really?" Reath Silas appeared at Avon's shoulder. "If you can predict the blight's path before it appears—Avon, that would be an incredible breakthrough."

These words made Avon's cheeks flush pink. Affie could see that the younger woman had a crush on Reath, who luckily seemed to understand how to be warm and encouraging without ever becoming *too* encouraging. "Okay," Affie said, "we'll make room for the lab supplies, but I warn you, if we have to leave behind Leox's spice supply, he's gonna be grumpy."

From within the *Vessel* they could hear Leox call, "It's *strictly medicinal!*"

Next a Coruscant security vehicle landed on the far side of

their docking bay, red lights flashing but absent any siren. *Oh, crap,* Affie thought, *maybe Leox's stash isn't considered medicinal here.* This was a problem they'd run into before.

But the authorities hadn't come to arrest her pilot; they were doing something much worse, which involved walking out a cuffed prisoner who turned out to be none other than Nan.

"Why is she here?" Affie demanded. "Why isn't she staying in jail where she belongs?"

"You'd like that," Nan said. "Me trapped, while you fly around the galaxy at your will."

Affie exaggerated her shrug as she replied, "Yeah, basically! Criminal in jail, noncriminal doing her job—I'm not seeing the problem with this picture."

This won no verbal response. Nan wore a shawl that probably cost as much as Affie cleared in the average month, plus a smirk that begged to be slapped off her face. Yet Reath came to Affie, not nearly as apologetic as he ought to have been, saying, "Nan is part of the mission. She claims to have defected from the Nihil, and to have knowledge of the blight and its recent . . . evolution. If she's on the level, her help may prove invaluable to us."

"She's not on the level," Affie said. "Nan's never been on the level with us. Not once. Why do you think she'd be any different now?"

Reath sighed. "Believe me, Affie, I'm not taking anything Nan says for granted. You'll notice she's wearing cuffs, and she'll be curbed by a sentry bracelet throughout the mission. That should keep us safe."

"What would keep us even safer is *leaving her here.*" Affie crossed her arms. "I could decline this job, you know. Or simply refuse her passage."

"I hope you won't," Reath answered, stepping slightly closer to her and speaking in a lower voice. "I know the risks, but they're risks worth taking. You understand how dire the situation is. Nan's told us that there's a top Nihil operative likely headed to Kashyyyk, a scientist under Ro's command, and if that's true, we obviously need to track this person down immediately. If there's any chance that Nan is being honest with us, we have to take it. Even if she's being dishonest, we might learn a lot from the lies she attempts to tell."

"What if she's already told all her lies and she's leading us straight into a trap?"

"On Kashyyyk? I doubt it."

Affie had to grant him that. The Nihil loved bullying and con-quering, but they had never once made landfall on the Wookiee home planet. They might be a horde of pirates, but apparently they preferred to keep all their limbs attached to their bodies. That wasn't entirely enough to reassure Affie, though, given her history with Nan. "We ran into each other on Starlight Beacon, you know. Not long before it fell. We fought. She'd have killed me if she could."

Reath's expression became more serious. "If she singles you out in any way—if I see the slightest hint that Nan's gunning for you—we'll figure out a way to confine her on the ship. An energy-field cell, if that's what it takes."

"Nah, we can just toss her in a cargo hold and lock the door," Affie replied. "Actually, that sounds like fun."

It took Reath a couple of moments to answer. "I don't think the Jedi Code would allow me to agree with that, but I'm not *disagreeing*."

Affie laughed. She was aware, of course, that she had just been talked into doing something that she would've sworn, ten minutes earlier, she would never even contemplate. Reath had persuaded her, calmly, intelligently, and fairly—demonstrating his authority over this mission rather than simply declaring it. He'd come a long way from the uncertain young apprentice she'd first met three years ago. This conflict had changed them all.

Just as Reath took Nan's elbow to usher her inside, a local Jedi transport zoomed up along the side of the platform. Reath stopped walking. Affie assumed this was just another of the Jedi Knights or apprentices assigned to the mission, another person to meet, greet, and get on board.

Then, from the transport stepped one of the most unnerving individuals Affie had ever seen. He was human, and once, perhaps, he might even have been handsome; some ghost of that still clung to him. But now he was a ruin. She could make no estimate of his age—his skin was wrinkled, but that might have been from desiccation more than age, and his hair contained both brown and silver. His eyes were missing, which on its own would not have greatly shocked Affie, though she would've wondered why he wore no enhancement visor or other device. Yet his face was scarred by deep ghastly gashes that suggested someone had actually gouged the man's eyes out—and somehow, without being told, she understood that he had done it himself.

"Azlin," Reath said. "Welcome. Everyone, this is Azlin Rell, a former Knight of the Order with experience that may prove useful to us on this mission."

Rell said nothing, only wrapped himself deeply within his robe. Nobody else spoke either. Avon didn't look thrilled about this addition to their party; Burryaga growled softly; Kelnacca's light-brown fur stood on end. Affie could take some satisfaction from the fact that Nan didn't look smug any longer; she seemed just as uneasy as everybody else.

Reath took Rell's arm, led him to Nan, and marched them both into the *Vessel*. Affie followed and found both Leox and Geode standing there, looking down the corridor where their less savory passengers had gone. Geode was uncharacteristically cold. Leox muttered, "I don't like the cut of that guy's jib. Plus what's that Nihil girl doing here?"

"She's pushing her luck," Affie said. "Let's hope luck's on our side."

"If so, it's about time," Leox replied.

Fortune still seemed to favor the Nihil. Affie hoped that the motley crew of the *Vessel* could change that.

If anyone could.

SIXTEEN

Marlem Glay, green-skinned Nikto and Cloud leader among the Nihil, had no ambitions of rising within the ranks—achieving the status of Tempest Runner or even Storm leader—or meeting the great and glorious Marchion Ro. She'd joined the Nihil for one reason only, as she always put it: getting rich and blowing stuff up. The underling who'd pointed out that this was actually two reasons got a blaster bolt to the face. No discipline problems since, Glay liked to say. Some people overthought this stuff. She, on the other hand, just pumped up her music as the Nihil ships sliced through the outer atmospheric level of the planet Baori Minor.

"All right, everybody!" Glay shouted into the comm, her leather-gloved hands tilting her ship down for an epic dive. "Only things worth having on this rock are in the Republic warehouses. We hit 'em, we quit 'em, we party. Who's with me?"

Cheers echoed through the comm as Glay cackled and the Cloud ships dove. The sky paled, and the percussion vibrated in her chair and controls. Today was gonna be a *great* day.

Baori Minor had been a modestly prosperous manufacturing world until a few centuries ago, when the combination of an uncharted asteroid and a faulty satellite detection net led to a devastating impact. Most of the population had been killed and the ecology severely damaged. The Republic had relocated almost all the survivors of Baori Minor generations ago and left the planet to heal itself, or not. Only the smaller island continent on the opposite side of the planet from the asteroid strike remained active, used for massive storage warehouses containing lower-value Republic tech supplies, and inhabited by lots of hauler droids and no more than a handful of sentient workers.

Not exactly the juiciest target to hit, in happier times. These days, however—with the Stormwall slicing trade routes into shreds and creating supply problems across the galaxy—even this tech would fetch high prices. Combine that with comically low security, and what did you have? Painless profit.

Well. Painless for Glay. If she wound up hurting anybody else, that was just a bonus.

The ships of the Nihil Cloud dove at a sharp angle, each of them broadcasting fake distress signals, effectively masking themselves as an automated asteroid-belt patrol that had fallen victim to a faulty nav system and was about to crash. Glay bared her sharp teeth in a grin as the stony surface of Baori Minor came closer and closer—then she pulled up sharply, coming so near the surface that dust clouds swirled up around her and the rest of the Nihil ships. She skimmed over the ground, the targeting holo projected over her viewscreen illuminating the warehouses on the horizon.

Still no response from planetary security, or what passed for it here. Glay began assigning individual targets to various ships, saving the richest stash for herself, of course: a massive barn reportedly filled with prototypes for the latest starpath model. Starpaths were small enough that she could load up with thousands of the things, maybe tens of thousands. She cackled again, imagining the credits she'd get in exchange filling the holds instead, gleaming and heavy.

One of her ships sent a warning signal—not because of a planetary security response but because there wasn't any. Glay's scales rippled in irritation at first: Why put everyone on alert due to having no problems whatsoever? But within a few seconds, she became wary, too. Low-level security or not, they ought to have met with *some* resistance by now.

Instead, nothing.

Glay kept going, pulling up to her target and landing outside just as she'd planned. This was where she and her crew were meant to don their masks, throw their gas canisters, and charge in with blasters blazing. Yet nobody appeared to oppose them. The only moving thing in sight was a staircase droid, so devoid of intelligence it barely counted as a droid at all; indeed, it rolled up to her ship to provide assistance, as welcoming to an invader as it would've been to anyone else.

To her crews, she said, "Masks on. Weapons at the ready."

The hatch swung open, revealing the grayish stone-ash surface of Baori Minor, dotted here and there with heavy black boulders of igneous rock, remnants of the asteroid strike on the other side of the planet. A few dusty speeders and haulers sat parked in odd positions, almost as though they had been abandoned in the middle of a shift. They couldn't have been left that long ago, Glay realized; ashy as this place was, the machinery would've looked much worse after many months, or even a few weeks. The workers here had probably fled within the past several days.

Which, of course, raised the question of why they had fled, and whether Glay and her Cloud ships ought to flee, too.

Nikto were generally wary by nature. Had Glay not already imagined all those lovely credits shining in her cargo hold, she might have aborted the raid that moment. Instead, she began moving forward, gas canister in her hand, speaking into the comm in a low voice: "Take it slow, everybody. Looks like we have time to be careful." Careful was boring, but *careful* also often meant *alive*.

Glay moved around the corner of the warehouse, her masked breath loud to her own ears. Her boots crunched in the ash underfoot with every step. Seeking potential resistance, her reptilian eyes darted all about—cargo crates stacked here, someone's canteen lying on the ground there—but found no motion beyond that of the dust in the wind.

Finally, they cleared the corner, the warehouse door coming into sight . . . and surrounding it, reaching up the walls and into the distance, was the decay and desiccation of the blight.

"So we lit out of there fast as we could," Glay said later that day in a tavern on the planet Zeitooine, sitting across from a Koorivar who ran one of the Strikes within her Cloud. "Nobody understands how that stuff spreads, so every single scrap we could've taken had to be treated as a contaminant, plus we had to scour ourselves down like we were sanding wood. Made the whole raid for nothing. Nothing! I mean, it's out of the way, but it's still in the Occlusion Zone. If Ro targeted Baori Minor, why weren't we warned about it? And why is he targeting planets in the area he controls?"

"He's never been great at sharing information, has he?" the Koorivar griped. "Doesn't care if we get ours, as long as he gets his."

Glay was still fuming. "Fuel costs credits. Ro doesn't seem to remember that. My entire Cloud is poorer, all because we went on a wild muunyak chase. It could've been avoided if he'd just kept us in the loop."

The Koorivar snorted. "I bet he doesn't even know. I bet he doesn't even care where the blight's spread to now. He's happy to let it eat up the whole galaxy, as long as he gets his chance to kill a few Jedi."

"I don't care if he sends his monsters after the Jedi," Glay replied. "Everybody needs a hobby. But this blight hurts all of us it touches, Nihil and Republic alike, and it's spreading too far, too fast. If you ask me, Marchion Ro's lost sight of what matters."

Only a couple of years ago, both of these captains had been among the crowds of Nihil cheering Ro; like the others, they had believed in him wholly and completely. Back then, voicing discontent like this would've gotten a person fried or pushed out of the nearest airlock. These days, people complained vocally and often, with little fear of being opposed, much less reported.

This would've been good reason for Ro to reconsider his tactics . . . if he had known about it. He did not. His eyes remained on the Jedi, and he could imagine no fall but theirs.

※

The electric-blue gleam of hyperspace illuminated the interior of the *Vessel* as the ship hurried toward the stricken planet Kashyyyk. Affie Hollow had dimmed the inner lights at Reath's request; by the time they had taken off, it had been nearly nightfall on Coruscant, and he'd reasoned that a nap would help everyone avoid hyperspace lag. Privately, Affie suspected that really he had wanted to keep people quiet and separate as much as possible, because otherwise the tensions already simmering on the ship might boil over into awkwardness, hostility, or even worse. No way was anybody sleeping easy.

She made her way through the ship, supposedly checking instruments, really making sure she had an eye on where everyone was and how they seemed to be. The Wookiees, Burryaga and Kelnacca, had slung up hammocks, in which they lay, disconsolate; even though Affie spoke no Shyriiwook, the mournful tones of their growls and whines told her that their thoughts were all for their wounded planet. Beneath them, on the floor, Amadeo Azzazzo and Dez Rydan lay on their bedrolls, not sleeping but meditating—or at least trying to.

Cohmac, she realized, had set himself up in a seated meditation pose just outside of the chamber where Azlin Rell—the name of the *creepy, creepy guy*—was being held. Standing guard, Affie figured. She was glad somebody was guarding Rell, but it seemed like this mission was too important to have included multiple people who counted more as prisoners than team members.

No doubt Rell was the more dangerous of the two prisoners, but he wasn't the one who set Affie on edge.

She went to the second makeshift cell and poked her head in. Nan, wide awake and still cuffed, looked bored for the brief moment it took her to notice Affie at the door. "Of course," Nan said, "it's you. I figured you'd want to have your say now, while I'm on your ship and my hands are still tied."

Affie didn't like being accused of cowardice, but she knew better than to let Nan dictate the terms of any conflict between them, even a verbal one. "As the owner of the ship, I take onboard threats seriously."

"And I count as a threat? Even now?"

"You tried to kill me."

Nan smiled. "Don't take it personally. I try to kill a lot of people."

"I don't try to kill people often," Affie replied. "But when I do? It's *very* personal." It was past time for Nan to remember that Affie had given as good as she'd gotten in their battle aboard the dying Starlight Beacon.

"Noted," said Nan, still maddeningly untroubled. Affie might have been goaded into an argument, after all, had Reath not then appeared at the far end of the corridor, gesturing to her. She walked away, refusing to so much as glance backward at Nan.

When she reached Reath, he said—in a low voice, one that would not carry to either of their prisoners' hearing—"Everything all right?"

"You tell me," Affie said. "Who needs enemies when you've loaded up my ship with a bunch of people who hate each other?"

Reath looked as though he would like to argue this point, but instead he sighed. "Nobody hates the Wookiees. Or Dez."

"But that one"—Affie jerked a thumb back in Nan's general direction—"has done us all dirty and has the nerve to be proud of it. And *what* is *up* with that Azlin Rell guy?"

"He's a Jedi Knight, or a former Jedi. . . . I'm honestly not sure which category we should put him in. But he suffered from an early attack by a Leveler, and it warped his mind terribly. The fear that took him over then has turned him toward the dark side of the Force. You probably feel the effect of that darkness, so strong, so close to you. The fear you're experiencing—the combativeness—trust me, I understand. I have to work through it, too. Everyone on the ship may be affected, at least to some extent."

Affie had seen how devastated Stellan Gios had been by his encounter with a Leveler, or a Nameless, or whatever they were called. For a Jedi, apparently, this was about as painful as it got. But Stellan Gios had pulled himself together enough to steer the plummeting remnants of Starlight Beacon away from a city to crash relatively harmlessly in the water. Whatever had happened to Azlin Rell wasn't inevitable, then. "If he can warp the rest of us just by being near, why did you bring him along, again? Because all that sounds like a great reason to *not* bring him."

"Because I believe Azlin Rell still has a path to follow that might lead him beyond darkness." Reath sighed and leaned against the corridor wall. "Recently, I had my first encounters with the Nameless. The fear that I endured—the sheer horror of the Force draining away, of this separation from all life—Affie, it's the worst thing I've ever felt. The worst thing I can imagine anyone feeling. And for a Jedi, I'm not exceptionally strong in the Force. For those who are, like Azlin, the effect of the Nameless is even worse. So I understand how he got so messed up. But I pulled through it, so maybe he could, too. And he deserves the chance. I can't just say that because he was hurt by one of the Nameless, he ought to be thrown away."

She realized then that Reath was giving Azlin Rell the same compassion he'd had to give himself to recover from the horror he'd endured. Reath had a good heart.

But that good heart better not cost me my ship, Affie thought. *Or my life.*

SEVENTEEN

The great wroshyr trees of Kashyyyk reached far into their planet's sky, weaving a thick canopy of leaves that shaded the entire surface, save for the oceans. The landing pads were built in the trees, platforms of wood suspended far above the surface with the leaves thinned out above—though not entirely removed. So the *Vessel* settled down onto a landing platform amid rustling green, a handful of leaves spiraling up in the gusts that surrounded the ship's descent.

Burryaga had witnessed such landings before, many times; he even remembered the arrival of the Jedi ship that had identified him as strong in the Force during his childhood and carried him away to Coruscant. Yet the repetition could not diminish his wonder at the perfect harmony of nature and technology, and not even the crisis at hand could take away his joy at returning home.

Next to him, Kelnacca snuffled in equal happiness. They shared a glance of understanding. The other Jedi knew no home but Coruscant, no family but their fellows in the Order, and to be sure, this fostered both camaraderie and loyalty among them. Yet all Wookiee Jedi knew that those of most other species were the poorer for not feeling such a bond with a planet, an ecosystem, their own species. This attachment, in Burryaga's view—this vaster feeling that encompassed an entire world—*this* was the sort of attachment that showed how very small and selfish other attachments had to be. Such enlightenment could only be more difficult to accomplish among those many Jedi who seemed determined to pretend attachments should not, did not matter at all.

Burryaga strode along the platform, raising one arm and howling a greeting to the many Wookiees who had come to welcome him. When they howled in return, joy shivered along his skin, fluffed his fur. Whatever else might come to pass—at least he had, once more, come home.

Reath followed Burryaga from the *Vessel*, taking his first-ever look at the fabled forests of Kashyyyk. Next to him Kelnacca growled his pride in its beauty, and Reath nodded. "You're right—if more people could spend time on worlds like this one, I think it would be a happier galaxy."

Yet the cool, crisp scent of aromatic wood and the dappling of sunlight on rippling tree leaves only heightened Reath's anxiety for the fate of Kashyyyk. If they had any chance of saving this planet from the blight, they needed to seize it swiftly. He quickened his steps to catch up with Burryaga, who was being met by a small welcoming party.

"Greetings," he said as he approached. "I'm Reath Silas, the Jedi in charge of this mission. Whom do I have the honor of meeting?"

The elder matriarch, a black-and-white-speckled Wookiee, introduced herself as Pruzzalla, the leader of the local clans. Next to her was an adult female in her prime with pale golden fur, Lohgarra, who usually worked as a pilot offworld but was serving a term of duty to her home planet as Pruzzalla's principal aide. Beside them stood a very young male called Nevakka, perhaps the equivalent of a human toddler, who practically wriggled with excitement; his mottled gray fur was draped with flower chains and crowns he seemed to have made for the visitors. With an amused growl, Pruzzalla informed Reath that Nevakka had very much been looking forward to seeing him again.

"Again?" Then it hit Reath. "The transport, three years ago— the one that caught fire—you're the Wookiee baby!"

Nevakka chuckled with delight at having been recognized, and Pruzzalla said how happy she was that the boy had been reunited with his savior. He who saved one Wookiee, she told Reath, would forever have the gratitude of all Wookiees.

"Seeing him well and happy is thanks enough," Reath said. In truth his memory of the rescue focused primarily on the uncomfortable moment when panicked little Nevakka had bitten off Reath's Padawan braid—but that sting had been temporary, and the amusement would stay with him forever. Nevakka held up one of the flower crowns; without hesitation, Reath knelt and lowered his chin so the young Wookiee could settle the crown on his head.

It was Lohgarra who gently whined to say that, as enjoyable as these pleasantries were, a member of the Jedi meditation team wished to speak with Reath as soon as possible.

"Really?" Reath knew the team had traveled ahead, understanding the importance of confining the blight as soon as possible. Because of this, he had expected all those Jedi already to be in deep meditation, essentially out of contact. If one among that team had delayed entering the meditative state, they could only have done so because the information to be shared was critical. Dismay quivered within his gut, but he shoved the ominous feeling aside. "Okay. Let's get down to the blight area—that's where the team is, right?"

Pruzzalla growled that this was correct. The meditation team had surrounded the small patch of blight on the forest floor.

Traveling down to ground level was a significant task even for the Wookiees. Out of respect for the nerves of the smaller, more breakable persons who had come to their world, Pruzzalla had decreed that they should not ride the great mylaya steeds down but would climb—simpler and easier all around, surely. For humans, even those strong in the Force, the trip was . . . well, neither simple nor easy but certainly an adventure. Reath found that he rather liked swinging on a vine, but clambering down the trunk of a wroshyr tree, even one of those with steps and footholds cut out for smaller species, children, and elders, required considerable concentration. It definitely helped to not look down.

Above, Reath could hear the other Jedi following (save for Azlin, who remained in custody alongside Nan under the supervision of the *Vessel* crew). When Amadeo gasped, Reath paused and said, "You looked down, didn't you?"

Amadeo didn't deny it. "I never thought buildings on Coruscant would seem small," he said, his voice strained. "But I'd rather dangle off the side of Five Hundred Republica than climb one of these things. And I can levitate! I mean, I can a little."

"Let the fear flow through you and past you," Cohmac said gently. "All non-arboreal species are born with a fear of heights; it is as natural as the beating of your heart. But you are more than the instincts you were born with. Your conscious mind will take control and restore calm, but you can only begin by accepting your fear, not fighting it."

Burryaga chimed in, adding that even he found this difficult going. On most of Kashyyyk, the underbrush of the forest was a distant sort of netherworld, a place of deep legend and unsettling darkness. This village had sacred forestry responsibilities, tending wroshyr saplings and other flora, so they took the considerable efforts required to create a path downward, thin out the underbrush below, and overcome their instinctive dread of traveling so far beneath the treetops.

"So that's why"—Dez Rydan panted, someplace farther back—"why we have this easy path set out for us?"

Either Wookiees were immune to sarcasm or Burryaga had simply decided to ignore it, because his only response to Dez was a sympathetic purr.

The jokes and banter buoyed the group's spirits somewhat, but Reath knew they all felt the same disquiet he did. To him it seemed to go beyond the natural dread of approaching the blight, though he tried to dismiss the idea.

By the time the group reached the forest floor, the sunlight had been so dimmed by layer upon layer of leaves that it seemed nearly twilight. Reath's boot stepped down onto ground so thickly carpeted with fallen leaves and needles that it felt springy underfoot. The Wookiees bounded down from higher overhead, landing with an agile grace that was striking for creatures of such size. Reath felt a brief pang of sympathy for Burryaga, who spent so much of his life in habitats so little like the one he had been born into.

Cohmac came next, then a highly relieved Amadeo, and finally Dez Rydan—who, to Reath's surprise, carried Avon Starros on his back. *No wonder he was panting!* Reath thought. Avon's arms were wrapped tightly over one of Dez's shoulders and around his waist, and her hands gripped each other at his breastbone so desperately that they had turned white. When she let go and dropped to the ground, she breathed a sigh of profound relief.

"I offered her a harness," Dez said to Reath, gently amused.

Avon, however, was already adjusting her hip pack of equipment. "We'd have had to go back to the *Vessel* to get a harness, and we don't have any time to waste. Besides, if I'd fallen, you could've caught me with the Force, right?" When nobody answered her, her eyes widened. "Right?"

"In theory," Reath said. "Come on, let's go."

By this point the Wookiees had moved several strides ahead, and with their long legs, it took the humans some catching up. Reath noted that all the Jedi and Avon wore flower crowns or necklaces resembling the one still on his head; Nevakka had been thorough.

As they entered a small clearing, they saw a Jedi standing there: Belka Poiryn, an elderly Pau'an meditation master, renowned through the entire Order for her deep connection to the Force. Legend had it that she had spent so much time in deep meditation that she had actually aged more slowly than others of her species. Reath had never put much stock in this particular rumor, but there was no denying that Master Belka had lived far longer than most Pau'ans.

She stood motionless as Reath and his team approached. Though he and Master Belka had never met, her gaze found him instantly. Nobody had needed to tell her that he was the mission leader; she just *knew*. "Master Belka," he said, going to her with a short, respectful bow. "I am Reath Silas. How does your team fare?"

"They are in place, doing what they can," Master Belka replied. Her gravelly voice alone betrayed her years. "Soon I must rejoin them. But you must know—all of you—that the blight is not the only source of darkness on Kashyyyk."

Burryaga whined in dismay. Reath wondered what she

could mean. Of course the dark side of the Force was present on Kashyyyk; this was true of anyplace with any life at all. But Master Belka would not have bothered mentioning this. "What do you mean?"

"It sleeps," Master Belka said. "No more can I tell you. The darkness sleeps here, because it must—" Her pale face crumpled into a scowl of effort and confusion. "My words are useless, worse than useless, and yet they are the only truth I have to offer. I can but warn you, Reath Silas: Darkness haunts this land, barely slumbering, and if it should awaken . . . nothing we can do will hold it back."

Reath and Cohmac shared a glance of dismay. The warnings of the Force were gifts, one and all, but that did not reduce the frustration when such warnings were so vague. Reath said only, "Thank you for your counsel, Master Belka."

She nodded. "I must return to our task. Follow me, if you wish."

The entire group walked behind her toward a wider clearing; through the trees, they began to catch glimpses of the meditation team, all of whom sat on the forest floor, eyes closed. Amadeo was the first to see what they sought. "Oh, no," he whispered, his steps slowing in dread. "No, no—"

A shaft of light from above fell on an area ahead where the soft greens and browns of the forest had palled to a horrible gray. The Wookiees all came to a halt just short of the spot, and Kelnacca howled low and mournful. Reath caught up with them to see that the center of the clearing was already completely ashen with the blight. One of the streaks of gray reached out from the mass toward a nearby wroshyr tree.

The thought of these great trees, this forest, falling to the blight was more than Reath could bear. "Right," he said with determination. "Master Belka, thank you and your team for your efforts in keeping this at bay." Master Belka merely nodded. Already she was taking her place on the forest floor, completing their circle around the ugly gray splotch of the blight. Reath continued, "Avon, are you ready to get to work?" When she nodded, he gestured to his fellow Jedi. "Okay. Let's settle in at the Wookiee village and get started. We have a lot of searching—and a lot of researching—to do."

Avon Starros remained wobbly from the sheer adrenaline of their descent through the trees; her knees shook beneath her as she began walking around the blighted area, leaving as wide a perimeter as possible without stepping too close to the silent meditating Jedi surrounding the clearing. These Jedi had a job to do here— meditating at a depth that would allow them to hold the blight at bay—that would probably hold them in place for days or weeks to come. Her task would require more legwork, both figurative and literal.

The theory, she reminded herself as she made her way through the thick rustling carpet of leaves, *is that the blight is no natural ailment, that it is linked to the Nameless and their negation of the Force. If so, then it is highly unlikely that any scientific "cure" can affect it. Maybe by studying this patch of the blight—one that's literally only a couple of days old—I can confirm or disprove that theory.*

However, safely obtaining a blight sample was tricky. Avon had done her research and come prepared with specially engineered tools and tubes that were somewhat resistant to the effects of the blight. Not immune—these, too, would corrode as the blight inevitably overtook them—but she'd have several hours or even a couple of days to study before the risk of contamination would require her to bring all materials back to this same spot to decay in place.

She knelt on the ground and withdrew from her pack a miniature sampler droid. The tiny globe hovered above the ground, opening its retrieval chamber wide; it looked like a little creature that was almost nothing but mouth. Avon made a flicking motion with her hand, and the sampler droid shot forward to hang above the blight. Another poke downward with her fingers, and it descended into the fuzzy gray mess that had once been ferns or leaves and took a huge *chomp*. The second it had done so, Avon made the gesture that would seal the droid, then beckoned it back. It flew obediently into the larger sample vessel she'd taken from her pack; double seals meant double safety.

If anyone or anything can even be safe, she thought bleakly as she rose to go, before her thoughts were interrupted by a chirp from another of her instruments. Just the toolminder, warning her that she'd left a device behind—but she hadn't. She couldn't have. She hadn't taken anything else from her pack.

Stooping low, she ran her hands through the leaves, shivering at the proximity to the blight but wondering what on earth she might have dropped. Her fingers hit metal, and she brushed aside leaves to reveal a small sentry device. Very basic. Hardly the size of a human's big toe. Not Republic make, at least not any kind Avon knew.

She whispered, "Dr. Mkampa."

Avon did not dare pick it up or even put her face too near it; she didn't want Mkampa to know that one of her instruments had been found. When the signal was broadcast across the galaxy, Mkampa would take action immediately, whether that meant attacking the Jedi, accelerating the blight, or choosing some other equally murderous option.

Then Avon realized no signal was going to be broadcast far. This could only be an observer-scope—a local monitoring device meant to gather information about an experiment without disrupting it. Such scopes were weak by design, their signals reaching out no more than five klicks in any given direction.

Which meant Mkampa was indeed on Kashyyyk, just as they had suspected . . . and soon she would realize the Jedi had come.

If she hadn't already.

◈

In hyperspace, the *Innovator* shot through the waves of electric blue, borne on toward its target: Kashyyyk. The Drengir lay fallow in the ship's hold, irritable under the pale innutritious artificial light of the ship, the useless blue glow of hyperspace itself. How they loathed the need to go from place to place; it was enough to make one envy more rooted brethren, who had the luxury of remaining forever at home, sipping from sunlight, with no cares at all.

But those who stayed put were those who might be mowed down. It was better to be the reaper than the crop.

The trip took so very long, and they all felt so very wilted. What gave them the strength to continue, however, was the pull they all felt—strong as sunlight, all-giving, all-consuming—the inexorable force that pulled them toward Kashyyyk, that gnawed at them, that reminded them how badly they needed to eat and promised that the best meal of their lives awaited at the end of this journey.

It was all right to be so hungry, to have become so very ravenous for meat. The Drengir were ready to hunt for it.

EIGHTEEN

Apparently Wookiees were known throughout the Republic—a spiritual species from a beautiful planet, impressive in their strength and size, fearsome in battle but deeply loving toward those they cared for. Little kids in the Republic had Wookiee toys. Children's holos might be set on Kashyyyk, complete with songs about the tall, tall trees.

So Nan gathered. She, however, had grown up far beyond Republic space, scrounging for every meal and treated to exactly zero children's holos. Thus she had no sentimental notions about Wookiees. Kashyyyk smelled nice, like aromatic wood and those leaves that looked like needles, but all she was getting the chance to see of the planet was one particular hut that had been turned into her personal cell. The highly unnerving Azlin Rell was being held in the next hut over, and he hadn't stopped singing his eerie lullaby once in the past hour. Each door was guarded by a full-grown Wookiee, and Nan was both unarmed and the height of one of their species' small children. Briefly she had contemplated trying to make an escape through one of the windows, which were covered with nothing but woven blinds—but a glance out one of them had revealed the staggering drop to the ground. Plus the sentry bracelet she wore would begin to shriek—and to shock—as soon as she put any meaningful distance between herself and the Jedi. So she was stuck.

Not that she would or could have gone far. Nan knew what she needed to accomplish here with the Jedi, and she intended to do it. But it would've been nice to vanish for a bit, give them a good scare, then saunter back to Reath Silas not as a prisoner but as a free person and an equal. Instead, she got to sit here and hope Wookiees cooked their food.

Of course, she was also preparing in her own way: noting the sentries, learning the schedule of the village and the moments when the most people would be distracted, observing exactly what equipment and weaponry the Jedi seemed to have on hand. All this knowledge could be useful.

Then rising yowls and growls nearby suggested some sort of ruckus. Nan went to the door and pressed her ear against it, the better to hear; immediately she was rewarded with the sound of Avon Starros's voice. "—definitely, absolutely, short-range only—"

"But not anything we can definitely trace to the Nihil." That was Reath. "Could it just be a form of Republic manufacture you're not familiar with?"

"In theory? Sure. But who else's would it be? Your meditation team doesn't use devices like this, do they? They wouldn't need a device to monitor the blight when they're sitting only a couple of meters away. Dr. Mkampa has to be on Kashyyyk monitoring this personally. Somebody is monitoring it personally, anyway, and she's the likeliest candidate." Avon had come close enough by this point for Nan to hear her sigh. "I didn't pick it up or disturb it, but those devices are sensitive. We have to assume that Mkampa knows we're here."

"Of course." She recognized the new voice as that of Cohmac Vitus. "And that she has heard every word."

Nan had suspected all of this—had gambled on it—but the confirmation gave her strength. Her memory filled with the last moment she had spoken to Marchion Ro, the hand he had placed on her shoulder as a rare sign of trust, even liking. Proof that Ro—who believed in so few—believed in Nan.

She made up her mind and stood up straight. "Hey! Don't forget that if you want to find Mkampa, I'm your best bet."

◆

Reath sat near one of the campfire cauldrons on the Wookiee platform the team would be calling home for the duration of their stay. Apparently this open-sided canopy with a chimney spout at the top was to be his base of operations. A few of the Wookiees, including the aide Lohgarra, had declared themselves part of the team and had joined the assembly of Jedi; the crew of the *Vessel* had left their ship to also be with the group, at least for now. In other words, he had quite an audience for this conference with Nan.

"You know Dr. Mkampa's here," she said. "And she knows you're here. The difference is that she almost certainly knows where you are. If I were you, I'd want to know where she is, too, and fast."

"Of course," Reath said. "Are you now telling me that you know the location of her lab? Because that's information a trustworthy source would've shared with us from the beginning."

Yet again, Nan remained completely unfazed. Could nothing shake her? "I don't know the location of Mkampa's lab. I do know what model of portable shelter she'd probably repurpose as her lab, though, and the likely energy signatures of the support equipment she'd bring along. With that information, finding her should be a whole lot easier, don't you think?"

Affie Hollow crossed her arms in front of her chest and sniffed; over her shoulder, Geode looked equally skeptical. Affie said, "It's a forest planet. Shouldn't we just be able to look for *any* energy signatures and track her down on our own?"

"It's not that easy," said Cohmac. "Although the Wookiees use far less technology in their daily lives than most sentients, there are various droids, labs, even some factories scattered throughout the forests. Not many Wookiees own starships, but some do, and those ships may be moored on platforms across the planet."

Lohgarra murmured her agreement, pointing out that she was saving up to buy a ship herself. Energy signatures might not be as common on Kashyyyk as they were on most other worlds, but that did not mean there weren't enough to complicate a search.

Reath had understood this already; he knew that Nan's help—if it was on the level—was something they could truly use. So he asked the one question that really mattered: "Okay, Nan, if you're offering to help us, then what do you expect in return?"

"Nothing," Nan said. "Nothing at all. I want Mkampa stopped, too, you know."

"We do *not* know that," said Affie, scowling. Leox Gyasi put a calming hand on her arm, but the tension remained.

"I'm done with the Nihil," Nan insisted. "You have Avon Starros, daughter of *Ghirra* Starros, on your team, don't you? And some dark sider Jedi? You obviously believe people can change their allegiances, Reath. So why don't you believe I have?"

"Trust has to be earned," said Reath, "but I'm going to give you your chance to earn it. Come sit with me and let's work out exactly what we're scanning for." Nan's face remained impassive, but he could feel the impatience in her, barely beneath the surface; the emotion was so strong that a lesser person would have been screaming. What did it mean, that she wanted this so badly and yet could hide it so well?

Cohmac gave Reath a look that clearly meant, *Are you sure?* Reath *wasn't* sure—how could he be?—but he also knew that they'd have to put Nan to the test sooner or later. It might as well be now.

※

Elsewhere on Kashyyyk, but not terribly far away, a thick web of vines had been encouraged to grow in a dense waterfall of leaves that entirely encircled one small natural glade. Given a bit of specially engineered fertilizer and daily baths of UV rays, the vines could grow up to three meters in a single day. In other words, it had taken almost no skill whatsoever to conceal the *Firebringer* there.

"Feels a bit like cheating," Dr. Mkampa had said to one of her droids, which did not reply, as it was a nonspeaking model like all the rest of her droids. She had no use for conversation.

The *Firebringer* would house her during her search, its scanners and tools enabling her to scour Kashyyyk for what she sought. It lay somewhere within a ten-klick radius—a tantalizingly precise location within a vast galaxy, yet an area large enough to be searched for weeks on end with no success. The blight meant her time was limited, but Mkampa had to prepare to use every second of it. So she had found this fine hiding place and had scaled down onboard operations to prioritize her search. The Jedi would not find her with basic scans. Although bright light was available at every workstation, she used no overhead illumination so that her hiding place would not be revealed by any telltale glow. Wookiees had sharp night vision, after all.

That evening, over a steaming pot of tea, she reviewed the recordings from her various monitors and sentries, her red cybernetic eye briefly gleaming Loth-cat gold as she shifted the degree of her focus. The Jedi sat near the blight and prayed, or chanted, or whatever it was they did; Mkampa had to admit their methods had some efficacy against the blight, at least in the short term, but nothing and no one could stop it for long.

She had no good view into the nearby Jedi encampment, as it was part of the local Wookiee village—a site she had previously determined to be of no use to her. On the whole, Mkampa wasn't certain she needed to worry about it even now. That was merely where the Jedi would sleep and plan and flail. She made a few notes as to the various Jedi she saw, hoping to ID some of them through public records; if the Jedi were fool enough to be so transparent about their identities, why should she not benefit from it? Probably it did not matter which Jedi had come, but better to have more knowledge than less.

One familiar figure proved to be neither prisoner nor Jedi. Mkampa laughed out loud when she recognized that little Starros girl, play-pretending scientist, struggling to keep up with the more powerful figures surrounding her. "At least she has an excuse for being ridiculous," Mkampa said, to no one. She tapped the lab counter with her long fingernails. "Her mother can't say the same."

The real question was—how could Avon Starros's presence on Kashyyyk potentially be of use?

It might be fun to find out.

�⁂

At that very moment, not very far away, the *Innovator* set down on the surface of Kashyyyk.

The Drengir, still suspicious of technology and hardly comprehending it, understood enough to recognize that Kashyyyk was very little industrialized, still in its natural, clearly superior state. Their past hunts had sometimes been cut short or even aborted when satellite networks had informed the meat beings of the Drengir's arrival. That would not be a problem here!

They were further encouraged by the scene that greeted them as the ship's hatch opened to reveal a lush verdant landscape. The *Innovator* had landed within one of the small meadows between Kashyyyk's boundless forests, treating them to a fine patch of natural sunshine—very desirable, after such a long journey—and air thick with the pollen of a thousand species of brethren. Nor could the Drengir fail to be impressed by the scale of the trees no more than a klick away. These plants eclipsed the scale of virtually any animal being they had encountered; they testified to the superiority of the botanical.

In the end, however, those who were rooted had limitations. The Drengir did not. They went where they wished, to eat whatever they could claim. And they had wished to come here powerfully, so incredibly powerfully, as though they were swayed by the heat of their native sun.

The Great Progenitor, despite her own hunger, wondered why they should all wish to come to this particular planet so eagerly. Kashyyyk was not their homeworld; rich in plant life though it was, it was hardly unique in this way, and to judge by the faint scents they detected via their receptor cells, the meat beings native to this planet tended to be large and fierce, far from the easiest hunting available.

But such analysis lay outside the general thought patterns of the Drengir. None of them doubted their ability to slaughter all they came into contact with, and challenging hunting was enjoyable hunting. Beyond all else . . . the call they felt was too strong to resist. No matter where it drew them, the Drengir must answer. They had landed. Next they would hunt.

As they emerged into this new sunlight, unfurling their leaves to soak it in, however, the Great Progenitor understood something she had not before: They were not only drawn to Kashyyyk by the need to eat. This soil, this sunshine . . .

This was where they must sprout and spread their seeds.

This was where darkness should reign.

NINETEEN

Shrii Ka Rai, *Ka Rai…*

Then the singing was silenced by the sound of Azlin's own childish voice, sharper in memory than it had been in a long while.

"Master Elio—look! Look at the fancrest birds! They're every color at once!"

"That is called iridescence, Azlin."

All the younglings grouped together in wonder, looking out on the vast treetops of Kashyyyk stretching in every direction. All Azlin's friends, pointing at this flower, at that vine. Azlin holding a soft green leaf bigger than his head, tracing the delicate veins with the tip of his finger, feeling the brush of its fuzz.

The young Wookiee Pruzzalla affectionately patting his head. Arkoff in his prime, not yet Azlin's master, climbing the trunk of an impossibly tall tree with unbelievable speed, tiny wood shavings spraying out from his claws with every handhold he grasped. The sense that the galaxy was so much bigger than the Temple, than Coruscant, than any one mind could contain—

※※

Azlin awoke. Though he knew he had been dreaming, that particular dream was born of memory. He *had* been to Kashyyyk before, when he was just a youngling; he and all his crèche mates had been taken on a journey to see some of the other planets of the Republic. Yoda had said they needed to understand the vastness and diversity of the galaxy that they would travel within and serve.

Did the Jedi still do that? Take their younglings on such journeys of discovery? He felt a spark of genuine curiosity, untainted by fear—an emotion that had been lost to him, even in memory.

Arkoff had told Azlin of one of his crèche journeys once, a trip to the salt planet Crait. He said there were beautiful crystal-white foxes there, that he had begged to bring one back to Coruscant as a pet but the crèche-keeper nurse Yenlit Elio had told all the children that the fox would be happier in his own home, with his own friends. Azlin had always meant to get around to seeing one of those foxes someday.

"So much for that," he said aloud to no one.

He could tell from the general tenor of the sounds surrounding his hut that all had returned to this platform village for the evening, Jedi and Wookiee alike. The scent of cooking filled his nostrils, and the freshly recovered memory of his first trip to Kashyyyk told him that this was a kind of stew—spicy and rich—and one humans enjoyed every bit as much as Wookiees. (Though the Wookiees hadn't considered it spicy at all, had they?) Azlin's belly growled, a sound that startled him; he had become unaccustomed to paying any attention to the needs of his body, thinking of it only as a flesh prison that so far had not permitted him to die.

As long as he *was* hungry, he decided, he might as well eat. Azlin called out, "When is dinner?"

He expected the reply to be a terse report of the minutes that would elapse before a bowl was brought into the hut. Instead, after a moment, he heard footsteps, followed by Reath Silas's voice: "We'll be eating any second now. Would you like to join us?"

To Azlin, Reath's politeness sounded false, but—but perhaps it wasn't. Time to test him. "Yes, I would."

A rustle of robes and the nudge of Reath's elbow signaled that Azlin was being offered an arm. He took it and allowed himself to be led out into the twilight.

Memory joined with Azlin's strength in the Force and his other sensory impressions to create an image so strong in his mind that he might as well have been looking upon it with his long-dead eyes: the campfires blazing in their cauldrons, the thatched roofs of the huts clustered all around like ridgeshell nuts on the branches of the wroshyr trees, Wookiees loping across the long rope bridges that connected cluster to cluster. He could imagine a few of the human Jedi using the bridges, as well, though perhaps with less enthusiasm. As a child, how wary he had been to walk out on them! Arkoff had stooped low to hold Azlin's tiny hand.

Suddenly, his face felt strange. Azlin lifted one hand to his mouth and realized that he was smiling. Not the fevered expression that accompanied his laughing fits, not the smirk with which he dismissed everything and everyone he held in contempt. Just . . . a smile. The oddity of it disquieted him, and he remained silent while being given his stew and the entire time he ate. He felt the others near him, uneasy in his presence; that sensation, at least, was familiar.

As the meal began to draw to a close, Reath summarized all that had happened that day: the warning of the meditation team (fools who talked darkness without even understanding it), the discovery of instruments that suggested a Nihil scientist called Mkampa was potentially on Kashyyyk, and the ongoing study of the blight. He finally said, "And, as many of you know, Nan here has recently left the Nihil—"

A cough from the corner (female? Maybe the young woman who owned the ship, Affie Hollow?) wordlessly but clearly expressed skepticism; Azlin suspected she wasn't alone in that feeling, but no one spoke.

Reath continued as though he had not heard. "—and she has some thoughts about how we might find Dr. Mkampa. We'll get to work on those first thing in the morning. For now, everyone should just wind down, relax, and get some rest."

Azlin's senses were sharp enough to detect the exact sounds of people rising, adjusting, moving in their separate directions. What surprised him was that nobody immediately moved to imprison him within his hut. He supposed they trusted the strength of the Wookiees to contain him, which he had to admit was not an unreasonable supposition. Slowly he rose to his feet, curious about the limits of his freedom.

First he found one of the wood-and-rope railings that edged every platform and walkway and resolved to hold on to it. The wood had been smoothed by generations of Wookiees; he could trust in its strength and integrity. Secured, he began to walk through the village, his ears pricking at every snatch of conversation that was in Basic rather than Shyriiwook.

There—that was Affie Hollow again. "I just wish we had a proper hangar—that's all."

"The Wookiees trust their ships to the trees," drawled the pilot, Leox Gyasi. "They put their faith in branch and limb, in the wind and in the sky. Inspiring, if you ask me."

She answered, "I'd feel more inspired if my ship had walls around it."

"I don't blame you," said Azlin. Through the Force he could feel the sharp surprise and unease his interruption spiked within them both. "Particularly knowing the Nihil could be here. There's nothing to stop them from felling the trees from strike ships, and that would take your craft with it, wouldn't it?"

"There's no sign of the Nihil here," said Leox—defiantly but with a hint of uncertainty. The darkness within Azlin sipped that doubt like wine as he walked on.

It seemed the railing was leading him in a broad circle, because just as he began to arc back toward the campfire they'd eaten beside, he heard the girl Avon Starros, apparently talking to one of the Wookiees: "—taken all the readings I can for now.

It will take a few hours for any other potentially useful changes to take place."

Azlin relished the shock he caused when he spoke to her: "What do you think you'll learn about the blight that the Republic scientists haven't?"

"Since this appears to be one of the newest patches of the blight yet found—well, who knows?" How young Avon sounded, and yet not young enough to deceive herself that she could be uniquely situated to solve this problem. "Even if I don't find a breakthrough myself, the data I send back to other scientists might help them do so."

He tried to smile on purpose. It was harder to do when he was thinking about it. "It's good that you understand the odds against you. Best to be realistic about the possibility of making a difference—saves you from heartbreak later. Very sensible." Azlin walked away then, relishing the silence between Avon and her companion that stretched out long in his wake.

Then, for the first time, someone spoke to him first: "You're playing mind games."

"Nan, of the Nihil," Azlin said. "From what I've gleaned so far, you're rather an expert at mind games yourself."

She ignored this. "I don't know why you want to interfere with this mission, Rell, but I'm giving you fair warning—don't. Stop deliberately unsettling the others. Stop acting like some kind of monster, or phantom. You're just a person some bad things happened to, and the galaxy is full of bad things that have happened to a whole lot of people. You think you're unique? You think your own personal pain gives you the right to inflict pain on others in perpetuity?"

"Quite an unexpected comment from a member of the Nihil," he replied. "The motives you attribute to me would seem to be the Nihil creed"

"I left the Nihil," Nan snapped.

"So you say. But no one believes you."

She took a step closer, her weight making the planks beneath them creak ever so slightly. "Thought experiment—let's say I am still one of the Nihil. That I have a whole Tempest at my beck and call, ready to descend and destroy every single person I choose. If that's true, wouldn't it make more sense for you to avoid antagonizing me?"

"By speaking to the rest of the party?" Azlin said. "Interesting. In this thought experiment of yours, you see, there's no reason why you should care what I say to any of these people, or even whether I speak to them at all."

Nan's voice sharpened on her reply: "Don't analyze me."

"I don't have to," he said. The implication, of course, was that he completely understood Nan, needed no further clues or thought as to her nature. In actuality, he had barely been able to think of her at all. Azlin's mind was too caught up in the strange experience of being back on Kashyyyk again—of reliving memories that had nothing to do with the Nameless—

But no sooner had he thought of them than fear clamped its cold weight around him. Darkness was present on Kashyyyk, and it called to Azlin, reminding him that light was only an illusion; only the dark told the truth. The ugliness of mortal existence, the inevitability of pain and death, the way affection and friendship were nothing but breeding grounds for grief and betrayal—yes, he knew the truth that the Jedi feared to know. That truth would never change. And the darkness came for everyone.

Azlin's breaths came fast and shallow as he stumbled away from the gathering, singing under his breath, *"Shrii Ka Rai, Ka Rai...."*

Nan, for her part, could only think, *Why did Reath ever bring that man along?* On that point at least, she and Affie Hollow, Leox Gyasi, Geode, and Avon Starros were all in complete agreement.

He had interrupted Nan just as she'd been nearing one of Avon's scanning devices left on a nearby platform, one that Nan could possibly have tinkered with to deactivate her sentry bracelet. Already Avon had scooped it up again, eagerly taking readings as though the answer to the blight lay here in this very village.

Still, early carelessness was a good sign. The more comfortable this team became in their new surroundings, the more lax their security would become. Nan could be patient.

※

Not everyone on Kashyyyk shared equal patience.

Dr. Mkampa swore colorfully as her scans of the nearby mountain came up reporting nothing more than the expected mineral deposits. "The mountains are perfect hiding places!" she muttered to herself. "All but invisible to standard scanners. Almost no instruments other than mine could penetrate deeply enough to find anything. *Why isn't it there?*"

Apparently the Sith had thought differently. She did not

know enough of that ancient empire and sect to comprehend their thought patterns, much less replicate them. There was nothing for it but to keep looking.

※✦※

Early the next morning, Reath descended to the forest floor again, hoping to spend some time meditating along with the team of mystics at the blight site. Of course he aimed to help them in their task, but he also thought that, by achieving the same depth of trance, he might be better able to sense that specific "darkness" Master Belka had warned him of.

So Reath sat in the dawn-dappled glade, just slightly back from the ring of silently meditating Jedi, rested his knees against the loamy soil of Kashyyyk, and attempted to deepen his meditation. He had decided to use the breeze as his tool in this endeavor. When the tree limbs overhead rustled in the wind and the small rays of sunlight shifted with the leaves, he focused minutely on the faint patches of warmth scattering across his face. When the air caressed his cheeks and ruffled his robes, he filled his mind with that sensory input, allowing nothing as structured as actual thought.

When he'd been young, he'd told Master Jora that he didn't fully understand how emptying one's mind could be helpful. Wasn't thinking important? Didn't intelligence and learning matter? "Of course they do," she had told him. "But your education and your brain can't accomplish everything on their own. Meditation is about existing solely in the moment. About freeing your brain from the prison of thought, linking yourself to the pure Force. When that link is strong, then you will be without limit."

Given his love for the Archives, Reath had been slow to accept that entire realms of wisdom could lie in an experience impossible to capture within a Jedi holocron. Yet he had indeed come to understand it, and rarely had he been gladder of that understanding than he was on this mission. As he sat there, eyes shut, he was able to stand with the very trees of Kashyyyk; to feel the outline of the blight as keenly as the plants did, a sharp emptiness amid so much life; to meld his spirit with that of the life growing most closely to the blight, to strengthen it, to feel its purity standing fast against corruption—

A slithering sound tugged Reath's mind away for a moment. *Just a snake,* he told himself. Many serpents dwelled on Kashyyyk, and some of them were venomous, but the very harmony Reath sought with the life around him would no doubt camouflage him from the snake's exploration.

But then he heard it again, louder, and somehow no longer exactly like a snake. He'd heard it someplace before.

Reath's unconscious mind supplied the place he'd heard it: on the Amaxine station.

His eyes flew open as he breathed the words, "The Drengir."

TWENTY

Amadeo Azzazzo had only clambered half-way down from the treetops to the ground when he heard Reath Silas's distant shout: "We're under attack!"

Several steps behind, Avon Starros swore. "Do you think it's the Nihil?"

"No idea," Amadeo said. "But I'd better find out. Excuse me."

With that, he flung himself from the trunk of the wroshyr tree and fell.

Some few Jedi could levitate; Amadeo was one of them, though he wasn't terribly good at it. Still, he could use the Force to slow his descent enough to land safely—if bone-rattlingly hard—on the ground. Gasping, Amadeo shook off the impact, grabbed his lightsaber, and ran toward the sounds of battle, which became louder by the second.

Within moments he could see the fight. To Amadeo's shock, it was the Drengir attacking the Jedi, en masse. While half of the meditation team remained in deep trance, ignoring the danger, the other half had leaped up to fight alongside Reath.

They'd said there was a truce of sorts between Jedi and Drengir at present—but apparently that truce had expired. Amadeo had never fought the Drengir one-on-one before, but Master Mirro had reviewed all the available recordings and combat advice with him just in case. He knew what to do.

Or so Amadeo told himself. In truth, as he ran closer and one of the Drengir whirled toward him, every bit of that carefully assembled strategy seemed instantaneously to flee from his brain.

It's a plant, Amadeo thought, and it was as though he could process the information no further. Despite the recordings he'd seen, he had somehow continued to think of the Drengir as animalic creatures, just green, with appendages that looked leafy or vine-like. Confronting a Drengir face to face (so to speak) felt entirely different. Amadeo couldn't help understanding at last that this was a botanical creature, and on some level, his primal defense instincts simply did not respond to *a plant* as a predator threat.

Then the Drengir lashed out at him with a thorny whip, one Amadeo barely managed to duck.

Forget primal instinct. Amadeo called on the only thing that allowed humans to rise above such animalistic reactions: years and years of training. He ignited his lightsaber and swung upward sharply. The Drengir pulled back its appendage with great speed, but Amadeo's blade sliced through the very tip.

When the Drengir roared in surprise and pain, Amadeo couldn't resist a quick smile. Then he wished he had, because in the very next instant, another of its tendrils slipped around and slammed Amadeo across the back so hard that he fell to the ground.

✦

Thanks to the sharp hearing of Wookiees, the village became aware of the attack at the same moment Amadeo did. Burryaga bellowed a war cry, and dozens of fellow Wookiees followed suit.

Azlin Rell, who sat in his hut, had been incredibly bored and brightened at the sound of Wookiees preparing for battle. "Well, well," he murmured. "What might that be?"

"The meditation group must be under attack," said Dez Rydan, who'd just brought Azlin his breakfast. "Stay here." With that Dez ran out of the hut, making no effort to contain the prisoner within. He was pretty sure his Wookiee guard had left for a few moments, believing Azlin to be under Dez's supervision.

Did that make him no longer a prisoner?

Azlin had been in a real fight again not too long before. He'd missed the thrill of combat, had even taken some satisfaction in saving Master Arkoff, but best of all had been sending his power surging through that accursed Nameless, feeling its pain and anguish in the last moments before it had exploded with such a wet, sickening pop. He could almost taste the blood on his tongue.

Darkness relished combat. Azlin felt the call of it again, somehow deeper than ever before.

He stood, straightened, stretched. His joints popped and cracked in satisfying ways. Then Azlin walked from his hut, found the nearest railing on one of the elevated walkways, and simply rolled over it headfirst.

Some few Jedi could levitate; Azlin was not among them. However, the dark side had given him gifts of its own, gifts not entirely within his control but exhilarating nonetheless. He flung his arms wide, feeling electric bursts of power crackling all around him, each spark and bolt tethering him to a new branch or trunk, one after another, all the way down. Azlin could imagine what it looked like: a human-sized lightning storm in a forest, descending as slowly and gently as a falling leaf.

But if the Drengir nearby were fool enough to believe that gentleness was anything more than a mere illusion, it would make it all the sweeter to slaughter them.

Azlin rotated in midair, each crackling spark stinging his skin, so he landed on his feet. He could *feel* the Drengir near him, as darkness calls the dark. So he began running toward them, trusting the Force to steer him away from any fallen branch or unwieldy stump. That was what the Jedi didn't understand, that the dark provided its own guidance to rely on, clear and sharp, unfogged by hope.

As he ran, Azlin could hear the hum and whir of lightsabers moving through the air, the hiss and rustle of the Drengir opposing them. Within his mind, impressions of the Drengir began to take shape—nothing visual, because that was useless to him, but since removing his eyes he had learned how often vision could lie. Better to know the truth of a thing: its size, its speed, its heft. Its tone, temper, and fury. Its anger.

Its weakness.

A seeing person would have flinched from the whipping tendrils of the Drengir. Azlin simply slid between them, punching his blade-flat hand not at the Drengir's "skin" but at a point several centimeters beneath it. Skin and pulp gave way, and the Drengir screeched. Sticky sap flowed over Azlin's hand, gushed onto his body, but he simply twisted his hand until he felt the core stem of the Drengir, wrapped his fingers around it, and pulled back so hard he yanked a section out completely.

The Drengir made a wretched rustling sound—withering from healthy plant to crackling leaf in an instant—and collapsed.

Azlin felt a rush of pure bliss. How glorious, to face one's fear and destroy it, utterly and forever.

❧

Avon knew, of course, that she was no match for the speed of the Jedi, but she had rarely been so forcibly reminded of it as she was that day, painstakingly creeping down a wroshyr trunk, hearing the sounds of battle but as yet unable to join it.

Not that she was much of a fighter. But Avon was a scientist, one good enough to know that any interruption of the meditation group at the edge of the blight—much less something as violent as a Drengir attack—might well allow the blight to progress. Studying the blight just after one of its leaps forward, taking a sample from its first hour of existence, when it was still new, when some fragment of life might remain: that might allow her to confirm, or disprove, the latest theory about the blight. This was her big chance, assuming the Drengir didn't win.

They won't, Avon told herself. *The Jedi won't let them. Reath won't let them. The Jedi will win.*

When she was finally within a meter of the ground, she leaped from the tree trunk and literally hit the ground running. Avon raced toward the sounds of battle at full sprint, her sample kit banging against her side with every step. Even as she ran, it seemed to her that she heard fewer cries, shouts, and whip snaps. Was the battle over already? If so, that had to be a good sign . . . right?

At last she broke through a copse of slightly taller bushes and stumbled into the clearing where the Jedi stood. Amadeo lay on the ground near her, which struck pain into Avon's heart in the instant before she realized that he was alive and struggling to sit up, albeit injured, with blood seeping through the back of his robe. Reath, who stood at the center of everything, stared— along with all the other Jedi—at Azlin Rell, who stood panting and happy, like a charhound after a fun session of fighting with its favorite toy. Around Azlin lay the corpses of at least three Drengir. Maybe more.

I guess there was a good reason to bring him along on this mission after all, Avon thought, but she spared Azlin no more of her time. The Jedi could look after themselves; this was her chance to get a sample of brand-new blight.

And it was there to be had, for the dying gray patch they'd seen yesterday had leaped forward several centimeters. It was to this edge that Avon went.

It had seemed to Amadeo when he fell in combat that this was certainly the worst thing that could have befallen him and was likely to end his life. Instead he panted for breath as Azlin Rell stood nearby, eerie Force electricity still slightly crackling at his fingertips. "Funny, isn't it?" Azlin said. "How the Drengir came toward the blight instead of fleeing from it?"

"Hilarious," Amadeo said flatly. Azlin just went back to humming his creepy lullaby.

Amadeo struggled to his knees and was fighting for the strength to stand when Reath appeared at his elbow. "Easy," Reath said. "Your back's been cut, and we don't want to make your wounds any worse. Could you take my arm?"

"I think so." Amadeo gripped the crook of Reath's arm and allowed himself to be pulled to his feet. A dizzy swoon nearly overtook him, but as soon as he had taken a couple of deep breaths, he realized he would remain upright and could possibly even walk. There, however, was his limit. "I can't climb back up the trees," he said to Reath. "One of the Wookiees might have to take me."

Kelnacca had already appeared at their sides, but Reath put up a hand to take a quick pause. "I want the medic to take a look at your back before we make any decisions about how best to move you. If it's bad, we can fashion some kind of a sling, or even have the *Vessel* bring you up. If not, maybe a med-spike will do the trick."

As horribly winded as Amadeo had been by the blow, as much as his back hurt, he already thought the second alternative more likely than the first. "All right, then. Reath—I'm sorry I couldn't help more."

"What are you talking about?" Reath shook his head. "Amadeo, you ran straight into battle. No one could be braver."

"But I went right down. Immediately."

"That doesn't mean that you fought any less bravely. It doesn't even mean that you fought any less well—only that you encountered a truly dangerous adversary in the first moments of combat. That can happen to anyone." Reath spoke with conviction. "One of the most insidious illusions of war is that the winner in any encounter, small or large, was in some critical way superior. It leads to the conflation of *might* and *right*. In truth, chance always plays a factor. Often that's the *biggest* factor. Sometimes the strong fall and the weak stand. And sometimes, you just run into the wrong Drengir first thing."

Amadeo laughed, the sound surprising him. "Yeah, I found that out the hard way."

Master Cohmac had supported him both before and during this mission; now here was Reath Silas, providing all the wisdom and strength of a master despite his young years. How glad Master Mirro would have been to know that Amadeo would find other teachers, other guides.

In the distance, other would-be fighters were arriving; behind them, just now visible, was their mission medic. Amadeo had never looked forward to a med-spike more.

Azlin Rell stopped humming, turning his blank face toward Reath. "The Drengir are tied to the dark side. Do you think they hear the darkness calling them from the blight?"

"It hasn't before," Reath said, but his uncertain expression told Amadeo that—for all their worries about the Nihil and the blight and the Drengir—their true enemy on this mission, in this entire conflict, was darkness itself.

The surviving Drengir had collected in a shady glade not far from the *Innovator*, the better to soak up sun and let their wounds regenerate. Recovering after a fight was new to none of them, nor did they flinch from pain. Yet all were uneasy, and none had to say why.

They had intended to hunt, had intended to slay the animal life-forms they would find on this planet. They had not even been shaken to realize their adversaries included Jedi.

Yet the way that they had rushed into the fray—without tactics, without strategy, without even pausing to consider potential sources of escape or assistance for their foes—that, the Drengir could not understand. Their need for combat had become so overwhelming, so maddening, that they had been unable to think about their actions. It was as though they had been compelled to act. And the Drengir did not like being compelled.

Something else was at work on this world—something that worked against them. Something they could not resist.

TWENTY-ONE

Avon scarcely noticed the Jedi handling the wounded or the disposal of Drengir corpses. She noted that Amadeo was back on his feet, that Reath was helping him, and no more. All her attention was for the blight.

As she had predicted, the blight had crept forward during the interruption of Jedi meditation—only a few centimeters, but that was enough. After quickly snapping on protective gear, Avon deployed her little sampler droid again, which munched up a new bit of blight and held it safely in a containment field within. She didn't let herself think about the various ramifications of any potential discovery; the scale and scope of this would unnerve her, if she did. Avon knew the value of progressing step by step, looking no further forward than necessary.

While she was at it, she took some samples left behind by the Drengir, as well. Given the poisons they were able to generate, it stood to reason that a toxicity study of their sap might provide some insights.

By the time she was done, the Jedi and the Wookiees had rigged up a sort of sling lift to transport the wounded and the weary back to the village. Those who could rode the enormous, intimidating, vaguely feline mylaya steeds instead, but the beasts were so powerful that it required a certain degree of strength just to hold on. Avon first thought she shouldn't bother the Wookiees by asking for a lift; people were seriously hurt, after all, and hadn't she managed to climb up the wroshyr trees yesterday? She had . . . and her legs still ached and wobbled from the exertion. Maybe she could ride a mylaya. But after watching Kelnacca ride one upward, at an angle almost precisely ninety degrees with the ground, she felt like the situation was going to have to be a whole lot more dire before she did anything so dizzyingly bold. To her relief, Reath motioned for her to join the queue for the sling. Avon took her place at the very end of the line, after those who were harmed even slightly. *Lazy comes last,* she told herself. (This was an injustice to the very real exertion she was still recovering from, but she might as well start psyching herself up, because the Wookiees weren't going to give her a ride every single time, and it was going to be a while before she volunteered to ride a mylaya.)

All in all, it took her the better part of an hour to get back to her makeshift laboratory and get to work. Her samples went in front of the electromicroscope, and she carefully recorded all measurements, comparing and contrasting as she went.

A rustling outside Avon's window drew her attention for one moment, and she peered out to see a shadowy shape—indistinct, large, but no Wookiee—moving through the trees. The wildlife on Kashyyyk was notoriously dangerous; even though the most savage predators usually steered clear of Wookiee villages, the black-furred shape vanishing into the leaves was a reminder to Avon that wandering off on her own would be an extremely bad plan.

Not that she wanted to wander. She wanted to work. Even if her work proved that the doom of the Republic—and of the galaxy—was nigh.

High noon had come. As the medics worked with wounded Jedi, and the reconstituted meditation group got back to work at the blight perimeter, Dez finally had a moment to eat something and review the battle with Reath. Dismayed as they all were to find the Drengir on Kashyyyk, and as chagrined as they were to have been caught off guard by the attack, Dez's attention was fixed on one element of the fight beyond all others.

"The way Azlin Rell swept in," Dez said, "the way electricity was crackling around him—Reath, it was like some Sith legend we would've told as younglings late at night, before staying up until dawn because we'd scared ourselves so badly."

Reath nodded. "The dark forces Azlin has in his grasp go beyond anything I'd thought possible."

Dez had to give him a look. "Why are you saying that like it's a good thing?"

"It isn't. I mean, of course it isn't. All I'm saying is that we need to use every tool at our disposal, even if one of them is in league with the dark side."

"I'm not at all sure that's what that means," Dez said. He wished they could get Azlin off this planet, immediately, but apparently there was no arguing with Reath when it came to Azlin Rell.

"Dez, are you okay?" Reath said. "I know your confrontation with the Drengir back on the Amaxine station took a lot out of you—"

"You mean, it forced me into three years of the Barash Vow." Dez laughed mirthlessly. "The Drengir are tied to darkness. Sometimes I think they're *made* of darkness. And the darkness within them—it wasn't my imagination, was it? That the dark is with them more strongly here. Stronger than it ever was on the abandoned station."

Reath didn't reply at first. He sat quietly, a small crease forming between his eyebrows as he carefully considered what Dez had said; probably he was reviewing his own memories of the battle. Finally he nodded. "You might be right. But I have no idea *why* you're right."

"All I'm saying is, the dark side plays some role in this we don't yet understand," Dez said. "And until we do, we need to be even warier of Azlin Rell than we were before."

Reath opened his mouth to reply, but at that moment, a call came from Nan's hut: "If you want to know what's going on with the Drengir—you want to find Dr. Mkampa!"

Nan sat within her hut, biding her time. Sure enough, within moments, Reath came through the door looking grim. Nan didn't even give him the chance to speak before she said, "Dr. Mkampa has figured out how to influence—maybe even control—the Drengir."

"You could've told us this from the beginning," Reath replied. "Why didn't you?"

She shrugged. "I wasn't sure it would come up."

"What does Mkampa want with the Drengir? Is she just trying to interfere with our mission?"

"Maybe. In all honesty, I'm not sure what purpose they could serve, other than as a distraction. They've thrown you guys off, haven't they?" Nan smiled up at Reath as though she, too, could defend herself against a Drengir. She couldn't let him think she was afraid. Couldn't let him see anything she was feeling. "For a while, I served on Mkampa's science vessel within the Nihil fleet, the Lightning Crash. During my time there, I was expected to keep tabs on her."

"You mean, spy on her for Marchion Ro."

Nan did not intend to be baited. "That's my job. In the process, I managed to access a lot of her personal research files—the studies she hadn't shared with Ro. Some of them I reported to him. Some I didn't. Her research on the Drengir was information I didn't pass along, mostly because I didn't see the utility of it. Ro already has better ways of derailing Jedi Knights, doesn't he?"

Apparently, Reath didn't bait easily, either. "So Mkampa has set the Drengir on us, maybe to distract us from holding back the blight on Kashyyyk—"

Doubt it, Nan thought but didn't say.

"—or to distract us from noticing or pursuing her."

"And if you're trying to save a planet, distractions are the last thing you need," she replied. "So are you ready to let me lead a search team yet?"

Reath stared at her long and hard. Nan managed not to smile. At last he said, "You'll be tethered and sentried. Your physical liberty will be limited, and you'll have to remain in close contact with all of us at all times."

Nan tilted her head. "I'll have to stay in close physical contact with you? How very forward, Mr. Silas."

His expression didn't change, but she thought she detected a slight blush on his cheeks. "No more secrets, no more half-truths."

"You've already got most of it," Nan said, "and not even I know every secret Mkampa has up her voluminous sleeves."

"I mean it, Nan. If you honestly want to help us against the Nihil and the blight, it's time to prove it."

"I'm volunteering to go to the forest floor of Kashyyyk—which, once you get too far from a Wookiee encampment, is basically like a zoo and terrarium of the most poisonous flora and fauna in the galaxy—and potentially to fight my way through some artificially enhanced Drengir, just to expose myself to the blight. If that's not proof enough for you, I don't know what would be."

Reath remained silent a few moments, studying her. Trust was a funny thing.

Finally, Reath nodded. "All right. We'll have you tethered past the point of escape. You wanted a chance, Nan—well, you've got it."

Her momentary elation was interrupted by a rap at the door. Before either of them could reply, Avon Starros poked her head through, her face so pale, her eyes so teary that it shocked Nan beyond the ability to speak. "Reath?" Avon said. "Can I show you something in my lab?"

"Of course," Reath said, hurrying out without another word.

I don't know what that's about, Nan thought, *but it can't be good.*

A dark shadow flickered across her window, and she wheeled around just in time to see a large black creature darting through the tree limbs, barely visible, then hidden by the leaves. Just one of the many dangerous denizens of Kashyyyk, she supposed. It had startled her. That was the reason she felt so shaky, so scared. Nan refused to acknowledge any other.

※

Reath understood what this meant without having to be told. But Avon had worked hard to present him with evidence—the kind of scientific proof they might have to use to convince Lina Soh, eventually—and besides, he had to hear it for himself before he could begin to accept it.

In Avon's lab hut, she pulled up two samples of blight, visible within their stasis fields. "Okay," she said, sniffling slightly. "The first sample is the one I took just after we arrived. The second sample is the one I took after the blight leaped forward following the Drengir attack."

"I can see that the first is more decayed," Reath said.

"Right, sure, of course. What's more significant, to me, is that the sample has decayed equally throughout. No matter how small

I section the sample, the rates of decay are constant. The same goes for the new sample, though obviously that hasn't progressed as far. But the rate of progression is identical. This isn't the way diseases or contaminations work in nature. There, we always see some degree of variation." Avon shook her head slowly. "Here? This is as constant as the half-life of a radioactive isotope."

"In other words, it obeys fundamental scientific laws. Your findings match my research. We can surmise that the blight is tied to the Nameless, and to the Force, not to any other source in nature—"

"And that there is no 'cure,'" Avon said. "There never can be. It's impossible. The blight can't be stopped."

Reath had come to similar conclusions on his own—but it was one thing to sense the philosophical truth of the blight, another to confront the hard scientific fact Avon had just confirmed. They stood together in silence for a few long moments. Reath collected himself as best he could. "We'll have to share this information with Coruscant—and with the others, here—but maybe not yet."

"No," Avon said. In her voice he heard total comprehension. News this disastrous could wait, in fact should wait as long as possible before being shared. It could affect very little. All this information could do was incite despair, because now they knew of the impending destruction ahead for Kashyyyk, for the Republic, for the galaxy entire.

TWENTY-TWO

The black-furred creature Nan had seen outside her window was in fact a wuguttan. Zoologists disagreed on whether this species was more feline or ursine, a question that could not be definitively answered due to the extreme difficulty of even capturing a wuguttan, much less managing to study one. After the first several dozen zoologists had died in such attempts, scientific curiosity had moved on to other, less uniformly fatal creatures. Wuguttans were among the many deadly creatures of Kashyyyk that Wookiees warned their children about.

Of course the Drengir knew none of this. They could sense, however, the danger the wuguttan represented. Already they felt withered from their run-in with the Wookiees and Jedi. Other, less dangerous meat could be had if they continued to search—yet once again, after seeing the meat creature near, the compulsion came upon them and they attacked.

This time, two more among the Drengir fell, and even the Great Progenitor was so savagely clawed on one branch that she could scarcely move. Though the wuguttan had been extremely large, the carcass provided only scant sustenance when divided among all the Drengir in the party. Yet as the Great Progenitor looked down at the remains, cracking into the marrow with a tendril, she felt an entirely different compulsion: the need to bury what was left in shallow soil.

Her comprehension flooded into the rest of the Drengir at once. Of course. They needed to prepare enriched beds for the seeds to take root. Everything they could kill—meat or lesser plants—would serve a purpose: helping make Kashyyyk the next greenhouse nursery of the Drengir, the seedbeds of the next generation.

Why reproduce here and now? What was it that made this place so perfect, this time so critical? None could say. They were aware of a great pressure weighing on them, very nearly directing them, but this they could no more understand than disobey. The Drengir had to do as they were urged, or die trying.

※

As soon as Affie Hollow heard that Nan was to be part of the team hunting down Mkampa and her laboratory, she did two things. First, she volunteered to be part of the team herself, pointing out to Reath that they needed at least one non-Jedi around. "What if Dr. Mkampa has one of these Nameless or Levelers or whatever they're called?" she said. "You'll need somebody who won't faint dead away, right?"

"Hey," Avon protested. The young scientist looked pale this afternoon, and her voice was hoarse, but she had suited up for the search already. "I'm not a Jedi, and I'll be on the team."

Affie never even looked away from Reath, who didn't actually look that great himself. She didn't intend to get distracted. "Amended to, you'll need somebody who's not a Jedi who knows how to fire a blaster."

"How hard can it be?" Avon said, gesturing vaguely like a person who'd spent way too much time with their holonovels. "Point. Shoot. Done."

"She thinks that's all there is to it," Affie said. "So I'm guessing that pretty much makes me a lock for the team."

Reath had matured enough to be a true diplomat when necessary. "Avon, nobody doubts your courage, but we'll need you to target Mkampa's lab more than the doctor herself. You're the only one who knows what to steal and what to destroy. That means we'll need Affie with her blaster, too."

With that accomplished, Affie then volunteered again—this time to help fit Nan with a more mobile tethering device than the previous sentry.

"This is an S-thread transmitter bracelet," she said as she sat in Nan's hut, hard-soldering the ends of the bracelet around Nan's wrist. Any number of tools would remove it easily enough, but none of those tools would be lying around on the forest floor. "That allows us to track you at all times. If you get too far away from the primary sentry, you'll be hit with an electric shock. Take another step away, you'll get hit again. It won't take five of those shocks to knock you out. You'd be dead in ten—but don't be discouraged. Nobody's ever stayed conscious long enough to take ten steps past their barrier."

"Don't I need to know where that sentry is, then?" Nan asked. "Or who's holding it?"

Affie shook her head and grinned. "Leave the worrying to the person holding the sentry. If you stay on task and do what you said you were going to do? You'll be just fine."

It seemed almost certain to Affie that Nan wouldn't fulfill her promises, that inevitably she would try to pull a fast one. When she did, the bracelet would lay Nan flat—and Affie couldn't wait to see it.

⁂

Reath had in fact planned on asking someone from the *Vessel* crew to join the team for exactly the reasons Affie had suggested. And besides, his concentration, as well as Avon's, wasn't what it should've been. Their party needed members who didn't know what he and Avon knew about the blight. He wished he could have brought the whole crew along—Leox was a wily fighter, too, and even the Drengir hadn't known how to take down Geode. However, if the Drengir attacked or some other emergency arose, the *Vessel* needed to remain with enough crew members to perform a swift evacuation of as many beings as could fit on board.

He also wanted Wookiees on the team because both plant and animal life could be extremely dangerous in unsettled areas of Kashyyyk, and only a native would be able to identify them all. However, as Reath sought out Burryaga and Kelnacca to ask for their cooperation, he ran into Burryaga, who had been looking for Reath to explain that, for the moment, he and Kelnacca intended to join the meditation team on the surface. This surprised Reath. He hadn't taken Kelnacca for a mystic, and while he could see Burryaga traveling that path someday, he knew his friend wasn't there yet.

But Burryaga went on to say that their strong spiritual ties to their homeworld gave their thoughts a protective power no non-Wookiee could muster. At this moment, when the blight was in danger of rapid expansion, their participation in the meditation group was crucial. His suggestion was for Reath to take along a Wookiee who was not among the Jedi: the leader's aide, Lohgarra. She was strong and in her prime, used to dealing with non-Wookiees, and clearly eager to help in any way she could. Indeed, when Reath asked her, Lohgarra agreed to take part before he'd even finished his first sentence.

He went to Cohmac Vitus next, assuming his participation to be a given, but Cohmac surprised him. "I feel I should instead join the meditation team with Burryaga and Kelnacca. Obviously the presence of the Wookiees is more critical than my own—but I strongly sense that I should support them at this time."

Reath would have been more surprised to hear this from certain other Jedi; Cohmac had always been a mystic at heart, and if he felt called to a duty, then no doubt that was where he should be. Why then did his words rankle? As though Reath's leadership of the mission were being called into question?

But that was his own uncertainty, pretending to speak with Cohmac's voice. Besides, Cohmac had not yet fully returned to the Jedi Order, which meant he remained under no one's command. Reath simply nodded and said, "Then you must do as you are called." Cohmac smiled approvingly—Reath did not want or need approval—but he had the good sense to end the conversation there.

Amadeo could not possibly accompany them; he was healing well from the wounds he had sustained in combat with the Drengir, but it would be another day or two before he was fit for full duty. In the end, Reath decided that it didn't matter. They only needed one other Jedi to accompany them on the journey: Dez Rydan.

When Reath asked Dez, he at first received no response. Had the fight with the Drengir unnerved Dez even more than he was letting on? Finally, however, Dez said, "Of course. I wouldn't let you guys go without me."

Reath had one more person volunteer for the team whom he turned down flat.

"Come, now," Azlin Rell said, rocking back and forth in his hut. "Didn't I prove myself in the fight against the Drengir? Don't you think you might need me, if Mkampa puts up resistance?"

"I think you have greater power in the dark side than you ever revealed before," Reath answered, "and for that reason alone, I'm not getting you any closer to the blight than necessary. The blight is tied to darkness, somehow."

"Who better to tell you how than me?"

"Dr. Mkampa, for one. You're not going, Azlin. Not on this stretch. That's final."

"We shall see," Azlin said. The smile beneath his ruined eyes could be so terrible, when he chose. "We shall see."

For all Avon's protests, she was relieved not to be the only non-Jedi in the group. Though she was confident in her blaster ability—not brilliant, maybe, but not incompetent, either—she preferred to keep the scientific instruments in her hands and leave the weapons to others. (Besides, Affie Hollow could seriously shoot. You could tell just by looking at her.)

What does it matter? whispered the traitorous voice in her head that wanted to curl into a fetal position and give up. *The blight takes everything. It will take everything. We can't stop it.*

But Avon refused to listen. Maybe finding Dr. Mkampa would help, and maybe it wouldn't, but either way, the fewer Nihil who remained at liberty, the better.

Together the group descended to the forest floor and began their trek, Nan leading them westward in a nearly direct line. "We're getting some signals this way," she said, checking the limited scanning device they'd allowed her. "Nothing like the scale I'd expect to see from her lab, but they look right so maybe we're still just too far away."

"We'll find out," Dez said. He sounded skeptical that Nan would lead them anywhere useful, and in that, he spoke for the group. Certainly he spoke for Avon.

At first, to her, their journey seemed like no more than a hike, a long walk through pleasant woods. *Maybe Nan's not actively entrapping us,* Avon thought. *Maybe she's just trying to waste our time and energy.*

After a couple of klicks, however, the team reached the perimeter of what the local Wookiees considered their territory. Avon could see that the underbrush ahead became thicker and the leaf cover overhead denser—so much, in places, that it seemed to turn day into dark. Lohgarra paused before crossing the boundary, and the others stopped when she did.

"Wow," Avon said, "you even till the ground beneath your villages so that it's good for plants while still being traversable for Wookiees and their visitors."

Lohgarra said this wasn't exactly the case. Pruzzalla's village held a ceremonial position; they had a religious duty of forestry that required cultivation of the forest floor, a place Wookiees otherwise left alone. Many creatures lived off decaying plant matter found on the forest floor, creatures that formed a part of the great interconnectedness of life but were more safely kept far from the Wookiees.

"Like what?" Avon asked in the split second before Lohgarra's great furry arm shot out, blocking her path. Her eyes widened as she saw the enormous golden millipede, at least as long as a grown Wookiee was tall, snaking along the leaf-strewn ground.

Affie stifled a little yelp as she saw it, Nan scowled, and even Dez Rydan looked dismayed. Reath said, a little too casually, "So, on lots of planets, centipedes and millipedes are venomous to some degree—"

Lohgarra interjected that this was true on Kashyyyk, very, very, *very* true, and that the sting of one of these millipedes could kill a large Wookiee within five minutes. She wasn't certain how much faster a human would feel the effects, but she was confident that, no matter how long it did or didn't take, that human would most definitely die.

"Important safety tip," said Reath. "Beware of millipedes."

That wasn't all they had to look out for, Lohgarra added with a quick whine. They also needed to avoid flame beetles and slyyygs. Worst of all were the wyyyschokk, giant spiders that hid in the canopies to literally get the drop on their prey.

"I really, really wish you hadn't mentioned those," Affie said, staring upward into the leaves. "Okay, so, be careful of pretty much all animal life."

Not just animal life, Lohgarra hastily added, explaining that they must look out for the jaw plants that lay open on the ground, waiting to snap shut as soon as the unwary stepped on them. They needed to distrust flowering vines, as well, for those could prove to be saava, which looked innocuous but could follow you, very slowly, before latching on to drain out your nutrients. . . .

Lohgarra's growls trailed off as she took in the horrified faces of the humans around her. She tried adding that, really, the main thing they needed to do was exercise caution and they'd be fine. Probably.

"How about we just keep moving?" Nan continued walking, as though she didn't care in the slightest, but Avon could see that she glanced around more often than before. So did everyone else. After several tense, quiet minutes, she reminded herself that she was in the company of a Wookiee and two Jedi Knights, which was about as safe as it was possible to get, and the less time she spent thinking about giant spiders, the happier she'd be.

Don't think about the blight, either, she told herself. *Just keep putting one foot in front of the other.*

Moving past a fray of green leaves made Avon recall the Drengir—in fact, it looked very like the aftermath of their battle with the Jedi—but if the Drengir had battled something here, they had won. A low, long mound suggested a burial, but that had to be Avon's imagination running away with her. The Drengir didn't bury those they defeated. They ate them.

As she fell into step beside Reath, they exchanged glances. His mood seemed as bleak as hers; they both bore the weight of this terrible knowledge, and it wasn't an easy burden to carry. So she decided it was time to make him smile. "So—how long until we find the mad doctor's *Mkampment?*"

Reath stopped short and glared at her, almost but not quite suppressing an answering grin. "I refuse to know you."

Avon laughed out loud; to her pleasure, Dez and Affie did, too, as well as Lohgarra with rough, guffawing barks. Nan alone seemed immune to the pun. Or maybe she was just really scared of millipedes. Regardless, Avon's mood had lightened—not much, but enough, maybe.

And that was when she heard the first twig snap.

Reath felt the ripple through the Force at the very moment Avon laughed; before she'd even finished, he was already whirling around, his hand moving to his lightsaber. Igniting it instantly, he swung his blade up just in time to deflect the first blaster bolt. Then the second and third, then the fourth—

"The Drengir?" Affie Hollow cried. She'd hit the ground to buy herself some cover as she brought up her blaster. "Since when do they have blasters?"

"Not the Drengir!" Reath answered. "Enforcer droids. Be ready!"

The first enforcer burst into the clearing, its three glassy eyes fixed on three separate targets. However, it had not fully calculated the outcomes when a Wookiee was in the area, because it took no more than a swipe of Lohgarra's mighty hand to send the droid crashing into the nearest tree trunk. But two more droids rose from the greenery, altitude-tracer models hovering overhead, firing with deadly accuracy. By then Dez had come to his side, his lightsaber blazing, and between the two Jedi they could protect their small party . . . but not for long.

Look on the bright side, Reath told himself as he continued parrying energy bolts. *If we've run into this much resistance, we must be close to Mkampa's lab. Either this was pure coincidence or—or there's a chance Nan is actually on the level.*

Then an eerie violet light flooded the area, and to Reath's astonishment, one of the patches of greenery ahead suddenly began to rise upward. The violet light streamed through its leaves, then broke free. Reath's eyes widened as he saw a Nihil Spider Squall, modified and apparently armed beyond belief, weaving its way through the trees on its long snaky legs.

Affie said something considered rude on most planets; Reath and Dez flanked their group, while the mighty Lohgarra stood in front. The altitude droids stopped shooting, but Reath understood that this wasn't a good sign—only an indication that the attack would be left up to the Spider Squall.

As the droids flew back to their owner, the lights within the spider came on to reveal Dr. Mkampa standing at the front window of the central unit, her hands on what must have been the controls. Reath had never seen her before, but he had expected either a grave, sober, logical type like the researchers he saw in most schools and laboratories or a full-blown Nihil raider who just happened to handle scientific equipment. Instead, the figure illuminated within possessed her own unique outlandishness: curly black hair that stood out from her head in all directions, a blowsy lab smock with a metallic sheen, brilliant red tint on her lips, and fingernails so long and so green that Reath couldn't help noticing them even at this distance. Artificial, probably—he could now see that at least one of Mkampa's arms was covered in synth-skin, and one of her eyes was a cybernetic unit that gleamed red. Affie aimed her blaster directly at the spider—at Mkampa herself—but to Reath's relief, she had the self-control not to fire.

Mkampa's husky laugh rolled from a speaker attached to her spider. "Little girl, don't I know you from some Strike or other? I believe the name might have been . . . Nan. Did you come all this way to find me? Did Marchion send you to bring me home?"

"No," Nan said. But Reath didn't know if he believed her, and it took only a quick glance at the others to see that they definitely didn't. If Nan had come to set them up, to deliver them straight to the Nihil's mad scientist, she'd succeeded.

However, Mkampa made no further move to attack. "We'll have to speak soon, you and I. Catch up on old times." Nan stared up at Mkampa, her expression utterly blank as she shifted away from the lab, somewhat closer to Affie Hollow. "And Avon

Starros. Working against your mother's interests yet again. I wonder who would be more interested to hear that . . . your mother, or Marchion Ro?"

"My mom doesn't play any role in this!" Avon shouted back. "These are my decisions alone."

Mkampa laughed. "We'll see if Ro—"

In a flash—so fast even Reath could not block her—Nan grabbed Affie's blaster, not to take it away, just to pull the trigger. Energy bolts sizzled through the air, striking Mkampa's spider. The window in front of the zealot doctor's face held, but it sizzled and grayed. Mkampa wasn't smiling any longer.

Affie tried wrenching the blaster out of Nan's control; this time the fire hit a nearby wroshyr tree, doing no damage worse than blackening some bark, though that was enough for Lohgarra to growl in protest. "What are you doing?" Affie yelled.

"Trying to *take her OUT*!" Nan shouted even louder.

Mkampa wasn't sticking around; her Spider Squall flew away, whipping tree branches and limbs in every direction until it was obscured behind them, leaving the search team alone.

It was Affie who spoke first. "I didn't know she had a Spider Squall. Any reason you didn't mention that, Nan?"

Nan had let go of the blaster, and her head hung down. She cradled one wrist against her chest, as if injured, but she asked for no medical attention. "I didn't know, either. Only that she had some kind of private spaceship that was also a lab. But putting it in a Spider Squall? Gotta admit, it shows imagination."

"A sick, twisted imagination," Avon said. "That's the creepiest laboratory I've ever seen."

"A custom job on that scale would have cost an unfathomable amount of money." Nan turned to Reath then, realization dawning on her face. "Ro wouldn't have approved that."

Reath frowned. "Approved what?"

"The expense of refitting a Spider Squall to also serve as a mobile lab. He doesn't think about strategy in that context, and he doesn't spend money on anything that isn't designed to specifically harass the Republic and the Jedi." Nan scoffed. "Except, of course, the fancy wardrobe he's wearing these days."

"You're saying that Dr. Mkampa may have stolen from Marchion Ro?" Reath said. "If so, maybe we don't have to capture Mkampa ourselves. We could hand the proof over to Ro, and he'd turn the Nihil against her."

"We have to capture Mkampa ourselves," Nan insisted.

Dez Rydan had leaned against a nearby tree—resting, Reath had thought, though their exertions had been too brief to require much recovery. "Dez, are you okay?"

"Don't you feel it?" Dez turned to face Reath, his expression pained. "The darkness. Reath, it's close. It's here."

It took Reath a moment to nod. Amid the malign influence of both Drengir and blight, there was another strain of the dark side—something more foreign, and more powerful. This darkness only stained the edges of Reath's consciousness, but for Dez, who had suffered so much from the Drengir on the Amaxine station, it seemed to have struck a nerve.

What is it? Reath thought. *What other enemy is out there?*

TWENTY-THREE

Affie Hollow had been set up several times in her life—by her adoptive mother, to start—and although she'd gained a lot of knowledge and wisdom over the years, she still didn't always see the sucker punches coming.

You'd have to be insensate not to suspect that Nan might be up to something. First of all, Nan was *always* up to something; second, they'd just been led straight into a scenario in which their main adversary, Dr. Mkampa, had been able to taunt them and fly away unharmed.

So why was Affie beginning to believe that Nan *wasn't* setting them up?

As they made their way back toward the Wookiee village,

Affie was taking a long hard look at Nan (at least, when she wasn't checking the ground for millipedes). Usually Nan operated in one of two modes: Either she put on the "I'm hardly more than a little girl! I need your protection!" act that had worked so well on them all on the Amaxine station three years prior, or she smoothed her features into total inscrutability, with only the occasional hint of contempt. At the moment, however, Nan walked a few paces behind Reath, speaking to no one, her head drooping. She looked . . . dejected.

Mkampa wasn't expecting Nan, Affie considered as she clambered over a large fallen log. *She might have been faking surprise, but I don't think so. And what would be the point of leading us into an ambush if Mkampa didn't bother to spring the trap?*

Not to mention that Nan had tried to *kill* Mkampa, or had done an excellent job of pretending to do so. Had Marchion Ro maybe sent Nan as an assassin to murder Dr. Mkampa for whatever grudge was fueling him at the moment? And Nan had turned herself in to the Jedi so the Order would do the hard work of tracking the doctor down?

But Mkampa had found them, not the other way around. And it seemed likely that Nan could have thought up another way of searching for Dr. Mkampa that didn't involve becoming a prisoner.

Oddest of all: Reath hadn't said a single word about Nan's actions during the face-off. She knew better than to believe he was ignoring it, but whatever his thoughts were on the subject, he wasn't betraying them.

Affie shook off her curiosity. It would take more than one odd encounter to make her believe a single word Nan said.

Perhaps half a klick from the Wookiee village, Lohgarra tilted her head, stopped in her tracks, and whined—a higher-pitched sound than usual, one that carried a note of fear. Affie shivered (what could scare a Wookiee?), and when she glanced at Reath to check his reaction, she saw that his expression had turned grave. "Oh, no," Affie said. "What's wrong?"

"Is it Mkampa?" Avon asked. "Is she after us again?"

Most telling of all, Nan's face had paled. "Or her droids?"

Lohgarra took off running, bounding ahead of the rest of the group; when Wookiees ran, they could achieve tremendous speed. Reath said, "It's worse than the droids. It's the blight."

◆

Within seconds Reath had sprinted after Lohgarra, leaving the rest of the team to manage on their own. He didn't even think about Nan until he was within sight of the clearing beneath the village; luckily, they'd trusted Avon with Nan's tether on this first trip, or else he would have electrocuted her terribly. In the clearing he saw the entire meditation group, as well as other Wookiees, huddled together in evident distress; more than one Wookiee was howling. Burryaga's hands were clenched in his long hair, as if by pulling it he could use that lesser pain to distract from one far greater.

Had someone been killed by the blight? Touched it and been husked? Normally that took a long time, but perhaps the mysterious dark influence on Kashyyyk had accelerated the process. Reath dashed forward, calling out, "What is it?"

Cohmac Vitus emerged from the group, shaking his head in evident grief. "Suddenly—with no warning, for no cause we can determine—the blight expanded enormously."

Reath's gut sank. Yet he regained what calm he could as he came up to the group and was glad for it, because the pattern of the blight surprised him. He'd expected that any expansion would be roughly symmetrical around the outer edge of the blighted area, and that the enormous growth Cohmac spoke of would surely represent no more than a meter or so in any given direction. Yet as he walked up to it, the main patch of the blight seemed to be mostly the same—except for the spike.

One spike—not quite a meter wide—had shot out from the blighted path, scarring a swath of gray almost directly to the east. The blight touched not only the grasses and shrubs now, but also the roots of one of the wroshyr trees. Given the interconnectedness of the wroshyr forests, what afflicted one tree seemed likely to afflict them all.

Horrifying as that was, however, Reath had the distinct sense that this was not what most concerned the Wookiees. Burryaga gestured toward the east, as though in despair, and the Wookiees' cries shifted upward in pitch.

Lohgarra stood very near Reath, with her head in her hands. He said, "Is there another village to the east? Why is that the worst part of all this?" But Lohgarra merely growled, not even in Shyriiwook, just a sound of frustration and mourning.

Obviously the reason was something cultural—something significant. Just as obviously, the truth would not be revealed to Reath anytime soon. Best to wait until the Wookiees decided to speak up themselves.

For the time being it was enough to know that, despite all their best efforts at checking it, the blight on Kashyyyk continued to grow.

*

Dez Rydan remained as stoic as he could during this, knowing that his primary responsibility was to give the Wookiees strength, safety, and support at a dangerous and tragic time.

Yet he could not even pretend to be surprised that the blight had surged forward again. For a planet possessed of so much strength in the light, Kashyyyk emanated a distinct vein of darkness—

It probably isn't Kashyyyk, he told himself. *It's probably the blight itself. Or the Drengir. They got into your head once, cracked you open and let the darkness bleed in. You thought the Barash Vow would seal the cracks?*

Apparently not.

This wasn't a healthy way to think. Were Dez on Coruscant, he would have immediately gone into a session with one of the mystics, or perhaps a counseling master.

But he had a mission to fulfill, and Dez didn't intend to fall short.

At least he had his friends about him. With Reath, Cohmac,

and the others by his side, he'd find a way to make it through. Somehow.

⚜

Up in the treetops, the Wookiee village was in an uproar. Avon didn't understand Shyriiwook perfectly, but she knew grief when she heard it, and the Wookiees' sorrow was so terrible that it brought tears to her eyes.

"They didn't think it would come for them," said that creepy Azlin Rell in a singsong. He huddled on a stump chair, observed by no one, taking a foul pleasure in the despair of others. "Thought they could love back the blight, love away the dark. No such thing, not in all the galaxy. *Shrii Ka Rai, Ka Rai* . . ."

Ignoring this as best she could, Avon hurried back to her lab hut. She rested her head on the smooth surface of her lab table; it felt too heavy to lift. She could not exorcise the haunting resonance of Mkampa's vengeful words.

Marchion Ro had never respected Ghirra Starros, not really, no matter how hard Avon's mother tried to convince herself otherwise. Soon he would hear of Avon's "treachery" in supporting the Republic. If he saw Avon's disloyalty as Ghirra's failure—

Mom thinks she can talk herself out of anything, Avon thought. *I hope she's right.*

She could live with whatever consequences came from her actions, unless those actions set her mom up to fall, and to die.

Just a few hours prior, it had felt to Avon as though almost nothing was worth doing, as though all emotion had been drained from her by the terrible discovery of the incurability of the blight. Turned out her heart beat on, that she loved her mother as much as she ever had, and that still, ever, always—she would continue to fight to protect those she loved.

Even if that was a fight that couldn't be won.

※

Another member of the mission felt as disconsolate about the interaction with Mkampa as Avon did, if not worse. Nan Hague sat in her own hut. Nobody had bothered locking her in or guarding her this time, probably because of the bracelet she wore, but it wouldn't have mattered if there had been no security on her whatsoever. There was no place else Nan needed to be.

Mkampa's gloating face still seemed to hover in the air overhead, taunting her from above. So Mkampa had remembered her name after all . . . barely. Of course Dr. Mkampa knew nothing of anyone's duty within the Nihil other than her own; she cared little about any sense of loyalty or freedom save for what she personally needed to conduct her bizarre experiments. It might have been said that she lay on the fringe of the Nihil, except even that gave Mkampa more belonging than she actually possessed, much less deserved.

The thought of Mkampa reporting on Nan to Marchion Ro—that was farcical. Mkampa had gone rogue, and while Ro might not care that much about losing her, she would never again be anything but an enemy to him.

The greater problem was that whatever credibility Nan had

gained among the Jedi—and she was not fool enough to think she'd ever gained much—was entirely lost. Reath might be willing to follow her out into the deep forests of Kashyyyk again, but who else would volunteer? Inevitably he would question her regarding the attempt to kill Mkampa, and Nan had no idea how much she was willing to say about it, if anything.

How am I supposed to do this? Nan thought. *How do I make this happen?*

One answer suggested itself: the sentry bracelet on her wrist. By cradling her arm close, Nan had kept anyone from seeing that the bracelet had taken some slight damage. Not much—not enough to set her free—

But it might be a place to start.

※

In a small hut far up in the trees, set off from the rest of the village, a very private meeting was being held. Humans were all well and good—fine friends and companions—but some topics needed to be discussed among Wookiees. Only one offworlder had been invited to their gathering as an objective listener and calming presence.

Geode stood alone in the center of the hut, considering in turn each Wookiee present. Burryaga and Kelnacca of the Jedi could scarcely stop growling their fury at Marchion Ro and the blight, though they caught themselves over and over, battling against their tempers as Jedi should. The fair-haired Lohgarra remained more focused on the direction the blight had traveled.

Most interesting was the reaction of the elderly matriarch Pruzzalla, who had been braiding her gray hair into plaits that, in Wookiee culture, could signify either a readiness to engage with the divine or the willingness to go to war.

Once the Wookiees had calmed themselves enough to pay attention, Geode pointed out that their dismay clearly focused on whatever it was that lay to the east of this village. Why had they not spoken of this to the Jedi?

Lohgarra roared that it was none of their business, that its meaning was reserved for Wookiees alone. This was not only secret; it was sacred, and non-Wookiees had a tendency to profane nearly all they touched.

Geode considered this somewhat unfair but was wise enough to remain silent. These Wookiees, different though they might have been as individuals, all possessed considerable intelligence and honor. They'd talk their way through this, given time. His job was to be the sounding board.

It was Burryaga who contradicted Lohgarra first. He knew many non-Wookiees who respected that which was sacred, both to themselves and to others, and the Jedi were among that number.

Kelnacca chimed in that the Jedi were here to provide protection—and was not that which lay to the east deserving of more protection than virtually anything else on Kashyyyk?

With a whine and a shake of her ash-gold fur, Lohgarra admitted that they each had a point, but that this secret was one that had been long held for the best reasons. They could not breach the seal of silence without due consideration.

Finally, the elder Pruzzalla gave her verdict: Yes, this was an important secret. But if the choice was between secrecy and survival—then there was no choice at all. They would take this to the entire village and put it to a common vote; all must be in agreement before revealing something so vital.

Burryaga roared his support as Kelnacca nodded. Geode watched Lohgarra struggle for a moment longer before she finally gave her assent, as well.

So at last the secret would come out. Geode decided not a word of it should come from him.

TWENTY-FOUR

Avon worked straight through to dinner, analyzing Drengir sap—maybe not the most useful research at the moment, but something constructive she could do. It proved absorbing work, as the sap had certain properties she wouldn't have expected from anything organic, though organic it certainly was. She might have continued through the meal had not her grumbling stomach finally demanded food so much that her thoughts began to cloud. "Damned meat machine," she muttered. "Always has to stop thinking for maintenance." Then she thought she probably sounded a lot like a Drengir. Maybe that particular figure of speech could remain private for a while.

She lined up for the meal of the evening—a kind of savory vegetable that could be tugged apart into strings almost like noodles, topped with a spicy sauce (yes, please); some sweet star-shaped fruit in vivid shades of purple (stained Avon's fingers and tongue; worth it); and a porridge-like substance that the Wookiee chef helpfully explained was made of ground-up wood grubs (pushed to the side of the plate so it wouldn't touch anything Avon intended to eat). A small bench area remained unoccupied halfway through the meal break, so Avon claimed it as her personal domain. Better if she didn't talk to anybody for a while yet.

But then Reath showed up—and, of course, he was the exception. "Whoa," he said as he settled his plate on the high table and glanced at hers in return. "You took some of the grub gruel?"

"Just to be polite," Avon said. "I mean, I'm pretty hungry, but I don't think I'm ever going to be *that* hungry."

"I've eaten insects on a few worlds," Reath said. "Where they're normal foodstuffs. There's one planet where they oil and toast bugs, eat them out of bags at parades and outdoor festivals and that kind of thing. That's where I tried my first one."

Avon raised an eyebrow. "And?"

"And honestly, they're not too bad. More crunch than flavor, you know?" Reath grimaced at the grub gruel. "Here, however, I draw the line."

"Maybe I could find a place to leave mine out for the birds. They like grubs, right?"

"Yeah, I think so." Reath studied her face intently; she hoped she didn't blush. "How are you holding up, Avon?"

Her first impulse was to refuse to think about the blight; distraction was the only thing that had helped so far. But this was Reath asking, and he was one of the people in the galaxy with whom she felt the greatest need to be honest. "Better than I would have thought. I mean, the galaxy is a big place. No matter how terrible the blight is, it can't destroy it all . . . probably."

"Probably," Reath agreed. "Maybe the Republic won't look the way it did before the Nihil conflict began. Maybe we'll lose even more to the blight. But it's our job to go on. Even if we wind up on just one safe world, then that's an entire world to protect, and to serve."

"Just one safe world," Avon repeated. It was as good a mantra as any.

Reath cocked his head. "Is something else getting to you?"

Avon sighed. "Yes, though it feels ridiculous to admit it. And it doesn't compare with, like, the fate of the galaxy. It's just . . . I'm worried about my mother. If Mkampa reports that I'm here, Ro might take revenge on her."

Reath considered that carefully. It was so much easier to be open with people who took you seriously, Avon decided. He finally said, "Your mother fulfills a very specific role for Marchion Ro, as chief negotiator with the Republic. That's not a role he can afford to get rid of right now, or probably for a long time to come."

"Do you think Ro knows that? Because I'm not so sure he credits anybody with helping him—not his Tempest Runners, not Mom, no one." Avon combed her hair back from her face with her fingers. "He might *regret* killing her, but he still could kill her."

"You've been working with us for a while—"

"But it's different now. Ro is . . ." This was hard to admit, but it had to be said: "Ro has the advantage. He thinks he's winning.

So maybe he thinks he doesn't need Mom anymore, and if he thinks that, why wouldn't he punish her for my actions?" Avon swallowed hard. "She's made some of the worst mistakes a person can make, but she's still my mother. I still love her."

"I'm not going to lie to you to make you feel better, mostly because I don't think it actually would make you feel better," Reath said. He rested one hand on her shoulder in a totally platonic, supportive, casual gesture that nonetheless made her cheeks flush with warmth. "Your mother is in danger as long as she's with the Nihil, yes. But after seeing Ro at work these past three years, I've learned that he's not very interested in 'justice,' even his version of it. He doesn't care what his underlings do as long as they're useful to him; as soon as they're no longer of use, it's all over. In other words—if Ro ever does kill your mother, it will be for his own reasons. It won't have anything to do with any actions of yours, or probably even any actions of hers."

This wasn't much comfort, really, but it was genuine. Scrap though it was, Avon could treasure it because it was true. She smiled shakily at him. "Thanks, Reath."

His attention seemed to have been diverted; she followed his gaze to see the huddles of Wookiees eating nearby, all of them entirely silent. They remained shaken by the blight's bizarre expansion earlier that day.

If she didn't keep busy, she'd wind up just as depressed, Avon decided, and wolfed down the rest of her food so she could get back to her lab. Except for the grub gruel.

That night, Azlin Rell dreamed of blood.

In his feverish mind, he was small enough to exist within a Nameless—to float within its blood vessels like some malignant corpuscle, or a microscopic pellet of poison. The pulse of the creature thunder-hummed all around him, a constant drumbeat urging him ever onward.

You will pay, he thought as he traversed the innards of the creature, ignoring the fact that it breathed and moved like any other living thing. *You will pay for what you did to me. You will suffer as I have suffered. I need your pain.*

Finally, the heart of the Nameless welled before him, fat and red as a sunset. Azlin imagined himself made of spikes and spears, ready to shred the flesh, loose a tide of blood, hear the Nameless scream one final time—

"Look, Azlin, look!" One of his crèche mates ran through the maze of Wookiee bridgeways—one that to them seemed the height of adventure, that would only in retrospect reveal itself as a sort of obstacle course built for children. "Can you do it? Bet you can't!"

He stood amid green trees and soft breezes, sunlight playing on his cheeks, a child once more. With a grin he called back, "Watch me!"

Azlin dashed after the young girl, forgetting his own timidity about heights as he leaped from rope bridge to rope bridge, laughing out loud. How nimble his friend was! The way she landed on a post on one foot, then rose on tiptoe—it had been as though she weighed no more than a feather. Although Azlin had never been granted any such grace, he was strong and agile enough to follow.

When finally he caught up to her, they had reached a net made out of vines that hung down like a curtain, pink and gold flowers bursting from the green here and there. Unsecured at the bottom, the net drifted and waved gently in the breeze. At the platform near its base, the Wookiees had set out treats—little curlicues made of sweet wroshyr sap hardened in ice. The candies had to be eaten quickly before they melted, because they were *soooooo* good.

"I'm going down the net," his friend said. What was her name again? He couldn't remember. He only knew that she had hair as pale and golden as sunshine. "Come on! Follow me!"

Azlin hesitated. The net stretched down so very far. It would not be impossible to fall, to miss the platform, and to tumble down to the forest floor and death. Yet she stood ahead of him, a ray of sunlight piercing the foliage to surround her in light, her smile urging him onward.

I could miss the platform, he told himself, but then he grinned and thought, *but I won't miss the candy!*

So he and the little girl—whose name he *must* know but could not recall—began clambering down, laughing as the net rippled in the breeze. Azlin watched her as he went, marveling at her ability to keep her balance and her courage. If she could do it, so could he!

She jumped down first and held up one piece of candy, beaming triumphantly, welcoming him forward—

Azlin awoke to darkness. He always awoke to darkness, of course, ever since excising his own eyes—but he could tell nighttime in other ways, too: the relative silence surrounding him, the cool touch of the air on his skin.

The dream was only that—a vision—for he remembered all his crèche mates, and the golden-haired child was not one of them. Why should he dream of a child he had never known? And why should she interrupt a dream in which he again got to take his revenge on one of the Nameless?

※

After releasing Avon back to her work, and as night darkened and the tiny insects of the trees began to chirp their evening songs, Reath knew the time had come to speak with Nan.

He went to her hut and rapped on the door. After only a short pause, Nan called back, "If this is about the grub gruel, no, I definitely have not changed my mind about having some, thank you."

Reath couldn't help laughing. "Trust me, I don't come bearing grub gruel."

Nan opened her door. She wore a loose white shift that, while modest enough, reminded Reath that this was in fact her night-gown. Yet the outline of her sentry bracelet beneath her shift's long wide sleeves reminded him of her status as a prisoner, and that was enough to keep the tone level.

She said, "Are you coming in or what?"

Reath went inside, walked past her, and sat on the one small stool in the corner. He had not fully reckoned with the fact that this would leave Nan to sit on her bed. His own mind remained correctly aligned, but he couldn't help feeling that if anyone else were to enter, he might have some explaining to do.

"I'm guessing this is about what happened with Mkampa during the search," Nan said.

"You would guess correctly," Reath said. "You played it off as an accident, right up until the moment you tried to kill her."

Nan swept her thick brown hair over one shoulder and began plaiting it. "She's a villainous Nihil scientist. She seems to be connected to the poisoning of an entire planet. You wouldn't consider that a capital crime?"

"No, nor would any of the other Jedi."

"There are plenty of star systems that would disagree," Nan said.

"You're not acting on behalf of those systems, are you?" Reath said. "You're doing this for Marchion Ro. You haven't left the Nihil; you're actually on a secret mission for him. Your job is to assassinate Dr. Mkampa."

Nan didn't directly reply. "So, let me get this straight. You trust the bizarre dark-sider former Jedi who murders Nameless with his bare hands, but *I'm* the security risk on this mission?"

She had a point. "Unfortunately, there's room for more than one security risk on this mission. If you're here to execute one of Ro's enemies for him—and using us as your transportation and your shield—you need to understand that we're not going to allow that to happen."

"You still think I'm following Ro's orders," Nan said, seemingly paying more attention to her hair than to Reath. "Let me ask you this. Do you still trust Avon, despite her previous ties to the Nihil and her lie about her identity?"

"Of course I do," Reath said.

Nan nodded. "You must find it believable, then, that a person might want to distance herself from the Nihil."

Reath sighed. "I find it very believable that Avon would. It's harder to believe that *you* would."

"Why is that?"

"Because—your deceit aboard the Amaxine station, the way you came after us as an enemy, even when we'd shown you nothing but help and friendliness—"

"I don't trust people as easily as you do," Nan said. "I don't think that means I'm untrustworthy. I think it means I have more common sense."

Enough of this, Reath decided. "Just tell me. Why are you trying to kill Mkampa?"

Nan's expression tightened. "How about this: After I've killed her, you'll get to hear the whole story."

Reath didn't leave the conversation there, but nothing he said mattered; he knew, even before Nan spoke that last sentence, that he would get no more information out of her that night.

He walked out of Nan's hut weary and discouraged. Thus far it seemed like they had accomplished little on this mission besides getting Amadeo hurt, confirming that the blight was unstoppable, and possibly transporting a Nihil assassin to her target. Reath rubbed the bridge of his nose and blinked hard; drowsiness had begun to overtake him. Maybe he needed to stop thinking for the day and get some rest. *Things won't look brighter tomorrow,* he thought, *but at least I won't be so tired.*

As he walked back toward his own hut, he saw that, a couple of levels below, many of the Wookiees were gathering together in one of their larger centers, a wide circular structure that hugged one of the massive wroshyr trees. Among them he glimpsed Kelnacca and Burryaga, the latter of whom looked up and spotted Reath in return. Burryaga simply gave him a brief nod before entering the gathering, which appeared to be rather large. If there was private Wookiee business underway, he had best leave them to it.

"Reath!" Azlin Rell called out, sending shudders along Reath's backbone. "Reath! Come here!"

Although at that moment Reath would have more gladly eaten tree-grub gruel, he went. Azlin stood at the door of his hut, shivering despite the warmth of the night. "Azlin. What's the matter?"

"Don't you feel it? The pull? The call? The cry?"

Oh, no. Whatever darkness it is that is so affecting Dez—Azlin feels it, too. That influence could not be good. "We know there's some . . . ah, source of the dark side here on Kashyyyk that is—"

"Not *that,*" Azlin scoffed. "I speak of the light. *Do you not feel the light?*"

TWENTY-FIVE

Azlin rocked back and forth, frustrated at the need to discuss this at all, frustrated at Reath's lack of comprehension, and—above all—frustrated that this was true.

He did not want or need a call to the light, and yet, it called.

"You're less afraid?" Reath said, not for the first time. "You've faced the Nameless, and you've emerged triumphant, and—"

"I'm not less afraid of them, and if you have the sense the Force gave a mynock, you're not any less afraid, either," Azlin shot back. "Are you, Reath? Less afraid, after you've felt one of them leach the Force from your very bones?"

"No," Reath quietly replied. "But if you aren't less afraid, how has darkness released its grip on you?"

"It hasn't." It wouldn't. Azlin had to believe that. Fear kept him safe. Anger kept him whole.

"Don't they take you on crèche journeys any longer?" Azlin's face was turned toward Amadeo Azzazzo, quite as though he were watching the Padawan, which in Amadeo's opinion was unnecessary. At least he was finally wearing his goggles again. "No enjoyable little trips for the younglings?"

"We had them sometimes," Amadeo said. He had come out to this walkway between the village huts this morning in the hope of practicing some lightsaber combat stances; the next time he faced the Drengir, he intended to be prepared. Instead, he had somehow wound up answering questions about the care and feeding of younglings. "One year we went to Jakku. Turns out there's not much there. At all. I don't know who picked that place or why, but it wasn't what you'd call enlightening. Mostly just very hot. Also dry."

"Sounds vile," Azlin said with relish. Amadeo sighed inwardly, thinking that at least *somebody* had gotten some enjoyment out of that trip to Jakku. "They brought us here to Kashyyyk, to spend a week among the Wookiees."

"Beats my crèche journey for sure," Amadeo agreed.

"With a century's experience, I can say—it seems to me that the Jedi Order isn't quite what it used to be," Azlin said. "They took more care, back in the day. They thought more deeply. They'd never have taken us to Jakku, of that I am certain."

Amadeo wanted to argue with this. The Jedi Order had

rarely, if ever, served the galaxy as tirelessly and valiantly as they had these past years of the Nihil conflict. Greater promise beckoned from a future free from the Nihil, if they could only reach it.

. . . but his crèche journey *had* been a trip to Jakku.

I shouldn't listen to this man, Amadeo thought. *He's deep in the dark side, and that's reason enough to turn and walk away. Except— except Reath brought Azlin on this mission. Reath's our mission leader. He knows what he's doing. If Reath thinks Azlin's worth listening to, then shouldn't I listen?*

Azlin leaned closer; Amadeo did his best to suppress a shudder as the man whispered, "You have sensed a destiny beyond the Jedi Order, have you not?"

"What do you mean?" Amadeo wondered if his stance work looked sloppier than he'd thought, before recalling that Azlin couldn't have seen it.

Still whispering, Azlin said, "You must have longed, sometimes, to be following your own path instead of forever answering to a master—"

"What do you think you're doing?" That was Cohmac Vitus, who must have been standing closer than Amadeo would've thought; it was a testament to Azlin's perverse magnetism that Amadeo hadn't been able to notice anyone else. Cohmac stepped between the two, his ire wholly directed at Azlin. "Corrupting young minds?"

"That, I leave to the Jedi," said Azlin.

"Hey." Another, sharper voice from behind jarred all three of them into turning toward Reath Silas, striding forward with

purpose. "Azlin, stop trying to undermine this mission and everyone on it. Amadeo, ignore him. Cohmac, I've got this."

Cohmac gave Reath a look that dangerously bordered on . . . hostility. Azlin wheeze-cackled as he wandered back to his hut. To Amadeo this seemed like a prime opportunity to mind his own business and be someplace else.

Reath and Cohmac came face to face. The irritation rising within Reath felt stronger than any he had known for a while, but he was determined to keep his voice, at least, under control. "I'm in charge of this mission," he said, "and that puts me in charge of Azlin."

"If you are in charge of him, then you must monitor him appropriately," Cohmac said. "Azlin Rell seems determined to make those around him uneasy. Given how recently Amadeo lost Mirro Lox, he is particularly vulnerable to the kind of manipulation that Azlin seems to enjoy."

"Amadeo's stronger than you give him credit for," Reath insisted. "The fact remains that I'm leading this mission, and that makes it my responsibility to keep the peace."

"It is all our responsibility to keep the peace," Cohmac said, "and I know that in your heart you have not forgotten that. You know this was no challenge to your authority. You are still angry with me, and this is how your anger has expressed itself."

Reath wanted to deny Cohmac's words, but he could not. "I apologize. I let that get to me when I shouldn't have. But . . . I thought I was over this. That we'd found peace about everything that transpired in our past."

"To some extent, we have," said Cohmac. "Yet when I left the way that I did—I know that I wounded you, Reath. The wounds of the spirit heal in their own time, and in their own way."

"I guess," Reath said. "Down deep, I know you had to fight your own demons, find your own way back to the Jedi Order and to the light. I've forgiven you. I'm moving on. But on the surface, where it barely matters—when it comes to pride or vanity—there, sometimes, the littlest things get under my skin. It's not how I should react, I know."

"There is no 'should' when it comes to such things," Cohmac said. "Forgiveness is not a linear process, Reath. It is not accomplished in one moment, immediate and complete. It grows between two people, over time. We have traveled far along the path together, you and I, but it is not so strange that the journey is not entirely complete. Forgiveness cannot be rushed."

"But it comes," Reath promised, and finally, Cohmac could smile.

In this moment, Reath realized, Cohmac had served as his teacher one last time, and the lesson was one of the most important he could have been taught: Small failures were not the destruction of progress. Sometimes they were what progress was made of.

❖

Dr. Mkampa's expertise covered many fields of science: botany, biology, chemistry, and such. Rarely had she had cause to dip into astrophysics, but recently she had taken it up. Unfortunately for the well-being of the galaxy at large, she possessed a mind more than sharp enough to grasp the concepts most important to her plans.

Different stars shone at different brightness, emitted numerous forms of radiation, produced light at varying wavelengths. The astute could learn much about a star by studying a plant for which it had been the life-giving sun (controlling for atmospheric and other planetary conditions, of course).

The star of the Drengir homeworld turned out to be rather unusual. Mkampa's first studies of Drengir samples had led her to believe that they had evolved beneath the light of a red supergiant, before she realized that the findings didn't quite match up. Instead, they seemed to have come from a world that orbited a rare sort of star indeed: a compact neutron star surrounded by a large, diffuse envelope of hydrogen. They looked just like red supergiants, but their spectra contained uniquely strong lithium and heavy-element lines. The Drengir had proved that they could thrive on many different kinds of worlds, even lie dormant for decades or centuries . . . but they would always have a powerful instinct that drew them to this unique form of light. How lucky, to find such specificity! Mkampa had not wasted it.

Broadcasting certain wavelengths in the direction of the Drengir affected them powerfully. The stronger those broadcasts, the more inescapably compelled the Drengir would be. Already she had managed to madden them past their truce with the Jedi and had drawn them all the way to Kashyyyk. Once she fine-tuned the process, there might be no limit to what she could force the Drengir to do. They would be her servants—her very deadly, nigh-unkillable servants in the darkness.

And when her search was complete, of course, her power over them, and over the galaxy, would be boundless.

�※

The *Vessel* crew had, throughout the journey to Kashyyyk, bunked on their ship. "The Wookiees are an obliging folk, bounteous in hospitality," Leox had said, "but that doesn't mean we should importune them unnecessarily. They'll be busy enough housing and feeding and bathing all the Jedi and scientists. We can take care of ourselves."

Affie had agreed, and they didn't even have to ask Geode, who would always prefer his own bed.

So they had spent most mornings, post-briefing, hanging out on the *Vessel*, taking care of maintenance, letting Affie catch up with Byne Guild business, and eating some of the snacks they had in stores that were most definitely *not* grub gruel. That didn't mean they weren't mingling with the Wookiees, however, or volunteering for tasks when they could—or noticing some of the undercurrents that went unspoken.

That morning, as they all tuned up the fuel field-balancing system, Leox said, "Do any of you have the distinct sense that the Wookiee leaders are . . . up to something?"

Affie frowned. "What do you mean? You don't trust them?"

"I'd trust just about any Wookiee farther than I'd trust the average human," Leox answered. "Theirs is an honest species, uncompromising in their nature and unwavering in their loyalty. But I feel like they're hiding something. Not something to hurt us or confuse us. Just . . . something they're not telling."

"Where are you getting that from?" Affie asked.

With a shrug, Leox said, "Last night, seems like there was some kind of late meeting. A whole lot of chitchat going on between the matriarchs and the other leaders of the village. And don't think *for one second* that I haven't noticed how quiet you've gotten, Geode."

Geode seemed to be taking a sudden, acute interest in the fuel gauges, or doing a very good job of pretending to. Leox and Affie shared a glance they'd shared before: *Geode knows more than he's telling.* But there was no getting him to open up before he was darned good and ready.

In a low voice, Leox added, "Something is most definitely and most decidedly *up.*"

Marchion Ro enjoyed having his slicers pull up recordings from various droids the Jedi had deployed to search for him, to see all the endless, useless wastes they had been forced to explore. How pleasant, to see a group of Jedi trudging through a foggy marshland, damp and discouraged, while Ro himself lolled on his couch, next to a dining table laden with dishes from across the galaxy, and feasted on the finest mussels the galaxy had to offer.

This was no exaggeration. Although Lina Soh would have said that the Republic stood together, unified, against the Nihil threat, at least a handful of planets had begun to hedge their bets. Among those was the planet Cato Neimoidia, which had sent Ro an entire cryovat of manax mead, "with compliments." Sibensko had offered up the mussels. These cowardly planets hoped to win mercy with beverages and *appetizers*? Republic people could be so very funny. He would, in the end, eradicate Cato Neimoidia and Sibensko if and when he wished. Until then, however, Ro intended to eat, and to enjoy himself.

Among his greatest pleasures was observing the progress of the blight on the affected planets. When those worlds lay within the heart of the Republic, Ro's worthless underlings were not always able to place a small satellite droid—but with Kashyyyk, they had succeeded. The pathetic furry brutes that lived there would never evacuate, it was said; Ro could not wait to watch them die.

He brought up the image of Kashyyyk, hoping to see a larger swath of gray. Instead, he saw a small blinking alert; further investigation revealed a distant image of one of his Spider Squalls, none of which he had ordered to the planet.

Who could have taken one of these from his fleet? No sooner had Ro asked himself this than he knew the answer: Dr. Mkampa. His pet mad scientist had finally gone too mad for her own good, it seemed.

Little pleased though he was to find her on Kashyyyk, ignoring the task he had given her, he found he was somewhat relieved, too. He had begun to believe that Mkampa was realizing the truth of the blight, and the lie of his so-called cure. But if she had suspected this, surely she would not have gone straight to the latest planet to be infected. No, she would have hurried far away.

Ro took another deep quaff of mead. If Mkampa did not doubt him, then why would she be on Kashyyyk?

Ghirra needed something to do besides calling for "strategy sessions" that turned out to be nothing more than her seeking reassurance in his bed. Let Ghirra bring the mad doctor back into line.

If she failed—he needed neither of them much anymore.

TWENTY-SIX

Wartime was difficult for most independent pilots, if not deadly, but it was an absolutely *fantastic* time to be a spice runner.

Captain Marot Luriel and his ship, the *Purrgil Wake*, had always had a knack for evading Republic patrols, even back in the days when those patrols didn't have nearly as much to do. Now that the Republic's resources were focused on Nihil attacks? The living was easy. The Nihil themselves didn't care much about small solo ships—sure, some of them were spice runners like himself, or carrying other valuables, but most weren't, and it wasn't worth the Nihil's time to try to tell the difference. So for now, Captain Luriel had the run of the galaxy.

And that wasn't even getting into the sharp rise in demand!

The *Purrgil Wake* didn't run the seriously hard stuff—Luriel considered himself less "amoral," more "keenly aware of market fluctuations." No, his specialty was death sticks: banned on many worlds, rendered hugely expensive by tariffs on others, but craved by shortsighted oxygen breathers everywhere. He skipped from world to world, purchasing them from unregulated markets, laying in stores of some premium brands, sometimes wrapping generic stuff in counterfeit packaging for the premium brands, then selling it all at a markup that guaranteed he had it made.

On this particular run, Captain Luriel was heading toward Pamarthe—a planet of hardy folk, some of whom took it all the way to *fool*hardy and thus thought they could smoke death sticks with impunity. This made Pamarthe one of his more reliably profitable runs. Even better, they knew how to mix a drink on Pamarthe. Just after exiting hyperspace at the edge of the star system, Luriel was lounging in his captain's chair, dreaming of his first glass of Port in a Storm, when the proximity alert began to blink red.

"Dammit," he muttered, sitting up straight. Pamarthe didn't have many patrols—the entire planet operated on the assumption that nobody was foolish enough to attack them, which was largely correct—but the few they had could be fierce. He might have to hide out amid the rings of one of the uninhabited outer planets, running on low power to look like just another bit of debris, until the heat was off.

But when he fixed instruments to take a look at what was happening, he realized that this situation was simultaneously not as bad as he'd feared and a whole lot worse.

The Pamarthe patrols were out, yes. They weren't out looking for him.

They were in battle with the Nihil.

Captain Luriel hesitated. The smartest thing to do was get out of this system before anybody saw him. (The Nihil might not target small independent ships, but that didn't mean they wouldn't sweep one up if it happened to get in their way.) But even running away might draw their attention. He studied the battle for a moment. It looked like a bigger cargo hauler headed for Pamarthe had been the original Nihil target, but the Pamarthe planetary patrols had responded, turning it into a larger fight. Now, if the Nihil won, they wouldn't satisfy themselves with just that hauler; no, they'd hit the planet surface hard. They'd meet fierce resistance, but bloodshed was certain.

And to Luriel's surprise, he realized he wanted to help.

That's ridiculous. How would you ever make a difference, in your little skimmer?

At that moment, as though he had been heard, an entire squadron of small skimmer ships appeared at the edge of the fight—lower-mass freighters, too, even a tug—a motley collection of vessels that had to belong to independent traders but one that had organized and acted as a team. They began hammering the Nihil hard, scattering their ships, upsetting their battle plan. Luriel watched, a grin dawning on his face. He might not be a fan of Republic rules, but he knew who the enemy was.

Almost without consciously deciding to do so, he pushed the *Purrgil Wake* forward, flying toward the battle. One particular

Nihil craft seemed to have taken a hard hit, if not hard enough to take it out of the fight. All it would take was a few blasts—

He fired. The blue bolts hit the Nihil craft dead center, and within seconds it exploded.

Over the comm came a message from one of the independent ships: *"Nice shooting!"*

"I try," Luriel replied. "Good job taking out the trash." By this point, the surviving Nihil had begun to scatter.

"Yeah, we make it our specialty."

Curiosity got the better of caution. "So how do a bunch of independent ships wind up taking on the Nihil?"

"Tell you what—let's meet up on Pamarthe and we'll buy you a drink and tell you about the Byne Guild."

This might be leading somewhere that involved risk—real danger—and scariest of all, actual commitment. But, *man*, had it felt good to blow that Nihil raider out of existence.

Captain Luriel grinned as he spoke into the comm. "Make that Port in a Storm, and you're on."

❧

On Kashyyyk, Affie Hollow learned about all this from the Byne Guild members' viewpoint around midday, and she wasn't sure she liked what she heard. "I don't know—we've taken on plenty of people who fly a little close to the regulatory edge—but an out-and-out spice runner?"

"Just death sticks," said the pilot on the other end, who sounded extremely hungover. "I mean, who cares if he's running death sticks?"

"Not me," Affie admitted, "but this is where the phrase 'slippery slope' comes into play."

Leox Gyasi, who sat beside her in the cockpit, munching on ribbonfruit, said, "Maybe during wartime we don't worry too much about how slippery the slopes are going to get. You ask me, any help against the Nihil is worth having."

What happened when the war ended, though? Affie sighed and decided she'd worry about that once peace returned. "We can bring the *Purrgil Wake* in, but on a provisional basis only. We're not admitting this guy as a full member right away—but we'll defend him if he defends us."

As soon as the communication ended, she turned to Leox, expecting him to hold forth on what he'd just heard. Instead, his gaze remained fixed on the distant treetops of the village. From their docking platform they could see the general outline of what was going on, including a small mass of Wookiees deep in discussion . . . which seemed to include all the Wookiee Jedi.

"You think that's about whatever secret the Wookiees are keeping?" Affie asked. "The one Geode's in on?"

"Note that our mineral-based navigator is mysteriously absent from the *Vessel* at this time," Leox pointed out.

With a start, Affie realized he was right; Geode sometimes became so quiet that it was easy to forget he was, or wasn't, present. "Okay, seriously, what's going on?"

Through a mouthful of ribbonfruit, Leox said, "I have a feeling it won't be long before we find out."

Reath Silas would have taken note of Geode's absence from the village—and that of several of the Wookiee leaders—had he not been deep in conference with Azlin Rell.

Though Azlin had not realized, Reath had in fact been deeply intrigued by his assertions that both a dark and a light form of the Force were at work on Kashyyyk, and powerfully so. In fact, it made a great deal of sense. There had been moments when he had sensed a low, ominous undercurrent of darkness, and yet this had never grown more powerful or more dominant. Something was counteracting the dark, but what?

"Your bonds to the dark side should allow you to sense the Drengir," Reath said. "Do you think the Drengir are connected to these phenomena in any way?"

"I know of the Drengir, and they know of me."

Determined though Reath remained to work with Azlin, this was difficult to hear. "You mean you could have warned us earlier and simply chose not to?"

Azlin shrugged. "Bygones. Suffice it to say, the powerful tides at work within the Force on this planet are far beyond the strength of the mere Drengir. I imagine they can feel it, but they're no more in control of it than we are."

Reath tried to keep himself centered rather than giving in to frustration. "If you understand the Drengir so well, do you also know how Dr. Mkampa summoned them here?"

It took a moment to recognize the expression on Azlin's face as thoughtfulness. Although Azlin Rell remained aligned with darkness, remained eager to upset and undermine those around him whenever possible, he had at least become less crazed, more rational. Reath hadn't heard that lullaby once today. Was it possible that Azlin was actually . . . trying? Did the benign influence of this other power within the Force actually hold sway over the darkness that had imprisoned this man for so long?

"I don't understand the means she is using," Azlin finally said. "Not yet."

"So she's *not* using the dark side of the Force to summon them."

"How would she? According to you, she's a mad scientist, not some Sith Lord from five thousand years ago." Azlin cackled with contempt before settling down again. "No, it's not that. But whatever method she has used to call them, I can feel the pull it exerts upon the Drengir, and it is a powerful one. More Drengir beyond these may arrive, if they can."

"Luckily for us they're not great with technology," said Reath. "So I'm not too worried about that. Still, Azlin, if you can feel the same call that Dr. Mkampa is using, could you possibly track it? We need to track down her Spider Squall lab, and sooner rather than later."

If Azlin cared about others, he gave no sign—yet it seemed to Reath that if they'd had this same conversation a week ago, Azlin would have angrily denounced the idea that he might be concerned for the various planets and peoples of the galaxy. Even silence suggested progress.

We're getting somewhere, Reath thought, and he grinned.

Azlin opened his mouth to speak, but in that same instant,

one of the great signal horns of the Wookiees sounded. Then another.

Reath knew a summons when he heard one.

Avon Starros would've ignored the horns, no matter how many or how loudly they blew, had she not just set her Drengir samples in an infrared chamber for an exposure test that would take at least half an hour. Whatever the Wookiees had to say would at least keep her mind occupied during the test's run time, so she quickly put on a fresh shirt and headed out into the Wookiee village.

There, all the non-Wookiees had begun to gather. Geode, it seemed, had been standing there for a while, as Nevakka and several other Wookiee children had already formed a ring around him; Cohmac, Amadeo, and Dez were walking up to the central hearth cauldron, murmuring to each other as to what it all might mean, with Affie and Leox not far behind them.

It was the elder Pruzzalla who climbed atop the speaking dais, her yowls loud enough to carry to the ears of one and all. The visitors had noted the most recent, strangest development of the blight—its sharp turn toward the east. No doubt they had also noticed that this news troubled their Wookiee hosts greatly. It had taken them a while to decide if the outsiders could be trusted with this, which the Jedi must not consider a sign of distrust; this information was sacred, perhaps the most sacred in all of Wookiee belief, and they did not speak of it lightly even among themselves.

Avon hadn't thought of the Wookiees as possessing a spirituality that had canon, secrets, and the like; she'd seen it as something simpler, sweeter, forest-based. Her cheeks flushed amid the realization that she had unconsciously been condescending to them.

"What is this truth?" Reath said, speaking for the group. "I promise you, all of you, that this information will be treated with absolute secrecy, delicacy, and respect."

Pruzzalla sighed, then took the woven headband from her forehead. In the center of the complex braid was an enormous opal of meryx, one of the most precious jewels in the galaxy—valued not only for its iridescent beauty but also for its rarity. There was no need for her to tell anyone present what it was; meryx was a synonym for luxury and elegance across the galaxy, and had been for many hundreds of years. Pruzzalla explained that meryx was amber from the long-extinct white wroshyr trees of Kashyyyk, the last of them dead for more than three millennia . . . or so everyone believed.

"They're still alive," Avon breathed, not realizing she had spoken aloud until others turned to look at her. "The white wroshyr trees. They still exist?"

Only a small grove survived, Pruzzalla confirmed, and on a planet where every tree was sacred, these were the most sacred of all. The secrecy surrounding their existence was partly to protect the white wroshyr trees from those who would have attempted to harvest their sap and synthesize new meryx jewels—but mostly, she confirmed with a growl, because the sacredness of this grove was so very great, so pure, that its existence had never before been shared with offworlders. The white wroshyr grove represented the very heart of the Wookiee religion, the core of the Great Forest. It was among the white wroshyr trees that the Wookiees knew themselves to be closest to the presence of the living Force.

And the white wroshyr grove lay to the east.

Avon cried out in dismay, just as several of the Wookiees moaned and whined in distress. The terrible realization was written on every face, but it was Reath who said the worst aloud: "That's what the blight is drawn to. It's headed for the white wroshyr grove."

Pruzzalla confirmed this, then added that to the Wookiees, this was as good as a knife held to the heart of Kashyyyk itself.

"I am so sorry," Reath said to Pruzzalla, holding out a compassionate hand. "We will fight the blight as hard as we can. Our meditation team will—"

Burryaga growled, telling them all that this was only half the problem. It was Avon herself who blurted out, "What's the other half?"

It was not only a question of the white wroshyr trees themselves, Pruzzalla said. They had also to consider the other part of their secret—namely, the danger that the white wroshyr trees protected them from.

The danger that now appeared destined to be freed.

TWENTY-SEVEN

Every member of the Jedi mission heard Pruzzalla's words with dismay—but for Dez Rydan, there was also a solid, almost tangible pulse within his chest that said, *I was right.*

Ever since arriving on Kashyyyk, he'd felt darkness haunting him. He'd attributed it to the Drengir, to the blight, and worst of all—most of all—to himself, believing it to be evidence that three years of the Barash Vow had been insufficient to cleanse him of the dark side of the Force that had taken such a terrible hold on the Amaxine station. But it wasn't true. Something else here had been affecting him. The darkness had been on Kashyyyk the whole time—not within him.

In the brief moment it took Dez to process this revelation,

Reath stepped forward. "What danger are you referring to, Pruzzalla?"

The Wookiee matriarch explained that they called it the Well of Night, but this name came from deep, ancient legend first told hundreds of generations ago. (*On Kashyyyk,* Dez thought, *that means thousands and thousands of years.*) No one knew when the darkness had arrived, only that it *had arrived*—it was not native to this planet. The only other truth they understood of the Well of Night was that the white wroshyr grove contained it. When the other white wroshyr trees had decided that it was time to go extinct, to allow their younger wroshyr cousins to inherit Kashyyyk in their turn, this grove had chosen to remain in order to continue their guardianship of the Well.

Dez and Cohmac exchanged glances. Under his breath, Dez said, "I never heard of a species choosing to go extinct before."

Just as quietly, Cohmac replied, "On Kashyyyk, it seems anything may be possible."

But it was Reath who made the leap. "If the blight destroys the white wroshyr grove, then the Well of Night—nothing will be holding it back. That darkness may even be calling the blight to it, attempting to set itself free."

"But what darkness?" ventured Avon Starros. "Like—a living thing? An object? Another phenomenon like the blight?"

"We have to find out," Dez said. This masked evil had made him second-guess himself, as though it had been laughing at him from the shadows. He was tired of shadows. Time to shine a light.

His eyes met Reath's. It was Reath's place, as mission leader, to request this—but no persuasion was necessary. Reath immediately asked, "Pruzzalla, you've trusted us enough to tell us of your sacred grove. May we ask you to extend that trust and take us there?"

Pruzzalla nodded, explaining that they had always intended to do so. The Wookiee Jedi themselves had asked to lead their party to the white wroshyr grove.

Dez realized immediately that Burryaga and Kelnacca had been waiting for this; they had to have known all along. (He also suspected Geode's inscrutable expression was concealing a definite lack of surprise.) No sooner had Pruzalla finished speaking than Kelnacca sprang for the nearest tree. Were they meant to follow? But Burryaga growled that Kelnacca was arranging their transportation. Dez peered after Kelnacca, who was already clambering higher; it was startling to see how high Wookiees could jump, how much more quickly they could climb when they weren't holding themselves back to accommodate non-arboreal species.

"Is everyone ready?" Reath said, glancing around the party. "We have no idea what we're about to encounter, which is why I'd like as many people as possible to come along. That includes your crew, Affie, if you're willing. There's no telling whose experience or insight might help us make sense of what we're about to see."

Affie looked at her colleagues. Geode's eagerness was apparent to all, and Leox nodded. "Not that I am exactly 'looking forward' to encountering something called the 'Well of Night,'" he drawled, "but the need is great, and the spirit is willing."

"What about us?" someone called from high above—Nan, Dez realized with a start. "We have experience and insight!"

Azlin Rell shouted, "This Well of Night—bring me there!"

"I don't think you were supposed to hear any of this!" Reath called back.

"Then maybe don't discuss everything out in the open!" Nan replied.

Dez had to admit, she had a point.

But Reath would not be so evenly swayed. "You two are both staying here."

"Tell me all about it later—if you survive," Azlin said.

"Um, everyone?" Avon Starros seemed unusually timid. "What exactly do they mean by our 'transportation'?"

At that moment Dez heard a deep, echoing yowl from much, much too close by. Then came the sound of tree branches creaking under immense weight, and each creak was nearer than the last.

Gently, Burryaga told them not to worry—they would love traveling by mylaya steeds. It was time for them to behold the last living white wroshyr trees, to see the greatest treasure, and true soul, of Kashyyyk—and to discover whatever it was those trees had contained for so many years.

※※

Burryaga had undertaken many thrilling adventures as a Jedi, had defied death in a dozen different ways—but he still believed almost nothing in the galaxy was as exhilarating as riding a mylaya steed. All the agility of a tooka cat, all the size of a mudhorn, all the power of a dozen Wookiees—they were the perfect creatures to move swiftly through the great forests of Kashyyyk.

He gripped the reins as his mylaya leaped from one tree to another, soaring over the wide gaps between the wroshyr trees. The mylaya's feline claws speared the outer bark, sending a fine spray of splinters through the air. Then the mylaya began climbing upward at astonishing speed, though to Burryaga's mind it was still not fast enough. With the fate of the white wroshyr grove at stake, no velocity could match the urgency he felt.

As the group leaped into another tree, Burryaga heard the human members of the party shout out in understandable delight. Then, glancing behind him, he got a glimpse of Reath's wide eyes and realized those shouts might not have been motivated by delight. In fact, the sounds might have been more accurately described as shrieks. But the humans were all holding on, and that was enough.

From a nearby branch, another mylaya came into view, this one ridden by Kelnacca. Burryaga roared to him, a mighty yell of comradeship and shared purpose—Wookiee Jedi to Wookiee Jedi, joined in creed and in mission. Kelnacca's answering roar was even louder, one that echoed off the trees.

As Burryaga had known they would, the mylaya steeds instinctively began to travel lower and lower through the trees as they approached the area of the white wroshyr grove. When they were perhaps half a klick away, they finally dropped to the ground, slowing their stride until they came to a stop.

"Are we here?" called Reath. "I really hope we're here." Like the other human Jedi, he looked rather windblown, perhaps shaken, but otherwise no worse for wear after their mylaya ride. Affie Hollow was another story: She knelt down, then lowered her forehead to the ground as though swearing allegiance to it. Avon Starros had turned slightly green, and her steps were wobbly. Geode remained stoic, but Leox Gyasi was grinning. Burryaga silently decided that, assuming they all survived this mission, he'd have to get to know Leox better. A human who could properly appreciate a mylaya ride was hard to find.

Kelnacca was the one who informed Reath that they were very near the white wroshyr grove but would have to make the rest of the journey on foot. The mylayas could sense the white wroshyr trees and instinctively kept their distance from a lifeform so much larger than themselves.

"Walking sounds good," said Cohmac. Next to him, Reath nodded a little too quickly.

Burryaga concealed his amusement, but it was short-lived. Nothing could long eclipse the threat to the trees, and the dread of discovering what lay beneath them.

❦

I have to admit, Affie thought as they walked on through the woods, *living on a planet has its charms.* Kashyyyk's natural beauty—in every aspect, from sight to scent to the sound of the birds trilling in the trees—filled her soul in a way that reminded her that her ancestors for countless generations had lived on planets of their own, had felt close to soil and sun. She intended never to give up her own place in the stars, but these days on Kashyyyk had taught her for the first time why so many chose never to leave their homeworlds, at least not for long.

Or maybe she was just really, really grateful to be standing on solid ground again after the wild mylaya ride. Her legs still shook beneath her, yet she'd rarely been happier to walk.

Their path had taken them up a gently sloping hill for several minutes, and Affie was beginning to feel how steep it really was via the burning of her calf muscles. Burryaga roared in encouragement as he gestured for all the group to follow him toward the ridge that lay a dozen or so meters ahead.

Affie did as he asked, though by now they were less walking, more climbing, making their way up a sharper ridge. Once she put her hand out to brace herself against a tree trunk and just in time saw that it was occupied by a woolly brown arachnid with a diameter larger than her own head. Lohgarra's warnings about the many fatally dangerous life-forms on Kashyyyk flooded Affie's mind, but after the mylaya ride, she seemed to be immune to fear. Besides, if Burryaga and Kelnacca weren't worried, she had to assume there was no need for her to be, either.

And perhaps they didn't have much farther to go. She realized that, beneath the sounds of feet tromping through the thick carpet of decaying leaves, she could hear the soft bubbly sound of running water over rocks.

They all clambered up the ridge, each one falling completely silent as they were finally able to take in the view for themselves. Here, a river flowed through the forest, ridged by high banks on either side. Though she could not tell how deep the river was, she could tell by the white foam along the edges and a few stray twigs and leaves caught up in the eddies that the current running through it was both very fast and very strong; also, the river was tremendously wide, perhaps fully half a klick. In the middle of that river, the currents had formed a small island, one the size of a ten-craft hangar, no more.

On that island grew the white wroshyr trees.

Their leaves were as green as those of any other tree on Kashyyyk, only slightly paler; no doubt the grove didn't look unusual from above. However, these trees' trunks and limbs were covered with snow-pale bark, and when shafts of light played on that bark, Affie glimpsed a faint iridescent sheen. It was as though the trees had been carved from the very meryx jewels derived from their sap. Not only were they breathtakingly beautiful, but the trees also had a distinct sense of presence. *As though,* Affie thought, *when you look at them, they look back.*

The island was not wholly isolated within the river, she realized. A low stone bridge connected the island to the bank. Burryaga explained to them all that, during certain rare religious ceremonies and of course on Life Day, the Wookiees would cross this bridge to commune with the great trees. Most of the year, they were content merely to behold the six surviving white wroshyr trees, the speakers to their souls—and to leave untroubled what lay beneath them.

"Beholding them ought to be enough for anyone," Reath said. "Burry, they're amazing."

Burryaga gave him a sharp-toothed Wookiee smile, and for a

moment Affie allowed herself to simply feel gratitude for the gift of seeing something so rare and priceless.

"But we can't actually just behold them," Avon said. "We have to investigate. How do we do that respectfully?"

The trees would understand their intentions, Burryaga insisted. All they had to do was follow him to the island.

※

As they made their way along the slim stone bridge leading to the white wroshyr grove, Reath expected to feel the undercurrent of darkness far more sharply—yet he did not. *We're closer to the Well of Night,* he realized, *but we're also closer to the white wroshyr grove. These trees must be incredibly powerful in the Force to mask and contain the dark side so well.*

The grove itself was even more beautiful than he had expected it to be from the riverbank. Long branches of pale leaves formed an arched ceiling overhead that reminded him of ancient temples he had seen; the rich, loamy scent of Kashyyyk became somehow even more fragrant here, nearly perfumed. The soft, mossy ground made every step feel almost like a bounce. Reath thought he might have wanted to stay here forever . . . were it not for what he spotted ahead.

Over the millennia, the roots of the trees had grown thick and long, dipping in and out of the ground in massive tangled knots. In the center of the grove, those knots formed almost a wall circling what appeared to be a sort of pit or cavern. Now, at last, Reath began to feel the dark side more strongly, a kind of tension all along his nerves, but the presence of the wroshyr trees gave him comfort.

He glanced over at Dez. "Are you okay?"

Dez nodded but said, "I might stand guard outside, if that's all right with you." Geode's appearance at Dez's side indicated that he had volunteered for this duty, as well.

"Great," Reath said. "Everyone else? We're going in."

Squeezing through the thickly interwoven roots—some thicker than his torso—took Reath a few moments; the Wookiees found it tougher going. But within moments, they all stood at the mouth of the Well of Night. Reath braced himself against the roots to climb down into it. To his surprise, the Well was only a few meters deep and was not substantially wider than its opening. Yet along one wall he saw small glints against a hard surface—rock of some sort but incredibly shiny, not black but the absolute darkest shade of purple. He realized that deep, deep within, the rock seemed to glow.

Avon whispered, "Is it some kind of crystal?"

"I think so," said Reath. *Could it be an Echo Stone?* he wondered, before rejecting the thought; the two gems shared the same color, and may be related, but their energy felt completely different. He activated his lightsaber for illumination, which cast dim green light through the entire Well. The crystal was revealed—nearly the size of a Padawan's bedroom in the Jedi Temple, if the side embedded in the ground was of similar dimensions to the side exposed. Its dull purple glow felt unmistakably malevolent, almost sentient. *The mirror of the trees above,* he thought.

Leox Gyasi dropped down beside them. "Why do I feel like that thing doesn't like me?"

"It doesn't like anyone," Reath said. "Are those *carvings*?"

Avon nodded. "I think so—the crystal's been etched with symbols, maybe images—"

Reath stepped closer and saw, carved within the crystal, only slightly softened by time, four faces of four different species.

And he had seen those faces before.

"By the Force," he whispered. "This is a Sith artifact. This is a *Thornseed*."

TWENTY-EIGHT

"Where *can* the Thornseed be?" Dr. Mkampa smacked the wall of the *Firebringer*, after yet another set of scans had come up empty. "Where would they have placed it? Why can't we find it?"

Her droids could only watch as she paced restlessly through the Spider Squall, muttering curses in a few languages. She wondered whether she would have to wait for the blight to destroy this entire area of the Kashyyyk forest, presumably laying the Thornseed bare. But the blight would then consume the Thornseed, too.

The Sith holocron she'd found had given her information about the Thornseed and its tremendous capabilities—but that information did not extend to any explanation of which sites

were more potent and powerful, and certainly it made no refer-
ence to the blight. There was nothing to be done but to continue
the search.

Mkampa set new parameters and activated another set of
scans. For the next many minutes, she would have nothing more
to do here on Kashyyyk—so perhaps it was time to take advantage of the few useful things she had learned on this planet thus
far. "Open communications with the *Gaze Electric*. Dr. Mkampa
for Ghirra Starros."

It took several minutes for Starros to appear, and when she
did, her holo revealed her to be disheveled. "Dr. Mkampa. What
can you possibly want?"

"Forgive me. I had not thought it would be the middle of a
night cycle aboard your ship. Do not tell me I have disturbed the
sleep of our lord, as well?"

"You haven't," Starros said. Apparently she didn't wish to
betray what anyone remotely close to Ro's inner circle had long
known, which was that Ro spent many of his nights elsewhere.
All Mkampa had needed to learn was whether Marchion Ro was
in Starros's chamber, and he was not. Excellent. Starros snapped,
"Is this about a potential test site? If so, honestly, that could have
waited a few hours until—"

"This has nothing to do with any test site," Mkampa said. "It
has to do with the location of some of the Eye's many storehouses
of riches. For all his talk about distrusting the Republic, the banking guilds, all of that, he's taken advantage of the sophisticated
ways in which they hide their money, hasn't he? At this point, Ro
must be hoarding so much plunder that he would never miss, oh,

a few million credits here or there. Wouldn't it make more sense to distribute that wealth more widely? For instance, to me?"

Ghirra Starros stared at her, incredulous. "I can't be understanding you correctly. Do you expect me to ask Ro to give you millions of credits for services rendered? Because those are no less than what the Eye of the Storm should be able to expect from any among the Nihil."

"No, you do *not* understand me correctly. Ro would never pay me such riches from his own pocket. That's why you'll have to steal them for me."

"Why would I do that?" Starros snapped.

"Because if you do not, I'll be forced to send my enforcer droids out to eliminate this one." Mkampa sent over the images of young Avon Starros taken during her one confrontation with the Jedi mission. Hopefully her mother would not identify which planet they were all on—that could lead to complications—but Mkampa was gambling that whatever vestiges of maternal instinct remained within Ghirra Starros would carry the day.

"Avon," breathed Starros. "You haven't hurt her?"

"Not yet, but I can, and I will unless properly compensated for my restraint. Let us say five million? Little enough that I doubt Ro will miss it at this point in his highly successful career of plundering—but enough for me to make my own destiny elsewhere."

Ghirra Starros was clearly furious, yet even more frightened. "What do you expect me to do? Meet you under a bridge on some Outer Rim planet, hand over bags of money?"

"Don't be ridiculous. You couldn't carry five million in bags. No, all I ask is that you send me the appropriate account and authorization codes that will allow me to withdraw the funds myself. If the accounts you send me provide slightly over or under five million, I completely understand. It's sensitive information, and were Ro ever to find out—well. Better not to talk about that possibility, isn't it? And make sure that the amount isn't too far under five million, or I will have to see to it that your daughter never leaves this planet alive."

"Don't—Wait, surely there's something else I could—"

"Five million. You have twenty hours. Farewell." Mkampa lifted one hand to wave goodbye, her shiny green fingernails tearing small ripples in Ghirra Starros's holo in the instant before she cut communication.

She had either just made herself a great deal richer or developed an excellent excuse for blasting the Starros girl to atoms. Either way, Mkampa decided, it was a wonderful use of her downtime.

※

Leox Gyasi said what everyone, including Avon, was thinking: "What the blazes is a Thornseed?"

"An ancient Sith artifact," said Reath as he paced back and forth, gazing up at the gigantic crystal as the glow from his lightsaber lit each facet and carving in turn. Burryaga dropped down to join them, then whined in both wonder and dismay. Apparently Reath was too fascinated to notice as he continued speaking:

"Essentially, a Thornseed had the power to turn plant life to the dark side. The Sith could embed one into a planet, and within a short amount of time, all the flora in a wide area—even a continent, sometimes—would be irrevocably turned to darkness."

Avon gaped. "You mean, the plants would get up and attack people?"

Reath shook his head. "Nothing that dramatic, at least not so far as I know. But the Sith—this was an ancient empire led by dark side Force users, by the way, long extinct—the Sith could then harvest deadly poisons and toxins from those plants. They could use it to devastate a planet's crops, to cause famine and starvation. According to the lore, apparently they would sometimes lure opponents into battles on terrain corrupted by a Thornseed, giving themselves an advantage—particularly against any Jedi, who would be strongly affected by such a powerful presence of the dark side."

"If all this happened thousands of years ago and the people who used them aren't even around any longer," Leox said, "how do you know about all this?"

Reath turned around with the biggest grin Avon had ever seen on his face. "I know about Thornseeds because I read about them in the Archives." He laughed out loud in what seemed to Avon like triumph. "Adventures are all well and good, but in the end, there's no substitute for *research*! While my friends were playing wrestling and gymnastics games, I was holed up in the Archives, and one of the records I wound up studying for months was on crystallography and gemology as they related to the Force. I never thought about whether or not I'd need to use that information someday—I just wanted to know it, for the joy of knowing. *You* understand, Avon."

She would treasure that comment in days to come, but at the moment, an idea was beginning to bubble in her mind, one that felt important to tease out.

By this point, Cohmac Vitus and Affie Hollow had joined them in the Well of Night. Affie hung back, clearly awed by the size and strange glow of the Thornseed, but Cohmac went to Reath's side. "The faces," he murmured. "The ones carved into the crystal—they're the faces of the idols we found on the Amaxine station."

Reath nodded. "The ones that kept the Drengir dormant."

The moment Reath said the word *Drengir*, Avon understood the connection she'd made, as well as the more important one she might be about to discover. "So," she said, "obviously this is a very dangerous crystal, but the white wroshyr trees have kept it from having any effect on Kashyyyk, right? They keep it in stasis?"

"They must," Reath said. He looked up to the pale leaves so very far overhead, dappled with the sunlight that could not penetrate the Well of Night. "Their power in the Force must be even greater than I'd imagined." Burryaga growled his assent.

Avon took a deep breath. "In that case, do you think it's safe if I take a very, very small sample of the crystal material? Or would even a small sample be super evil? Or just a little bit evil?"

"An evil rock," muttered Affie. "Geode's not gonna like the sound of this."

Reath, Cohmac, and Burryaga exchanged glances. Leox asked, "Was that information in that record you studied?"

"Not explicitly," Reath said, "but if I remember correctly, and I think I do, a very small shard ought to be safe. The main thing is not to threaten the structural integrity of the Thornseed unless and until we can destroy it completely. If we merely damage it, while leaving it whole—make no mistake, the dark side *will* lash back at us, violently."

Avon wasn't sure what he meant by that, and she profoundly hoped she would never have to know. "Okay. I've worked with crystals in labs before. Let me take a crack at it."

She went up to the very surface of the Thornseed. Somehow its glow seemed brighter up close; the multifaceted translucence shifted in the light from Reath's lightsaber, appearing nearly alive. Avon told herself not to be silly. It was important to concentrate, especially because she didn't have the ideal tools for crystal sampling in her pack. But she had something that would work as a chisel, and a suspensor-field tube. Hopefully that would work. "I don't suppose you remember any specific mineral densities from that record, do you, Reath?"

"That's more detail than I recall," he answered. "I've been focused on the Echo Stones and their connection to the Nameless and the blight, not ancient Sith artifacts."

Cohmac stepped forward. "Thornseeds were thought to have been made from different types of crystals, though we don't know for sure," he said. "What mattered more than the exact mineralogy was the darkness infused into them by the Sith."

"Infused darkness," Avon muttered as she angled her tools just so. This particular little outcropping seemed more fragile—one of the few spots on the Thornseed that showed any sign of the artifact's incredible age—

She delivered one hard, decisive tap. A crack forked through this tiny piece of gem—like pale lightning—before the fragment of crystal fell into her tube. Before Avon could celebrate, the Thornseed momentarily glowed brighter behind the eyes of the idols, as though they were glaring down at her.

"Okay, that was off-the-charts creepy," said Affie. Nobody argued. "Can we get out of here?"

Burryaga growled that this was an excellent idea, the best he'd heard in a while, and they should follow her suggestion *right now*.

So they all set out for the village, leaving the Well of Night and walking back across the stone bridge toward the massive mylaya steeds that would bear them the rest of the way. Avon hardly saw any of it. All she could think about was the sliver of evil she carried with her.

TWENTY-NINE

For a man with *thousands of discontented under-lings and the entire Jedi Order searching for him,* thought Ghirra Starros, *Marchion Ro sleeps far too well.*

He lay sprawled across his bed, still on his back, face tilted toward her but unseeing—at the moment. His mask sat dark and empty across the room. His posture left little space for Ghirra, who generally curled into a ball on the edge of the mattress and wondered how to best bring up the subject of perhaps fitting his cabin with slightly larger sleeping accommodations.

Tonight, however, she was glad for the depth of his slumber.

Silently she rose and slipped on a wrap that could feasibly be worn in the corridors of the *Gaze Electric* but could also simply serve as a warmer layer over a nightgown. Ghirra ran her fingers through her hair so it would not look so obviously disheveled. Then, holding her breath, she stepped out of the bedchamber, then into the corridor beyond.

Go, she told herself. It would not do to run—that would attract too much attention—but time was short. She could not count on Marchion remaining sound asleep for too long, and besides, her twenty hours were almost up.

Avon's twenty hours.

When she reached the most secure data area, Ghirra straightened herself more, in case anyone was inside. Unlikely—not even five people aboard the *Gaze Electric* had access—but not impossible. She was almost dizzy with fright as the doors slid open, and she breathed out a sigh that was half a sob once she realized she was alone.

Banking information: not difficult to find, mostly because Ghirra was the one who had told Marchion how many more possibilities existed for storing one's money, and just how creative and lucrative such possibilities could be. Secret accounts had proved a revelation for a Nihil raider who had once kept most of his wealth in a single vault. Yet she lost precious seconds typing in the codes, simply because her fingers trembled so.

Of course she feared being pushed out of an airlock. Worse by far, however, was the prospect of anything happening to Avon. Ghirra knew Dr. Mkampa too well to believe that the threat to her daughter was idle; she also knew that if Mkampa could ensure that Avon's death was not a merciful one, she would. It would be just like that demonic scientist to send Ghirra the recording of some ghastly, torturous—

Stop it, she told herself before taking a few deep breaths. *Avon will be safe, as long as you get this done.*

Within another two minutes, Ghirra had the information on a datacard, tucked that solid into her pocket, and hurried out of the data center. Her nerves still jangled, but less with every step she took. The hard part was over. All she had to do now was find an isolated transmission—

She gasped as she turned a corner and nearly ran bodily into Thaya Ferr.

"Good evening," Ferr said, as cool and calm as if they were on the bridge conducting business. "I wouldn't have expected you to be up at this hour."

It took all Ghirra's political training to steady her voice. "Insomnia. Happens to the best of us. I thought a quick walk might help me clear my mind."

"An excellent idea," said Ferr. "Rest well." With that, Ferr continued walking on her way.

Ghirra resumed her own journey, but she was even more frightened than before. Thaya Ferr hadn't been walking off her insomnia; she had been dressed as normal, carrying around a datapad, apparently still taking care of Ro's business. (Did the woman not sleep?) They had not encountered each other so close to the secure area that Ferr would necessarily know or assume that Ghirra had been there—but close enough to it that Ghirra could not be certain Ferr wouldn't guess.

And if Thaya Ferr guessed the truth, even thought Ghirra's presence in that area to be remotely likely, that information would be reported to Marchion Ro.

The only way to absolutely save herself, Ghirra knew, was to destroy the datacard and transmit nothing. To accept no future communications of any kind from Mkampa. To trust that, whatever Avon was doing, she could either take care of herself or rely on the Jedi to help her. In short, to wash her hands of her daughter.

Ghirra had to think it over. She was not proud of this. The various possibilities played themselves out in her head for the several moments it took her to get to a potential point of transmission, and then for several moments longer as she stood there, panting, trembling, frozen.

Then she jammed the datacard in, input the codes for Mkampa, and sent it.

If this was the end of her—at least it wouldn't be the end of Avon.

∆|∆

Mkampa's comms aboard the Spider Squall *Firebringer* immediately chimed to inform her of a new message, but she paid it no mind. Something far more fascinating had appeared on her scans only moments before. A brief energy surge within her search area—too close to the blight for comfort—was smaller than she would have expected but bore the exact wavelength signatures the holocron had cited.

"Who has found my Thornseed?" Mkampa murmured. Whoever it was, they hadn't taken it with them; now that she'd spotted it, she could trace its location easily enough. It remained very much in place on a small island within a river. Certainly the finder hadn't possessed a clue about the potential of what they'd found, or else they would not have contented themselves with generating such a brief, modest spark of energy. Not when the Thornseed was capable of so much more.

Soon she would be able to retrieve it for herself, and after that, the possibilities were endless. Digging it out and securing it safely might take time, forever. Best to ensure that her work would remain uninterrupted.

Grinning, Dr. Mkampa moved to her sunlight generator, the one attuned to the native star of the Drengir. "Let's make them very, very angry," she whispered, "then point them straight at the Jedi."

◈

Avon Starros hadn't slept particularly well the night before. Her dreams were filled with eerie carved faces, glowing dull violet, angry at her for wounding them; every few hours, she would startle awake from yet another vision of them. Waking was worse, though, because it reminded her that this wasn't just a dream. There was every chance the Thornseed really felt anger, that it directed its malevolence toward her, and that—if the blight reached the white wroshyr grove before it descended into the Well of Night—that malevolence could be unleashed. So, around dawn, she had given up on the whole idea of rest. Instead, Avon went to her lab table and worked on analyzing the shard of crystal she had chipped from the Thornseed's surface.

The first studies she'd run, the previous evening, were basic crystallographic studies. To gauge by its hardness, density, and rhombohedral crystalline structure, Avon would assess the material of the Thornseed to be similar in many respects to that of dolomite. However, this stone had certain peculiar resinous characteristics, as well—which ought to have been impossible, given its crystalline nature—yet Avon found herself unsurprised. After all, she'd seen this before.

By the time Reath Silas appeared around breakfast time, Avon had not only been at work for a couple of hours but also proved the theory she'd reached while staring at the Thornseed the day before: "Guess what," she said as he stood in her doorway. "The Thornseed crystal turns out to be derived from the sap of the Drengir."

"What?" Reath's surprise was gratifying, but so was the comprehension that quickly dawned on his face. "Of course it was. We knew that the Sith used the Drengir; we knew that they contained them. We should also have realized that the Sith might develop something *from* them."

"I think we have our answer as to why the Drengir are so drawn to this place," Avon said. "Maybe it's not just the dark side of the Force calling to them. Maybe the Thornseed reaches them on, I don't know—an ancestral level."

Reath went very still. "And it's not coincidence that Mkampa showed up here with the Drengir. At this exact time, in this exact place? No."

It hit Avon then, a wave of pure horror crashing into her and over her, nearly knocking her down. "You think Dr. Mkampa knows about the Thornseed?"

"And I think she means to take its power for herself." For

one of the only times during their acquaintance, Reath Silas had begun to look almost . . . angry. "And I think we might have known all of this days ago, if someone had just been honest with us."

⚘

Nan had only just awakened when she heard the thumping on the door of her hut. "We need to talk," called Reath.

He spoke calmly, and yet something in his tone set Nan on edge. Hurriedly she finished pulling on her clothing, tugging a sleeve over the tethering bracelet she wore. "Come in."

When Reath entered, she knew. He didn't even have to open his mouth. The game was up.

"You knew about the Thornseed before we arrived on Kashyyyk, didn't you?" He came closer to her, studying her face as though he'd never seen it before. "You made it sound like you were just giving us Mkampa. But you knew what she was after from the beginning. What else would draw anyone to a planet afflicted by the blight?"

Nan kept her cool. "Yes. I knew. Dr. Mkampa learned about it years ago; I learned about it from certain private records of hers I accessed while serving on the Lightning Crash."

"Records you accessed to turn over to Marchion Ro," Reath said.

"Some of them," Nan admitted. "Not all."

"You claimed you wanted to help us catch Mkampa." Reath raked one hand through his sandy hair, as though he were attempting to calm himself. Jedi didn't rattle easily—and Reath wasn't exactly rattled now, but he also wasn't displaying the usual equanimity expected from a Jedi Knight. "Really, you wanted to stop Mkampa from getting the Thornseed. And once you'd done that, you'd have its location, and you'd feed that information straight to Marchion Ro. This power-hungry warlord who's already split the galaxy in two and taken millions of lives—you would have given him the power of the Sith?"

"Ro's no Force user," Nan said. "The Sith were Force users, right? I don't know if you remember the Nameless, but they're not exactly the weapon of choice for somebody who wants to use the Force more, right?"

Reath's eyes met hers; his expression could have been etched in stone. "I remember the Nameless. I could've lost my life to them, and more than once. I know the horror they inflict. That's one of the many reasons I wouldn't put anything past Marchion Ro. And if I know anything about Ro, I know that there's no way he would pass up a chance to get his hands on anything as powerful as the Thornseed."

"I never told Ro about the Thornseed," Nan said.

"Why should I believe that? Why should I believe anything you say? I took a chance on you, Nan. I really thought you might be on the level—or, at least, that you weren't in a position to do us harm. Instead you could've done more damage than anyone dreamed possible, not even the people who argued the hardest that you should just be thrown in a cell and forgotten."

"Do you do that, Reath?" Her voice sounded smaller than she would've wished. "Throw people in cells, lose the key, never think of them again?"

Reath breathed out as he steadied himself with an arm against one wall. For an instant she saw how tired he was, how much responsibility he bore—how much he had changed from the boy she'd met three years prior. "Of course I don't," he said. "Not to anyone, not even to you. That's not how the Republic does things, and certainly not the Jedi way. I'm sure they'll deal with you humanely and fairly, once we take you back to Coruscant and the prison sentence you've earned. In the end, Nan, the only thing I know about you is . . . that you're not my problem anymore."

With that he left, and she was glad. That way he didn't see how badly his words had stung her.

Azlin Rell cackled with glee as Reath departed Nan's hut, so disquieted that Azlin could almost trace his shape in midair. Some senses were far more profound than sight. He called out, "The crystal and the trees. The crystal and the trees. We've all been doing the dance, haven't we, my boy? Me more than the others."

Sure enough, Reath swiftly came to his door. "What do you mean?"

"They've been calling to us the whole time. Both of them." Azlin rocked back and forth, grateful for the understanding but still feeling the twin pull on him, threatening to rend him in two. "Sometimes the dreams came from the trees. But the Drengir—when I got to kill the Drengir, when I recalled killing the Nameless—those dreams came from the Thornseed. It understands me, Reath, and I understand it."

He hoped to tempt Reath with knowledge—the only true

temptation that had power over the boy—but Reath surprised him by saying, "Tell me about the dreams that come from the trees."

Being a child again.

Running across rope bridges with his friends.

The sound of laughter.

"You need to know more about the Thornseed," Azlin insisted. "You want to learn all about it, don't you? To delve into its secrets—"

"Enough." Reath's tone was calm and yet firm enough to silence Azlin. "Yoda understood one thing about you—that you still wanted to serve. You fear and dread the Nameless, the Drengir, and the blight; you ought to be bound to them in darkness, but *you aren't*. You claim to be tied to the Thornseed, too, but *you aren't*. You're lost. You've jabbed at all of us in turn during this mission, even Amadeo, trying to manipulate us and sow discord. Really I think you're looking for a companion in the dark so you won't be alone any longer. But the only way you'll ever cease being alone is if you again dare to step into the light."

Azlin could not respond. Reath left without another word.

Slowly Azlin lowered himself back onto the grass mat on the floor of his hut. Normally, to comfort himself—to target his anger and fear toward their rightful place, the Nameless—he began to sing the lullaby once more. But he didn't feel like singing now.

The trees had called to him. After he'd spent so long in darkness, after he'd traveled such a vast distance from the light—still, the trees had known him, given him dreams of beauty and sunlight. It was as if they alone remembered his name.

Nan couldn't muster up the appetite for breakfast. Instead she sat on the edge of one of the more distant walkways of the village, her legs dangling over the side as she stared into the abstract patterns woven by the green leaves all around her. The sentry bracelet wound around her wrist looked less like a manacle all the time; it might as well have been mere jewelry.

All along, her plan had been to inform the Jedi of only so much, to hold her knowledge close, to trade toward her ultimate goal—

And what had come of it all? The Jedi had enlightened themselves with very little help from her, and her goal seemed as far away as ever.

The wroshyr leaves rustled, and Nan shivered at the beauty of the sound. Did those who had lived their whole lives on planets, surrounded by greenery, share her wonder at such things? More likely they took it for granted. Their lives were as unusual to Nan as hers must be to them.

I have to restrategize, she thought. Marchion Ro's face swam in her mind, a memory that became hazier all the time. *I have to reconsider. I have to figure out what's still possible.*

Again the leaves rustled in the breeze—but that was when it hit Nan: There was no breeze. No wind at all.

She scooted back from the edge and got her feet under her as she stared into the trees. One of the vines rippled. No—it moved.

Nan screamed out, "The Drengir! They're *here*!"

THIRTY

Nan's cry echoed through the Wookiee village, followed almost instantly by multiple howls of alarm and fury, then again by the war horn that summoned everyone to the fight. Reath, who had been speaking with Burryaga, whirled around just in time to see a Drengir spring onto one of the rope bridges, tendrils lashing in every direction at once. He managed to activate his lightsaber and swing upward just in time to intersect with a Drengir tendril, which fell, sizzling and still thrashing, electric impulses moving tissue that had not yet had time to fully die.

With a great roar, Burryaga leaped toward the Drengir. Reath discounted that one immediately—it was taken care of—but he knew the Drengir almost never attacked alone. He ran in the direction of Nan's shout, even though other shrieks and screams had begun to sound all around him, because those cries were followed by other sounds: the hum and whir of lightsabers, the silvery percussion of blaster bolts, the mighty growls and howls of Wookiees going into battle.

Dez Rydan somersaulted into the fray, his lightsaber blade swirling in a vortex that slashed through one Drengir tendril after another. Leaves and vines sprang out all around him, almost like he was a greens trimmer. If the shrieks of the wounded and dying Drengir even reached Dez's ears, he showed no sign. Whatever hesitation or inner weakness had driven him toward the Barash Vow had been fully conquered.

As Reath swung around the curved walkway, both Nan and the Drengir came into view. With a jolt he realized that this was one of the largest Drengir he had ever seen, with at least two dozen tendril tentacles writhing in multiple directions. Nan, small as she was, appeared dwarfed by it—but she had pried loose one of the boards from the walkway and was whaling on the Drengir with it as best she could while still remaining far enough away to avoid becoming entangled. It hit Reath at that moment that, even though Nan *had* turned out to be deceiving them all yet again, he respected her grit and her guts.

Not that he had any time to meditate on this, because already he had called on the Force to help him leap the several meters over various walkways and gaps to land right next to Nan. With one fierce slash upward, he severed two of the Drengir's thickest tendrils; the answer was a furious hiss.

"Look out!" Nan shoved Reath down just before the Drengir

spat copious greenish fluid at them. The foul gunk landed on the wooden walkway, which promptly began to sizzle and dissolve. Reath was very glad the Drengir venom hadn't hit his face but not thrilled to realize it was currently eroding the structure that kept him from plummeting several dozen meters to the forest floor.

He stabbed forward with his saber, piercing the Drengir with its point; it crumpled, browned, and fell off the side of the walkway, crashing against multiple tree limbs as it tumbled to the ground. From the corner of his eye, Reath saw a vine and nearly grabbed it before realizing it was actually another Drengir tendril; more were coming to replace the one he had just killed.

Azlin Rell's cackling laugh echoed through the battle. Nan gasped. Reath had to look—and Azlin was doing whatever that thing was with the lightning again, electricity crackling between his levitating body and the trees as he hovered eerily amid the fray. When a Drengir fought through the charge to seize Azlin, he cackled and plunged his hands into its core, wringing out the pulp from within. The Drengir shrieked, a terrible sound, one that only made Azlin grin wider. His power in the dark side allowed him to kill quickly and ruthlessly, and to enjoy it.

"He's buying us time," Reath said, deactivating his saber and grabbing Nan about the waist. "Hang on."

His fist then closed around a real vine, and with a leap, Reath swung with Nan across the clearing. She clutched him as they arced through the air, her grip tightening as they reached the far edge; Reath let go and used both their momentum and the Force to bring them back up onto the next platform. The only Drengir there were—thanks to Burryaga and Azlin—dead.

The battle clearly belonged to the Wookiees and the Jedi, and the Drengir knew it. Already many were slithering away, rustling down tree limbs and trunks, disappearing into the vegetation.

"Oww," Nan said, hugging one arm to her chest, but when Reath turned to her, she shook her head. "I'm okay. Just wrenched it, that's all." In the distance, Kelnacca bellowed as he brutally cuffed another Drengir and sent it plummeting all the way down to the forest floor.

Avon staggered up to Reath, a livid welt from a tendril graze marking her forehead. "Okay, those were the most ridiculous Drengir ever," she gasped as Burryaga and Dez drew near, as well. "Why would they attack a Wookiee village? I guess they had a death wish." Burryaga growled his assent.

Dez straightened, his gaze distant. Whatever lingering tie he felt to the Drengir appeared to be serving him now, rather than haunting him. "The Drengir *wouldn't* attack a Wookiee village. They're fierce, but they understand that prey can be fierce, too. Beings as large and powerful as Wookiees—Drengir would only attack them one or two at a time. Not dozens of Wookiees at once."

Whatever Dez had glimpsed, Burryaga now saw, too. He urged them all to consider that, if the Drengir were willing to attack Wookiee villages, they would surely have done so before now. Also, for all their contempt for "rooted" creatures, the Drengir stayed close to the ground as a rule. What could have driven them up so high? What had changed?

"Mkampa," said Avon, realization dawning. "We know she's somehow able to influence the Drengir. She sent them after us."

The question following that, Reath knew, was: Why now?

"She wants to distract us," he said. "Which makes me think—she's found the Thornseed. That's why she's on Kashyyyk. That's her number one priority. She saved the attack on the Wookiee village until she needed it most."

"Agreed," said Dez. Avon nodded, and Burryaga yowled his agreement. But Reath wanted to hear from the one person most likely to know.

He turned to Nan. Although she still hugged her arm in pain, she spoke clearly: "I think you're right. At any rate, if I were you, I wouldn't take the chance of being wrong."

". . . okay," Reath said, then shouted, "We have to get back to the white wroshyr grove, now! Burryaga, Dez, Cohmac, Kelnacca, you're with—"

One last Drengir, which had been lurking on a tree branch, camouflaged within the leaves, unwilling to give up the fight, then launched itself toward Reath from the treetops above. He grabbed his lightsaber once again, ready for battle—but then energy bolts from even higher up hit the Drengir, incinerating it almost instantly. He looked up to see the *Vessel* hovering just overhead, close enough for him to see Affie Hollow grin and wave.

He waved back. "And here's our ride."

⚜

The Drengir could not understand why they had felt so compelled to undertake that hunt. They were not unfamiliar with the principle that the ripest fruit was sometimes found on the highest branch—nor did they doubt their own strength and ferocity—but attacking so many Wookiees at once could only lead to the shedding of leaf and sap, and the loss of many kin, as indeed it had.

And yet, even as they attempted to collect themselves afterward, the strange, irresistible pull that had summoned them to Kashyyyk in the first place took hold of them again, demanding that they follow, regardless of how wounded they might be, how much they might desire to cease the fight.

The pull could not be resisted, and so they would go.

As the Drengir made their way through the forest beneath the Wookiee village, it occurred to more than one of them how very much they liked the trees found here. The wroshyr trees existed on a scale deeply impressive to the Drengir; rooted though these plants might be, they dominated their world. Throughout their time on Kashyyyk, they had often thought how fine a thing it would be to liberate these great trees from the infestation of large hairy meat beings, and from the pestilence of the Jedi.

Was this why the planet called to them so? Was it the trees, summoning the Drengir to win them their freedom?

Win they would—Jedi or no Jedi. For their opponents had made a critical mistake, assuming that the Drengir's departure meant a retreat, the end of fighting. The very concept of "retreat" relied on the idea that it was preferable to remain on one particular patch of ground. That was the sort of folly one would expect only from the rooted. The Drengir knew better.

※

I have to get on that ship, Nan thought. The rush to board the *Vessel* and reach the white wroshyr grove was great enough that she figured she had a good chance of hurrying on with the rest; the others would assume Reath had given her permission, at least until it was too late. As long as she could avoid attracting Reath's attention until they were in the air, it ought to work.

And if it didn't? She'd steal a mylaya if she had to. Under no circumstances would Nan allow herself to be left behind.

Besides—she was a lot freer to act now.

As the Jedi and Wookiees gathered together beneath the descending *Vessel*, Nan allowed herself to be pushed toward the far side of the crowd, next to one of the wroshyr trunks; almost nobody could see here there, even if they were watching her, which at the moment she suspected no one was. This gave her the chance to check her injured arm.

When Reath had leaped toward the Drengir to save her, his lightsaber had come too near her wrist. It hadn't actually made contact, which was the only reason she still had both hands; however, the blade must have come within microns of her skin, because she had a long welt that looked like a bad sunburn.

More significantly, she also had a sentry bracelet that had been badly damaged, almost burned through. It took only one tug for the charred remnants to fall away, leaving Nan unbound.

Quickly she took the leather strap she used as a belt and wrapped it around her wrist. Tying it was difficult with one hand, but Nan managed, and even contrived to allow a little bit of the burn to show. Anyone who looked at the leather around her wrist would assume it was a makeshift bandage and would be unable to see that she wore the sentry bracelet no longer.

After that, it was just a matter of forcing her way back into the throng currently leaping from the rope bridge through the *Vessel*'s hatch. That jump didn't appeal to her, but she wound up next to Kelnacca and simply grabbed onto his arm; as she had gambled, he didn't even look at who he was helping in, just made the leap without even feeling her weight. Only moments later, the ship began to wheel around and the hatch to close. The chase was on.

Nan's body still shook with adrenaline from the sudden Drengir attack and their escape from it; she'd learned from long experience that it was better to burn through fear by action than to let it burn its way through you. If it betrayed the absence of her sentry bracelet, so be it. She'd gone to Coruscant and met with Reath Silas for a purpose that remained unfulfilled, and Nan wouldn't stop until it was done.

THIRTY-ONE

Azlin Rell at first believed that he had managed to get aboard the *Vessel* without anyone noticing. Then he reckoned again with his appearance—which he understood, from various reactions, to be strikingly ghoulish, and which was at the moment capped off with the enormous goggles that covered his eyes—and understood that he had of course been noticed. That his presence here and in the battle to come was allowed, perhaps even desired.

To find even this bare minimum of acceptance was rare for Azlin, but he was not much surprised by it. Killing the Drengir was a pleasure, and the others could not have failed to note his abilities in battle.

His prowess in combat with the Drengir must have

outweighed their concerns about bringing him so close to the Thornseed. Would Reath and the others have reached that same conclusion if they'd had ample time to consider the matter? Azlin suspected not.

He greatly anticipated the chance to kill again, relished the thought of feeling warm Drengir sap running down his arms as he crushed their innards and yanked them out. This malevolent glee—so divorced from his fear—must be attributed to the power of the Thornseed. He was eager to experience its direct influence at last, but he also wished to know the true power of the white wroshyr grove.

These two powers—aligned with opposite sides of the Force— had been battling for control over Azlin ever since his arrival on Kashyyyk. He was curious to learn which was the stronger.

(Before coming here, he would have been certain that the darkness was the stronger path. After his dreams on Kashyyyk, however . . . Azlin was no longer sure.)

※|☘

Dr. Mkampa took immense pride in all the modifications she had made to the Spider Squall *Firebringer*, but none so much as the replacement of the shorter, thicker "legs" with the tall, willowy stalks on which the *Firebringer* moved. Perfect for looming over one's enemies, dropping inefficient droids on rocks to watch them shatter, and here on Kashyyyk, moving smoothly among the wroshyr trees. By increasing walking altitude and reducing overall diameter, she was able to steer her craft so it stalked easily along the forest floor. Every once in a while, she spotted some of the large arachnids native to this planet; the fun part came when they spotted her in return and scurried away in terror of a spider so much more enormous than themselves.

She had elected to walk through the forest rather than fly in order to avoid attracting the Jedi's attention, not that she expected them to have much left over from the Drengir attack that was probably taking place at this very moment. Also, the Jedi had arrived via a civilian craft—one only lightly armed, but Mkampa had no intention of being sidetracked by ship-to-ship combat.

Not now, when her ultimate prize lay so close.

The *Firebringer* reached the edge of a river and waded out into it. Mkampa felt the faint shudder of the current against its spindly legs, but the craft could handle the pressure. Not too far ahead, just around the bend of the river, scanners had at last detected the island where the Thornseed must lie. The scans found nothing of particular note about these trees aside from the color of their bark, and that seemed likely to be a random genetic mutation, hardly uncommon when one fraction of a population was somehow cut off from the larger group. Nor was the island sufficiently isolated to protect the Thornseed from discovery. What could have led the ancient Sith to select this unremarkable location?

Dr. Mkampa reminded herself that the terrain might have looked very different when the site was chosen thousands of years ago. Still, it might prove worth her while to investigate the island and its trees more thoroughly. All she lacked was time. (Between searching for the Thornseed and summoning the Drengir, Mkampa had been extremely busy. She reasoned that she didn't have three hands, after all . . . though thanks to cybernetic enhancements, maybe she could change that.)

Well, soon the Thornseed would be hers. Once it lay in her hands and the Jedi on this planet had been destroyed, she would have all the time in the world.

"Let's get this done," Dr. Mkampa whispered. Even she could not have said whether she spoke to herself, to the Drengir, or to the Thornseed she had longed for these many months. All that mattered was that she and the Jedi were locked in a race, one only she could win.

Under Leox's deft piloting, the *Vessel* swung around neatly to settle on the riverbank across from the island of the white wroshyr grove, next to the stone bridge. Lacking any clear spot to land on the island itself, this was as close as they could get. To Reath's immense relief, there was as yet no sign of the *Firebringer*, nor any other evidence that Mkampa had already reached their location.

Dez Rydan, who was walking from the hatch onto the riverbank by Reath's side, said, "Do you think that was a false alarm? The Drengir could've just been especially hungry. We don't know for certain that Mkampa sent them after us."

"Maybe," Reath answered. "I wish we had time to reach out to Master Byre—she'd almost certainly know. But I doubt it, and regardless, it's not worth taking the chance. Now that we know Mkampa is aware of the Thornseed and trying to take it for herself, we should be guarding it, and this island, nonstop."

The rest of the party began to disembark, overseen by Geode, who stood at the side of the hatch. Reath was glad to see Azlin prepared and ready—even if he was possibly too eager to engage again in fatal combat. At this point, though, Reath saw Azlin's willingness to fight alongside them, to more or less behave normally, as progress. It seemed to him that there might be changes at work within Azlin at last.

He was less glad to see that Nan had somehow wrangled a place on the *Vessel*, as well. Then again—who had her tether at this moment? Probably still Avon, who was disembarking alongside Amadeo. Nan had had no choice but to follow along. Reath felt a pang of guilt: Yes, she had greatly disappointed him, and yes, stopping Mkampa from obtaining the Thornseed was now his top priority, but that was no excuse for endangering a prisoner in his custody. He should have looked out for her—but Nan never failed to look out for herself.

Already Avon had begun checking the area, and a frown appeared on her face. "I'm picking up more energy signatures in this area than I should. More than were here when we first came to this island—was that only yesterday? The day before? It's all starting to run together—"

"What kind of energy signatures?" Reath asked

"Very small ones," Avon replied. "Little devices, but many of them."

"Mkampa," said Cohmac, who was among the last to step out of the *Vessel*. "Who else could have placed them there? We can no longer doubt that she knows the location of the Thornseed. She must have sent ahead mobile monitors or sentries, to warn her if we arrived before she did."

Azlin laughed grimly. "That means she's ready for us. What of it? We're ready for her."

Reath considered what he knew of mobile monitors; while some might possibly have embedded themselves in tree branches, most would probably have dug into the ground. Stooping low, he began to search; some of the others were already following suit. Once they had some idea what they were looking for, it didn't take long for something to turn up. He pointed toward a small metallic device amid the grassy underbrush next to the riverbank. "There. What's this?"

"It's not a monitor," said Avon, who stepped closer to it. "To me it looks like a . . . light intensifier?"

Dez nodded. "Yeah, that's what it is. I used some on a mission in the underwater caves of Manaan once. But what would even Mkampa want with one of those here?"

It was a fair question. Such intensifiers—which, when activated, shone at a brightness closer to that of an astronomical object rather than any mere lamp or spotlight—were generally used only in deep caverns, on asteroids in empty space between systems, or in other places so dark that a device was needed to very nearly play the role of a sun. Why should Mkampa have planted one of them on a planet with ample sunshine and a bright blue sky?

Reath picked up one of the intensifiers to study it more closely. Given the sunny day, it had taken Reath a while to realize that the light enhancer device was active, even though not nearly at full power. Its light shone ever so slightly bluer than that of

Kashyyyk's sun, though not so intensely as might be expected for a signal, much less—

"Bluer than Kashyyyk's sun," Reath whispered.

Nan had been standing close enough to hear. "What do you mean?"

"All plants that photosynthesize are drawn to light," he said. "And plants are always drawn most strongly to light that matches the sun under which they first evolved."

"Which means . . ." Nan looked from Reath to the light emitter, then back to Reath again with wider eyes. "You think these light amplifiers are tuned to the wavelengths of the Drengir's original sun?"

"That would explain the extremity of their reactions." Reath nodded grimly. "Dr. Mkampa's figured out how to draw the Drengir to and from different locations."

Avon's quick mind was already a few steps ahead. "The light may also energize or irritate them into a sort of frenzy. That might explain why they attacked the Wookiee village, right?"

"Did you know this, too?" Reath asked Nan. "How Mkampa was influencing the Drengir?"

"I knew she was interested in learning how to do it," Nan admitted. "Not that she had succeeded."

"After they attacked the first time, you didn't consider mentioning that?" Reath wasn't sure what difference it made, but he didn't intend to let Nan off the hook even one more time. "You deserted from the Nihil to tell us *almost nothing*? That was worth your stunt on Coruscant?"

"I didn't desert the Nihil by coming to Coruscant!" Nan said it as though she could contain the words no longer; despite all her previous deception, Reath could not help feeling that, at last, she was telling at least some fraction of the truth. "Marchion Ro sent me there on a mission. But I was supposed to lead you into an ambush in the Dinwa system, not accompany you here. I disobeyed Ro by helping you. And no, I wasn't able to help you nearly as much as you wanted—or as much as I suggested—but that was the only way I was going to get a crack at Dr. Mkampa."

"A personal vendetta, then." Reath's curiosity was piqued. "Why do you have it in for Dr. Mkampa? She barely seemed to remember you."

"That's the whole point!" she cried.

He would have asked why—had that not been the moment they heard the telltale whine in the sky and looked up to see Mkampa's Spider Squall coming around the river bend, suddenly and appallingly close, nearly as tall as a wroshyr, its shadow now blocking the sun.

Reath's hand went to the hilt of his lightsaber as Dr. Mkampa's voice rang out from the speakers of the Spider Squall. "Well, if it isn't my friends the Jedi. We meet again!" In a less belligerent, almost confidential tone, she added, "I've always wanted to say that."

No point in replying. Reath calculated trajectories, positioned himself, and in one move both activated and threw his lightsaber almost directly upward. The blade sliced through three legs on Mkampa's Spider Squall, sending a shower of sparks down on him, Nan, Dez, and all the others. The severed metal legs toppled down into the river with a mighty splash. Yet as Reath reached out to catch his lightsaber by the hilt, he realize that he had not inflicted enough damage to cause a crash, because Mkampa's craft had simply begun to hover instead, drawing its remaining arms up underneath. The smoldering scars left behind did nothing but taunt him, much like Mkampa herself.

From the *Vessel*, Affie called out to Reath: "We can take her! There's not a lot of visible weaponry—how much firepower can that thing have?"

Dr. Mkampa had heard her and cackled with glee. "I don't require much firepower. Just enough to do *this*."

From the floating lab came a slim violet ray—a scanner turned to extreme amplitude, perhaps—which was pointed directly at the island. *No,* Reath realized with dread, *it's aimed at the Thornseed.*

She's activating it. Waking it up.

"Now," Mkampa continued, "all I need to do is turn on the lights."

With that, light arrays surrounding her lab turned on—and their glow was almost lost in the sunlight save for that faint hint of blue.

"She's calling the Drengir," Dez said, taking his lightsaber in hand and getting into battle stance. "She's summoning them here."

Sure enough, the branches of the trees lining the river had begun to thrash as though in cyclonic wind. Rustling came from the underbrush in every direction. Reath's gut sank as he saw the Drengir begin to appear from the green surroundings that had camouflaged them so well. They burst forth, already in a frenzy, maddened by the call of what seemed to be their sun, the urge to plant new Drengir, and the boundless desire for meat.

Dez said what everyone else was thinking: "We're surrounded."

THIRTY-TWO

From the greenswards and the underbrush and the branches they came—hordes of Drengir bursting forth, tentacles thrashing, thorns slashing leaves and trunks alike as they barreled toward the Jedi and their companions. Dez Rydan brandished his blue lightsaber as Reath's green saber flared into brightness. The hum and vibration were reassuring, reminding Dez of the countless hours of combat practice that had gone into his right to bear this weapon.

I am one with the Force, he thought, drawing on the depth of calm mindfulness he had learned while observing the Barash Vow. *The Force is with me.*

The Drengir were not uniquely powerful in the dark. They had had no influence over him during his time on Kashyyyk.

Even though Dez knew the malign power he'd felt was real—and, he could sense, sharpening even now—he knew it had nothing to do with the Drengir. Time to face his fears.

He spun forward toward the closest approaching Drengir, the angle of his moves bringing his lightsaber blade slashing through the trunk of one and the tentacles of another. High-pitched shrieks and a faint smoldering smell like burning grain testified to the deadliness of both hits. But Dez could not even press his advantage against these opponents because more of them were spilling out of the woods, rushing forward, mad for meat and blood.

Cohmac managed to parry the next Drengir attacking them, but barely, and Dez was obliged to follow Cohmac's strike with his own. Kelnacca had two Drengir attacking him at once; so far he was holding them off with his blade, but he could help no one else. Nan had run almost knee-deep into the water. What was she doing? But there was no time to think about her.

"Get back into your ship!" Reath called out to Leox, Affie, and Geode. "Avon, Nan, you too! Protect yourselves!" Dez felt a moment's gratitude that the non-Jedi might be spared this. Already Leox and Avon were headed back inside. The *Vessel* would provide some measure of safety.

At least, he'd thought it would, but a Drengir's vines began to snake into the ship's hatch, preparing to pull the entire creature inside, where those attempting to enter would have no opportunity for concealment or escape. But that was when Burryaga sprang at the Drengir, lightsaber blazing. Another shriek cut through the air as leaves and sap flew from Burryaga's mighty swipe.

Affie Hollow had taken cover behind Geode, who shielded her from direct attack. She leaned out just long enough to get off a few shots, hitting most of her targets, but there were just so damned many of the Drengir coming at them—more than Dez would've believed existed.

"To your left!" Reath shouted, and Dez wheeled around just in time to swing his blade into one more Drengir. But that one had gotten way too close.

The enemy was closing in.

✵

Decades of blindness, and an equal amount of time spent learning the gifts of the dark side, had attuned Azlin's hearing to a sharpness almost unknown among humanoids. So, for him, the sounds of battle were as informative as the sights of it could be for any other.

He spent so much of his life afraid—remembering the vile Nameless, the emptiness of existence they had revealed to him—but there was no need for fear now. Only the chance to attack the Drengir anew and give vent to some of the pent-up hatred in his heart.

Master Arkoff had always said anger and hate had no place in a Jedi's heart, and if they could not always be avoided, these emotions had to be kept at bay during combat—then above any other time. Arkoff had warned that this was where darkness lay. Yet darkness surrounded them constantly, insinuated itself within every fold of existence, between the molecules, within the air. The only way to avoid the dark side was to die, and Azlin didn't feel like dying today.

He heard the huff and pant of a fighter in trouble—young Amadeo, Azlin suspected—and launched himself at the Drengir with all the power and malevolence the dark side could give.

And it seemed to be giving so much more, now. . . .

~*~

The last time Affie had felt this cornered, she'd been on the burning hulk of Starlight Beacon as it crashed through planetary atmosphere on the way toward destruction, trapped behind durasteel doors that wouldn't open. Here, she stood on a planet, but the open sky above and the rushing river behind only seemed to taunt her with what ought to have been avenues of escape— but were cut off by the Drengir and Dr. Mkampa.

A Drengir spat acidic venom in their direction, but Geode took the brunt of it. He'd have died before he let the Drengir know how much that hurt, but Affie sensed the tension in her Vintian friend. How much longer could he hold himself together like this?

"Gah!" Dez Rydan staggered backward, clutching at his thigh; a slash in his trousers and a streak of gory red revealed that a Drengir thorn had hit him hard. Reath Silas fought back the Drengir—a whirlwind of green leaf blades—even as Dez wobbled on his feet and dropped his lightsaber. It fell at the very edge of the water.

And Nan lunged for it.

A strap of leather, loosely tied around Nan's arm, fell off and into the river. Affie gasped as she realized Nan's sentry bracelet was gone. It was just like Nan to use this opportunity—the wounding of a man who had been fighting to save her life—to escape, and to steal a lightsaber while doing it.

But Nan didn't run along the riverbank or fling herself into the water. Instead, she ran toward the *Vessel*.

※

Every step over the jagged riverside stones jolted all the bones in Nan's body, and more than one Drengir spat venom in her direction, barely missing her. Nan refused to pay attention to any of that. *Get to the* Vessel, *get on top of the* Vessel, *go go go go GO.*

Burryaga roared out that they must try to reach the island—that the trees would save them if only they could reach the island. Nan thought she'd probably heard a more ridiculous plan at some point in her life (she knew Ghirra Starros, didn't she?) but could not remember exactly when. Stupid Wookiees, putting their faith in trees. Stupid Jedi, putting their faith in the Force.

Nan put her faith in weaponry, and the unfamiliar heft of the lightsaber in her hand promised to be the greatest weapon of all.

The *Vessel* wasn't a large ship, and even more than most spacecraft, it was outfitted with various rungs and ridges, as well as tool pockets, to aid in hull repair between voyages. She scrabbled to open one tool pocket, which ought to have something magnetic— yes! *A metal repair tether!* As soon as Nan had the tool in hand, she tucked it and the lightsaber into her shirt and began clambering toward the top. Overhead loomed Dr. Mkampa's hovering Spider Squall, the comm still broadcasting her cackling laughter as the people beneath her struggled for their lives.

Nan remembered the first time she'd heard Dr. Mkampa laugh, just over three years prior.

"You awakened the Drengir, just as I hoped," she'd said as Nan stood there, scarcely more than a girl. "The texts I studied—I knew it was more than a legend. All unfolded according to plan."

"But it was an accident," Nan had blurted out. Their whole Cloud had been caught in the Hyperspace Disaster, with Nan and Hague as the only survivors. Even Hague had died before escape from the Amaxine station had been possible. "We weren't supposed to be there."

"Of course," Mkampa had said blithely. "Of course. I misspoke. Still, I suspected the Drengir had existed, that they still existed, and you've proved it."

Nan had chosen to believe this—Dr. Mkampa was certainly capable of delusions of grandeur—and had even attributed her later assignment to the Lightning Crash, then under Mkampa's command, to the "luck" she'd had in encountering and awakening the Drengir.

Yet Nan's time on the Lightning Crash, and her interest in gathering clandestine information from both ally and foe, had eventually led her to Mkampa's private records of the event . . . which began well before the event. Mkampa had known, from the start, that Nan and Hague's Cloud would be caught up in the Great Hyperspace Disaster. She had counted on at least one ship surviving—and only one had—but all the others had been considered acceptable losses. Hague, too, was no more than a detail for Mkampa to ignore. All to see if the Drengir existed. All before the Drengir could have possibly played any role in the plans of Marchion Ro.

She didn't think Mkampa even remembered Hague's name.

Nan reached the top of the *Vessel* and got to her feet. The magnetic tether she'd taken would generate a magnetic feedback loop—not the strongest one possible, but she thought it might be just enough.

Her body tensed as the *Firebringer* came closer again, whirring near. The dark scars in the metal that Reath Silas had inflicted gave Nan her target. As soon as Mkampa was directly above, Nan jumped as high as she could, holding the tether overhead, and clicked it to start the magnetic loop.

The lift it provided wasn't much. If Mkampa hadn't been flying so low, the plan would never have worked. As it was, though, Nan had just enough height to reach the lower part of the lab and grab on to one of the jagged metal edges, then pull herself into the gaping hole left by one of the legs that had been shed after Reath had severed it.

Blood dripped from her hand as she struggled to her knees; the metal had cut her deeply. It didn't matter. Nan could only crouch in the narrow space she'd accessed. She was surrounded on all sides by wiring and power conduits, the innards that allowed this thing to fly. Having no idea which to attack first, Nan decided to destroy them all.

With shaking bloody hands, she pulled out the lightsaber and ignited it. Nothing could have prepared her for the way it felt in her grasp, the vibration that seemed almost to be alive. Nan put the sensation aside and began slashing with it indiscriminately, just trying to burn or sever as much as she could. Sooner or later, she'd hit something critical—

A hot shower of sparks sprayed across her right side, burning her cheek, ear, and shoulder. Nan cried out in pain, but she felt joy, too, because the *Firebringer* had begun to shudder and smoke. Already they were losing altitude. Amid all the noise of the Spider Squall's wounded workings, Nan thought she could make out the sound of Dr. Mkampa's scream.

Something on the far end of the ship's underbelly exploded. Nan was hit with a wave of compressed air and searing heat; that, combined with blood loss and dizziness, made her swoon. She slumped forward, falling through the gash in the bottom of the lab and tumbling toward the river that waited to swallow her whole.

⚜

Reath watched Dr. Mkampa's Spider Squall going down with relief—at least, until he saw Nan fall, seemingly unconscious, from the lab into the river. He used the Force to push the nearest Drengir fighters violently away from him, then reached his hand toward Nan, pushing her limp form out of the rapids, guiding her closer and closer to the dry land nearest her, namely the shore of the island.

Nan was finally telling the truth, he realized. *She wanted to take down Dr. Mkampa, and now she might have done it.*

However, the Drengir didn't require instructions from Mkampa to fight, and her fate made no difference to them.

Maddened by the still-shining light amplifiers, they were perhaps incapable of stopping their attack. The two Reath had managed to push back were already writhing toward him again, the wide maws of their mouths taunting him. Dez could barely stand. He'd be no help—

What was that sound? It was growing closer—a mixture of rustling and growling.

Not more Drengir, Reath thought. *There can't be!* But already they were bursting forth, reinforcements outnumbering the Jedi and Wookiees, overwhelming them entirely.

Burryaga roared again for them to run for the island. Reath was loath to bring the Drengir closer to a source of dark side energy . . . but if there was any chance of the white wroshyr trees having some kind of influence, or even of finding more favorable fighting ground, they had to take it.

"To the island!" Reath shouted. "Let's *go!*"

THIRTY-THREE

Avon was no warrior, but she understood when a battle was going badly—and this one was undoubtedly being lost.

She, along with the Jedi and a handful of Wookiees, was running with all her speed along the stone bridge that led to the island of the white wroshyr grove. Unfortunately, Avon's speed didn't come close to that of the Wookiees—but the Drengir appeared reluctant to cross the bridge right away. She suspected the maddening effect of the sunlight would drive them onward before long; still, they at least had some short respite from the fight.

As soon as Avon had reached the island, she went to a half-rotted log on the shore, thinking to sit down and catch her breath, but the wood was so black and soft it crumbled with a touch. The others were pausing to collect themselves and take stock of their situation.

On the one hand, they'd bought themselves some time. On the other, they were now on an island from which they could not readily escape. Avon wasn't sure they'd improved their odds.

Then she gasped. A few meters downstream, a supine figure lay at the very edge of the water, seemingly unconscious. Avon swiftly realized it was Nan. She'd considered Nan the enemy and therefore probably the last to be attacked; how foolish to have thought that the Drengir respected any alliances. To them, every being in the galaxy besides the Drengir was prey.

Mkampa's Spider Squall seemed to have crash-landed on the river bank, perhaps fifty to seventy meters downstream. It was impossible to tell whether Mkampa had lived through the crash. Who knew what information might lurk on that craft? A lot of evil science, Avon suspected—but science that might potentially be put to better ends. She resolved to reach that wreckage as soon as possible, assuming she managed to survive.

Burryaga roared over the din that they must reach the white wroshyr trees and speak to them—beseech them? Commune with them? Avon's Shyriiwook wasn't totally fluent, but she didn't think it mattered if she was missing some nuance. When your best hope was praying to foliage, that meant there wasn't much hope at all.

Reath stared across the river at the Drengir, who thrashed angrily but had not yet begun to cross the stone bridge to attack the Jedi on the island.

"Are they afraid of the water?" Amadeo said. "Because if so, that really is information I wish we'd had a lot sooner. Very easy workaround."

"I don't think that's it," Reath replied. "Cohmac, Burryaga—you feel it, too, don't you?"

Burryaga growled his assent, and Cohmac nodded, saying, "The darkness urges them onward, but the light repels them, powerfully so."

With a huff, Burryaga pointed out he had *told* them multiple times that the trees would protect them.

"We should've believed you right away, Burryaga—my apologies." Reath patted his friend's shoulder and received a friendly gruffle in return. "But I'm not sure even the white wroshyr trees can keep the Drengir back forever, because the darkness has become more powerful, too."

"Oh, yes," whispered Azlin Rell, who stood not very far away, his face upturned to the sky. "I feel them both, I do."

Leox was leaning hard against Geode, who didn't seem to mind bearing his weight. "That purple light Mkampa shone toward this island—it reminded me a whole lot of the color of the Thornseed."

"Me too," Reath said. "I worry that she may have activated the crystal in some way. It held a faint glow when we saw it for the first time; that might have been some residual charge from a beam she had sent in its general direction longer ago."

Burryaga said he wondered whether this might be the reason the Drengir had come to Kashyyyk in the first place, the method Mkampa had used to draw them here. The striated light signatures she was using on this planet wouldn't have been sufficient to call to the Drengir across the vast void of space, but who could say how far the malevolent influence of the Thornseed might reach?

Reath made up his mind. "Okay. So far, the balancing effect of the trees is keeping the Drengir from reaching us and the Thornseed from having undue influence. There's no saying how long this pause will last, so let's use what we've got. We can take a moment to get our bearings, but after that, I want us to head to the center of the white wroshyr grove and the Well of Night. Keeping Mkampa from collecting the Thornseed isn't enough. We have to figure out if there's any way to destroy it."

With a frown, Amadeo mimed slashing to and fro with a lightsaber. "Can't we just, you know, slice it up?"

"Dark side artifacts tend to protect themselves," Cohmac warned. "When we strike at it, it will strike back. We must be ready for anything."

Reath took advantage of this brief moment to walk to the place on the riverbank where Nan lay. Her head had lolled to one side; her wet hair obscured her eyes. She was so motionless that Reath thought she might be dead—but no. A flicker of the Force remained, a tiny candlelight that testified to life, and to hope.

Swiftly he knelt by her side. "Nan, can you hear me? Can you get up?"

"Mmmph." Nan pushed her damp hair back from her face,

squinting up at Reath as though she couldn't focus. Blood seeped from her injured hand. "I—I don't know."

Reath bent down and scooped Nan into his arms. With the help of the Force, he was able to move almost as quickly carrying her weight as he would have without her. As his boots sank beneath each stride along the waterlogged sand, he said, "Pretty impressive, how you took down Mkampa."

"Is she dead?"

"I'm not sure."

Nan gave him a crooked, drowsy smile. "I *really* hope she's dead."

Reath spared one glance backward to see that the Drengir were beginning to amass near the far end of the stone bridge. Perhaps the protective effect of the white wroshyr grove was reaching its limit.

When he looked back down at Nan, she was still smiling at him. "My knight comes to the rescue," she said. "Mr. Silas, I could almost believe you liked me."

Reath had neither the time nor the mental space to think of an appropriate response. Luckily, Kelnacca came up alongside him then, roaring that Reath shouldn't be straining his human muscles with such a burden. Kelnacca grabbed Nan by the back collar of her shirt, hauling her up the way he might've lifted a Wookiee baby by the scruff of the neck, and plopped her across his shoulder. Someday, Reath would be amused to know what Nan had made of that.

For now the group needed to get on the move.

Azlin Rell could not tell whether he felt very strange indeed—or in fact felt very well, perhaps the best he had felt in years. Perhaps ever.

All around him, the team was beginning the trek into the white wroshyr grove. Azlin could hear the Wookiees murmuring among themselves as they led the way, the whir and hum of some scientific device the Avon girl held, the metal-on-leather sound of the human members of the *Vessel* crew holstering their blasters, and even—a high, high silvery sound, beyond the frequencies detected by human ears uninfluenced by the Force—what Azlin believed to be the sound of the Vintian's magnetism at work on the ground beneath him, moving him forward. (He sort of liked the Vintian.)

What, oh, what might this secret grove contain? Azlin couldn't begin to guess, but already he sensed an intensifying of the Force all around them, as though shining down from above. Life within life. Age within age. Every blade of grass, every flatfish in the nearby river, each tiny spark of existence lighting at once— illuminating even the darkness Azlin had for so long carried within.

Yet with this illumination came shadow. Even as the benevolence of the white wroshyr trees shone down on them, an insidious evil leached into the soul, shadowing their footsteps. What caverns might lurk underfoot? How far beneath the surface could he go? Maybe it didn't matter. The poison was not deep. It lurked near to them, very near indeed. He imagined every impression of his boot instantly killing the moss and grass beneath, turning them black.

That's not happening. That's not real. Azlin often felt the need to clarify this.

Both darkness and light beckoned him forward. The only difference, in this moment, was which he chose to follow.

Slowly—to his own astonishment—Azlin lifted his face toward the sky and felt the warmth of the sun on his cheeks.

For now, he was not running away from anything any longer. Not the Drengir, not even the Nameless. Azlin was finally walking *toward* something again. He had forgotten how good it could feel.

⚜

Not for the first time, Avon wished there were some scientific way to measure the Force.

She didn't mean anything as mundane as an individual's M-count, which only spoke to their potential to use the Force. No, she longed to observe some of the power her Jedi friends called on for insight and strength—though that would probably mean also having to observe the darkness of the Drengir. Maybe she was better off.

As Avon entered the white wroshyr grove again, she amended that thought: She was *definitely* better off not witnessing the Force. It might have been glorious to see whatever it was that came from the white wroshyr trees, but she 100 percent did not want to see whatever was coming from the Well of Night.

Besides the creepy purplish light, anyway. The light that hadn't been there before but now throbbed within the Well of Night like a slow, ominous heartbeat.

"It wasn't doing that before, right?" asked Affie Hollow.

"Most certainly it was not," answered Cohmac. Burryaga's whine made it clear that he was unhappy to agree.

Reath walked to the very edge of the Well before glancing back at the others. "Nobody happened to bring a thermal detonator, did they?"

"No such luck." Dez joined Reath at the side of the Well. "Whatever Mkampa did to the Thornseed, however she managed it—she's woken it up."

Avon felt obliged to add, "I might have done that. Remember how it literally glared at me when I took that sample?"

"It was awakened already," Reath said, in a tone that suggested she should find this comforting. Comfort felt very distant at that moment. "It wouldn't have been glowing otherwise. But Mkampa seems to have sent it power."

Cohmac said, "That power, it intends to use."

"Yes," said Reath. "I feel that."

He jumped into the Well then, which made Avon gasp. She ought to have expected it, but somehow it seemed impossible to just walk up to anything as palpably evil as the Thornseed. Still, as Dez and Burryaga followed, Avon went to the edge of the Well to see for herself.

Reath asked his fellow Jedi, "Could we use the Force to pulverize it? Even one strong crack might be enough to weaken it."

Burryaga growled that it was worth trying. But even as the

Jedi lifted their hands, the Thornseed sent out a tremendous pulse of energy and light, one that turned the whole world purple for an instant. Avon imagined she could feel it scouring her skin, or maybe she didn't imagine it, because the wounded Nan groaned in fresh pain.

Azlin Rell shuddered, though it was impossible to tell whether he shook from horror or delight. "They're coming," he said. "The Drengir are coming."

THIRTY-FOUR

Reath could've stabbed the Thornseed with his lightsaber in frustration. Then again, maybe that was a good idea. They'd have to try it, at any rate. His thoughts felt fuzzy now, not entirely clear, and though the Force remained his ally, he could tell that the Thornseed's influence would make any call upon the light side more difficult.

He ignited his blade and told Burryaga and Dez, "Come on. Let's try to cut this thing down to size. Count of three?"

Dez and Burryaga fired up their own lightsabers in unison, then went into combat stance on either side of Reath.

Bracing himself for a potentially explosive reaction, Reath counted it down: "Three, two, one—"

He stabbed his blade into the heart of the Thornseed crystal at the very moment Dez and Burryaga did. The crystal didn't shatter. Worse, it began to glow even more brightly and steadily. Reath's heart sank as he realized that not only had they not managed to destroy the Thornseed, but they also seemed to have given it even more power.

"Damn!" he swore as all three of them pulled their blades back. "Any other ideas?"

Before anyone could reply, Kelnacca roared a warning—and only a second later, Reath heard the telltale rustle that meant the Drengir were coming. They'd have to tackle the Thornseed again later. For now, the fight was back on.

Reath leaped up from the Well of Night just in time to see the masses of Drengir storming into the grove, tendrils thrashing. Kelnacca, who had dumped the semiconscious Nan into a nearby bush, went at them with his lightsaber, as did Amadeo. Reath rushed to join them, then felt something fly just past his face to strike Dez, who cried out in pain: "Poison!"

Instantly the grove—which had once seemed so beautiful and serene—devolved into the melee of combat. Reath threw himself into it, slashing as best he could; to his side, Burryaga did the same. From the corner of his eye, Reath could see Leox Gyasi had managed to climb one of the smaller, non-wroshyr trees that also ringed the glade, and from this vantage point was firing his blaster as quickly as he could take aim. Not so far away, both Avon and Affie had taken shelter behind Geode, who was immune to the Drengir's poison thorns. From that cover, Affie ducked out to fire her own blaster as often as she could.

Even as electricity crackled around Azlin Rell, who savagely wrestled with one of the Drengir, even as Kelnacca bellowed his victory over a Drengir he'd literally just ripped in two—Reath knew that the Drengir numbers were too great. With the weight of the Thornseed's malign influence on them, the Jedi would not be able to overcome this enemy.

Reath kept fighting, would keep fighting until the end, even as he thought, *I've just gotten us all killed.*

✺

Affie fired another few shots at the Drengir before ducking back behind Geode, by Avon's side. Avon said, "Are you sure Geode's immune to poison?"

"It won't kill him," Affie confirmed. "But it hurts him." Geode hid pain well, but she had learned to recognize the signs. He was suffering mightily to protect them.

"I'll take other cover," Avon said. "So then maybe Geode can take cover, too."

"Good plan!"

With that, Avon threw herself toward the nearest white wroshyr, literally jump-rolling until she could scramble behind its wide trunk. Affie wasn't sure how long that would protect her—the Drengir were so many, and they were so few—but she appreciated the effort. Time she made some effort of her own.

When Affie could bear Geode's agony no more, she patted his side in farewell and then ran away from him as hard as she could. She could almost feel his horrified gaze on her as she left, but she couldn't just let him take hit after hit of venom to protect her. On his own, Geode was of no interest to the Drengir; sometimes it paid to be inedible. Maybe at least one of them would get out of this unscathed.

Affie instead ran for the tree where Leox had found a high perch, hoping that she'd have a better vantage to fire on the Drengir. *Hey, who knows,* she thought, *in the flush of battle, maybe they'll mistake the tree for one of their own. That might buy us a little time.*

"Affie!" Leox called as she clambered up the branches toward him. A couple of Drengir threw prickly spines in their general direction, but for the moment they were far more engaged in battling the Wookiees and the Jedi. "You all right, Little Bit?"

He hadn't called her by that childhood nickname in a while, mostly because she'd threatened him with bodily harm if he ever did it again. At this moment, though, Affie had bigger problems. She reached his side and braced herself in a fork among the branches, able to take her blaster from its holster again. She had a good view of the battle, which helped—and a good view of the throbbing, evil Thornseed crystal, which didn't help at all.

What else can we do? Affie was desperate for any possible solution. "Can we try a remote start on the *Vessel,* bring her here? If one of us could manage to get inside, we'd at least have the laser cannon to work with."

"Hard to set that up, and not much time to maneuver." Leox shook his head. "I can try with the remote devices, but—I don't know."

Affie knew. It wouldn't work. They'd have had to plan that long in advance, and how could they have?

More and more Drengir continued swarming the grove; they'd spawned or sprouted or whatever they did until they were at least a hundred in number. As valiantly as the Jedi and the Wookiees fought, she knew they couldn't hold out for long.

They're losing, Affie thought. Her gut clenched with a dread she hadn't felt since the death of Starlight Beacon. *The Drengir are going to win.*

"Wait," Leox said, his drawl suddenly sharp with fear. *"Geode?"*

Affie scanned the battle scene and realized that Geode—usually the furtive type—was tumbling, as though in a rockslide, toward the Well of Night. Either his momentum or his will took him over the edge, into the Well itself, to land directly in front of the Thornseed. Only then did Affie understand that Geode definitely had done that on purpose. But why?

Her first shock-giddy thought was that Geode was staring the Thornseed down, demanding that it knock off this dark side stuff or else.

Her second thought—sickening in its horror—was that Geode was beginning to glow.

Leox's voice had gone up a half octave in pitch when he said, "Geode's heating up really hot. Hotter than I've ever seen." Sure enough, Geode was brightening into redness, light tracking the small veins in his surface stone, as though he were turning into lava.

But what was happening was even worse. "He's heating to superconductivity," Affie breathed.

"He can stop," Leox said, even though a faint whining vibration had begun to shiver through the air. "He can stop until the last second."

"He can stop," Affie repeated. But why would Geode stop

unless the tide of the battle turned? And it wasn't turning. It was only getting worse.

He won't stop. He won't stop.

Affie couldn't restrain herself any longer. She jumped down from the tree, heedless of her own safety, running toward the Well of Night, toward her friend. "No! Geode, no, *don't*! Don't—"

Geode exploded. White-hot gravel and crystalline shrapnel sprayed in every direction, up and out, forcing Wookiees, Jedi, and Drengir to duck low or be wounded. Affie went down only as long as she had to, then resumed running to the Well. Looking down through tear-filled eyes, Affie saw remnants of the Thornseed lying in shards like so much broken purple glass. Briefly it glowed—one swift pulse—before going dark, forever.

Of Geode, only pebbles remained.

⁂

Burryaga knew immediately what Geode had done, the sacrifice their friend had made. But he also felt the impact of what Geode had accomplished. In an instant, the dark influence of the Thornseed had vanished almost as though it had never been.

The Drengir slowed, deprived of some of their power, but their assault did not cease. Within minutes they would be fighting as furiously as ever, unless they could be stopped . . . and Burryaga thought he knew who might stop them.

For the first time in millennia, since the Thornseed had first been planted in Kashyyyk's soil, the white wroshyr trees no longer had to bear its burden. Who knew what they might now be capable of?

Burryaga went to the edge of the former Well of Night and leaped down inside. The great white wroshyr trees stood in a circle all around it; for all these thousands of years, they had focused their energies on this spot, now cleansed and consecrated by Geode's noble sacrifice. He knelt briefly in the grayish dust that had been his comrade to give thanks, but Burryaga did not forget what he must do.

The Wookiees were sworn to protect these trees with their lives, even with their souls. The trees were sworn to protect them, too. To ask this of them—to commune with them—it was both the riskiest and the holiest act possible in the life of any Wookiee.

And Burryaga intended to ask for even more. To ask for something that, so far as he knew, no Wookiee had ever requested and no wroshyr had ever granted.

Kelnacca then jumped into the former Well to land by Burryaga's side. The wild eyes and fearsome toothy grin Kelnacca usually wore in battle had given way to an expression of the greatest humility. Evidently he understood what Burryaga wanted to ask, and intended to ask alongside him.

So the two of them stood face to face. A gentle breeze, untainted by the fighting still taking place above, stirred the white wroshyr grove as the Wookiees closed their eyes. Burryaga called on all his knowledge of the Force—

Every lesson Nib Assek had ever taught him—

Every time he and Bell Zettifar had laughed in friendship—

Every occasion when Burryaga had learned from Yoda, or Stellan Gios, or Avar Kriss, or Orla Jareni, or even Reath Silas—

Everything that had ever made him a Jedi.

And to the trees he said, *Let them know you.*

The answer did not come in words, but Burryaga sensed exactly when to open his eyes. It was the very moment when the white wroshyr trees began to radiate pure light.

※

Reath gasped—in astonishment, yes, but also in something far closer to wonder—first believing that the whole trees were glowing. Then he realized that, in fact, the prismatic illumination came from the slender cracks within the trees, amid the silvery bark, and from the veins in the pale green leaves. Even Reath, who had both witnessed and worked incredible feats through the Force, thought he'd never before seen anything that could so accurately be called magic.

In the former Well of Night stood Burryaga and Kelnacca, deep in meditation. Their communion with the trees was so deep, so profound, that they seemed oblivious to his presence. This alone would have won Reath's respect, but the greatest miracle was the trees themselves. They were not merely alive, not merely conscious, but sapient. They thought, they felt, and they knew their planet on a level and at a depth that could be matched by almost no other form of intelligence in the galaxy. Without the burden of the Thornseed, their immense power in the Force was at last freed.

No wonder the Wookiees kept this a secret, Reath thought, panting for breath, awestruck by the vision of this grove carved from white light. *People would try to understand this. They'd try to analyze it. And in so doing, they'd destroy it.*

Reath, at least, was wise enough to know how futile it was to attempt to analyze magic. In the light of the white wroshyr grove, he thought all the others must know it, too.

Including, somehow, the Drengir.

The Drengir had any life-form's instinctive aversion to fire, and the explosion of the Inedible One had seemed enough like fire for them to hesitate a few moments to take stock. From their first arrival on the planet, they had admired the trees of Kashyyyk, which existed on a scale that ought to humble any meat creature. These were beings of nature and dignity. They could be respected.

But—like all other plants the Drengir had ever found, on any world—the wroshyr trees had remained silent.

Until now.

The Drengir lifted their faces and fronds toward the glittering leafy canopy above. Distantly they noted the presence of the meat creatures, but this was no longer a time to hunt. Who could think of eating when there was a sight such as this to be seen? Conversation such as this to be had?

Not that the white wroshyr trees communicated through anything so crude as words. But the scents they released in the air, the microscopic bubbling of nutrients just beneath the soil, made their way into the Drengir minds. They spoke of another form of existence—one that repudiated the lesser joys of the hunt and the kill in favor of higher consciousness, one that honored other life instead of preying on it—and in the nature of this sort of communication, the information could not be given without also imparting the joy that could result.

The Great Progenitor sank her tendrils deep into the ground, harkening back to the ancestral instinct for roots. As soon as she had done so, the other Drengir began to follow suit. They reached upward with their leaves in unison, swaying with the breeze, answering the call of their most ancient genes. One by one, their thorns softened, turned green, and began to blossom into flowers.

The meat beings might remain as near or go as far as they wished, for they were no longer prey. They were fellow links in the great chain of existence that bound all life together. How could the Drengir not have seen it before? For this revelation—this sacred truth—they would eternally be grateful.

No longer would they fight and kill. No longer would they pollute their beings with meat.

From now on, forever, the Drengir would be creatures of the light.

THIRTY-FIVE

"The Drengir have been—converted?" Avon suggested as she and some of the others wandered around the stationary Drengir, who even now were sprouting fragrant buds that seemed likely to bloom into flowers. "Brainwashed? Enlightened?"

"Whatever it is," said Reath as he wiped sweat from his brow, "it's a welcome change. Hopefully a permanent one."

Burryaga warmly growled that the change would certainly endure. None could share consciousness with the white wroshyr trees and leave unaltered. He wished he had conceived of this solution to the problem of the Drengir long before, but the centuries-old tradition of secrecy around this island and its sacred grove could not have been broken lightly.

"I promise you won't regret doing so." Reath turned to each of the Wookiee Jedi in turn. "Burryaga, Kelnacca, I hereby promise you that neither I nor anyone else on this mission will breathe one word about this grove, not even to the Jedi Council, unless you and the other Wookiees decide that we should."

Gruffly, Kelnacca said he thought such a decision unlikely. This was a Wookiee secret and should remain so—but he trusted Reath, the other Jedi, and even the civilians to honor the access they had been given by keeping their silence about it for all time.

"Then how do we explain about the Drengir?" Avon asked as she set to work bandaging Dez Rydan's wounded leg. Nearby, Amadeo and Cohmac exchanged glances that hinted they'd been wondering the exact same thing.

"We don't." As Reath gazed at the flowering Drengir, he began to smile. "We just say they've . . . seen the light."

But his smile faded the instant he saw Leox Gyasi hurrying to Affie Hollow's side and was reminded of what this transformation had cost.

※

As soon as Affie had been sure that—whatever they were doing—the Drengir weren't trying to commit homicide any longer, she shook off Leox's arm and hurried to dive into the former Well of Night.

The last place Geode had been.

Affie fell to her knees as she took in the fine gravel and a particularly shiny sort of sand that lay all about; this, she knew, was what remained of her friend.

The heavy sound of someone dropping down beside her proved to be Leox. Affie expected him to hug her again—or maybe he expected her to hug him; she just knew they both needed hugs—but all Leox said was, "Help me look."

When he got down onto all fours to comb through the sand, Affie did the same, though she thought he must be fooling himself. "I know what you told me about Vintians—about how they sometimes remineralize after injury—but after an explosion like that? It can't be possible."

"Probably not," Leox admitted, "but that's no reason to give up."

It took another few minutes of searching amid soil, shards of crystal, and a few stray Drengir clippings before Affie finally found it: a small gleaming gemstone in dull slate blue with a kind of cabochon star at the center. Its shape roughly approximated Geode's, at one one-hundredth scale. "Is this it?"

"Gotta be." Leox took the stone, reverently cupping it in his palm. "Every Vintian's got a heartstone. When they've been damaged, the heartstone helps them regenerate. And after—" His voice broke, and she realized how hard he'd been holding on to that last bit of hope, how fully he now understood that hope was probably in vain. He swallowed hard before he managed to continue: "After they die, the heartstone is all that's left behind."

Affie knew, deep down, that Geode couldn't regenerate from a fragment so small. Even as she wept, though, she was grateful they had found this, that they had something of their friend to keep forever.

One by one, the other members of their party joined them. The dark shards of the Thornseed were trod upon and forgotten, powerless and meaningless. Yet first Reath, then Amadeo, then all the others, knelt beside Leox and Affie, silently helping them collect as much of Geode's sand and gravel as they possibly could.

"Thank you," Affie choked out. "He'd want us to thank you."

"We're the ones thanking him," said Reath. His voice was hoarse. "By destroying the Thornseed, Geode saved us all." That was when Avon started to cry. Affie suspected she wasn't alone.

Geode always did touch people, she thought.

Finally there came a point when they'd gathered together as much dust as possible, placing all of it save the heartstone in a sack Cohmac had been able to provide. "We'll have a service in a couple of hours," Affie said. "At sunset, by the riverbank." It was Vintian custom to commemorate the dead at dusk, and by the nearest shore. The others nodded their assent and one by one made their way back up out of the former Well of Night—they should call it the Well of Geode from now on, she thought— giving Affie and Leox one final moment alone in the place where their friend had given his life.

Leox slipped the heartstone into the chest pocket of his shirt and leaned against Affie's shoulder. For several breaths, neither could speak or move. The shock was too great. It felt as though the whole universe ought to stop spinning. *Like it's all been torn in two,* Affie thought.

Finally Leox said, voice shaking, "Once we've got ten seconds to spare, I've got some leather cording on the *Vessel* that I can use to turn this into a necklace. That way I can keep him close to my heart until . . ." His voice trailed off.

"I get to wear him, too," Affie said, leaning against Leox's shoulder. "No hogging Geode."

"No hogging Geode," Leox agreed before they embraced and gave in again to their tears.

⁂

Once Avon was able to stop crying, she decided the best thing she could do to honor Geode's sacrifice was live up to it—which, in her case, meant tracking down Dr. Mkampa's lab. The knowledge contained within it needed to be either turned to good purposes or, if that was impossible, destroyed. Above all, they had to find out whether the mad Nihil scientist had survived; if so, she could not be allowed to escape.

Leox did not yet feel capable of flying, so it was Cohmac who piloted the *Vessel* toward the place where the Spider Squall had crashed. Avon sat beside him, still haunted by Geode's death. She whispered, "The ship seems so quiet without Geode here."

"I know," said Cohmac. "I know."

It took only a few moments for the *Vessel* to travel perhaps two klicks downstream to the place where the *Firebringer* had crash-landed next to the water. It had cut a gouge in the sand and stones that measured a few dozen meters; Avon was surprised the force of impact hadn't torn the thing apart. Certainly the ejected remnants of its long legs lay scattered all around. The craft still seemed to have its power; in fact, the bluish lights that had once manipulated the Drengir continued to glow. But that light had been powerless to influence the Drengir when compared with the great light of the white wroshyr trees, and Avon suspected it would remain useless forever after.

The central section of the Spider Squall was more or less intact, which meant Dr. Mkampa had likely survived. Had she already made her getaway?

You might run, but you can't hide, she thought toward Mkampa. *You survived the crash. Maybe you think you're going to get away with it all. But you aren't.*

"Look out for her enforcer droids," murmured Cohmac, who was moving forward by her side.

"I think if they were active, we'd have seen them by now." Avon felt more confidence with every step.

As Cohmac searched in one direction, Avon looked in another. Anything on the ground might present a danger—or a clue as to whether Mkampa remained alive. It seemed safest to thoroughly search the exterior before attempting to enter the *Firebringer* itself.

But the one item of interest Avon found was, unfortunately, seriously damaged. *Some kind of pyramid . . . something,* she thought, peering at it. To her it slightly resembled a Jedi holocron, or at least it had, before something had smashed through it and hollowed it out. When she reached out to touch it, the remnants crumbled into so much junk. *No repairing that thing, whatever it is.* She moved on.

Finally Avon reached the Spider Squall's hatch, just as it

swung open with a terrible creak. From the shadows stepped Dr. Mkampa—disheveled, bruised, and angry, but not at all intimidated, not even when Cohmac hurried to Avon's side brandishing his lightsaber.

"My dear traitor child," Mkampa said, staring directly at Avon. "Your mother already paid the ransom for your safety, but I believe I shall have to renege on our bargain, after this."

My mom paid Mkampa to try to protect me? Avon felt a lump in her throat, but she'd have to think more about what this meant for her mother later. "Dr. Zadina Mkampa, the only person whose safety you should be worried about is your own."

"My Drengir will arrive any moment—"

"They are not your Drengir any longer," Cohmac interjected. "Nor will they be able to help you claim the Thornseed, which no longer exists."

Mkampa blinked. "What?"

Avon couldn't hold back her smile any longer. "What he means is, by the authority of the Galactic Republic embodied . . . not in me but in the Jedi—you are now under arrest."

※

"You'll need to be seen by a medic," Affie Hollow said to Nan as she checked some device or other that would've revealed hemorrhaging or a concussion or whatever. "But you're okay to be flown back to the village."

"Will this medic have a med-spike filled with some extra-special drugs?" Nan murmured. "I want the good stuff."

"I don't think that's how licensed medics work." But Affie paused, then added, somewhat grudgingly, "Nice work taking down Mkampa's lab, though."

Despite the pain of her wounds, Nan couldn't help smiling. "I think that's the most fun I've ever had."

"You know, you could've just told us you hated Dr. Mkampa," Affie said. It took Nan a moment to recognize that her tone was genuinely friendly. Nan had heard that tone so rarely these past three years. "We could've worked together to take her down from the get-go."

Nan wanted to answer honestly, but she was out of practice. After a few seconds, she managed it: "When you grow up among the Nihil, you learn that your real feelings—nobody wants to hear them. The truth is something to be hidden. Any vulnerability you reveal might be the one that gets you killed."

"That doesn't sound like a fun way to live," said Affie.

"It isn't." Nan hesitated before adding, "I'm sorry about Geode. He was pretty much the only one I liked."

Affie took this in the spirit in which it was intended, shaking her head and attempting something like a smile. "He was the best, wasn't he?"

Then Nan was alone, lying on a bed of soft grasses near the newly flowering Drengir. Probably she could sit up, but Nan didn't quite feel like trying it. No. Better to wait for the village, the medic, and whatever amount of painkillers was deemed appropriate.

Reath Silas came to sit by her. "I can't give you sole credit for saving the day," he said. "The trees did most of it. Geode did a lot, too. But taking down Mkampa like that bought us time. That's one of the factors that made the difference between victory and defeat."

Nan wasn't nearly woozy enough to get sentimental. "As long as Mkampa went down hard. That's all I ever wanted."

"You did all of this—lying to us, coming on this mission, braving attacks by the Drengir—just to get your shot at her. Why?"

"Turns out she's the one who sent Hague and me to the Amaxine station," Nan said. "You have to understand, Reath. I'm not a convert to worshipping your Jedi Order, or singing the Republic anthem, or anything like that. I don't believe in a bit of it. But . . . I can't believe in the Nihil anymore, either. It started as a promise that the poor and isolated in the galaxy could finally have something for themselves. That the richest and most powerful would be taken down a peg. Now, though? It's just Marchion Ro's vanity project. Millions have died just so he could feel strong and pretend the Jedi are weak. It's disgusting."

"No arguments there," Reath said.

Nan continued, "In the end, I realized that there's just one thing I ever believed in that was good and true. One person. And that was Hague."

"The old man you were with on the Amaxine station," Reath said. "He really did raise you after your parents died?"

"He did," Nan said, then swallowed hard. "He didn't know much about kids, and he barely had two credits to rub together, but he did his best. In those first few days, when I was still so little—still missing my parents—he made me a doll. It was just rags knotted together, really, but it had a head and arms and legs, and to me it was—" Her voice trembled, and she couldn't bear to speak any longer.

But Reath was kind enough not to point out her vulnerability. "That's why you've taken his name as your surname. To remember him."

"And for a long time, that's why I served the Nihil," Nan said. "I've had other reasons, over the years. Other ambitions. But it was Hague who taught me that the Nihil were our only chance at becoming something more than starving vagabonds lost in the galaxy. Even when my own belief wavered, I followed *his* belief. I thought it was the least I owed him. Lately, though, I think what I actually owe Hague is to live my life as honestly and happily as I can. And once I started looking at it that way, the Nihil didn't seem to be the right path anymore. I don't think I believe in . . . 'beliefs' any longer. To me it seems like we should only believe in people. And I believed in Hague." She met Reath's gaze again as she said, "Mkampa *wanted* us to wind up on that Amaxine station to awaken the Drengir. Hague died on that errand, and she didn't even remember his name. I wanted revenge for him. I got it. Now my war is over."

Reath nodded. "I wish you peace, Nan Hague."

Her voice was no more than a whisper when she replied, "You too."

※※

Azlin Rell sat quietly, taking stock of the fight that had just ended, and of his own role within it.

It had felt good to lash out against the Drengir—but why? On one level, he knew, he had relished the chance to strike, to hurt, to kill. Yet Azlin had dwelled in darkness for a very long time, and he understood the shape it took within him. Normally he did not want to cause physical harm for its own sake, only to defend himself against the Nameless, or against anyone or anything that might bring him back into contact with them. Malevolent as the Drengir had been, they had never threatened him in that way.

Was the zeal he had felt in battle the result of the dark influence of the Thornseed? Or was it the influence of the white wroshyr grove, calling him to the light and therefore encouraging him to defend this mission, the Wookiees, and Kashyyyk itself? Azlin did not know. He wasn't sure he wanted to know.

As he sat alone amid the post-battle activity, his restless hands brushed against the ground, a self-soothing activity that ended the moment his fingers found a strange, sharp shard of crystal. It still felt slightly warm.

Was this a fragment of the fallen Vintian? If so, he should offer it to his comrades . . . but it wasn't. A flash of recognition told him that he'd found a small piece of the Thornseed. Perhaps the faintest echo of the dark side remained within.

Azlin might have cast it aside. He might have called out for Reath or one of the others, turned the shard over to them.

Instead he slipped it into a pocket, where it would remain safe, secret, and wholly his own.

Finally, after everyone was more or less patched up, and once the chagrined Mkampa had been secured within one of the *Vessel*'s cargo holds, they gathered together at the riverbank to remember Geode.

It was Leox who knelt by the water and emptied the bag containing all of Geode's dust and gravel, save for the heartstone he already wore around his neck. With great care, he ensured that the remnants fell exactly where the water met the land. Hoarsely he explained, "The Vintians erode as they age, growing smaller and smaller over time. The goal is to someday become small enough to fit in on a beach, to help create the shoreline anew for generations to come. And when they suffer untimely deaths, well, we scatter them here. This is where they will forever feel both the coolness of the waves and the warmth of the sun. This is where they will watch daybreak and nightfall. For Vintians, the shoreline is paradise. This is their heaven."

Affie had wanted to say something, as well, but she was sobbing too hard to do so. Burryaga hugged her tightly. In her stead, Reath stepped forward.

"I met Geode on my first journey to this part of the galaxy," he said. "At first, I wasn't sure what to make of him. I didn't even want to go to Starlight Beacon in the first place—to me, Coruscant seemed like the only place in the galaxy worth being. That journey opened my mind, and Geode was a big part of that. He taught me that we can find both friendship and the living Force in places we might never expect. And that's why our minds, and our hearts, must always be open. Geode helped to teach me this lesson, and I thank him for it. But most of all, I thank him for all our lives."

With that, the final pebble fell at the water's edge. Leox rose and clutched the heartstone for a moment, then said, "All right. Let's get on home."

※

Reath collected himself as best he could during the short flight back to the Wookiee village. Now that Mkampa had been caught and the Drengir had been . . . dethorned, their mission had reverted back to its original parameters: namely, investigating the blight and, eventually, attempting to persuade the Wookiees to evacuate. It would take a great deal of persuading, and after only a few short days on Kashyyyk, Reath could understand why this planet would be especially difficult to leave. The Wookiees might be able to find work and homes somewhere, but nothing would ever be able to restore their pristine forests, or the communion they shared with the trees.

As the *Vessel* settled onto the landing platform, Reath saw that Pruzzalla and many other Wookiees, as well as Master Belka, were hurrying forward to meet them. *Oh, no,* he thought. *The blight must have leaped forward again. Was it the energy released by the Thornseed?*

As soon as the hatch opened, he hurried out. "What is it?" he said. "What's happened?"

Pruzzalla reached out, picked Reath up, and hugged him tightly to her massive chest. How had he done this miraculous thing? What wonders had the Jedi performed?

"What?" Reath asked, his voice somewhat muffled by a lot of thick hair. The others were exiting the *Vessel* to join them. "What are you talking about?"

It was Master Belka who said, "We felt a great disturbance in the Force, and then an even greater . . . I can only call it a celebration. And when it was done, the blight was gone."

Pruzzalla held Reath out, his feet still dangling from the ground, in order to grin at him. He couldn't believe his ears. "What do you mean, gone?"

"You mean, it's not growing any longer?" Avon asked. "It's ceased moving forward?"

"Not just that!" Master Belka explained. "The place damaged by the blight has completely healed!" By way of example, young Nevakka toddled forward, bearing a small wroshyr sapling in a pot, vibrant green. Hadn't they said they discovered the blight on Kashyyyk when a sapling had been found dead?

Now it lived again.

Reath managed to drop to the ground, to face Cohmac, Burryaga, and the others. He began, "The tremendous power of the white wroshyr trees—"

Which had been maintained and reserved for centuries, Burryaga pointed out, all in the service of restraining the Thornseed—

"Was at last set free," finished Dez Rydan, who had limped up to join them. "A once-in-a-lifetime, once-in-a-galaxy explosion of the light side of the Force—"

"Eradicated the blight," Avon said. She shared the group's

wonder, even as she shook her head. "We're not going to be able to replicate that, ever."

No, Burryaga conceded, but for today, perhaps for a long time—Kashyyyk was saved.

At first the joy was too great for expression. Then Reath didn't know what to say or how to feel, particularly when the red-eyed Affie Hollow pushed forward to his side.

Then she set him straight, poking a finger into his chest. "My friend sacrificed himself for us. Turns out he also sacrificed himself to save an entire world. And knowing Geode like I did, I know this for sure: He would expect every Wookiee and every Jedi on Kashyyyk to throw *the best damned party* this planet's ever seen!"

THIRTY-SIX

Everyone in the galaxy knew that when Wookiees were angry, their wrath was fearsome to behold and their opponents' extremities were endangered.

Everyone also knew that when Wookiees were sad, they could moan so low and mournfully that it brought tears to the eyes of almost any person from a species with tear ducts.

And—as the Jedi confirmed that night on Kashyyyk—when Wookiees were happy, they could *party*.

"Yesss!" Amadeo shouted for maybe the fiftieth time that night. He, several other Jedi, and at least a couple dozen Wookiees were all dancing to the deep percussive beat of the celebratory drummers. Dancing, in this context, meant bouncing up and down on a rope bridge that was both stronger and more flexible than Amadeo would've thought. Also a lot of swinging the arms around; that seemed to be a key dance move for Wookiees. Whatever it was, Amadeo was game for it, because it was possible he'd never had this much fun in his entire life.

Kelnacca appeared to be one of the chief percussionists; he stood at the head of the group, banging on an enormous drum as high as his waist and nearly as wide as it was tall. On another rope bridge nearby, Burryaga and Cohmac were leading some sort of line dance that snaked halfway around the village. Reath and Avon had joined another group of dancers near the central fire, along with Lohgarra, who supported the still-healing Dez with one of her mighty arms. The meditation team, now shed of their task, had formed a dance circle around Master Belka, who turned out to possess some serious freestyle moves. Nan, along with some of the other injured, had been nestled into cozy hammocks where they could watch it all. Even the grieving Leox and Affie had accepted glasses of mead and submitted to Pruzzalla's comforting embrace. The village children, excited past any control, swung from limb to limb, their flower crowns making them seem like sentient confetti.

This is the greatest thing that's ever happened, Amadeo thought. *Literally! This might be the single greatest thing anywhere ever! And I get to be a part of it!* Surely every person present was caught up in this shared elation, bound together by the light.

In his hut, away from it all, sat Azlin Rell.

He knew what had been accomplished, heard the sounds of celebration, understood the enormity of what had just happened. One planet had been saved from the blight. Even though this miraculous "cure" could never be enacted on any other world, the news would spark celebrations throughout the galaxy. Ro and the Nihil would never again seem as invincible. Kashyyyk's healing would give the entire galaxy new hope. Even more remarkable: Azlin had played a small role in this. In so doing, for a brief time, he had turned back from darkness—the same darkness that had so long consumed him.

In his mind's eye, he saw his crèche journey again, saw that long-lost sunlight—or what it represented. All Azlin had to do to stand in it once again was set aside the fear and hate that had consumed him these many years. It was that simple. All he had to do was step into the light.

Where the Nameless might find him.

Fear clamped down on Azlin, stronger and colder and harsher for its brief absence from his soul. His guts quivered as he remembered the soul-wrenching anguish of being cut off from the Force forever. No, no, no, *no*. Azlin curled into a ball, clutching his knees to his chest, and began to sing again: *"Shrii Ka Rai, Ka Rai . . ."*

The image of the Kashyyyk sunshine faded from his mind, swallowed up once more in the dark.

The next morning, unsurprisingly, most people in the Wookiee village slept very late. Reath was not among them. He had drunk very little, and as tired as he'd been after all the dancing, he was eager to begin putting things in order for their return to Coruscant.

His first priority was to check on Leox and Affie. They'd soldiered on valiantly yesterday, cheering on the celebration, but he knew they must both be bereft. So he went to the landing pad to visit the *Vessel* and its remaining crew. To his surprise, when he arrived, Affie was not only up and working on her ship but also talking with the bandaged-yet-standing Nan.

"It's not like I'm offering you a job, really," Affie said. Her fingers played with the slate-blue heartstone she wore on a cord around her neck. "We're not ready to replace Geode. I don't know when we ever will be."

"Of course," Nan said. She had the faint shadows of a black eye; Reath wondered whether she would have the med droid clean it up later or whether she intended to wear it as a badge of honor. "I understand completely. You just need someone at nav for this voyage."

Affie nodded. "Possibly just for this voyage. I mean, we just need somebody for a *little while*, which is where you come in. You were once part of a two-person crew, so I'm assuming you're competent at navigation; if I'm wrong, this would be a really good time to mention that."

"No worries, I'm competent at navigation. A few weeks sounds fine." Nan nodded, and Affie . . . didn't smile, exactly, but certainly seemed to be welcoming Nan aboard. This war had made stranger allies, Reath thought, but not many—and few that had made him as happy to witness.

✺

As he walked away from the platform, he encountered Amadeo Azzazzo, very clearly just awakened: robes a bit disheveled from having been slept in, eyes blinking against the sunlight, hair sticking out in several directions at once. This grogginess did not keep Amadeo from beaming at the sight of Reath. "Good morning. Great morning. Absolute best morning in years, right?"

"Right," Reath said as they fell into step side by side. "The best in a long, long while."

"When I first woke up, feeling so upbeat—I nearly stopped myself, thought, 'Oh, the whole galaxy's in trouble, can't forget that.' But then I realized it's not about forgetting that. Celebrating joy doesn't mean ignoring trouble. It's about giving each thing its due, isn't it?"

There was true wisdom in Amadeo's words. Reath realized that the wide-eyed young apprentice was maturing more fully into the Knight he would become; he hadn't been prepared for how poignant this would feel. He *liked* that wide-eyed young apprentice—but, he reminded himself, all things pass. It was just as Amadeo had said: grieving one thing did not make it impossible to celebrate another.

"Each thing its due," Reath repeated, smiling back at Amadeo. "Absolutely right."

Meanwhile, Avon was also up early, having a conversation of her own—but one that was much less enjoyable.

"The blight cannot truly have been eradicated, then," fussed Professor Hastmon Chross via holo. "Not without any treatment whatsoever."

"I swear to you, Professor Chross, it's gone," Avon said. "Completely vanished, like it was never here."

"Then you must learn the Wookiees' methods and report them to us!"

The discussion had been going in this particular circle for several minutes at this point. Avon wanted to thump her head repeatedly against the wall, but her grades still depended on Chross, so she gritted her teeth and remained polite. "There are no 'methods' to learn. The eradication of the blight on Kashyyyk was a one-time, miraculous event that took place through the Force. I'm afraid it can't be replicated."

Chross sniffed. "Nonsense. Transmit all your data back to Kashyyyk, and experts will take a look at it. Some hint of the cure for the blight must lurk within, even if you lack the acumen to spot it."

Galling as this was, a larger concern weighed on Avon, and she had to confess it: "Professor Chross, given the nature of the blight—or rather, the fact that the blight is wholly separate from nature and proceeds at a predictable, regular rate of decay akin to the half-life of certain isotopes—I believe that there cannot be a cure for the blight. It exists outside of nature and the life cycle as we know it. That's why we can't touch it. Unfortunately, it can touch us."

"Defeatist thinking," sneered Professor Chross. "Fortunately for the galaxy, its fate does not lie in the hands of a pessimistic student who assumes she already comprehends all that science has to offer. Transmit your data." He did not seem to consider it an afterthought when he added, "This will not affect your grade, though you must understand your conduct in this matter will be taken into account when lab-assistant assignments are made next semester!"

Avon nodded wearily. "Okay. Transmitting data now."

She sent off the data packet calmly. Chross couldn't stand in the way of her intelligence forever, and besides—she envied him, this ability to believe that a cure still existed. Let Professor Chross and the others like him dwell in that pleasant nonreality a little while longer. They'd learn the truth on their own soon enough.

Don't forget what you accomplished here, Avon reminded herself. She had made a significant discovery regarding the link between the Thornseed and the Drengir. She'd seen Dr. Mkampa go down in literal flames and enjoyed the satisfaction of arresting her. She'd witnessed the miracle of the blight being cured.

And Avon had discovered that her mother had risked her life to protect her.

Avon wasn't about to completely forgive Ghirra Starros on that basis alone. Her mom's actions had helped destabilize the entire galaxy and played a role in literal millions of deaths.

But it was enough to tell Avon that something of the mother she'd known endured within the person Ghirra had become. As long as that was true, there was some chance for understanding, maybe even for redemption.

Sure, it would take a miracle. Yet Avon had seen for herself that miracles were possible.

Nan hadn't been lying when she'd said she understood how to work nav controls, but she was more than a little rusty. It had been three years since she'd spent much time in the cockpit of a starship, so this involved a little studying and a lot of racking her brain to remember.

"Don't sweat it," Leox Gyasi told her after she'd stumbled her way through her first simulated landing, which ended with her badly scraping a pylon. "Memory traces paths within the brain that, while sometimes lost, never cease to be. You must become the cartographer of your own history and, therefore, of your own destiny." Nan's eyes must have glazed over, because he switched to easier phrasing: "It'll come back to you with practice. Just like riding a blurrg."

Both he and Affie were being extremely patient with her, so much so that Nan might have been wary of a trick; on Nihil ships, people didn't get cut nearly as much slack. Yet she had noticed that Leox and Affie took turns wearing Geode's heartstone, frequently enclosing it within their hands as though to commune with their lost friend. Maybe it was Geode's influence encouraging them to give Nan a chance.

This made Nan wonder whether she maybe needed to give someone else a chance—a chance that might have powerful consequences.

So finally, later that afternoon, when both Affie and Leox went out to talk with the Jedi about their predicted departure the next morning, Nan activated the comm and sent the last signal she would ever have expected to use. It took the better part of an hour before a response came, but finally, a soft fuzz of static alerted Nan to look over and see the small holoprojection of Ghirra Starros.

"You," Ghirra said. "Why are *you* calling me?"

"I'm as surprised as you are that this call needs to happen, but it does," Nan said. "Maybe Ro already knows this, maybe he doesn't, but if it's not clear already, it will be soon: I've left the Nihil and joined the Republic cause."

Ghirra kept her composure—or, rather, she tried to. But if Nan was any judge, the emotion behind Ghirra's facade wasn't betrayal or even the satisfaction of outlasting a rival. It was . . . envy.

"You want out, too," Nan said. "Right now you don't see any way besides helping Marchion Ro win this war so you might have new status in the galaxy. Don't you think it would be wise to prepare a plan B?"

"What is that supposed to mean?" Ghirra snapped.

"If you provided certain intel to the Republic—intel I'm willing to be a courier for—your life would be a lot easier after a Nihil loss. I'm not saying you'd completely avoid jail time, but cooperation like that could make the difference between a few months in a cushy low-security joint and a life sentence some-place a lot less decorative."

Ghirra hesitated before answering, and that hesitation told Nan everything she needed to know. "That's very presumptuous of you."

"You know I have a point," Nan said with a smile.

"I'm not having this conversation with you right now."

"You mean, we'll have it later?"

Ghirra Starros shut off her comm, fading away before Nan's eyes. But Nan suspected that particular negotiation was far from over.

⁂

Cohmac Vitus found himself unexpectedly grateful that the Jedi team did not leave Kashyyyk immediately after the end of the Drengir crisis. Though he had thought at first that he would feel impatient to rejoin the fight against the Nihil, he'd swiftly real-ized that the *Vessel* crew needed time to make repairs—a task that would be somewhat slowed by the grief they felt—and that the injured could use another day or two to heal.

As for himself—after years of crisis after crisis, urgent mis-sion after urgent mission, Cohmac had been given a moment of peace. He would not waste it.

After a session of meditation with Master Belka's team before they departed Kashyyyk, Cohmac allowed himself to stroll the many treetop bridges and pathways surrounding the village, to watch the play of sunlight between the leaves, and to simply breathe in and out as he existed wholly in the moment.

Consciously, he thought about almost nothing. This was how the best decisions were always made.

Cohmac was roused from his walking meditation by the sound of footsteps on the nearby walkway; he looked up to see Reath Silas approaching him. It almost took him a minute to recognize Reath, so changed was he from the boy Cohmac had first met more than three years prior. The changes were all for the better. How rarely this was the case!

"Taking a moment?" Reath asked. "If so, I can—"

"The moment has been taken," Cohmac replied. "I'm done."

"What do you mean?"

Although Cohmac had not pushed himself to make this decision on this day—or this month, or possibly ever—he found that the answer had come to him. "I would like to rejoin the Jedi Order, fully and completely. I must speak with the Council."

Reath grinned at him. "Congratulations, Master. We're the better for having you with us again."

"I don't know about that," Cohmac said. "I might be rusty, after so much time away. They might ask me to become a Padawan once more."

"They wouldn't . . ." Reath's voice trailed off as he seemed to realize that Cohmac was joking. "A Padawan, huh?"

Cohmac nodded. "Any chance you're looking for an apprentice?"

Reath laughed out loud, and Cohmac felt the last cloud

disperse within him, knowing that the final remnants of the breach between them had healed, for good.

✼

Aboard the *Gaze Electric*, Marchion Ro was receiving his morning briefing . . . and for once, it contained news he had not expected to hear.

"That is impossible," he said to Thaya Ferr, who stood before him with her datapad, calm as ever despite the words she had just spoken. "The blight was seeded on Kashyyyk. Our surveillance droids confirmed the site. Once seeded, the blight does not simply vanish."

Thaya bowed her head respectfully, the way she generally did before delivering bad news. "On that planet, it has."

Ro stood from his chair, agitated beyond the ability to remain still and dignified in the way Ghirra always urged him to be. "The Republic cannot have a cure." He took care not to say why. "If they even believed themselves to possess one, Lina Soh would be crowing it from every platform in the galaxy."

"I entirely agree, my lord," said Thaya. "The loss of this one world, for whatever mysterious reason, should not represent a major tactical difficulty, should it? Or do I need to inform the Tempests that—"

"Tell *no one*," Ro said, returning to his seat. "As you say, this is merely some sort of fluke. The blight may have been improperly seeded. That planet is not part of our core agenda. So there is nothing to tell."

"Of course, my lord." Thaya smoothly continued going through the day's business. "You'll be happy to know that the diversionary rumors about the Thraisai system worked precisely as you had hoped. Several transports of Jedi are even now searching through the fogs in vain—"

"Leave me," Ro snapped.

Unfazed, Thaya simply gave him a deep nod that was almost a bow. "As you will it, my lord." With that she exited his chamber, leaving Ro alone with his thoughts.

He was not afraid. He knew how many worlds suffered under the blight, how desperate they were for an answer, how certain he was that only he could provide one. His weapons remained deadly. His authority remained absolute.

Only the slightest element of doubt had entered his mind, no more than a sliver. Nothing that would not be dispelled by the next Nihil victory, which would not be long in coming.

But for the first time in a long while . . . Marchion Ro had a really bad day.

❖

On their final night on Kashyyyk, Reath took Avon along with him as they climbed to a little spot in the highest treetops of the village, where he had already arranged to meet with the crew of the *Vessel*. Wookiees didn't have "restaurants" as such, but they had places like this one, where hospitality was offered to those who visited, in proportion to their contributions to the community. Given the eradication of the Thornseed and the blight, he expected they'd eat and drink very well.

Reath understood that as soon as they returned to Coruscant, their war would begin again. Yet that made it all the more important to stand in the pure light of Kashyyyk's joy.

We saved one world, Reath thought. *When we're fighting on a near-galactic scale, it's easy to think of one planet as something small. But it's not. It's an entire population. An entire culture. Primeval forests, including one wiser and more powerful in the Force than even the Jedi Council. "Just one planet" means something.*

It means everything.

Leox and Affie had arrived first, snagging a table right at the edge of the railing, where they could look out over the treetops toward the distant river. Though weariness shadowed their smiles, they welcomed their friends with warm embraces.

"Bubblewine?" Avon said as they sat down. "You know I'm only fifteen, right?"

"This is for the adult celebration," Leox specified. "For you, we've requested a ribbonfruit smoothie. Sound good?"

"Yeah, actually." Avon sagged down into her chair, trying to smile.

"This has to be pretty much the only bottle of bubblewine on all of Kashyyyk," Reath said. "In all honesty, I wouldn't have thought there was even one." It didn't seem quite *sturdy* enough for a Wookiee drink.

Unexpectedly, Leox grinned. "We broke this out of the *Vessel*'s own stores, because no matter how big a party we had yesterday, this night deserves a celebration all its own."

Reath watched—first in curiosity, then in delight—as Leox reached under his shirt and pulled out the Vintian heartstone he wore on a cord around his neck. Before, the heartstone had been completely smooth and uniformly blue. Now a few flakes of rougher sediment had formed on the edges—not much, but definitely a beginning.

Avon looked like she might burst into happy tears. "Does this mean Geode's regenerating? He's still alive?"

Leox answered in words that Reath would never forget, words that would sustain him through the fight still to come: "With hope—anything is possible."

ACKNOWLEDGMENTS

I dedicated the book to the whole *High Republic* writing and editing team, but I have to add here: As great as it has been to work on this initiative, as many fantastic things as we've gotten to do (SKYWALKER RANCH!), the single best part of it all has been the friendships that have grown along the way. My editors and fellow writers were always there to help and listen—not only regarding *Star Wars* stuff, and not only regarding work stuff. Writing is often a very solitary profession, but with *The High Republic*, thank goodness, I never had to go it alone.

Thanks also to all the fans out there who embraced this series, who created amazing fan art and cosplays inspired by these stories, and who have come up to me at conventions, sharing their love for the story and the characters. (Shoutout within a shoutout to you Geode cosplayers, and the Leox Gyasi gender-swapped cosplayer who saw a Geode plushie where others witnessed only a gray throw pillow.) You're the reason we did this, and I hope the saga is one you'll always cherish.

Just as a fan of *Star Wars*, I've got to send my love out to Tony Gilroy, the rest of the writing and directing staff, and the whole cast of *Andor*, which I've loved more than anything else in canon since *The Empire Strikes Back*. I keep rewatching it and finding even more to love in it. Thanks for making me a giddy fangirl again!

Finally, thanks and love to my husband, Paul, who held my hand every step of the way.